THE
SAMURAI
AND THE PRISONER

HONOBU YONEZAWA

YEN
ON

New York

THE SAMURAI AND THE PRISONER

HONOBU YONEZAWA

Translation by Giuseppe di Martino

KOKUROJO
©Honobu Yonezawa 2021
First published in Japan in 2021 by KADOKAWA CORPORATION, Tokyo.
English translation rights arranged with KADOKAWA CORPORATION, Tokyo through
TUTTLE-MORI AGENCY, INC., Tokyo.

English translation © 2023 by Yen Press, LLC

Yen On
150 West 30th Street, 19th Floor
New York, NY 10001

Visit us at yenpress.com
facebook.com/yenpress
twitter.com/yenpress
yenpress.tumblr.com
instagram.com/yenpress

First Yen On Edition: July 2023
Edited by Yen On Editorial: Rachel Mimms
Designed by Yen Press Design: Andy Swist

Yen On is an imprint of Yen Press, LLC.
The Yen On name and logo are trademarks of Yen Press, LLC.

Library of Congress Cataloging-in-Publication Data
Names: Yonezawa, Honobu, 1978– author. | Di Martino, Giuseppe, 1989– translator.
Title: The samurai and the prisoner / Honobu Yonezawa ; translation by Giuseppe di Martino.
Other titles: Kokurojo. English
Description: First Yen On edition. | New York : Yen On, 2023.
Identifiers: LCCN 2023002881 | ISBN 9781975360504 (hardcover)
Subjects: LCSH: Kuroda, Yoshitaka, 1546–1604—Fiction. | Itamijō (Itami-shi, Japan)—Fiction. | Castles—Japan—Fiction.
   | Samurai—Fiction. | Japan—History—Azuchi Momoyama period, 1568–1603—Fiction. | LCGFT: Detective and
   mystery fiction. | Historical fiction. | Samurai fiction. | Light novels.
Classification: LCC PL878.O54 K6513 2023 | DDC 895.63/6—dc23/eng/20230120
LC record available at https://lccn.loc.gov/2023002881

ISBNs: 978-1-9753-6050-4 (hardcover)
         978-1-9753-6051-1 (ebook)

10 9 8 7 6 5 4 3 2 1

LSC-C

Printed in the United States of America

THE
SAMURAI
AND THE PRISONER

Contents

Prologue   What Is Sown

Advance to reach heaven. Retreat to know hell.

Their fervid shouts hurtled across the Bay of Naniwa, spurring the men to fight and do battle and promising them that battle alone was their road to salvation. A century had passed since the Onin War, which precipitated this epoch of civil strife, and not a single corner of Japan lay untouched by bloodshed. During this time, sundry clans both flourished and fell to ruin. Starvation, disease, and war begot one other, suffusing the world of the living with unceasing misery. If one wished to escape this suffering, they were to march and engage the enemy, then perish in combat. Then they would doubtless find peace in paradise. The shouting continued without pause: *Advance to reach heaven. Retreat to know hell.*

In Osaka's Settsu Province, followers of one True Pure Land Buddhism offshoot gathered and constructed a large edifice for their prayerful devotion to *Amida*, or the Amitabha Buddha. They dubbed it Hongan-ji. Because they had been impelled by the tumult of the times to build ditches and earthen ramparts, it was now difficult to tell if their stronghold was a temple or a castle. Eight years had passed since arms, armor, and provisions were carried in, and eight years had passed since the head priest issued his proclamation expelling all those who deigned not to participate in this battle to protect the Buddha's teachings. They aimed to defeat their would-be conqueror, Oda Nobunaga.

The notoriously rascally and gossipy youths of Kyoto sought distraction through rumors and tittle-tattle. Though there was much anxious pondering as to which side would win, Hongan-ji had no real chance of victory, no matter how impregnable Osaka proved, and so Hongan-ji joined forces with the Mouri clan. Oda Nobunaga, who was on the heels of driving off Takeda and Uesugi, was on the upswing. The great Mouri clan, meanwhile, had already laid claim to ten provinces. None yet knew how this battle would unfold. According to the gossip, it would be a spectacle either way.

The year was 1578, or the sixth year of the Tensho era, and it was the eleventh month.

Osaka was a city surrounded by fortresses and fortifications.

Oda stood victorious against the True Pure Land *Ikko-ikki* Uprising in Echizen Province and Ise Province, but he was as yet unable to rout Osaka. His forces built numerous fortresses surrounding Osaka and reconstructed the castles that were already there to be more robust— almost as though to stem the torrent of *nenbutsu* chants flowing out of Hongan-ji. The strongholds of Tenno-ji and Owada had changed as well, but there was no greater such change than was carried out in the castle of the town of Itami, which lay half a day by foot north of Osaka. Not just the drudges and laborers but also the samurai hauled the stones to fashion the new castle, the thinking behind which differed from the former iteration.

In the Land of the Rising Sun, the purpose of a castle was not to defend a settlement. Rather, it was to lodge one's forces and to fend off enemy attacks. As such, many castles were built along highways, atop peaks, or at other places removed from the habitations of the common folk. The new castle at Itami, however, was different. Ditches and wooden fencing totally encircled the town, and abatis on the perimeter cut the town off, effectively making it part of the castle as its outer citadel. The enormous castle on the gently sloping land of Hokusetsu, or northern Settsu, might have been confused for a hill made by human hands. The Jesuit padre Luís Fróis called the fortress superb and utterly splendid. Its name was changed to Arioka Castle.

At present, people, horses, and cattle were forming lines and lugging heavy bags into Arioka. The contents of those bags were varied, from rice to salt to miso; wood, charcoal, bamboo, lead, gunpowder, and iron; from leather to gold, silver, and copper currency to everything in between. Relief colored the faces of the people who finished their deliveries, and they quickly fled the castle, for they knew that this stockpiling portended imminent battle.

Even those with their wits about them were puzzled as to who exactly would be battling. The lord of Arioka Castle was allied with Oda, and the only force in opposition to Oda around these parts was Hongan-ji in Osaka—but word had it that Hongan-ji's priests and monks were so walled in that there was no way they could launch some kind of onslaught on Arioka. It didn't make sense to them, but the cargo bearers were too afraid of the potential consequences to go about asking anyone whom they would be fighting, so they simply set right back off.

From Arioka's innermost tower, a figure gazed at the traffic below.

He was a hulking boulder of a man with a swarthy complexion and somewhat drowsy-looking, deep-set eyes, which might lead one to believe him dull brained. Yet once he was in the field of battle, he fought with blazing intensity. He was a warrior of a tempestuous era who found himself talking various people into crafty schemes as necessary. A man in his midforties, he was considered a great hero of the age, and as the lord of Arioka Castle, he had been assigned the lordship of Settsu by the Oda clan. He was Araki Murashige.

The sound of footsteps coming up the stairs. The watchmen braced themselves. The warrior who arrived went down on his knees behind Murashige.

"I come bearing news, Your Lordship," he said, his voice throaty and hoarse. "An emissary who claims to be with the Oda has appeared."

For a short while, Murashige said nothing. What number of envoys did this make? There was something a touch off, though. This messenger "claimed" to be with Oda? What did that mean? Murashige turned to face the man.

"Who has come?"

"My lord?" A tinge of confusion was in the samurai's voice. "The name he gave was Kodera."

"What?" Murashige frowned. "I thought the Kodera forces left the Oda to join the Mouri. How can a Kodera claim to be with the Oda yet send me a messenger?"

"My lord, that may be so, but he said his name was Kodera. Kodera Kanbei."

Murashige's eyes widened slightly, and his frown dissipated. "Oh, so 'tis Kanbei. I haven't seen him since we last parted ways. Bring him in."

The samurai bowed his head and informed Murashige that Kanbei was waiting in the mansion.

Kodera Kanbei's erstwhile name was Kuroda Kanbei. Bestowed with the surname of his master, he now went by Kodera in public.

The man was known for many proficiencies; he was a master of the spear and an adroit horseman. He employed good retainers and steadfastly defended his stronghold. By Murashige's estimation, if Kanbei was made to command troops, he would wreak havoc on the battlefield. In short, Murashige thought him a great general. Yet he also thought that such a superficial summation fell short of a full account of the man.

Murashige allowed Kanbei through to the spacious reception hall of his residence. In a set of staggered shelves was a yellowish tea jar entitled Torasaru. This urn was so well-known that it was said one could buy a castle with it alone. Having it in the room was a sign of respect for Kanbei on Murashige's part.

Murashige bade an attendant open the sliding-screen door before entering the room. Kanbei was sitting cross-legged with his fists to the floor, prostrating himself deeply. Murashige had the attendant fall back, and then he sat down himself.

"Raise your head."

"Yes," Kanbei replied, shifting to comply.

As Kanbei was now past age thirty, he could no longer be called a young warrior. Yet he didn't look his years, and his countenance was easy on the eyes. His lips were firmly drawn, yet there was a whisper of a smile there, and his slender physique could even be described as meek. However, Murashige knew that this man with such delicate features was the most cunning individual in Harima Province. He had induced the Kodera clan to ally with the Oda.

"Pray allow me to express my sincerest gratitude at being granted the honor of this audience."

Kanbei's voice carried far. By contrast, Murashige's voice was invariably somewhat leaden.

"'Tis been a while, has it not, Kanbei?"

"Indeed, Your Lordship."

These two had fought side by side in the past. Murashige was the head of the Araki clan, while Kanbei was nothing more than a vassal of the Kodera clan. But although there was a gap between them with regard to status, Murashige nonetheless spoke to Kanbei often, and that was because he could tell Kanbei was no ordinary man.

Kanbei bowed reverently. "It doth please me greatly to see the good Lord of Settsu so hale and healthy."

Murashige smiled wryly at the effusive politeness. "Good to see you're doing well yourself. Is the Lord of Mino in good health, I wonder?"

"My father has not opted for a comfortable retirement, the times being what they are. He yet serves as the defender of Himeji. As of late, he carries on about nothing save for his anxiety regarding the hostages given to the Oda, and I fear senility may already be taking him. Though I speak of my own father, I believe him to be ever so slightly unreliable."

"Oh-ho. So you brought hostages to the Oda, did you?"

Kanbei looked surprised. "Was Your Lordship not aware? I certainly did."

"Harima's been entrusted to Hashiba Chikuzen, and he does not inform me of every little detail, such as whence he gets his hostages."

"Is that so, Your Lordship?" Kanbei straightened his posture. "I gave my son, Shojumaru, to Hashiba as a hostage for the Oda some time ago."

"I see. No wonder, then, that the Lord of Mino should be so anxious."

"Not at all—as long as Takenaka Hanbei is a Hashiba retainer, I do believe it shall, if anything, be better for his training concerning both the pen and the sword."

Murashige didn't reply to that. It was true that Hashiba Hideyoshi,

Lord of Chikuzen, was not rough with his hostages. His vassal Takenaka Hanbei, on the other hand, was too sharp and shrewd a man, and
Murashige often couldn't fathom what was going through his head. As
far as Murashige was concerned, Kanbei trusted in Takenaka because
the both of them were, in some respects, birds of a feather with more
than one thing in common.

Kanbei looked slightly abashed. "I humbly beg Your Lordship's
pardon for wasting your precious time discussing my son. I did not
come here to talk to you about such trifling matters." Then a faint smile
curled his lips. "I regarded the town, and well, I did espy the battle preparations that are transpiring. I heard tell that Your Lordship is gathering supplies in order to barricade yourselves inside the castle, but I
replied that this could not possibly be the case, and that it must be the
fault of careless scatterbrains spreading exaggerated rumors. I was in
error. It would appear Your Lordship truly is standing against the Oda."

Murashige said nothing, for it went without saying: He was indeed
bucking the Oda army he was once part of.

Before long, Arioka Castle would be besieged by tens of thousands
of Oda forces.

The rays of sun shining from beyond the transom bore a red tinge.
At last, Murashige spoke.

"Have you come to persuade me, too? I haven't yet told you how many
already came here for the same purpose."

Kanbei nodded. "Forsooth," he said unhaltingly, "I must say Your
Lordship committing such treachery is a bolt from the blue. The Oda
clan is currently in a state of uproar not unlike the prodding of a beehive. If it would serve to change Your Lordship's mind, then they would
send as many as it takes."

"And so you, too, have come before me, is that it? I hardly think it
can be on the orders of Tounohyoue—am I wrong?"

Kodera Tounohyoue Masamoto was Kanbei's master, though in
recent years, Kanbei had been working for both the Kodera and Oda
clans. Serving two masters wasn't uncommon throughout history, but
Kanbei's expression turned sour at the mention of the Kodera name.

"Yes—as the Kodera clan wishes to work together with Your Lordship, then it stands to reason I would not have come here under his orders. Therefore, as long as I remain here at this castle, I should like to put aside the Kodera name. Prithee call me simply 'Kanbei.'"

"Very well," said Murashige magnanimously. "So then, Kanbei, state your business. 'If you relent now, you'll be forgiven.' 'If you have complaints, air them.' 'Come to Azuchi and apologize to Nobunaga.' Prior visitors all said the same things before running back home. Are you here to parrot them?"

"I should like to say as much. If parroting prior visitors was effective, then I would do so, but that would be a somewhat arduous task."

"Then what *do* you have to say to me?"

Kanbei smiled. "Firstly, I tell Your Lordship that I am dumbfounded. Going against the Oda must mean Your Lordship sides with Honganji and the Mouri. While I would not even dream things would come to this, if Your Lordship joins hands with the Mouri, then indeed, the Oda would be greatly troubled. Hashiba's troops, who advanced to Harima, would be dead in the water. I can see how Your Lordship would seize upon this singular opportunity to deal such a blow."

"Then why don't you come under me, too, Kanbei? I'll give you a weighty position."

"I humbly decline," said Kanbei, still smiling. "This would be a brilliant tactical move only if Your Lordship can in fact force back Oda's advancing forces. I have no intention of telling Your Lordship that ye ought to apologize to Nobunaga. However, there is one thing that I would tell Your Lordship at once."

"One thing, eh?" Murashige stared at Kanbei. "Very well. Speak it."

"I shall." Kanbei's expression turned serious again. "This is not a fight that Your Lordship can win," he asserted solemnly.

For a fleeting moment, the room fell dead silent. Murashige was without words. That remark alone was reason enough to cut Kanbei down.

Nonetheless, Murashige told him, "Go on."

Kanbei didn't hesitate to do so.

"I am but another warrior in these turbulent times; if I thought Your Lordship would win, then I would join your side without a second thought. But is there anyone who would say that the Owada forces are a motley of cowards? Oda has proven that he possesses uncommon strength and numbers, enough to win battle after battle even amid the chaos. And in all of Hokusetsu, the only bastion that would hold out against the Oda is Arioka Castle. However strong this castle may be, 'tis but a single fortress. 'Twould be repeating the failure of the lord who relied on Shigisan Castle, Matsunaga Danjo."

Matsunaga Danjo Hisahide, the veteran general, had turned against his army in Yamato Province the year prior, only to get swiftly outnumbered and defeated. He died after setting fire to his own castle.

"Danjo lacked a rear guard," said Murashige. "And for that, he saw his defeat."

Kanbei replied instantly, as though he had been waiting for that response.

"I surmise that the rear guard that Your Lordship is trusting in is the Mouri. Your Lordship believes that Mouri troops shall dash through the San'yodo to save Arioka Castle. They shan't," he said bluntly. "The Mouri—and Mouri Terumoto—are not the kind to do such a thing. Nobunaga may have gone all the way to Mikawa in order to save Nagashino Castle, but Mouri Terumoto cannot do the same. Your Lordship will never hear me say that the Oda are guileless, but the Mouri exceed even them in that respect; they are a clan with many a scheme. Why does Your Lordship trust in Mouri Terumoto? I find it vexing."

Murashige's eyes had looked heavy this whole time, but now he grimaced slightly. Kanbei's words had touched a nerve. These were his best-laid plans, and if the stratagem succeeded, then taking Nobunaga's head was not impossible. He had vowed an oath in writing alongside the Mouri and Hongan-ji and come to multiple accords. Moreover, there were many commanders under the Mouri umbrella whom he had faith in. Hokusetsu more or less followed Murashige's command, and many among the Harima samurai went along with the plan. Such was the meticulousness worthy of the reputation of the famed general Araki Murashige.

Yet it all hinged on one point. How trustworthy was Mouri Terumoto, head of the Mouri clan, now? Murashige himself wasn't convinced the Mouri would help, something Kanbei had just indicated.

Kanbei awaited Murashige's reply with bated breath. The former's gaze held a certain ardor, and Murashige saw deep within them how confident he was that he was right.

I knew it, thought Murashige.

Kanbei could not be summed up by the phrase *great general*. In this age, the generals who excelled at archery and horsemanship numbered many, as did the generals who were skilled in battle and the generals who excelled at adjusting the structure of villages. Kanbei's talents soared higher. He could see the larger picture and thus stab where it hurt. Not many could do likewise. And much to Murashige's chagrin, Kanbei himself knew he was a sagacious man.

No matter what Kanbei said, the die was cast. The grand-scale machinations were already afoot, and the whole endeavor was not under Murashige's sole discretion. The only reason Murashige heard Kanbei out despite that was to determine whether Kanbei would hamper the cause—and Murashige had come to his conclusion.

"Kanbei," Murashige said sorrowfully. "Your words have struck a chord within me. 'Twould seem that I can hardly afford to let you go back. If you were to return to Harima, then the Kodera—not to mention the samurai of Harima now that the region has shifted to the Mouri—may just bow to the Oda. And that would be a thorn in my side." Then he shouted with gusto: "Come!"

The sliding screens on three sides of the room opened, and ten armored warriors surged inside. These men were the elite troops handpicked by the Araki clan to defend Murashige's person. They were collectively referred to as the *gozenshuu*—the lord's guard.

Kanbei was instantly surrounded by spearheads.

In the face of impending death, Kanbei smiled. "So it came to this after all."

Murashige knit his brow at Kanbei's calm and gentle timbre.

"Are you saying you came here knowing you might die?"

"I marched right into what amounts to an enemy castle. I was never under the impression that I would return with my life."

"Then why did you come? We have stood side by side in the battle-field; I wish not to torment you to no purpose. You should have stayed away from this place."

"Hashiba Chikuzen told me to come, and I could not refuse. No, insooth, that is not the reason." Kanbei craned his neck, as though awaiting his decapitation. "The truth is, I've grown slightly weary of this era of war. If I die doing my duty to Hashiba, then 'tis with a war-rior's dignity I die, and the Kuroda will be left with a chance to survive... 'Tis a respectable fate, if not a grand one."

Murashige admired the man's grace and courage.

"I shan't kill you," he said.

Kanbei frowned; this puzzled even him. "In that case, I shall be tak-ing my leave."

"Oh, no—I'm not sending you back, either."

The guards surrounding Kanbei didn't so much as twitch, their spears still pointed straight at the man.

The blood drained from his face. "What is Your Lordship saying?"

"'Tis not hard to understand. Kanbei, I'm capturing you. You'll remain here in Arioka till the war's end."

For a brief moment, Kanbei knew not what to say. Snapped back to his senses by the shining of the spear tips before his eyes, he at last spoke.

"But why? Is it not the warrior's code to return the messenger or, if one cannot do so, to cut him down? If Your Lordship commits that which runs counter to the ways of the world..." Kanbei turned a little pale. "Ye shall reap what ye sow," he squeezed out.

"This is just a part of my tactics. I grant you your life; are you not satisfied?"

That moment, Kanbei stirred.

"Yes! Greatly!"

He then unsheathed his blade. The guards, not having received orders to kill Kanbei, wavered momentarily. One barred Kanbei's path for-ward, intent on protecting Murashige. Kanbei feinted a slashing attack, only to stab behind the guard as he turned around. He hadn't aimed at anything in particular, but it hit the guard in the flank, causing blood to spray. Too much blood for him to survive.

Seeing their comrade's blood shed, the guards grew incensed. "Damned cur!"

"Do not kill him! Take his sword!" ordered Murashige.

One of the guards pinned Kanbei from behind. Falling prostrate on the blood-soaked floor, Kanbei was deprived of his blade, but he shouted all the same.

"Why won't you take my life?! Kill me, Murashige!"

"You dare issue orders to me?! Kanbei, you fool! You killed a retainer. I was going to treat you as a guest, but if you killed a vassal, that's no longer to be!"

"Pray hear me, Your Lordship—if you do not kill me..."

"Silence! One of you, shut him up!"

The second they heard Murashige's command, the guards poured blows and kicks on Kanbei. They gagged him, and though Murashige hadn't told them to, they went as far as to blindfold him as well. Even through all that, Kanbei was shouting, but none had ears to hear.

One of the guards fell to his knees before Murashige.

"My liege. Where shall we take the man?"

Murashige's mind was made. His expression turned sleepy once again.

"Toss him in the dungeon. Do not let anyone see him and do *not* kill him. Keep him alive until I say otherwise."

Kanbei continued to struggle; belying his usual reputation for being gentle as water, he flailed and writhed so desperately that it was hard to watch. Yet with his sword taken and his limbs held in place, he had no means of escape. Murashige had already turned his back on him.

Thus did Kanbei become a prisoner of Settsu's Arioka Castle.

And thus did the wheel of karma begin to turn.

Chapter I

Stone Lantern on a Snowy Night

1

The threat of battle hung over Hokusetsu. It was winter; needle ice dotted the ground, and thin sheets encased the waters.

The folk who inhabited the lands toiled over their farms in order to prepare for the season of withering. Even if they knew there must be enough food stockpiled to weather the cold months, there were none who, when faced with the sight of barren trees, didn't harbor doubts they would live to see the spring. And it was even worse when the winter saw a war.

Wood and charcoal extracted from places like Minoh and Mount Kabuto were stored in both the homes and castle storehouses of Itami, but nobody knew whether it would be enough. The sizable Oda army, which had all but conquered the capital region, was currently flooding toward Arioka Castle in great hordes as though they'd found a fertile field. No man nor woman alive could say with certainty how long this battle would drag on.

Dry winds blew down from the peaks of Rokko, swaying the dead reeds and rocking the tops of the evergreens. The biting cold robbed the elderly of their last remaining strength and ravaged mewling babies' lungs, kissing them both with death. Able-bodied wayfarers and traveling priests cinched their straw coats tight, ducking their heads and looking up at the dark gray skies, grumbling it might snow.

The frigid winds blew along the Ina River and against the abandoned Ikeda Castle. Much of the populace had fled to the mountains to avoid the bloodshed, and the winds chilled both the robbers who scoured the now uninhabited villages for valuables and Oda-allied undercover agents maneuvering to ascertain the movements of Araki troops. The wind blew unimpeded through the gentle slopes that characterized Hokusetsu.

The wind also reached Arioka Castle, causing the sentries straining their eyes atop the watchtowers to quiver with a start and causing the watch fires of the foot soldiers cooking rice all day to flicker. The wind then hit the castle keep towering over the Ina River and blew through its crenels and brattices. But the zeal seething within the tower was so heated that it refused to let even the winter winds penetrate. And the name of that zeal was rage.

On the first floor of the tower, the main commanders from around the castle had assembled for a war council. On this, the twenty-fifth day of the eleventh month, the commanders were kicking up a commotion, up in arms over the tidings. Five *ri* to the east of Arioka Castle, the daring general who'd been defending Ibaraki Castle, Nakagawa Sehyoue, had thrown open the gates without firing a single arrow upon seeing Oda forces close in, surrendering the castle to the Oda.

"Damn him! Damn that Sehyoue!" spat a young samurai in the front row of the Arioka camp. "He swore up and down that he could win, only to surrender immediately! He was all talk! The biggest coward the world over!"

Speaking was Araki Kyuuzaemon, who had only just reached thirty years of age. A man following in the wake of the Ikeda clan, which once held sway over areas in the vicinity, he was a leading figure among the vassals, as not only did he have a lofty social standing, but he was also possessed of prudence beyond his years. Cautious and thoughtful though he normally was, on this day, he raised his voice.

Some among the other commanders arrayed there voiced their agreement. "That's right!" one said. "That yellow-bellied bastard!" shouted another.

Murashige was sitting cross-legged on a cushion, his sleepy eyes idly watching the men speaking their minds. The commanders were all red in the face rebuking Nakagawa for his betrayal. Their indignation was justified—Nakagawa was the commander who'd enthusiastically recommended Murashige rebel against Oda. It was only natural they'd be angry that Nakagawa returned to the Oda's service without even putting up a fight. But Murashige saw behind the wrath in his commanders' faces. He saw how terribly shaken they were.

Prior to Nakagawa's betrayal, Takatsuki Castle, defended by Takayama Ukon, surrendered on the sixteenth day of the month. Takatsuki and Ibaraki Castles were supposed to be the twin shields keeping the Oda troops pouring in from the capital at bay. Of course, the commanders knew that there was hope yet for this war, and that Murashige had a plan that would earn them victory. All the same, the commanders began nursing misgivings about the future prospects, and they were being overbearing with all the invective they were hurling at Nakagawa, which they were doing mostly to hide their fear and unease.

Murashige said nothing as he scanned the faces of his commanders. He saw anger, he saw disbelief and distrust, he saw trepidation...but among their number, he spotted one man who was smiling. Perhaps that man derived strength from meeting Murashige's gaze, for he suddenly raised his voice.

"My fellows!" the man cried. "Nakagawa was only a *yoriki* in the first place. He was not one of us Araki. For this war, we cannot put our faith in the likes of a Nakagawa. The only thing we can depend on is the direction of our lord, the most battlewise man in all of Settsu, no, in all the region! We have but to defend this castle and our victory be assured. Am I mistaken?!"

Speaking was Nakanishi Shinpachirou, a fierce warrior who was just shy of thirty years old and a newcomer among the ranks of Murashige's retainers.

Upon hearing Shinpachirou's rant, some among the assembly grunted "aye."

"Too true, too true! Shinpachirou, ye rascal, ye sure know what to say for an underling! Nakagawa was a foolhardy man who talked big against the weak but quailed when facing the strong. We already knew he would not remain with us."

Next to speak was a large-framed commander in his forties, a man by the name of Nomura Tango. He'd taken Murashige's younger sister in marriage and was treated with warmth on par with Araki kin. He was entrusted with the fortification named Fort Hiyodorizuka constructed at the southern tip of the castle.

"I know that our lord anticipated this would happen," said Tango. "As such, there is naught to be so panicked about. What says Your Lordship?"

The commanders' eyes were all trained on Murashige now. In this reception room inside the castle keep, one could hear a pin drop. The rays of the winter sun shone in.

Calmly, Murashige spoke.

"Tango's correct. Nakagawa Sehyoue was not a retainer of mine, and placing the untrustworthy at the front is a common war tactic. And 'tis of no great consequence that Ibaraki fell. If they're turned away inside Arioka, they'll lose the battle. That's why they cannot breach Arioka. We have them holed up in Ibaraki Castle."

If one placed potential traitors at the rear, then if and when they turned coat, it would turn into a pincer attack. However, if they were placed at the front, then even if they switched sides, the fight was still on.

Upon hearing Murashige's reasoning, the commanders erupted with joy.

"Ohhh, my liege!"

"So Your Lordship saw through Sehyoue's scheming!"

"I stand in awe of Your Lordship's deeply laid plans!"

With a brief wave of his hand, Murashige immediately hushed the war council.

"Nonetheless, I can't say I was expecting that rat fink to fold without a fight. I've known him a long while, but the bastard must have gotten old, because he was even weaker in the knees than I'd thought."

The commanders were listening to Murashige's words with rapt attention. The tone of his voice contained both scorn and loneliness, impressing upon those listening the irony and the fickleness of the shifting tides of the world.

The only one who didn't take Murashige at his word was Murashige himself.

Nakagawa Sehyoue was neither a coward nor, as Tango had called him, foolhardy. He was now and ever a brave warrior—unmanageably so, even. Murashige knew that.

Murashige had brought prosperity to the Araki clan, and he owed the boldness of Sehyoue, his cousin and childhood friend, a great deal for securing his place as ruler of the whole of northern Settsu. Yet while Murashige ascended all the way to Lord of Settsu, Sehyoue was never more than a *yoriki*—a midrank samurai—under Murashige, the castle Sehyoue attained notwithstanding. Murashige reckoned that rather than living forever in Murashige's shadow, Sehyoue preferred to make a name for himself swinging a spear as a retainer for the Oda.

When Murashige heard that Ibaraki Castle had surrendered, he'd chuckled to himself: *That Sehyoue never changes.*

Needless to say, Murashige had hoped in his heart of hearts that Sehyoue would continue to fight under him. Ibaraki Castle being as small as it was, it could not withstand the Oda's brute force. Nevertheless, Murashige had thought that Sehyoue would battle on until he was bloodied and bruised and that he'd quip something to the effect of "Ack, you win. I see Oda's not to be taken lightly, either!" before withdrawing to Arioka. Murashige had even hoped he would cherish the day they won the war alongside Sehyoue. Though he knew this was just the way things were in this era of internecine conflict, Murashige was not so unfeeling that he thought nothing of breaking relations with an old friend.

Yet he didn't speak what he truly felt, for to him, the war council was not the place for that.

"I knew it," said Nakanishi Shinpachirou. "Our lord's decision was utterly flawless."

The sky visible through the crenels was getting covered in low-hanging clouds.

2

The snow that began to fall on the advent of the twelfth month descended to the Ina River, melting vainly.

At the river's western bank lay the castle named Arioka, constructed in the land of Itami. To the east stretched a vast marshy expanse. Those who sought to reach Arioka Castle from the capital would see its tower standing tall beyond the barren reedbeds.

South of the castle lay Osaka by way of Owada. North of it lay the steep natural defenses of Tanba by way of Ikeda, while to the west ran the long road to Harima. Now that Osaka was the scene of a battle, Itami was a key position linking the capital to the lands in the west.

Murashige ascended to the top floor of the castle tower and surveyed his surroundings. There were noticeably fewer people traveling down the highway. Looking down, he saw the outermost enclosure of the castle circling the town with earthen walls and wooden fencing, which gave him a good deal of heart. The war preparations, such as provisions and ammunition, looked satisfactory. Even if thousands upon thousands of Oda's crack troops were to advance, he was certain the castle would hold.

"Be that as it may…," Murashige muttered to himself.

He recalled what the famed Takeda Shingen purportedly said: *"The people are your castle."* It was true; what kept a castle fortified and steadfast wasn't the depth of its moat or the height of its fortress. It was the belief of the officers and men confined inside it that it was impregnable.

The castle was known as one of the strongest fortresses under the heavens ever since the days it was dubbed Itami Castle. Yet Murashige had taken Itami Castle extremely easily. Because the troops had doubted the skills of their general and the toughness of the structure, Itami Castle had been weak. Murashige refused to repeat that mistake. He reckoned that whether Arioka Castle was strong enough to hold hinged wholly on the spirit of his officers.

He heard hurried yet measured footsteps coming up the stairs. Murashige surmised it was Kyuuzaemon. Sure enough, Kyuuzaemon's lean face peeked through the door. Upon seeing Murashige there alone, Kyuuzaemon called for him quietly.

"My lord."

"What's the matter? Why so pale?"

"We have bad tidings."

"I had a feeling. Speak."

Kyuuzaemon gulped and bowed his head.

"Owada Castle has fallen."

"What did you say?!"

Murashige's voice was uncharacteristically tinged with shock.

Murashige had predicted that Takayama Ukon of Takatsuki Castle and Nakagawa Sehyoue of Ibaraki Castle would lose. Ukon was a devout Christian and had denounced the idea of Murashige splintering from the Oda from the beginning, and Sehyoue wasn't the type of man who would throw his life on the line out of loyalty to the Araki clan. But Murashige hadn't dreamed that Owada Castle would capitulate as well.

The commanders who were informed of the loss of Owada Castle at the hastily convened war council had much the same reaction. Their expressions weren't angry or contemptuous so much as they were disbelieving.

Even the stouthearted Nakanishi Shinpachirou was struck dumb. "You claim that the Abe brothers have surrendered?" was all he could say.

The other commanders were also in a tizzy, whispering among one another. Some even speculated this news was a groundless rumor sown by the Oda faction.

The Abe brothers, defenders of Owada Castle, were zealous believers in the True Pure Land sect of Buddhism; while they had refrained from allying with Osaka when Murashige was a retainer under the Oda clan, if the Araki ever threatened to attack Hongan-ji, it wasn't clear whose side they would have taken. They had encouraged Murashige, a Zen Buddhist, to invoke the *nenbutsu* chant, which was the hallmark of True Pure Land Buddhism, at almost every opportunity. When Murashige brought in a concubine connected to Hongan-ji, the Abe brothers all but clapped for joy. Murashige was never going to be swayed one way or another by the words of the Abes, but when the brothers heard that he would be switching allegiances from the Oda to Hongan-ji, they were in tears.

"*Your Lordship has finally, finally resolved himself!*" one had said. "*The head priest of Osaka shall no doubt be delighted to hear this. With this,*

Your Lordship shall certainly find rebirth in paradise. This is truly cause for celebration. Prithee place us at the vanguard when we cross spears with the Oda. We shall bring you the head of that damnable enemy of the Buddha called Nobunaga."

Murashige couldn't for the life of him understand why the Abe brothers would surrender to Oda without a fight. He listened to a messenger who had made it out of Owada Castle by the skin of his teeth. According to him, it hadn't been the Abe brothers themselves who decided to surrender but rather a son of theirs by the name of Niemon, who deceived his father and uncle by making it seem as though he was fighting the Oda, only to strike when the brothers had their guards down. He took their swords and bound them, sending them to the Oda as hostages.

"Abe Niemon," growled Murashige. "I never thought him terribly wise, but what an odious little rat."

They'd been so sure the castle wouldn't surrender, and yet it had; when their subsequent shock subsided, it dawned on the commanders more and more what Owada falling to the Oda meant for them.

Owada was on the highway connecting Arioka and Osaka. Rescuing Osaka Hongan-ji now that it was surrounded by such multitudes would have been difficult to do in a brief span of time, but as long as Owada remained in the hands of the Araki, the path from Arioka Castle to Osaka would have remained unobstructed. If Osaka came under attack, troops could have been sent from Arioka, and vice versa. They could have helped each other bedevil the Oda.

Now, however, the Oda had driven a nail in their vitals. They could attack Arioka without any misgivings. It was all thanks to Abe Niemon's betrayal.

"My lord," said Kyuuzaemon with a heavy air. "One of Abe Niemon's sons, Jinen, is being kept in this castle as a hostage."

"I know."

"Then let us make haste. Shall we go with a *hatamono* for him?"

Kyuuzaemon asked because there were a number of ways to punish an enemy using a hostage. *Hatamono* was a form of crucifixion that involved tying the victim to a post and stabbing him with spears for all to see. A beheading was a relatively painless death, and if one wanted to show the hostage compassion by allowing him to go out like a warrior, one could order him to commit suicide. No matter how one went about it, killing the hostages of a traitor was just what one did during times like these.

However, Murashige had something else in mind.

"Throw Jinen in the dungeon."

Kyuuzaemon goggled at him. "The dungeon, my liege? Does Your Lordship truly mean to keep Jinen alive?"

Murashige said nothing. The war council was astir.

Kyuuzaemon leaned forward. "My lord, prithee reconsider. If Your Lordship lets such cowardice go unchecked, the retainers of the Araki shall be tarred as being unable to kill their hostages."

Others among the commanders present also called Murashige into question.

"Kyuuzaemon speaks the truth. Prithee put Jinen to death!"

"My liege, I humbly bid ye reconsider."

"This is the hostage of that detestable Abe! Why hesitate?!"

Amid the din, Murashige lowered his voice a tad.

"Enough."

That was all it took to cow the commanders, and the room once again fell totally silent. Murashige spoke gently and deliberately.

"I'll give Niemon an upside-down crucifixion for you in due time. I'm sending overseers to the branch castles in jeopardy. I won't kill Jinen for the time being. Kyuuzaemon, follow your orders."

Kyuuzaemon had more to say, but he couldn't defy Murashige's aura of authority. He could only fall prostrate.

"Yes, my liege. As ye command."

Murashige saw the puzzled looks on his commanders' faces. Just one man's gaze was devoid of doubt and apprehension—Nakanishi Shinpachirou. It was the look of someone who spared no thought as to whether the hostage should be killed or not, as he would simply go with whatever Murashige decided.

3

As long as the people who presented the hostages didn't turn traitor, then those hostages were valued guests. Murashige placed the hostages in the custody of vassals he could trust, and they were often allowed to reside in their estates. Abe Jinen was young and had a weak constitution, so there was hesitation when it came to entrusting him to others. As Murashige had a concubine who was a True Pure Land believer, Jinen was placed in Murashige's own residence.

The district containing the castle tower, known as the inner citadel, was dotted by stables, as well as warehouses storing gunpowder, guns, and long spears. Murashige's residence was situated in the inner citadel's eastern tip, built in the innermost section of the castle.

After the war council, Kyuuzaemon accompanied Murashige on their way to the residence.

"Your son's name is also Jinen, if I recall," said Murashige.

Kyuuzaemon was walking a few paces behind him. He strained to hear his lord's voice against the wind.

"It is, my liege."

"Niemon's son is eleven. And yours is, I want to say, thirteen?"

"Yes."

"Same name, almost the same age. Do you not see your son in him?"

Kyuuzaemon looked cross. "I can scarcely believe the words coming out of Your Lordship's mouth. Showing mercy to a hostage whom it is only right to kill, merely because he shares a name with my son? I have never heard of such a thing."

"I suppose so."

Kyuuzaemon continued, at something of a loss, "My liege, I shall of course follow Your Lordship's orders, but I must say I do not understand. Your Lordship let Takayama Ukon's hostage live as well."

Murashige kept walking without a word.

Takayama Ukon of Takatsuki Castle's son was still a baby who could hardly speak, and he and his older sister had been submitted as hostages. Murashige hadn't killed either of them.

"I understand the reason Your Lordship let Ukon's hostages live. Though the bastard surrendered to the Oda, Ukon's father—Dariyo—and Dariyo's faction are here as allies, so sparing their lives does make sense. Even so, I do hear people opine that with Ukon's betrayal, they ought to have been killed regardless."

Murashige didn't bother asking who had said that, as he thought it was only natural that some should make that case.

"There are others still," Kyuuzaemon added, "who say we ought to have taken a hostage from Nakagawa Sehyoue. They claim that had we done so, the bastard would not have surrendered so easily. Pray forgive me for asking now after all this time, but why did you refrain from taking a hostage from Sehyoue?"

At last, Murashige spoke.

"Sehyoue isn't the type of man who would not surrender because of hostages. Once he decided to follow the Oda, he would've done so anyway, hostages or no."

"My lord, that's…," Kyuuzaemon said haltingly. He, too, had fought alongside Nakagawa Sehyoue in the past, so he knew Sehyoue's nature. "That may be so, but that reasoning does not hold for Your Lordship's not killing Abe's hostages. I realize this goes without saying, but while mercy and benevolence are all well and good for a bonze, they are not part of the warrior's creed. If we do not kill whom we must kill, the military clans of this world shall fall."

Murashige stopped in his tracks and turned around. Kyuuzaemon promptly bowed his head, and Murashige spoke, his voice as quiet as always.

"Kyuuzaemon."

"Yes, my lord."

"You think I spared the hostages' lives out of mercy and benevolence?"

Kyuuzaemon didn't know how to reply.

Originally, Murashige was nothing more than a vassal of the Ikeda clan. Back then, he was named Araki Yasuke. Naturally, the road to becoming the Lord of Settsu, Araki Murashige, had been neither smooth nor without its troubles. Kyuuzaemon had also been a vassal of the Ikeda clan, back when his name was Ikeda Kyuuzaemon. He had witnessed firsthand how Murashige had distinguished himself within the Ikeda clan, taken it over, and established his own.

He'd done this through double-crossing, scheming, war, more war, and more double-crossing. By means of bloodshed and strife did the lowly Araki Yasuke become Araki Murashige. Would the Murashige whom Kyuuzaemon knew let hostages live out of the kindness of his heart?

"...I do not believe so, my liege," Kyuuzaemon replied. "So please, I bid Your Lordship tell me: For what ploy are we letting Abe Jinen live? That way, if anyone in the castle should express doubt, I shall quell him, or my name is not Kyuuzaemon."

Murashige stared at him intently. He opened his mouth for a moment before closing it anew. The cold winds kept blowing.

"We'll toss Abe's hostages into a storehouse or some such," Murashige said at last. "You'll create a jail for the hostages. Wood is precious, so use bamboo. Don't make it too big; we'll soon be needing bamboo, too."

Kyuuzaemon dipped his head, but he nevertheless tensed his stomach to project his voice.

"Yes, my liege," he replied.

Murashige looked up. Heavy, low-hanging clouds were quickly shrouding the sky.

"Have it made by midday tomorrow. Now go."

His head still bowed, Kyuuzaemon stepped back before turning on his heel and marching away. It then started snowing.

When Murashige was a retainer of the Oda clan, visitors called on his residence in unceasing droves to seek an audience with him. Invariably, they would marvel wide-eyed at the art on the wooden doors and sliding screens, at the high-class coffered ceiling. They would express their admiration, telling Murashige that the mansion of the Lord of Settsu was splendorous enough to live up to his name.

That intricate design, however, was for appearances' sake. The inner rooms where no visitor was allowed were decidedly more modestly constructed. While Murashige paid handsome sums for tea utensils, he was not the type to otherwise indulge in extravagances in his daily life.

Murashige, having returned to his residence, opened the shoji door to the inner room, where his sole concubine, Chiyoho, was doing needle-work, mending Murashige's battle surcoat. He did not have a legal wife. She was on the wooden floor in a short-sleeved cotton garment with frayed hems, and she wasn't even using the brazier for warmth. She put her fingers on the floor and bowed deeply.

"Are you not cold?" asked Murashige.

Chiyoho lifted her head and smiled. "I am not."

Beautiful though she was, she also lacked the glow of life. Her skin was white; it was so pale, in fact, that one could make out a hint of blue. Furthermore, there was a touch of sadness that never left her eyes. She was in her twenties, and as Murashige was in his forties, they could have been mistaken for father and daughter.

There were townsfolk who called Chiyoho a beauty on par with the famed Yang Guifei, but Murashige sometimes found himself thinking that he'd have liked her to have Guifei's willfulness and zest for life as well. He also felt that Chiyoho's beauty stemmed from her having given up on life. She wasn't frail or in poor health, and she wasn't racked by a grave illness, yet she still left one wondering whether she might be gone the next day.

Murashige stayed on his feet.

"Where's Jinen?" he asked.

"He is doing his brush practice." She tilted her head slightly in con-fusion. "I heard that Abe has betrayed us."

"Nothing gets past you, I see."

"A mansion attendant informed me. I am told that Niemon changed allegiances and bound his own father."

Chiyoho apparently learned of events through the rumors told to her by the attendants and ladies who worked at the mansion, so she picked up on things surprisingly quickly despite seldom ever leaving the residence.

"Alas, such sorrow... Jinen is the child of a warrior. He must be resigned to his fate."

Murashige was about to tell her what Jinen's actual fate was to be, but just then, they heard someone speak from beyond the door.

"Honorable Lord of Settsu. 'Tis me, Abe Jinen. Prithee grace me with an audience."

His voice was still high-pitched, as he had not yet hit puberty, but it sounded somewhat restless and shrill on top of that.

Murashige raised his eyebrows and frowned.

Though Jinen was now a resident here, it was ill-mannered to come to an inner room like this without prior permission. But then Murashige thought twice when he realized that Jinen must be that shaken and upset. It was understandable.

"Enter."

"Yes, sir."

Jinen opened the door, his face stiffening upon spotting Chiyoho there. He hastened to prostrate himself.

"Pray forgive my rudeness."

Jinen had yet to go through the coming-of-age ceremony for boys of the era. He was slender of frame and gentle of facial features; nowhere was the mien of a warrior's child, and it seemed he knew that others saw him that way, for he woke up before sunrise to devote himself to studying and the military arts, stopping only at sundown. Though he was young, he was an ardent True Pure Land believer, never neglecting his chanting. In that respect, he resembled his grandfather.

"Never mind that. Raise your head."

Jinen did as he was told and sat up.

His complexion wasn't great at the best of times, but now he was white as the driven snow. Nevertheless, the boy was stout of heart, for he spoke loudly and confidently.

"I beg pardon for requesting Your Lordship's audience."

"What's this about?"

"'Tis about my father. I heard that he disregarded his debt of gratitude to Your Lordship and handed the castle to the Oda. Is this true?"

"'Tis," said Murashige bluntly.

Jinen's breath caught in his throat, and he cast his eyes downward. Tears streaked down his face.

"Though I speak of my own father, I can scarcely believe his cowardice. He always used to adhere to Amitabha's vow. But after Your

Lordship rightfully said, 'Advance to reach heaven, retreat to know hell,' he instead surrendered as soon as the enemy approached. The thought that might happen never crossed my mind, nor how my father bound my grandfather and delivered him to the Oda."

"So I heard myself."

Jinen wailed and broke down crying. Murashige shuffled his feet and positioned himself between Chiyoho and Jinen, his eyes fixed on the sword at Jinen's waist. Murashige was always vigilant that he might get assaulted whenever he talked to anyone with a blade, no matter who.

Jinen didn't raise his head. He just kept talking through his tearful voice.

"...It cannot be helped. O Lord of Settsu, I offer my person to punish as Your Lordship sees fit. I shall then ascend to paradise."

Murashige did not decide the fates of his hostages based on their wants and desires, and he did not find Jinen's words to his liking. Graciousness was noble and manly in the eyes of a warrior. Warriors who clung to life despite a lack of hope or prospects were looked down on. Jinen's manner of speaking *sounded* gallant. But to Murashige, Jinen's resolve was not the resolve of a warrior.

Kanbei, who was currently in the dungeon, had also demanded that Murashige kill him. However, Jinen's point differed from Kanbei's. A true warrior would never ask to be killed in order to go to heaven.

Murashige released a bit of the tension in his body. Meanwhile, Chiyoho mediated from behind him.

"My lord," she began. "I did not expect I would interject in a matter involving military clans, but may I ask you to heed my request? Though he speaks with such courage, Jinen is but eleven. He still lacks discretion. He is of my sect, so if you could please..." Her clothes rustled. "If you could please take his life out of consideration for him, I would be most obliged."

Murashige glanced behind him; Chiyoho's forehead was on the floor. It was rare for her to voice her desires. Murashige even considered granting her wish for a peaceful death for Jinen, but he stifled that thought.

"That won't do. Jinen will be thrown in jail."

"In jail?!" cried Chiyoho. "My lord, ye don't mean the dungeon, do ye?"

Unable to understand the meaning of this, Jinen stared at Murashige, his face still stained with tears. A little while later, Murashige spoke again.

"The dungeon is occupied at present. I'm having Kyuuzaemon build a jail, which will be finished on the morrow. Jinen will remain here in the building until then. Jinen, give me your sword. You won't be allowed a dagger, either."

Jinen's pale-white face turned red. "What is the meaning of this, Your Lordship?! It is too much!"

To have one's sword confiscated wasn't just humiliating for a warrior. It would be humiliating for anyone. But Murashige showed no mercy.

"Do not misunderstand. You are Abe's hostage, and now that Abe has betrayed us, your fate is in *my* hands. I've decided you will live, so I forbid you to die, however much you may desire death. Now hand me your sword."

Jinen hesitated, so Murashige shouted for his attendants, who appeared at once, pinning Jinen without effort. They thrashed him and snatched away his sword. Murashige looked down at Jinen, who was on his hands and knees.

"Throw him in the inner storeroom," Murashige commanded. "Let no one get near him."

Jinen was carried off. When the room quieted down, Murashige stooped before Chiyoho and touched her cheek.

"That must have alarmed you. Forgive me."

Chiyoho shook her head slightly. Her eyes were as melancholy as always. The doors had been left open, and the winter sky was already a light blue.

4

Hatamono.

Executions. Crucifixions. String them to the posts and kill them. Five of them. Ten of them. More. More!

There's not enough wood. Carry logs from the mountains. Make posts for crucifixions the second the bark is peeled off.

Bind the women, bind the children. Then crucify them. Ten of them. Twenty of them. More. More!

Stab them in the flanks. Stab them with the dull spear tips dripping with blood and fat.

These are orders from Oda Nobunaga himself. Crucify them!

String 'em up.

Stab 'em.

Crucify every last person in Kozuki Castle and line 'em up in rows. Oda's orders.

A hundred of them. Two hundred. The old, the young, men, women, it matters not. Line them up for all to see.

Have mercy, they say. Have mercy? Bwa-ha-ha! Idiot bonze. You ask for mercy now? At this stage of the war?

String them up.   ·

Stab them.

"I've never heard of a war like *this*, not even in fantasy."

Murashige groaned as he stirred from his sleep. Outside the doors, it was twilight.

A figure sitting on his knees could be seen in silhouette through the shoji screen. Murashige reached for the *wakizashi* short sword near his pillow.

"Who goes there?"

The man bowed his head. "My sincerest apologies. Abe Jinen has perished."

Murashige sprang to his feet.

5

The storeroom where Jinen had been locked away lay in the back of the residence. It was not typically put to use. Jinen's sword had been taken from him, and he had not been bound. He had even been given scriptures as a small mercy. To make absolutely sure the boy could not escape—and to make absolutely sure a vassal who hated Abe Niemon couldn't kill or harm him—Murashige had attendants guard the storeroom during sunup and his own personal guards watch over it when the sun was down. Those guards had lit a watch fire and kept strict and sleepless watch over any and all traffic coming from and going to the room.

And yet Jinen had died all the same.

Dawn was breaking, and cocks were crowing in the distance. Murashige took his guards and attendants to see Jinen's body for himself, ordering them to secure the scene from prying eyes.

Abe Jinen's face had been pale in life, but the complexion of a corpse was still different from that of the living. There was an unmistakable difference between the face of a person on death's door and the face of a cadaver. Murashige gazed at Jinen's face and felt pity. The boy's eyes were wide-open. Murashige himself was a Zen adherent, yet he clasped his hands and prayed the *nenbutsu* for the young True Pure Land devotee.

The storeroom was a confined space with a wooden floor and walls on three sides. The remaining side was a door leading into the covered, four-sided square corridor surrounding the residence, looking out onto the outside. When Jinen's body was discovered, the door was open, and Jinen was on the floor, crossing the frame of the door and facing up with his feet pointing toward the corridor. His robe was soaked in blood from the chest to the stomach.

Murashige knelt by the body's side and removed the robe. The attendants were aghast.

"No, my liege, you mustn't!"

"Pray leave such chores to us!"

But Murashige wasn't swayed. The bloody robe had a hole in it and, under that hole, a deep wound. Murashige looked at that wound and muttered to himself.

"Hmm… What is this?"

Murashige recognized it as an arrow wound. He had seen more arrow wounds than he would have liked to on the battlefield; there was no way he could be mistaken. He could even tell the arrowhead wasn't a hunting arrow, which was meant to be taken back. Otherwise, the wound would have been far messier.

Murashige placed the body facedown. There was no blood trail on his back, and no wound in his pallid skin there. The arrow hadn't penetrated his back. Jinen's chest was scrawny and weak, and he'd been wearing nothing more than a simple robe to boot. Had a bow with a heavy draw weight been used, then the arrow would have easily come out the other side of him, Murashige surmised.

He turned Jinen's body faceup again, then looked up.

"Juuemon, are you there?"

"Yes, my liege. I am here," came the instant reply.

The warrior stepped forward, his armor clinking, and he knelt near Murashige.

His name was Koori Juuemon. Originally part of the Itami clan, he'd been adopted into the Koori clan. He had made it over the thirty-years-old mark, and while he wore a somewhat blank expression, he was a deft hand with horses and with weapons from the bow to the sword to the gun, to say nothing of his facility with arithmetic and Chinese classic literature. The reason Murashige held Juuemon in such esteem lay elsewhere, however. He valued how Juuemon excelled at quickly realizing what needed to be done, as well as the man's broad view of things. Juuemon wasn't of high familial status, but Murashige liked the way he worked so much that he'd appointed him the leader of his personal guard.

"You were the ones who watched over that storeroom last night, yes?"

"Indeed, my liege," said Juuemon, hanging his head. "I apologize profusely for our mishandling Your Lordship's command."

"Who did you use?"

"Apart from myself: Akioka Shirounosuke, Itami Ichirouzaemon, Inui Sukesaburou, and Mori Kahei were all on watch."

"Hmm."

Murashige stroked his chin. Those men were hailed as the Five Spears of the Araki Lord's Guard, formidable soldiers who stood out even among Murashige's retainers. Juuemon was well versed in all things, while the other four formed the finest among the retainers when they made use of the weapons they were each most skilled at.

"If you used the Five Spears, there was no other way. I won't hold you responsible."

"My liege… I thank Your Lordship!" Juuemon prostrated himself immediately.

"Yes, yes. Never mind that; answer me this. Who found the body, and when was it found?"

Juuemon replied right away.

"Akioka Shirounosuke and I found it. Around the sixth hour of the morn, I heard a cry of shock and hastened alongside Shirounosuke to Jinen, only to find him collapsed on the floor. As Jinen was still drawing breath, I made to tend to his wound, but he murmured that he was 'heading West' and then perished. I stood watch over the body while Shirounosuke checked to see whether there was anyone suspicious lurking nearby. I asked my comrades who rushed to the scene after us to go give word to Your Lordship."

West was where heaven, Amitabha's Pure Land, was said to be located. For a young Buddhist devotee's dying words, mention of "heading West" was not particularly strange.

"Did you take something off Jinen's body?"

Juuemon's eyes opened wide. "Your Lordship's words shock me. What does Your Lordship think I took?"

"An arrow."

"My lord. An arrow, you say?" Juuemon replied blankly. "Nay, the moment Jinen cried out, we came running, and we saw not an arrow. Shirounosuke shall also attest to that." His face blanched. "My lord, was Jinen, by some possibility, shot dead by an arrow?"

"……"

"But, my liege, there was no arrow. I am sure of it. Did someone take it out? No, even more so than an arrow, there was no way we could have failed to see a *person*! Does Your Lordship suppose that Jinen was shot by an invisible arrow?"

Murashige didn't reply. He just looked outside, where the light snowfall was piling up.

The storeroom was facing a spacious garden, as it was originally installed into a room whose purpose was to provide a view of the garden. While Murashige, a master of the tea ceremony, loved the art of landscaping, this garden had yet to be completed. The evened-out, flat lot was vacant, with one lonely stone lantern being the only thing placed there as of yet.

The garden was covered in a blanket of snow. The lantern, too, was topped by white.

The snow shrouding the garden was smooth and level, with no traces of footsteps. There was nothing there. Murashige strained his eyes, but over and over again, he saw that there was nothing amiss whatsoever.

Rumors flew faster than arrows regarding Abe Jinen's mysterious death; by noon, everybody at the castle had been told. Word was that Abe Jinen had been shot dead at the dawn's light, yet the arrow vanished without a trace despite the watchmen running to his side immediately. It was as though he'd been shot by an invisible arrow.

Soon, some were crowing that this was divine retribution, a punishment from the gods and the Buddha.

They appealed to powers unknowable. The gods, the heavens, the Buddha, *oni*, demons—there were any number of beings who could have wrought this divine reckoning.

Abe Niemon had bound his father and uncle, forsaken his son, and betrayed the Lord of Settsu and the high priest. They posited that, as punishment, an arrow of lightning struck Jinen. Some even started claiming they saw a soundless bolt of lightning split the skies. Some among the True Pure Land believers broke into dance out of gratitude to Amitabha, and more than a few among the samurai believed that the gods and the Buddha had exacted the proper vengeance. The warriors who didn't agree that Jinen's death was divine retribution thought otherwise.

At the war council, Kyuuzaemon spoke, keeping his emotions in check.

"This is just as expected of our lord's greatness. When Your Lordship ordered us to keep Abe's hostage alive, I must say I wondered why, but he was in fact punished in the end. This is the very reason the Araki name is known for its military renown. I am truly relieved."

Some of the other commanders gathered there began expressing their agreement with Kyuuzaemon. Among their number, some seemed to come to the conclusion right then and there that Jinen's death had been by Murashige's hand. If Murashige had ordered his guard to slay Jinen, then the testimony that there was no arrow to be seen was just a lie told by the guard, and there was no mystery. Murashige was sitting cross-legged on his cushion, staring at no one in particular. He kept in mind who had said what.

When at last the din abated, Murashige spoke.

"'Tis not so. I did not kill Abe Jinen."

Kyuuzaemon looked flabbergasted. "What?! Could it be? Does Your Lordship, too, think it was divine punishment?"

"Do not speak such bilge. If that was the case, the punishment would fall on Niemon, not Jinen."

The war council was abuzz with murmurations. "Indeed," whispered one. "'Tis true," whispered another.

Kyuuzaemon shook his head, lost. "So 'twas neither Your Lordship nor the heavens. Then how *did* Abe's hostage die?"

"The answer is obvious," Murashige said, glaring at his commanders. "Someone else killed him."

The commanders quickly realized Murashige was furious. He had told them to throw Abe Jinen in a jail and keep him alive, only for him to end up a dead body that morning. Jinen's death had wounded Murashige's honor and prestige.

Though he feared the wrath of his lord, Kyuuzaemon raised his voice all the same.

"Your Lordship, you say that someone killed Abe's hostage, but I heard that the arrow that shot him dead could not be seen. This cannot have been the work of an ordinary person."

"Mightn't this be the work of a *Christian*?" grumbled Nomura Tango with mild disgust. "If 'twas perpetrated by one of the Christians who brought guns to this country, they may know a means of firing invisible arrows."

Murashige was less than pleased by this statement.

"The wound was a common arrow wound. I couldn't fail to recognize it as such. If Christians could use such a technique, then Takayama Ukon, a Christian himself, would be undefeated. To claim otherwise is hogwash."

Tango's face flushed bright red. "But then, my liege," he said, raising his voice, "how was the boy killed?!"

"Curb your impatience, Tango. To answer your question: I do not know. Not yet anyway. But whoever did the deed stands in violation of my orders not to kill the boy, and they shall pay a price for their actions," Murashige continued, his voice now a deep growl. "We will launch an investigation. Within the next few days, we'll get to the bottom of who killed Abe Jinen, and how they did it. Until then, do not spread any groundless rumors. Those who disobey will be punished."

At their lord's orders, the commanders prostrated themselves.

However, there was an air of dissatisfaction among them, and Murashige wasn't such a lackwit that he failed to notice.

6

Two days passed. Unbroken clear weather melted the snow, making the paths in Arioka Castle slushy.

Weak spots in the castle's defenses were repaired, and the umpteenth letter was sent to the Mouri or Hongan-ji. The scouts were trying to ascertain the movements of Oda forces, and an overseer was sent to a branch castle to exercise authority over it. As war approached, there was a plethora of matters for Murashige to attend to, but more than any of them, he was the most eager to get the investigation surrounding Jinen's murder over and done with. Yet the more he looked into it, the more the mysteriousness of it all came to the fore.

After writing another hurried letter and entrusting it to an attendant, Murashige made his way to the storeroom for the hundredth time, Koori Juuemon by his side.

Murashige's residence contained a square corridor that looked onto the outside. As the closet was encased on three sides by solid walls, the only way to enter or exit was through the shoji door that led into the square corridor. As they trudged through the hallway, Murashige asked Juuemon a question.

"Is there a way to approach the storeroom besides passing through this corridor?"

"There is, Your Lordship," said Juuemon without hesitation. "One could enter through the ceiling by removing its boards. One could also enter through the floor by removing the floorboards. In addition, the closet's walls are not very thick. I believe that if armed with an ax or a hammer or the like, one could break through one or more of the walls."

"Very well. If that's so, then I suppose the culprit used one of those methods to enter the closet."

"I must disagree," said Juuemon. "There are no signs the floorboards or ceiling boards were removed or destroyed. Judging by the spider-webs and the dust, as well as the guard's surveillance that night, I scarcely imagine the culprit could have been under the floor or above the ceiling."

"In that case, the culprit must have approached the closet by passing through the corridor."

"Myself and the other guards were watching over the corridor, and we allowed no one to get near the boy. I do not believe the culprit could have come through the corridor, either."

"Then nobody could approach Jinen from any direction. Is that it?"

"'Tis as Your Lordship says," said Juuemon, pained.

The Lord of Settsu and his retainer stood in front of the closet. Jinen's body had already been given a warrior's burial. Murashige opened the shoji door and entered the closet, then turned around to look past the corridor at the level ground that would one day be a garden and the stone lantern installed there.

These lanterns were a gift from Furuta Sasuke, a retainer under Oda and the brother-in-law of Nakagawa Sehyoue. Furuta, himself proficient at tea ceremonies, had an eye for elegance if his gift was any indication; from the slope of the lantern's shade to the roundness of the finial topping it, it was most definitely charming. Murashige had cut ties with Oda, but he couldn't bring himself to discard the lantern. The firebox in the lantern was supposed to have a lamplight placed in it at some point, but it was still empty.

Just beyond the garden, waist-high camellias had been planted to outline the border when it came time to landscape it in earnest. Beyond the camellias towered unrefined plaster walls dividing Arioka Castle from the outside world. These walls were fitted with embrasures: triangular openings for gunfire as well as vertical slits for arrow fire.

Murashige exited the closet and stood in the square corridor once more. He looked to the right to see that the corridor turned right about four *ken* ahead of him; one *ken* was roughly equal to three paces of an adult male. He looked left, and the corridor turned left four *ken* ahead of him as well.

"Where were the corridor guards stationed that night?"

"The part of the corridor to the right was watched over the entire night by myself and Akioka Shirounosuke, who stoked a watch fire. The part to the left was watched over by Itami Ichirouza and Inui Sukesaburou. As they are both conscientious men, I do not doubt their word that they saw not anything unusual during their sleepless vigil."

"I don't doubt it, either." Murashige had already ascertained these things many times during the past two days. He stared at the stone lantern. "Then what about the outside? Could they have perhaps crossed the unfinished garden, climbed up to the corridor, and entered the closet that way?"

"That, too, would be impossible, my liege. As Your Lordship has said that ye have yet to work on the garden, none of us have dared to tread there for fear of ruining the land. However, Mori Kahei patrolled along the plaster walls all night long. Kahei is honest to a fault; I do not believe he would ever shirk his duties."

"What about the lights? Did Kahei light a watch fire?"

"As Your Lordship ordered Kahei to watch over the closet, he did not light a fire, lest his eyes never get used to the dark of the night."

"Hmm."

"Moreover, it was snowing that night, ceasing during the small hours of the morning. The garden was totally covered in snow when Jinen was killed, but there were no footsteps. I would venture to say that no amount of acrobatics would allow one to leap over the garden and leave no footprints behind."

As viewed from the closet, the garden was five-by-eight *ken*. The lantern was at the center, straight across from the shoji door. If one was to use the lantern as a stepping stone, then maybe someone on par with Yoshitsune—the man said to have jumped across eight small boats during the Battle of Dan-no-ura—could have cleared the garden. However, the lantern was not rooted to the floor, and while one could clamber atop it without it toppling, one could not jump off it and say the same. Furthermore, when Jinen was killed, there was still snow atop the lantern. No individual could have possibly jumped from it.

Murashige stared at the camellias outside the garden.

"Kahei could have shot Jinen, couldn't he?" he asked.

A warrior as knowledgeable as Kahei could easily have struck Jinen from near the ramparts. He was often said to have the strength of ten men, and while that was an exaggeration, his physical might *was* immense. Murashige had never seen him use a bow, but underling or not, Kahei was a warrior, so Murashige figured there was little chance he couldn't use one at all.

"Kahei is not the kind of man who would do such a thing," Juuemon replied. "But if it is a question of whether he *could* have done it, then yes, my liege, I believe so... However—"

"He couldn't have made the arrow disappear afterward, right?"

Juuemon hung his head. "Indeed."

Jinen's body had an arrow wound with no arrow. If Kahei had shot him from across the garden, then what of the vanishing arrow?

There was no way the murder arrow could have been shot from outside the castle zone. Putting aside the whereabouts of the phantom arrow for the time being, the eaves lining the outer corridor blocked any and all incoming arrows. Granted, shooting an arrow through the gap bored in the rampart was not unfathomable. On closer inspection, there was an embrasure directly across the garden from the corpse, conveniently enough. However, Murashige did not think for a second that was how Jinen was killed. The embrasure was wider on the inside to prevent outside arrows and bullets from penetrating the rampart. A hundred thousand arrows could be shot from outside the castle zone, yet Murashige highly doubted a single one would ever fly through that gap and pierce Jinen.

A watchtower could be seen far to the right. It was around forty *ken* away, and the fact that it was visible meant an arrow could have been shot from it. A skilled enough archer was capable of shooting a victim from a sixty-*ken* distance.

"Juuemon. Who was in that watchtower?"

For the first time, Juuemon couldn't answer immediately.

"I know not. Forgive me, my liege."

This hypothesis had the same problem as with Kahei—it failed to explain the disappearing arrow. Jinen had died during the dawn's early light. It was so dark, one could just barely see their hand if held outstretched. Murashige understood that one couldn't have seen Jinen from forty *ken* away, but he issued his orders nonetheless:

"Find out who was there."

"Yes, my liege."

Suddenly, war drums sounded throughout Arioka Castle. Murashige's eyes glinted, and Juuemon raised his head, his face tensed.

The sounding of the drums meant different things depending on the rhythm. This particular signal meant that enemy forces were close at hand.

7

As previously planned, Murashige headed for the keep. The members of his guard assembled one after the other, and Araki Kyuuzaemon, too, came rushing. Attendants carried Murashige's armor, which was stored in his mansion. Murashige's first priority was to try making sure what direction the enemy was coming at them from. That was the point of the tower. He spotted skirmishes to the west of the castle. It seemed Oda hadn't brought the full might of his army to bear, which was a relief. He could see the insignia on their banners, but it was too far to make out who was fighting who.

With the assistance of his attendants, he donned his *haramaki* armor and strapped up his shoulder straps. While he was putting on his tassets, bracers, and other pieces of his armor in turn, a messenger rushed in panting.

"Attention! Nakanishi brought thirty of his troops west of the castle for a patrol, where they encountered the troops of Oda clan retainer Mutou."

"Souemon, was it? He never learns his lesson."

Mutou Souemon Kiyohide, Lord of Tsuruga, was a general of wisdom and courage serving directly under Nobunaga. He was the first to invade Settsu, his forces having crossed spears with Murashige's the month prior. That fight had ended when Mutou withdrew after it turned into a melee that threatened to take the heads of both generals.

"How many of the enemy are there?"

"I caught sight of around forty, Your Lordship."

Mutou couldn't be wanting to attack the castle with numbers that low. Murashige reckoned this was reconnaissance in force.

Once again, he looked west. Judging by the battle standards raised next to the commanders' horses, both Shinpachirou and the enemy commander were alive and well. He couldn't hear gunfire. Both sides most likely carried guns, but for a close-up confrontation, forged weapons like swords and spears took precedence, as there was no time to load or reload.

"Shinpachirou's pushing them back," said Murashige after eyeing the battle for a short while.

If the messenger wasn't wrong about the enemy's numbers, then Shinpachirou should have been at a numerical disadvantage, but Murashige knew that on the battlefield, the enemy's numbers always *looked* greater than they actually were. He concluded that their numbers weren't inferior to the Oda forces after all. Shinpachirou's standard was moving right and left, right and left, while Mutou's wasn't moving much—this told Murashige that Mutou was gradually backing off and that Shinpachirou was pushing his forces away, albeit not decisively.

"My lord," said Kyuuzaemon. "Your orders? Shall we go to battle?"

"Wait."

Murashige strained his eyes toward the north, east, and south. He was used to the landscape of northern Settsu; he was making absolutely sure that there weren't any troops hiding in ambush amid the reedbeds or the sparse woods. Luring out castle troops with a small contingent and then raiding when the castle gates were opened was a well-known rudimentary tactic. Murashige would never be fooled by such a ruse.

It was difficult to fully conceal troops. There were many tells, from the swaying of the branches to the startlement of the birds, to the glinting of spear tips, to the rising of the smoke from the fire used for cooking. Well acquainted with the topography of Hokusetsu, Murashige was confident he could spot troops if they were numerous enough to be able to take Arioka Castle, and so it was with confidence that Murashige concluded that there were no troops in ambush.

This battle was not premeditated. Instead, both Nakanishi's and Mutou's lines of sight had been blocked by the slight undulation of the land, leading to them bumping into each other unprepared.

This afforded Murashige a golden opportunity.

"Excellent," he murmured. "Go take Souemon's head. Send plenty of men from Fort Jorozuka."

"Yes, sir," replied Kyuuzaemon.

Fort Jorozuka, located at the western tip of Arioka Castle, was in fact a gathering place constructed for the warriors in Arioka more than it was a fort. If they sent troops from there now, they ought to make it in time. The war drums were sounded apace. It was the signal ordering the samurai in charge of the foot soldiers to depart for battle.

No matter what type of battle it was, the time to strike could change in the blink of an eye. The time it took for one's orders to actually get troops moving was always intolerably long. With bated breath, Murashige watched the progress of the battle intently. Getting hit with Abe Niemon's betrayal on top of Takayama Ukon's and Nakagawa Sehyoue's defection had sapped the castle of its vigor. If they could defeat or slay one of Oda's generals here, it would greatly increase the troops' morale. More than anything else, Murashige wanted that general's head.

"Juuemon, stand watch over the north. If you catch the faintest glimpse of the enemy, then inform me immediately."

"Yes, my liege."

"Where are those foot soldiers?"

His gaze went to Fort Jorozuka; the troops there hadn't moved. They weren't even getting ready to move out. They were simply stationary.

"Kyuuzaemon, my orders haven't reached Fort Jorozuka. Issue the orders once more."

Kyuuzaemon swiftly conveyed Murashige's commands. Once again, the war drums were sounded, and this time, the *horagai* trumpet shells were blown as well. At last, Murashige saw Fort Jorozuka spring to action. The tips of the long spears the foot soldiers gripped glinted in the distance, but they were being slow. This was not the pace of men going out to do battle.

Looking back at the battlefield, Mutou's forces had been crushed, and they were retreating northwest. Nakanishi Shinpachirou must have gotten exhausted from the unforeseen battle, for he didn't attack the routed enemy. The battle could be called a victory, but to Murashige's chagrin, it appeared Mutou's head was not going to be taken.

Upon seeing the enemy retreating, the troops packing the castle tower cried with shouts of joy. Kyuuzaemon, too, was smiling broadly.

"My lord, victory is ours! Shall we raise our voices in triumph?"

Murashige wasn't smiling in the least. "Only after we welcome back Shinpachirou."

His eyes were fixed squarely on Fort Jorozuka.

When a warrior took a head in battle, the general always inspected it. Identifying a severed head was the way of war.

Murashige decided the head-identification session would take place in the inner citadel. By having Shinpachirou and the others walk to the inner citadel, he was showing them off in their moment of triumph for many pairs of eyes to see, thereby boosting morale. Fresh from battle, Nakanishi's forces passed through the castle gates and crossed the town of Itami and the samurai quarter before ascending to the inner citadel, basking in the jubilation of the crowds the whole way there. While it may only have been a skirmish, seeing the men who'd defeated Oda's troops brought joy to not just the townsfolk or the warriors but to all the people in the castle area—just as Murashige had planned. Shinpachirou's face and body were drenched in the blood of those he'd slain; the warriors looked frightful, smeared with mud and dust, but all that filth served as proof of their bravery.

Of Nakanishi's forces, one horseback warrior had sustained an injury, but they had taken the head of a commander. The Mutou foot soldiers who were taken prisoner were asked for the head's name; it came to light that it belonged to a samurai from Wakasa Province. The warrior who had distinguished himself in battle was given a sword and a letter of commendation, winning him great honor.

With the head now identified, Nakanishi's forces were treated to drink below the castle tower, irrespective of rank. They sat in a circle on the bare ground, while Shinpachirou sat on a camp stool, clapping gleefully like a child.

"A treat of *sake*! Ah, how delightful! That Mutou was easy to deal with. I remember his face, so next time, I'll take his head and show it to His Lordship!"

Murashige watched them from within the castle tower.

He hadn't had an opportunity to take off his armor, so he still had his stomach band and bracers on, although he'd removed his helmet. Kyuuzaemon had already taken his leave, so the only ones there were Murashige and his guard.

The Nakanishi troops pouring one another drinks didn't realize Murashige was watching them. Shinpachirou gulped down the booze that was poured into his unglazed sake cup, then laughed and engaged in some flippant boasting. The other warriors, meanwhile, were not as simpleminded. In the eyes of the men drinking and the eyes of the men brushing off the dust of war, there was a vague gloom. They weren't drinking with spirit or cheer. Murashige sensed that their depression was rooted in their dissatisfaction with their leadership.

This won't do, he thought.

"Juuemon."

"Yes," said Koori Juuemon. "I am here."

"We must hurry the investigation of Jinen's murder along. Though to you, I'll give a different mission."

"Yes, my liege. Whatever Your Lordship asks."

"Good."

The troops were brooding over how they'd been made to fight a purposelessly close battle because the castle hadn't sent reinforcements.

"The foot-soldier commanders of Fort Jorozuka were moving sluggishly. Shinpachirou had the edge, so it did not lead to anything serious, but if we had gotten pushed back, they might have been seconds too late to prevent a total rout."

So long as the general's orders could only be transmitted through messengers, trumpet shells, and war drums, it was only natural for it to take time for those orders to be carried out. But even accounting for that, Fort Jorozuka had been slow to mobilize. Murashige was the only one who nursed suspicions that something was amiss.

"If there are traitors, then we must slay them. If something untoward happened with the conveyance of my orders, then we must investigate. The foot-soldier commanders are, as you well know, Yamawaki, Hoshino, Oki, and Miyawaki. Go look into why there was such a delay. As for who shall guard me in your place...let's go with Inui Sukesaburou. Call him for me."

Juuemon bowed his head at once. "Yes, my liege! I shall do so. If you would excuse me."

With that, he drew back, and when he'd gained enough distance from Murashige, he broke into a run.

There were many in the guard who were even more proficient at the military arts than Juuemon. Murashige had chosen Juuemon as their leader not only due to his superior tact and arithmetic prowess, but most of all due to his speed.

8

It was quiet that night, and freezing cold.

Once the sun set, there was nothing they could do. There was only so much oil to fuel the votive lights or torches, and they could not waste their resources. If they stayed awake until late, their sleep would become too deep, and it would take time for them to awaken in the event of an emergency. Going to sleep early was a warrior's pearl of wisdom. On this night, however, Murashige was still awake. He lit the votive lights in the hall with his statue of the Shakyamuni Buddha, then assumed the cross-legged *zazen* meditation position in front of the statue.

The clouds hung low and heavy. Murashige was waiting for it to snow. Before long, he heard footsteps approaching down the corridor.

"Sukesaburou, is that you?"

"Yes, my liege."

"Is it snowing yet?"

"'Tis, Your Lordship. Everything is just like that day."

"Aid from the heavens," Murashige muttered to himself.

Murashige entered the corridor to find the portly Sukesaburou, along with another, lower-ranked member of the guard, waiting there. As Juuemon had been ordered to probe the state of affairs in Fort Jorozuka, Sukesaburou had been called here in Juuemon's place. Sukesaburou's nature was the opposite of Juuemon's. He wasn't as thoughtful or perceptive, and he was slow about everything, but his physical might was on par with Kahei's, and he was surprisingly capable of using technique in a fight. And just like Juuemon, Sukesaburou was a trustworthy, loyal man who followed Murashige's words to the letter.

The reason Murashige was waiting for it to snow was, of course, to see how the scene looked on the day that Abe Jinen died. The boy had perished at the very break of dawn when it was still dark out. Right now, it was the early evening, and some sunlight remained.

Murashige made his guard hold a portable candlestick holder and stepped out into the corridor. Other members of the guard were already gathered around the storeroom that Jinen had died in, and they were holding torches, having lit a watch fire. Light snowfall accumulated on the flat plot of land meant to one day be a garden, and just like that day, the stone lantern that Furuta Sasuke had picked out for Murashige was topped with snow. Murashige opened the shoji door to the closet and contemplated for a short while.

Abe Jinen had died here. He had sustained a deep arrow wound to the chest and breathed his last before Juuemon's eyes. The arrow was nowhere to be found, nor were there footprints in the snow in the garden. The left and right sides of the square corridor each contained two members of the guard, and there were muscular and strong troops along the castle ramparts that sandwiched the garden.

Murashige had decided to lock Abe Jinen in this storeroom the day before he died. The arrangements for the guard were made after Jinen was ordered to be locked up. Until then, nobody knew where to place Jinen. Murashige himself didn't pick the storeroom for any particular reason. No matter who had killed the boy, they couldn't have had enough time to craft some elaborate trick or device.

Murashige glanced outside. He couldn't see it through the darkness, but a watchtower stood around forty *ken* away in that direction.

"Sukesaburou. That watchtower has lookouts, does it not?"

"It does, my liege…" For some reason, Sukesaburou seemed disconcerted. "Juuemon has ordered me to investigate who was the lookout in that watchtower the morning of Jinen's death."

Evidently, before heading to Fort Jorozuka, Juuemon had issued orders of his own as head of the guard. Murashige admired the man's scrupulousness.

"Did you investigate?"

"Yes, my lord. The lookout is a skilled gunman from Saika by the name of Sagehari. The other night sentries have corroborated that he was scouting throughout the night."

Murashige figured that the reason Sukesaburou's voice was so unsteady was because he hadn't reported to Murashige what he'd already found out. He didn't reprimand him. The dimwit had been a dimwit. Making good use of what little time he had was more important. The obscure light of nightfall was similar enough to daybreak to simulate the scene; there was no time to waste.

"A Saika, you say. Do you know whether he had a bow on him?"

"Sagehari apparently always brings his gun to his night shifts as a lookout. However, no one knows whether he did so on that night."

"I see." Murashige stroked his chin.

Though they were few in number, some men from Saika had been sent from Hongan-ji Temple to Arioka Castle as reinforcements. Many of the people who lived in Saika, a village in Kii Province, were pirates by trade. Those who had gotten their hands on guns relatively early on made for strong troops who were already used to battle from a young age. Their will to fight was high, and they were adept at steering ships. They were far from useless on the land, too, for they also knew their way around guns. They were not, however, samurai.

The main accomplishments of samurai warriors lay in their knowledge of archery and horsemanship. Some were more skilled than others, but there were no samurai who couldn't pull a bow or ride a horse. Murashige wondered whether that held true for the gentlemen from Saika as well. Bows were different from guns, and the amount of time required to learn the bow was long. Most could get the hang of how to fire a gun in a day or two, even if that didn't make them masterful marksmen. To learn how to fire a bow properly would take at least a month. Murashige imagined that the men from Saika, though great with guns, would find it pointless to try to learn the bow as well.

Besides, Abe Jinen had died when it was still mostly dark outside. There was no way someone in that watchtower could have made Abe Jinen out. It was a feat not even an archer like the legendary Nasu no Yoichi could have pulled off. Murashige discarded the notion that this Sagehari from Saika might be his man.

"...Hmm." Murashige had examined the storeroom, the garden, the castle ramparts, the corridor, and everything else. "I know 'tis impossible, but let's try it anyway. Sukesaburou, set up a straw post in place of Jinen. Make it straddle the shoji frame. Also, bring a bow and arrow and an archer's glove. And some hemp twine, too."

"Hemp twine, Your Lordship?"

"You heard me. Order a servant to find some twine that's long. Ten *ken* long."

"Right away, my liege."

Sukesaburou noisily dashed through the corridor. Murashige gave orders to the remaining member of his guard and made his preparations. He had the man hold his footwear and was about to descend to the garden when he remembered that there were no footprints in the snow when Jinen died, so he went all the way around the garden and stood by the rampart.

Soon, a straw post was placed where Jinen had been. Such posts of straw were usually used as targets for archery training. Murashige took the bow that Sukesaburou handed him and plucked it two, three times. It was a carefully maintained bow with a heavy draw weight. Murashige, recalling that the arrow hadn't penetrated Jinen's back, slackened his pull on the drawstring a little.

The area by the rampart where Murashige now stood was where Mori Kahei had been patrolling when Jinen died. Across the garden from that position sat the straw post. It was five *ken* away, which wasn't particularly close but wasn't too far for an arrow.

Murashige glanced at the members of the guard holding torches. Of the Five Spears, who were on duty guarding Jinen that day, only Inui Sukesaburou had been present to witness this place.

Sukesaburou knelt down. "The hemp twine has arrived, my lord."

"Good. Now tie twine to three arrows."

Sukesaburou's sausage-like fingers clumsily tied the string. Murashige nocked one of the newly twine-attached arrows.

"Now let's see what happens. For caution's sake, step away from the straw post."

The members of the guard fell back, and Murashige drew the bow.

The stone lantern stood in between Murashige and the straw post, blocking his shot. Murashige returned the bowstring to its original position, shifted where he stood a little, and drew the string again. It was a night of the twelfth month, and the area was dead silent save for the roar of the torch fire. It was dusk, and the straw post was shrouded in darkness. Murashige fired the shot.

With a *thunk*, the arrow pierced through the straw post. The second and third shots sank deep into it as well.

"Well done, my liege!" said Sukesaburou with wonder and admiration; it wasn't entirely to flatter his lord.

Murashige's expression was blasé. To him, it was obvious he'd be able to hit a target five *ken* away with three arrows.

He still held the three arrows' respective strings in hand.

"Now...," he murmured, pulling hard on one of the strings.

The arrow didn't come out. The string that Sukesaburou had tied came loose and fell limply onto the snow.

"Good heavens," muttered Sukesaburou.

Murashige ignored him and pulled on the second string. It was even worse than last time; not only did the string come off, but it also shaved off the arrow feathers in the process, leaving them scattered on the corridor floor.

Without a word, he pulled on the third string. This time around, the arrow came out. Murashige kept pulling, and the arrow slid across the ground before reaching his hand.

"Oh-ho," said Sukesaburou. "Your Lordship, you figured out how Jinen was shot, and how the arrow disappeared as well."

Murashige glared at him.

"Sukesaburou. A member of the guard can't get by solely on the military arts. Look closely. This solves nothing."

"But, my liege, the arrow was taken away, was it not?"

"Only one out of three separate tries."

Murashige looked at the straw post. The members of the guard who returned to its side, torches in hand, illuminated it for Murashige to see the two arrows still stuck into it.

"I couldn't remove two of them. 'Tis possible that the culprit devised some way for the string to stay attached to the arrow. Maybe they could have used a light-drawstring bow so that the arrow didn't penetrate too deep into Jinen's body. But have a look, Sukesaburou."

Murashige pointed at the ground. There was a line in the snow—the track left by the arrow when Murashige dragged it back to him stood out clearly and distinctly.

"An arrow with a string tied to it will invariably leave a mark on the snow. And there were no such marks on the snow that morning. I thought that perhaps one might be able to pull on the string hard enough to send it flying through the air back to himself, so I tested it out. But I knew it—'tis not possible. So this isn't it, Sukesaburou. The culprit did it not this way."

"Ha—ha-ha!" While Sukesaburou was always respectful and

obedient, he seemed glad. "Then, Your Lordship, that means it was not Mori Kahei's doing."

If the method had in fact been a string-tied arrow, then the only one who could have fired that shot was the man who'd been patrolling the area by the castle ramparts, Mori Kahei. As a fellow member of the Five Spears, Sukesaburou must have found the idea of Mori Kahei getting charged with this crime less than agreeable.

Murashige's expression was severe. "It couldn't have been the lookout in the watchtower—Sagehari, was it? And it couldn't have been Kahei, either. Which leaves one of you four—yourself, Koori Juuemon, Akioka Shirounosuke, or Itami Ichirouza."

"Is that indeed what this means?"

"Tell Shirounosuke and Ichirouza to come to my residence tomorrow morning. Call Kahei, too. And bring yourself. I'll be questioning you."

"Yes, my lord. And what about Sagehari of Saika?"

"Call him, too."

Looking pensive, Sukesaburou complied.

9

The sun hadn't emerged fully, but it was the start of a new dawn and a new day.

A scroll depicting the great bodhisattva Hachiman hung in the alcove in the reception room of the Araki residence. The people gathered there that day entered through a separate room and were called one by one into the reception room.

There were no watchmen, no guards. Each time Murashige questioned one of five men, the two of them were the room's sole occupants. Of course, strong and brawny warriors were waiting in the next room over in case the unlikely occurred. Even so, the only ones conversing were Murashige and the person being interrogated.

The first to be called was Sagehari of Saika. A small man, he was presumably around thirty years of age. His eyes were moribund and lacking vitality. Given Sagehari's low rank and status, one might expect him to hesitate to enter a castle lord's residence, but he didn't seem particularly timid. He just had a dispirited look in his eyes. *The eyes of a man who's always on the battlefield*, thought Murashige.

"I'm here on the occasion of your summoning me," Sagehari said, not entirely politely.

"You are Sagehari?"

"So they call me, Your Lordship."

"So is your real name different?"

"'Tis. *Sagehari* is a moniker. They said I could even shoot a *sagehari*, a needle held by string. However, since more people know me by Sagehari during battle, I call myself that now."

"A skilled sharpshooter, are you?"

"So I'm told, Your Lordship."

Sagehari must have already been informed of why he'd been summoned. Not wanting to get into minutiae, Murashige got to the point.

"On the morning Jinen died, you were the scout at the watchtower with a sight on the storeroom Jinen was imprisoned in, correct?"

"That is so. Only, I knew not that such an honored personage was trapped in that storeroom at that time."

"Did you take a bow up with you?"

Sagehari looked nonplussed. "Firing guns may be my strong suit, but I have never even held a bow. Please, just ask the Saika men."

Murashige nodded. *I figured as much.*

"So," he went on, "when Jinen died, did you see or hear anything?"

"Well...about that, Your Lordship." Sagehari straightened up his posture. "The servants told me that Abe cried out, but I did not hear any such cry. I heard the sound of armor and shifted my eyes to the residence, wondering what was going on."

"Hmm. Did you catch sight of anything?"

"I can see in the dark, but it was a little far. All I saw was a small fire."

"A fire, eh?"

Murashige raised an eyebrow. He hadn't heard about a fire.

Sagehari continued, not especially excited or worked up, "Yes. I believe that may have been a candlestick holder. If he was struck down and it went out, then maybe he sustained a wound and dropped the candle. After that, I saw a cluster of lights—torches, I assume."

The torches the guards were carrying, thought Murashige.

"How many torches did you see?"

"Two."

"Are you certain?"

Sagehari laughed.

"They say that in addition to my gun skills, I have a good memory. There were without a doubt two torches—or rather, the fires I think were torches—on that day."

Murashige paid him in silver for his time and dismissed him.

Next was Itami Ichirouza.

His full name was Ichirouzaemon, and he had a connection to the Itami clan, which had made Arioka Castle their stronghold back when it was called Itami Castle. At twenty-four years of age, he was a rather unimpressive-looking man of slim figure, but he was a crack shot with a gun, and he was more knowledgeable about the geography of Itami, where Arioka Castle was located, than anyone else. The Itami clan had placed enough trust in him to dispatch him to Sakai to buy guns, but because of that, he inspired envy in his peers, whose slander forced him to flee temporarily. Murashige overthrew the Itami clan, which made him the archenemy of Ichirouza's clan, but in this era, it wasn't uncommon to serve under the man who'd overthrown one's former master.

"You were on guard duty alongside Inui Sukesaburou?" asked Murashige.

"Yes, my liege, I was," Ichirouza replied calmly.

"Before daybreak on that morn, did you hear Abe Jinen's voice?"

"I heard a voice, but I know not if it was Jinen's."

Murashige was a bit surprised, yet he kept that to himself. By distinguishing between what he heard and what he thought, Ichirouza was being cautious and prudent. Murashige hadn't believed Ichirouza was that kind of samurai.

"Describe the voice you heard, then."

"I think it was a cry of surprise. I do not think it was a cry of anguish or death throes."

Murashige's eyebrow rose a little. That reply sounded a tad too crisp and well enunciated. It was likely because all the time that had passed since Jinen's murder allowed Ichirouza to prepare his testimony. While Murashige had been unable to give the investigation his absolute undivided attention, he realized it might have been a mistake to put off interrogating the members of his guard.

"What happened afterward?"

"I stopped Sukesaburou from running to the scene and told him I would go."

"Hmm. Why did you decide to go and not him?"

"My liege, Sukesaburou was holding a hand spear, so I thought it best for him to stand watch outside rather than enter the storeroom."

The hand spears that higher-ranked samurai used were much shorter than the long spears that bottom-rung foot soldiers used. Their length ranged from half to twice the user's height.

"Since I was carrying a gun and a sword, I put down the gun, used the watch fire to light a torch that was on hand, and grasped my sword's hilt before rushing to the scene."

Murashige acknowledged the truth in Ichirouza's testimony—if a scuffle had played out at the storeroom, Sukesaburou was too big and his spear too long to be anything but in the way.

"I see. Continue."

"Yes, my liege. When I hastened to the storeroom, Koori Juuemon and Akioka Shirounosuke were already there, and Jinen was lying faceup on the floor. I heard the two men's footsteps, as well as their shouting at Jinen to pull himself together."

Ichirouza had volunteered more information than he'd been asked for. It appeared he was telling Murashige in so many words that Juuemon and Shirounosuke didn't act suspiciously. Murashige understood that Ichirouza likely wanted to defend his comrades in arms; he promptly mulled over whether it might be a lie.

For the time being, he couldn't determine the statement's veracity one way or the other. His gut was telling him this probably wasn't a lie.

"Understood. Did you see or hear anything else of note?"

Ichirouza bowed his head deeply. "I must apologize, my liege. I was too preoccupied with Jinen and did not pay attention to our surroundings."

Murashige couldn't blame him. The attack had taken place within the residence, so under normal circumstances, their highest priority would have been to at least search for the culprit, but Ichirouza had been ordered to protect Jinen. Being concerned over Jinen's wound at the expense of scanning the area was not an indiscretion in this case.

"I see. Very well, then."

With that, Ichirouza was dismissed.

The next to be called in was Mori Kahei.

Though the Mori clan had a liaison with the Mouri clan, Kahei was descended from the Mori branch whose roots lay in Awa Province. He was thirty years of age, and he was a large man sporting the beard of a larger-than-life heroic figure. A zealous believer in Amitabha's Pure Land, he had holed up in Osaka Hongan-ji. When the Araki and Hongan-ji were deepening their ties, Mori had come to Arioka Castle as the messenger's guard, and he never went back. He was adept in all the martial arts, and his grasp of the spear bordered on mastery, but he was extremely lacking in perception, so he was by no means suited to a leadership position. Now that he was face-to-face with Murashige, his hulking frame was curled up with awe and humility.

"On the night Abe Jinen died, you were patrolling the area along the rampart, were you not?" Murashige asked.

"Yes, my liege!" Kahei shouted, falling prostrate and not lifting his head.

"Let me ask you—what had you patrolling there as opposed to outside the storeroom?"

Kahei had been standing watch over the sole ingress into the storeroom, but he hadn't been right in front of it. Instead, he'd been patrolling with the garden in between him and Jinen.

"My liege. I was following the orders of the head of the guard," he said, speaking of Juuemon.

"What were Juuemon's orders?"

"He said that if we all camped in front of the storeroom and watched outside, we would be with our backs to Jinen, which was too risky. Yet if we all faced the storeroom, we wouldn't notice any suspicious individuals approaching. As such, I was ordered during sunup to stand watch from a distance."

Murashige nodded. He reckoned he would have issued much the same command.

"Then let me ask you this: Why didn't you enter the garden?"

The garden visible from the storeroom—which was really a garden in name only—amounted to nothing more than a plot of land that would one day be crafted into a garden. Despite that, Kahei had avoided that mostly empty stretch during his patrol, as evidenced by the lack of footprints.

"An underling like me," he replied, his voice deep, "could never so much as think of trampling Your Lordship's garden. I swear that I did not avoid the garden out of dereliction of duty. I was simply intent on doing my duty without being careless or clumsy."

"I understand. I applaud your conscientiousness."

"I thank Your Lordship for this pleasure!" He banged his head on the floor.

"Raise your head, Kahei. Tell me what you saw and heard at the time Jinen died."

Kahei sat up. He was trembling. Then at last, he forced his words out.

"Before the dawn broke, I heard Jinen's voice. 'Ah,' he cried. I looked to see a candle, and though I couldn't make out much through the darkness, Jinen was on the floor. I considered rushing over, but I did not wish to trample Your Lordship's garden. While I was at a loss for what to do, when I saw that several of my comrades had already run to his side, I concluded I would be of no use there and that I ought to continue keeping my eyes peeled while remaining at my post."

"Did you see anything? The culprit, the arrow as it was in the air—anything at all?"

Once again, Kahei's forehead met the floor.

"I was born dim-witted; I did not see anything of that nature. I have no excuse, my lord."

"Very well."

The other members of the guard had been standing at the square corridor, with the storeroom past the corner out of sight. Disregarding how dark it was out, the only ones with a sight on the storeroom were Kahei and Sagehari. Sagehari's watchtower was too far to see anything. As Murashige had figured Kahei would be the only one to have witnessed the moment Jinen was murdered, his disappointment was sizable.

"I've heard enough. You're dismissed."

Kahei obeyed and got to his feet. Murashige realized then that he'd forgotten to ask one thing.

"Kahei. On that night, what did you have on your person?"

Kahei froze in his tracks as though he'd been struck by lightning, and he prostrated himself the second he turned around.

"Pray forgive my rudeness, my lord!"

"'Tis no matter. Answer the question."

"Yes, my lord. I was wearing my *do-maru* chest armor and had my sword."

"Is that all?"

"Yes, Your Lordship!"

It was a matter of course that he should carry a sword, and his equipment was light indeed for a man tasked with guard duty. Murashige had appointed him this role due to his connections; he figured Kahei lacked the money to complete his armor and weapons set.

However, that didn't mean Murashige would let him off the hook.

"You forget yourself. Your duty requires a fuller set of arms. Even if you don't have everything, you should at least be resourceful enough to fetch a long spear from the spear warehouse. We're in the middle of a war; the warehouses are not locked."

Kahei looked like he was on the verge of tears.

Next was Akioka Shirounosuke.

Akioka was part of a clan that served the Araki, and there were many more servitors from that clan besides Shirounosuke, but he was the unrivaled master of the blade among Murashige's retainers. He was slender, with eyes as sharp as a hawk's. Oddly enough, a large proportion of swordmasters were fastidious by nature, and Shirounosuke was no exception; he seldom associated with other people. Being a loner was a liability on the battlefield, as it meant that they had no one they could trust to have their back. But to the lord's guard, whose main duty was protecting Murashige, he was ideally suited.

"Shirounosuke, at Your Lordship's service." He prostrated himself.

For a short while, Murashige said nothing. Shirounosuke didn't seem to think anything of it, for he did not budge.

"...Raise your head. I'm going to ask you some questions."

"I shall tell Your Lordship whatever I know."

"During the break of dawn when Abe Jinen died, you and Koori Juuemon heard a voice you recognized as Jinen. You both ran for the storeroom, and Jinen died shortly thereafter. Did I get that right?"

"Ye did, my lord."

"Answer me carefully."

Shirounosuke placed both fists on the floor and listened obediently.

"Had Abe Jinen already been on the floor by the time Koori Juuemon rushed over? If not, then did Jinen collapse after Juuemon rushed over? Which is it?"

Shirounosuke didn't reply immediately. Murashige looked on that interval favorably.

"Actually, my liege, the one who was running at the head when we heard that worrying cry and took those torches was me. And since I was also the one who rounded the corner first..."

Shirounosuke chose his words carefully.

"...I was the first one to see Jinen, who was lying faceup on the floor. However, Juuemon must have seen what I saw, albeit a few seconds later. Upon seeing Jinen's chest covered in blood, I thought the culprit might be inside the closet, so I drew my sword and peeked through a gap in the door."

"Wait. Tell me—at that point, you were holding a torch in your left hand, yes?"

"Yes. That is so, my liege." After a little pause, he smiled faintly. "I have no difficulty drawing my sword using only my right hand."

"I see," said Murashige. "Continue."

"Yes, my liege. It was discourteous of me, but I opened the door with a foot and stepped into the storeroom. As Your Lordship is aware, 'twas entirely empty. Juuemon put down his bow and embraced Jinen, then attempted to tend to him as I inspected the storeroom."

"Hmm," Murashige intoned. "So Juuemon was carrying a bow."

"Indeed, my liege, that is the case. Since the sword is my strong suit, the leader of the guard brought projectile weapons." Shirounosuke raised his head. "Looking back on that day in detail like this, there is no doubt in my mind. Jinen had already collapsed before Juuemon hastened over to him."

"Understood." Murashige heaved a soft sigh. "While Juuemon was looking after Jinen, tell me what you saw and heard, and what you did."

"Yes, my lord. I had not yet let go of my suspicion that someone might be lurking in the storeroom, so I examined every nook and cranny. Then I found the fallen candlestick holder in the corridor, and as I presumed it to be what Jinen had used, I checked to see if it was still warm, as a precaution."

Murashige pondered for a moment.

"Where did that candlestick holder turn up?" he asked. "How did Jinen light the candle?"

Fires were mainly ignited using flints. On that day, Jinen had been rid of his sword and thrown into the storeroom with only the scriptures he was given and the clothes on his back. Unless he always concealed a flint inside the breast of his clothing, he shouldn't have had a way to light the candle.

"I know nothing of the candle, my lord," Shirounosuke replied swiftly. "The storeroom contained a brazier, so it might have housed a banked fire."

"I see."

Murashige hadn't ordered a brazier be placed in that closet, but he supposed it had been put there out of concern for the boy suffering in the cold of winter.

Last to be summoned was Inui Sukesaburou.

Sukesaburou had once been a ronin—a masterless samurai. Initially, he served under the Saito clan in Mino Province, but he drifted to Settsu after the Oda overthrew the Saito. Back then, Murashige himself wasn't a lord, so he lacked the wherewithal to have too many people under his employ, but he added Sukesaburou to his retainers because he saw promise in the man's prodigious strength. Many years later, now that Murashige was Lord of Settsu, Sukesaburou had become one of the Five Spears of the Guard hand-selected by the Araki clan.

Murashige didn't suspect Sukesaburou had killed Jinen. Sukesaburou followed orders with single-minded earnestness. If Murashige had ordered him to kill Jinen, he would have. Sukesaburou had a side to him that was a touch soft and mild for a warrior, so he would have worn a pained and sorrowful look while doing the deed, but he would've obeyed his orders and killed Jinen regardless. But the orders Murashige had issued were to *protect* Jinen. Therefore, Sukesaburou could not have been the culprit. That being said, Murashige still had to interrogate him.

"On the night Abe Jinen died, you were standing watch alongside Itami Ichirouza, correct?"

"Yes, my lord!" Sukesaburou replied enthusiastically, throwing his head onto the floor. "I was standing watch with Ichirouza!"

"I see. Did you hear Abe Jinen's voice before daybreak?"

"Yes, I did."

"What exactly did you hear?"

Sukesaburou's vigor deflated. His eyes wandered as he faltered. "My lord...it was a cry of 'ah'...or perhaps 'oh'..."

"Are you sure you heard him? Tell me the whole truth."

"Yes, I definitely heard him, my liege."

Murashige felt he had to give up on asking Sukesaburou for any more details. Every person had their uses. Sukesaburou was strong and loyal, and that was all he needed to be a capable samurai. If he wasn't as quick-witted as others, then that just meant his time to shine lay elsewhere.

"After you heard his voice, what did you do?"

"My lord!" he shouted, bowing his head deeply. "I was about to rush over when Ichirouza said I must not vacate the position, and seeing that he was right, I did not move, opting to let Ichirouza check what was wrong."

"I see. You acted with composure."

"I humbly thank Your Lordship for such kind words."

Sukesaburou's expression was sunny. He had probably feared a scolding for his negligence in not rushing to Jinen's side.

"While you were standing guard at your post, did you see or hear anything?"

"I did not, my lord," Sukesaburou said with pride.

"…I'm going to ask you once more. Did you pick up on anything odd? Did you hear something, perhaps? Did somebody come passing through?"

He hung his head timidly, but the answer was the same.

"No, nothing. Following the incident, I witnessed Your Lordship, Juuemon, and the rest with you all go through the corridor toward the storeroom. I did not see anyone else crossing nearby, and I was fulfilling my duty to watch with my whole heart."

Murashige made a mental note to remember that Sukesaburou obstructed the corridor the entire time.

"I see. I'll ask you one last question. That night, what did you and Ichirouza have on you?"

Sukesaburou threw out his chest.

"I was wearing my suit of armor hailing from Inui clan tradition. I had on my armored headband and my sword at my waist, with a spear in hand."

"And Ichirouza?"

"I cannot remember."

It was of the essence that a warrior be able to compare and distinguish the possessions of allies and enemies. One could ascertain the rank of an enemy through their armor, which in turn allowed one to prove their achievement when slaying a high-ranking foe. Lapses of memory were to be expected in the thick of the battlefield, but to forget what one's fellow guard was wearing or carrying after spending a whole night standing watch with him was unacceptable.

After admonishing him to that effect, Murashige dismissed Sukesaburou.

With that, Murashige had grilled all the people who had been close to that storeroom save for one.

Inui Sukesaburou and Itami Ichirouza had been together, and after they heard a cry that they assumed was Jinen's voice, Ichirouza ran for the storeroom.

Koori Juuemon and Akioka Shirounosuke both headed for the storeroom. While Shirounosuke examined the closet's interior, Juuemon was left to his own devices.

Mori Kahei had been alone, but the only way he could have been able to approach the storeroom without being seen was through the garden, and there were no footprints on the snow to incriminate him.

Sagehari was atop a watchtower at least forty *ken* away, and there were witnesses who corroborated that he had been serving as a lookout the whole night.

The only one with a bow had been Juuemon…

Alone before the scroll of the great bodhisattva Hachiman, Murashige closed his eyes.

Some time later, an attendant called out from beyond the door.

"Koori Juuemon wishes for an audience with Your Lordship."

Murashige opened his eyes.

"Let him inside."

10

Juuemon entered looking slightly dirty all over.

He sat cross-legged in the dim and gloomy reception room, placing his fists on the floor and bowing his head. He was covered in dust, and the clothes he was wearing were different from his usual attire; they were tattered clothes made of hemp, the kind of garb a common foot soldier might don. Murashige had ordered Juuemon to probe into the state of Fort Jorozuka. He thought Juuemon would take longer than two or three days to return, so his coming back so soon came as a surprise.

"I have returned, my liege," said Juuemon, bowing his head yet deeper.

"You're back soon. Did something impede you?"

"No, my lord."

Juuemon's expression had always been vaguely blank, but now that he was so crusted with dirt and wearing rags, one would never suspect this man was the head of the Five Spears. The glint in his eyes, however, was sharp.

"Fate smiles on me, for I have pieced together a general picture of the state of Fort Jorozuka and the reason the troops got a late start when our men were skirmishing with Mutou. For the time being, I shall first report my findings. I also came to receive Your Lordship's orders regarding whether I should investigate in more detail."

"You're telling me you know why?"

"Yes, my liege. I know that which I ought to inform Your Lordship."

"Good. Speak."

Juuemon straightened up a little.

"One of my servants is on friendly terms with a foot soldier in Fort Jorozuka, and it was through his good offices that I stole inside the fort. Araki Kyuuzaemon's thorough investigation revealed that all four of the commanders of Fort Jorozuka stated that they did not hear the war drums."

"…I see. So Kyuuzaemon conducted the investigation, eh?"

After the battle, Kyuuzaemon had railed against Fort Jorozuka for mobilizing so sluggishly, but he hadn't looked into the reasons behind it. That Kyuuzaemon had in fact questioned the foot-soldier commanders behind Murashige's back left him unamused. However, Kyuuzaemon was a chief retainer. Murashige decided he couldn't call Kyuuzaemon's behavior an overreach.

"What of the trumpet shells?"

"The trumpet shells, they said they *did* hear. They claimed that that was why they prepared to go into battle but failed to make it in time."

The outermost enclosure of Arioka Castle contained the whole town of Itami. It covered a wide area, and as such, it made sense that it took time for orders to be relayed. It was also plausible that they couldn't hear the drums. But in that case, why did they hear the trumpet shells? That didn't add up.

"Is what they said true?"

Murashige could tell Juuemon was choosing his words.

"I know not, my lord, but it is clear that they all talked beforehand to get their story straight."

"Hmm... Are they traitors?"

"Loath as I am to gainsay Your Lordship, it does not seem so. Oki Tosa-no-kami remarked that if he distinguished himself on the battlefield, he could see himself employed by the shogunate clan, and comments made by the other foot-soldier commanders were on the whole not much different."

Murashige crossed his arms.

The four foot-soldier commanders of Fort Jorozuka recruited men who were down-and-out in life by promoting their own strength and troop numbers. They weren't people one could trust, but judging by what Juuemon had divulged, it was too early to conclude they were turncoats.

Amid the dim light of the early morning, Juuemon continued, "Only..."

"Only what?"

It was rare for Juuemon to hem and haw like this. He glanced at Murashige's face, then summoned a deep voice as if screwing up his resolve to say what needed saying.

"My liege, this is exceedingly difficult to tell you, but there is gossip among not just the foot-soldier commanders, but also the foot soldiers themselves and even the other samurai defaming Your Lordship."

Murashige's bushy eyebrow twitched. "Gossip, you say."

"Yes, my liege."

"No matter. Speak."

Though it was midwinter, sweat was running down Juuemon's forehead.

"It revolves around the Abe hostage matter. The conviction that Jin-en's death was a divine reckoning runs deep, while among the foot soldiers, rumor is spreading that it was Your Lordship who killed him after all. They make the case that killing him more quickly either by *hatamono* or by decapitation would have been just, yet Your Lordship ordered for Jinen to be kept alive, then simply killed him in the same breath. Not only that, but they say Your Lordship is barking the deed was another's—and that such behavior is craven."

Murashige listened without a word. The breeze was cold.

"There were some who opined that, thinking about it, even if Jinen said he desired death and rebirth in paradise, he was too young to have been truly prepared for that. To be told that he would live, to be given that joy and that hope, only to then be slain anyway..."

Murashige simply stared at Juuemon, who cast his eyes down.

"...They say Your Lordship is just as callous as Nobunaga."

A dog could be heard barking in the distance.

"...I see," said Murashige. "Juuemon, are you saying that is why the four commanders of Fort Jorozuka did not follow my orders?"

"Nay, Your Lordship. I believe the reason behind the delay is that the drums and the trumpet shells were hard to hear, and that it would take time to recognize the signal as orders intended for Fort Jorozuka. I cannot say anything definitive as to whether there was doubt in their hearts."

After a brief pause, Juuemon continued:

"To foot-soldier commanders like Yamawaki and Hoshino, being craven is just another way to put food on the table. What they worry about is a general who *lies*. They fail to see the point in risking their lives in battle if their glorious deeds and reputation building come undone. That was what they apparently stated."

"You're telling me that there are those who criticize me for lying about not killing Abe Jinen myself, is that right?"

"As much as it pains me to say it, my liege."

Murashige knew that there was no way that talk hadn't spread beyond the foot soldiers. Most likely, similar conversations had been taking place among the higher-ranked samurai and the populace of Itami.

He felt a shiver run down his spine.

Murashige had no intention of showing Abe Jinen mercy; there was another reason he hadn't had Jinen killed. But no one would understand his reasoning.

"Very well," he said. "You're dismissed."

Juuemon left Murashige alone in the reception room.

11

Murashige had his eyes closed.

It was the people who made the castle. A castle where the officers and soldiers doubted their general had what it took would fall with ease, no matter how deep its moat. Troops abandoning the castle with every night's passing. Commanders getting taken in by the smooth talk of the enemy. Murashige didn't need to hear Juuemon's report to sense that Jinen's death had caused the officers' and men's faith in Murashige to waver. A small setback had come to pass in the war councils that, up to that point, had been going smoothly, and that was likely the reason the foot-soldier commanders had hesitated to follow their orders. Murashige's instincts as a general, honed by surviving this time of wide-spread war and chaos, were tingling. If Oda's forces were to close in on Arioka now, the castle would fall.

Murashige was a samurai. He didn't balk at the idea of dying in battle. In fact, he thought it an honor. He didn't entertain the notion he might lose this war, but so long as he still had the wisdom and the valor, then nothing could be finer, as a warrior's death, than cutting open his own belly inside his castle after fighting to the bitter end using every means available. Dying slowly after being forsaken by his men as a general no longer worth serving, on the other hand, would tarnish his legacy.

Oda forces, which numbered in the tens of thousands, were slowly but steadily approaching Arioka Castle. Oda would definitely choose to go with brute force for the first battle. If they staved off the Oda during that battle, then he could act on plans for what to do afterward. But if Murashige's men doubted their general to any degree, the castle would fall. Oda Nobunaga was not an opponent he could defend against while battling doubt and apprehension at the same time.

His intuition was telling him he still had time to resolve this. If he could uncover who'd killed Abe Jinen and how—if the investigation yielded a good result—then there was still time. Jinen had died by an arrow, of that he was certain, but how had that arrow disappeared? How and from what direction had the culprit approached that storeroom? Could it be that this *was* divine punishment after all?

Everything was still so unclear.

But Murashige had one option left.

In this castle, there were none who excelled at military tactics more than Murashige, nor had he any betters when it came to scheming and conniving. Furthermore, the wisdom of no man in the castle exceeded Murashige's own—except for one place in the castle. The underground.

Slowly, sluggishly, Murashige rose to his feet.

In the basement of the castle tower, a well had been dug as a precaution in the unlikely event that water access was cut off.

Of course, in this water-rich area, one would find water no matter where they dug, so the precaution was rather pointless. Murashige procured a portable candlestick holder and descended to the underground alone. He came to a stop in front of the well. A hoarse and husky voice called out to him from the darkness.

"My lord. How rare to see Your Lordship here."

The man was, at a guess, in his forties. He bowed his head, illuminated by the glow of the votive light. When he moved, the keys at his waist jangled.

"Let me in," said Murashige.

"Yes, my lord."

A small hinged door lay in a corner of the basement, locked. The man stood in front of that door and inserted the key into the padlock. With a dull *click*, the padlock came unfastened.

"...I shall accompany Your Lordship."

"No need. Wait here."

The man hung his head and withdrew.

Beyond the door was a descending staircase. The stairs were wet from the moisture soaking through from the earth. Murashige climbed down one step at a time, and it creaked with each step. The light shed by his candle kept frightening away insects that could have been centipedes or millipedes for all Murashige knew.

He reached the bottom of the none-too-long staircase and the bare expanse it led to. Murashige's legs splashed in the water that had collected. Then a sound Murashige couldn't immediately identify reverberated from within the darkness.

It was a voice. A *chuckle*.

"Keh-heh-heh."

Murashige shifted his candlelight in the voice's direction. What met his eyes first were bars of wood. The wood of the chestnut tree was hard as steel, and it had been cut into thick bars and latticed by a skilled woodworker such that one couldn't so much as slip a piece of paper through. It was a small, cramped cage that was made to fit the tunnel that had been dug here.

What met his eyes next was the squatting figure inside the cage. The figure had their back to Murashige. The fire was bright.

"Kanbei," said Murashige.

The shadows on the wall of the dungeon flickered, as there was a slight draft blowing the flame of Murashige's candle. The chuckling had stopped, giving way to a hush. It was so quiet, he could hear bugs crawling and the flame wavering.

"Kanbei," he repeated.

Amid the darkness, Kanbei stirred slightly and showed his face.

A month had passed since Kanbei had been taken prisoner. Only a month. And yet the man had completely transformed.

His facial hair had grown out, and his head of hair was now disheveled. While his limbs had turned thin, his cheeks looked puffy. His clothes were frayed, and his whole frame looked oddly curved within the confines of the cage where he was kept. This was no longer the unflinching warrior who had told Murashige to his face that his machinations would spell Murashige's end.

More than anything else, his *eyes* were different. He kept blinking and blinking against the light of the candle, looking up at Murashige. His eyes were turbid, and it was as though he was looking at nothing in particular—as though he couldn't even understand what he was seeing.

Murashige looked down at those eyes.

"Kanbei, I heard your laughter. What were you laughing at?"

His voice was hoarse. "Nothing clever, Your Lordship."

"I don't care. Tell me."

Kanbei hung his head. "Your Lordship's footsteps sound different from the jailer's," he murmured. "Right away, I could tell the Lord of Settsu had come to visit me."

"Ah. And what of it?"

"I thought that the next time I would enjoy an audience with Your Lordship was after this war was over. I cannot say I expected to see the Lord of Settsu again before a single month had passed, so Your Lordship caught me by surprise."

"And that made you laugh?"

"......"

"Kanbei, I'll hear no more incoherent twaddle. No man would *laugh* upon being surprised."

But Murashige exhibited no anger or irritation. If anything, he addressed Kanbei with a measure of warmth. Kanbei's eyes remained cast downward.

"...Though I do not know who shall win or lose this war in the end, I did anticipate that this would lead to the fall of Arioka Castle," said Kanbei. "As such, whenever I find myself wondering whether this act of rebellion sputtered after one month's sound and fury, and whether a senseless battle like this would be the Kuroda's undoing... For some reason, something about it amuses me."

Kanbei spoke without fear of reprisal. Murashige could feel his blood boil.

"Preposterous. Arioka has not fallen!"

Kanbei stared intensely up at him from behind his unkempt hair. His cloudy eyes looked vaguely amused, somehow.

"Does that mean...that it *might* fall?"

Murashige's wrath abated instantly. Kanbei had sensed that Arioka was in a precarious position just from the sound of footsteps. Though Kanbei's eyes were failing him, it appeared his mind was as sharp as ever. Murashige smiled.

"I expected no less from you, Kanbei. 'Tis true. I came to tell you that recently, a mysterious and nefarious crime was perpetrated, and if we fail to uncover the truth, then the castle will fall. And your life may be forfeit as well—if the castle does fall, then I'll take your head to bring with me to the realm of the dead. I'll listen to any last words."

"A visit from the honorable Lord of Settsu, just to listen to some dying words? What would Your Lordship have me do?"

"Hmph. Surely, you know."

Kanbei said nothing for a moment. He shook his head. "Can it be?"

"It can. I think you're the only one who can clear up this wicked act."

Kanbei didn't reply.

"I've come to know three rear vassals in this area whom I thought too talented to end up as pawns in others' hands. There's Ukita Naoie, the Lord of Izumi who served the Uragami clan in Bishu. There's yours truly, who served the Ikeda clan in Settsu. And there's Kodera Kanbei of the Kodera clan in Banshu... Ah, you told me put aside the Kodera name. I suppose you're Kuroda now. Kuroda Kanbei Yoshitaka. You're the one."

Murashige sidled up to the wooden bars boxing Kanbei into a ball.

"Kanbei. Lend me your wisdom."

"...Is the Lord of Settsu feeling faint? Why this drivel?" he spat.

Murashige understood full well that it was absurd, but the odds were on his side. The man was sharp as a tack. That was how he'd earned the trust of the lord of the Kodera clan over his elders. It was why Kodera had made the case that they should side with Oda. And it was why he was unsatisfied being the chief vassal of the Kodera, instead cozying up to the Oda and acting as a de facto vassal of Hashiba, Lord of Chikuzen. That was the measure of this man: Kuroda Kanbei, the man whose shrewdness Murashige could not help but praise.

That was the way warriors were. Just as those who excelled at swordsmanship used the sword, and those who shone at arithmetic used arithmetic, those who proved proficient at military tactics couldn't help but be tacticians. He couldn't speak for the samurai of the Kamakura period who devoted themselves to the defense of their territory, but the samurai of this day and age were more than willing to change employers whenever their skill wasn't recognized if that was what it took to make their reputation known far and wide. And to Murashige, Kanbei stood out among those glory seekers as particularly guilty. When given a challenging puzzle to solve, Kanbei couldn't sit by without proving that he was the cleverest of them all. That was his nature. By Murashige's estimation, while Kanbei was a man of high caliber who stood above the crowd, he was also a man who was easy to lead around by the nose if one caught on to his tendencies.

Murashige sat down cross-legged on the earthy ground. The dampness and chill of the dungeon soaked through.

"But never mind whether you actually solve the case; you must be tired of this cage. I'm here to relieve you of your boredom. It all started with the betrayal of the lord of Owada Castle, Abe Niemon. Let me fill you in."

Murashige told Kanbei in minute detail about how Takayama Ukon, Nakagawa Sehyoue, and Abe Niemon had switched sides; about Jinen's murder by means of a seemingly invisible arrow; about the arrangement of the sentries that night; about the structure of his personal residence located in the inner citadel; about the rumors that Jinen's death was divine retribution; and about the uproar at the war council.

Initially, Kanbei was facing away from him. He didn't plug his ears, but he strove not to listen to a word of Murashige's explanation. However, the more Murashige spoke, the more fidgety Kanbei became, and he looked up from time to time.

At last, Murashige told him about everything, up to and including what had brought him down here to the dungeon, before he finished talking. The flame of the candle kept on flickering, the sheer cold of the twelfth month sinking deep inside him.

"Heh."

That was how it started.

The next moment, Kanbei was laughing loudly enough to rock the dungeon. It was as though he'd been possessed by a demonic spirit.

The wooden door opened.

"What's that racket, my lord?!"

"Fall back," Murashige chided the guard. "'Tis nothing."

His voice, however, was shaking as he spoke. What had Murashige said that had churned the insides of Kuroda Kanbei to this extent? He had no idea.

A bug wriggled near Murashige's knee. He smashed it with his fist.

"Kanbei!" he shouted, his voice harsh and thick. "Have you gone mad?"

Kanbei suddenly stopped laughing. He crossed his legs and hung his head.

"Please forgive my insolence. To think, the great and magnificent Lord of Settsu, trifled with by this child's play and, on top of that, bracing for the fall of his castle over it! 'Tis just ever so comical."

Unhurriedly, Kanbei looked back up. His eyes had a crazed sheen to them, as if smeared with oil.

"I believe untangling the truth behind Jinen's murder shall be fairly easy for me."

12

"What? Are you saying you already solved it? Just from what I told you?"

"Of course."

Kanbei was wearing tattered clothes. His hair was a disheveled mess, and his beard long and scraggly. Despite that, his voice was drenched with pride, and it was breezy, betraying his amusement. Through the darkness, Murashige thought he could even make out a *smile* on his lips.

Was this the selfsame man who had, until moments ago, been hugging his knees, murmuring to himself with such murky eyes? It seemed Murashige's judgment of Kanbei as unable to pass up the chance to prove how ingenious he was had hit the bull's-eye.

It was almost *too* accurate.

A shadow formed in Murashige's heart. Kanbei had, as he'd expected, taken the bait. But was that actually because Kanbei was the man Murashige thought he was—the kind who took pride in his own ingenuity? Could Murashige truly chalk up Kanbei as a greenhorn whose brilliant mind was tempered by his susceptibility to dancing to the tune of anyone who primped his ego? And what had that burst of raucous laughter been about?

"Lord of Settsu," said Kanbei. "Earlier, you graciously offered to alleviate my boredom. However, as much as it pains me to tell Your Lordship, I'm afraid I'm not bored just yet. How would Your Lordship feel if we engaged in a moment's conversation?"

"About the truth behind Jinen's murder?"

Kanbei shook his head, and his tousled hair swayed.

"Please, do not make haste. Let us put that petty matter aside for now. There's something I have been dying to know for some time, and I would very much like to use this opportunity to ask Your Lordship."

Murashige was silent. The intuition he had forged on the battlefield whirred: *I mustn't let him have his way. Perhaps Kuroda Kanbei isn't the type of man who would dance in the palm of my hand. Perhaps I should not have come here. This man is trouble.*

Yet Murashige couldn't refuse him. If Kanbei left the dungeon now, the castle would fall. That, too, his intuition assured him.

"What says Your Lordship?" Kanbei urged, not failing to note Murashige's indecision.

Murashige wondered why Kanbei didn't just ask his question unbidden. Then he realized Kanbei was trying to draw the words *I'll allow it* out of Murashige's mouth. Steeling himself as if against an ambush, he said the words, though not before a pause.

"…I'll allow it."

"Your Lordship has my gratitude. Now, I shall ask you, Lord of Settsu." Kanbei's glazed-over eyes suddenly drew closer to Murashige. "Why didn't Your Lordship kill him?"

"What do you mean, 'why'?"

"So Your Lordship plans to play dumb. Very well, that's fine."

A grin curling his lips, he leaned back and sank away from the candlelight into the black.

"Then I shall ask my next question. In what way attained the Lord of Settsu such a lofty rank? With all due respect, when Your Lordship was with the Ikeda clan, your position was a humble one. Your master was the Lord of Chikugo, Ikeda Katsumasa. He was no dullard, but he was a tad short of the adroitness needed to bolster his clan in this time of war. I heard he would often equivocate or lie during battle… Well, as a retainer of the Kodera, I cannot say I know the details. What I do know is that an Ikeda retainer, a general, feared for their future and ousted Katsumasa…and that general is now known as the Lord of Settsu."

"Here in Settsu," said Murashige, "even children know all that. What are you trying to tell me, digging up such ancient history?"

Kanbei waved a hand dismissively.

"Pray do not get so angry, Your Lordship. Ye said ye are allowing me to ask questions. Ye banished your master, Katsumasa, without killing him. How are we to view this? As ye know, in these times, banishing one's former master is not uncommon. Saito drove out Toki, Ukita drove out Uragami, and Oda drove out Shiba. And in all those cases, they chased their former lords away without hurting or killing them. As such, we can call Your Lordship's sparing Katsumasa his life conduct befitting a samurai."

"......"

"Now, with the current battle, Your Lordship's actions led your son Shingorou to separate from his wife. I speak of the daughter of the well-known retainer of the Oda clan, the honorable Koreto Hyuuga-no-kami or, to call him by his prior name, Akechi Juubei Mitsuhide. When Your Lordship decided to antagonize the Oda, ye made an enemy of Koreto as well, and the daughter of an enemy could not remain in your home. That makes eminent sense. However, ye refrained from killing her as well, instead sending her back to the Oda. What are we to make of this?"

Kanbei inclined his head to the side, affecting puzzlement.

"Moreover, before Takeda assaulted the Imagawa, he returned an Imagawa woman. And I heard that before Hojo attacked Takeda, he returned Takeda's woman. Azai detained Oda's woman in the castle, but in the end, as one might expect, he returned her. Even if marital bonds become riven due to shifting allegiances, a samurai does not kill a woman out of spite. In that respect as well, Your Lordship's behavior was the way of the warrior."

"You're yammering on and on about things we both know. Don't get carried away, Kanbei!" said Murashige, his voice echoing.

Yet Kanbei showed no sign of being cowed.

"Now we get to the main point," he continued. "When Your Lordship was a retainer under Oda, ye were one of the generals who attacked Osaka. Ye constructed branch castles and set up battle encampments. The watertight way you waged war impressed me so. Each of those branch castles played host to one of Oda's castle overseers. Now, what did Your Lordship do with Oda's overseers after ye were swayed into siding with Hongan-ji and, by extension, the Mouri?"

Murashige could tell where this was going, but he remained silent.

"Your Lordship did not lay a finger on a single one of those people, sending them all safe and sound back to Oda's side. I heard that the Oda were shocked and astounded when those castle overseers returned alive, as they had believed they would have been beheaded as the toll of war. I may be unlearned and ignorant, but I have never heard of this punishment—sending the overseers who know all about the castles down to their construction out of the castle territory back alive. I shall ask Your Lordship—what precedent followed ye in doing so?"

When Murashige sent the castle overseers back alive, some of his retainers had expressed their concern. While the castle overseers had been underlings of his, they did become enemy officers the moment Murashige betrayed Oda. What's more, those overseers were in the know regarding the internal affairs of the Araki clan. If anyone was to be killed, it was them. Back then, when Nakagawa Sehyoue was still on Murashige's side, he had been furious. Even Takayama Ukon had regarded the affair with incomprehension.

Murashige had told them the following: *"When we cross spears with the Oda, the enemy will come in tens of thousands. Whether or not we slay ten or twenty castle overseers won't affect the war one way or the other. Just forget about them—they are nobodies. It won't cost us our victory."*

The other retainers, upon hearing that, clapped and heaped praise on their lord for doing something so bold and daring against an enemy like Oda. At least outwardly, Nakagawa and Takayama appeared more or less convinced, too. The officers and men were all elated, and they had absolute faith in Murashige. Murashige, for his part, understood that sending those overseers back alive was an eccentric move—and Kanbei had just thrust that eccentricity in his face.

Murashige's voice took on a bitter edge. "What do you gain by asking that? All I want to know is who killed Abe Jinen and how."

"And that stands to reason. Be that as it may, to my eyes, everything is connected like beads on a rosary. And I'm not done talking just yet. Earlier, Your Lordship said ye didn't take any hostages from Nakagawa, and that ye sent the hostages taken from Takayama back alive. As I heard that not killing Takayama's hostages sparked some dissent among your retainers, I shan't say anything. But what about Nakagawa? I'm sure Your Lordship said that because Nakagawa is a relative, you treated him as your kin and didn't take any hostages, to which everyone consented."

That was indeed how it transpired. None of his retainers had objected that he should have taken hostages from Nakagawa up until Nakagawa switched sides.

"Yet if we take into account the subsequent events, I believe Your Lordship may have had a different motive. From what I can see, Nakagawa is a peerlessly valiant warrior and more of a tiger than a man, and whether his lord is Oda or yourself does not matter to him. Even if you were to take hostages, he is not the kind of samurai who would pay that any mind. Thinking of it that way, one can get a vague sense for why Your Lordship didn't take hostages from Nakagawa. That is to say—"

"Enough, Kanbei."

"—the reason Your Lordship didn't want hostages from Nakagawa is so that ye wouldn't have to kill them when he betrayed you. Am I mistaken?"

Murashige looked behind him to check if the jailer was eavesdropping. Had he been listening in, Murashige would have no choice but to cut him down. Kuroda Kanbei's words had hit the bull's-eye. Were this to get out, it'd damage morale.

He could have drawn his sword and sealed Kanbei's mouth forevermore, but he hesitated. He was unshakably sure that he had to uncover Jinen's killer. Yet at the same time, he felt fear and hatred over Kanbei, the man who had picked up on his secret scheme just by listening to him speak. He was dangerous enough to kill but too valuable to lose. Murashige couldn't act.

Kanbei must have picked up on Murashige's hesitation, for he smirked again.

"And finally, there's me," he said, raising his right hand to his chest. "Why, may I ask, am I still alive?"

There was no doubt in Murashige's mind that the question had been eating at Kanbei this whole time.

Kuroda Kanbei had come to Arioka Castle as Oda's envoy and truce bearer. Murashige could have sent him back or simply slain him. It also wasn't rare to send back a military envoy alive but with their nose or ear sliced off. Yet Murashige had chosen none of those options, electing instead to capture him and imprison him in the dungeon.

Prisoners needed to eat and drink. If one wanted the prisoners watched, they had to use up troops as watchmen. There was no merit to the endeavor, but Murashige nevertheless didn't kill Kanbei.

"I understand ye couldn't afford to send me back. Though my talents be meager, I did know a little about how Harima was taking action, so if I made it back alive, I would certainly plot against the Araki in Harima. I know full well that doing so would be a thorn in the side of the Lord of Settsu. I myself didn't come as the envoy expecting to be able to return with my life."

Kanbei's glazed-over eyes glared at Murashige from within his cage.

"And to be treated this unthinkably abominably, too. All your retainers know that ye didn't kill me and threw me into a cage instead. O esteemed Lord of Settsu, why didn't ye kill me? For what purpose?"

"That's what you want to know? Did you want to die that badly?"

"I wanted to die, yes. I pled with you to be killed. Ye can't have forgotten, surely."

Of course, Murashige had not forgotten.

Kanbei suddenly leaned forward, whispering to Murashige as though the thick wooden bars weren't there. "However, that isn't what I want to know. After all, I know now why Your Lordship is unable to kill."

"You lie."

"I speak the truth. I know why. Oh, how I know. I had a month in this cell to think about you—what I failed to understand before, I came to understand more and more over time."

Murashige had half a mind to pull back right then and there, but he barely managed to stay the course. His pride as a samurai would not allow him to back away from a man in a cage, however slightly. Kanbei's gaze was at once impish and mad, but Murashige didn't evade it, either. Instead, he maintained his composure and asked Kanbei once more:

"Who killed Abe Jinen?"

Kanbei didn't answer, sinking back into the darkness. "Your Lordship departed from the ways of the warrior. Ye did not kill Oda's castle overseers. Ye took no hostages from Nakagawa. Ye neither killed nor released the envoy, instead throwing him in prison. And the chain of cause and effect eventually led to Abe Jinen's mysterious death. Hehheh. Your Lordship, allow me to inquire at last."

Kanbei's voice was distant and hoarse, yet it reached Murashige's ears all the same.

"Araki Murashige, Lord of Settsu. What in blazes are ye so afraid of? What has ye so afraid that ye must bend the warrior's creed and even rebel against the Oda? *That* is what I wish to know. That is my question."

The candle's flame burned on.

A drop of water dripped somewhere.

Murashige got to his feet.

"This was a waste of time. You don't know a thing about how Jinen was killed, Kanbei."

Kanbei didn't reply.

His mood dour, Murashige wondered whether he'd guessed correctly. Kanbei was clever, but not so much that he'd be able to get a clear picture of everything to do with Jinen's murder just from hearing Murashige talk about it. Murashige decided he needed to take a different approach. Oda forces had to be pressing close now.

That was what Murashige thought as he turned his back and headed for the wooden door.

"*Araki yumi itami no yari ni hi wa tsukazu, iru mo irarezu hiku mo hikarezu.*"

No fire lit on the spear of Itami nor Araki's bow; they're there but not there, retreating yet also advancing.

He looked back, but the flame of his candle was too feeble to illuminate the speaker of that cryptic message.

13

The cool and clear air of the twelfth month didn't ease even after sunup.

Scouts came one after the other to Murashige's residence to report the movements of Oda's troops. Now that they had laid claim to Owada Castle, throngs and throngs of Oda soldiers were closing in on Arioka Castle. Takigawa Sakon and Korezumi Gorouzaemon had advanced, reaching near the provincial border between Settsu and Harima, laying waste to the area behind Arioka. Many a temple was set ablaze, and countless men, women, and children had been slain. The highway to Amagasaki Castle, where Murashige's son was hiding away, was already blocked as well.

Murashige felt no urge to launch an offensive.

While he didn't foresee the battle progressing this quickly, he did anticipate that at some point, the battle would come to the defenders who relied on Arioka Castle. Oda was fixated on Arioka Castle, and the more troops he deployed to contain the castle, the more pressure would be taken off the shoulders of the allied troops in Harima, Tango, and Tanba Provinces, and Osaka Hongan-ji. If Arioka Castle's name became known far and wide as a tough stronghold to crack, then the samurai of the various lands repressed by the Oda would see this as an opportunity to start maneuvering behind the scenes. And if that bought enough time, the Mouri would arrive, as well as the Ashikaga shogunate clan. Murashige didn't doubt that Arioka was a grand fortress more than capable of holding out until then.

But even a stronghold as solid as Arioka was nothing more than a house built on sand if the officers didn't have faith in Murashige. He had to solve Jinen's murder by hook or by crook.

Murashige sat cross-legged in his Buddha statue hall, ruminating. He'd ordered his men not to let anyone inside except in case of emergencies. He was gazing at the statues of Gautama Buddha, while his mind roamed about the morning of Jinen's death.

Murashige didn't know how much time had passed.

"Someone come," he ordered.

The sliding-screen door opened, and a mansion attendant appeared.

"Accompany me," Murashige said.

"Yes, my lord."

They crossed the square corridor toward the storeroom. How many times had he visited that small wood-floored room now?

Murashige had questioned the six men because a thought had occurred to him. Abe Jinen had died of an arrow wound, but there was no arrow. However, Murashige had realized that in order to harm someone with an arrow, one didn't necessarily need to use a bow.

The sound of the war drums reverberated. Murashige stopped in his tracks, but he recognized the signal as the one for military training, so he started walking again.

To wound someone using an arrow, all that was needed was an arrow. One could simply hold the arrow and stab the victim. And doing so had one advantage over using a bow—when using a bow, the arrow couldn't be too short to be nocked. When used as a stabbing weapon, however, it could be as short as one needed for their purposes.

Murashige's conjecture was this: That dawn, when Abe Jinen cried out, he was still alive. At that time, he didn't have a single wound on him. Upon hearing Jinen's cry, the members of the guard came rushing. Then one of them pretended to be worried over Jinen and, swiftly so that the other members of the guard didn't notice, stabbed the arrow into Jinen's chest. If it was a long arrow, there'd be no place to hide it, but an arrow that had been cut short beforehand could be hidden inside one's helmet or armor. Thus, one could make the body bear an arrow wound with no arrow to be seen. Was that the truth behind this murder?

If that line of thinking was correct, then the culprit had to be Koori Juuemon. He'd been the only one who cradled Jinen in his arms and tended to him.

However, Murashige had to discard that idea that the culprit had killed Jinen in such a lightning-quick feat of agility. The only reason Juuemon had reached the storeroom before Itami Ichirouzaemon and Inui Sukesaburou was because Ichirouzaemon had persuaded

Sukesaburou not to leave his post. Moreover, Juuemon had been beaten there by Akioka Shirounosuke, and when the watchmen arrived, Jinen was already on the floor with his chest covered in blood. That couldn't have been it. Jinen wasn't killed by some sleight of hand...

"My lord," asked an attendant. "What did Your Lordship say?"

"...What?"

"Your Lordship was muttering the same words over and over," the attendant replied, visibly confused. "I thought perhaps I failed to hear your orders."

"What was I saying?"

The attendant looked down and replied with a shaky, uncertain tone.

"...I believe Your Lordship said, *'Iru mo irarezu hiku mo hikarezu.'*"

Murashige stood transfixed. He hadn't noticed that he'd been repeating the facetious poem that Kanbei had recited back in the dungeon.

Kanbei's poem was an allusion to another.

During the spring of that year, Oda-controlled Kozuki Castle in Harima became surrounded by large numbers of Mouri forces. The Oda forces threw in Hashiba Chikuzen and Murashige as reinforcements, among others, but the Mouri battle formation was too solid, and the Oda forces became disheartened.

In truth, Murashige's heart had already strayed from the Oda at that time. As such, the fighting spirit of the forces of the Araki was low, and they hadn't fought to their fullest potential. The satiric tanka that'd gained purchase on the Oda side of the field of battle was as follows:

> Araki yumi
> Harima no kata he
> oshiyosete,
> iru mo irarezu
> hiku mo hikarezu.
> *Araki bows*
> *pointed at Harima*
> *and pressing forward;*

they are there and yet not there,
they pull back yet advance.

Essentially, it was poking fun by saying that while the Araki forces had come to Harima, they couldn't do anything. Had Kanbei recited a play on that tanka merely to mock Murashige?

Something in Murashige's heart was telling him no; instead, Kanbei had given him a riddle to solve. He was toying with Murashige by hinting at the truth behind Jinen's murder. And unless Murashige humored this riddle, there was no way out of this corner.

That thought refused to leave Murashige, and the fact that it had leaked through his lips was a blunder. He gnashed his teeth, then returned to his usual composed self.

"Forget I said anything," he ordered.

But there must be something to it.

"*Iru mo irararezu hiku mo hikarezu.*" Those words could refer to the Araki forces who could neither stay nor retreat. But they could also refer to a bow that could neither shoot arrows nor be drawn. Was Kanbei's tanka alluding to a bow? A bow that couldn't shoot arrows nor be drawn could only be alluding to the murder by arrow. Kanbei, too, must have concluded that Jinen's murder was a sleight of hand on the part of Koori Juuemon.

But that wasn't all there was to Kanbei's tanka. It also included the words *itami no yari ni hi wa tsukazu.*

For the most obvious reading, "*Itami*" was referring to the location by the same name, but the fact that Arioka Castle was located in Itami was a given. As for the word *yari*, it was probably referring to a spear. The only man who'd had a spear that night was Inui Sukesaburou. And what could "*hi wa tsukazu*" mean? No fire lit? But the guard had been carrying torches, and Abe Jinen had been carrying a candlestick holder. If he recalled correctly, Akioka Shirounosuke had said that the flame of that candle had gone out, but…

Murashige shook his head and tried convincing himself it was all just Kanbei toying with him. But the more he pondered, the more his mind turned back to the same tanka.

In front of the storeroom, Murashige noticed the presence of another person. Somebody was in the closet, which wasn't currently in use for anything. Upon Murashige's command, two of his attendants loosened their swords within their sheaths, gulping as they came in front of the door. One of them slid the door open.

"Eek!"

It was a woman's yelp.

Unexpectedly, Chiyoho and two of her personal lady servants were in the storeroom. One of the maidservants had yelped, blanching in the face after seeing the half-drawn sword. Chiyoho, meanwhile, didn't even look surprised.

"My lord," said Chiyoho, bowing with her fingers on the floor.

The closet was used for neither public nor private business. While the women's presence caused no harm, it was nonetheless inexplicable. Murashige frowned.

"What are you doing here?"

"Well..." Chiyoho gently raised a hand and indicated the brazier placed in the corner. "We have come to retrieve that."

Oh, I see, thought Murashige.

"The brazier was yours?" he asked.

"It isn't usually in use. As I wished not to obstruct Your Lordship's investigation, I left it there, but now that three days have passed, I thought I would put it back where it was. Would that be hindering you, my liege?"

"No, I don't mind." Murashige's eyes were on the brazier. "Were you the one who gave it to Jinen?"

"Yes, I was. He may have been the child of a traitor, but Jinen was under my care, and I pitied him for the cold of the night, so I brought him the brazier along with his supper."

"I see."

Murashige had held no intention of extending Jinen that courtesy, but he didn't blame Chiyoho for worrying about Jinen freezing while trapped in the storeroom.

"The brazier must be heavy for you ladies to carry. Somebody give them a hand."

"Yes, my lord," said the attendant who happened to be the closest to the brazier in a delighted tone.

"I need to keep investigating for the time being. Leave us."

"Yes," replied Chiyoho, who took her leave alongside her maidservants.

Murashige had come here to examine the storeroom. However, his eyes were now trained on the lantern in the garden. The sun was shining, but the air remained cold, and the beautiful night snow still blanketed the garden. Murashige put on the proper footwear and descended to the garden. He left black prints on the level shroud of snow and drew nearer to the lantern. He didn't have anything in particular in mind. Maybe he was here because he didn't like how nobody else had left any footprints on the snow. Maybe it was because the beauty of the lantern Furuta Sasuke had granted him caught his fancy.

The lantern was, of course, there to place a light in. But it was also there to be appreciated for its look and feel. The lantern set up at Murashige's residence was awaiting the garden that had yet to be crafted in this lot; at present, it had no purpose. At the moment, a light cap of snow sat at the top, with a modicum left upon the spherical finial. Murashige had never soaked in the lantern this up close before.

"There's no light inside...," he murmured. "A fire not lit!"

Murashige brushed away the snow from the top of the lantern. He looked at the body of the lantern and brushed the snow from its base. Once he saw that it had never been lit, he raised an eyebrow.

It was faint, but the firebox had a bloodstain.

The firebox was a cube with holes on each of its four lateral sides. The blood was on the side facing the mansion. Murashige looked up through the firebox and saw the storeroom.

"Incredible..."

Why did it have a bloodstain? On the morning of Jinen's death, nobody was supposed to have been near the lantern, so what was a bloodstain doing there? The square corridor lay two and a half *ken* away from the lantern—too far for anyone to jump, and too far for blood to spray, realistically speaking.

Turning in the opposite direction, Murashige could see the camellias and the plaster rampart with its embrasures. The space from the lantern to the camellias spanned around two and a half *ken* as well.

As if struck by lightning, Murashige felt a shock run down his body. "*Itami no yari!*" he cried abruptly. "A spear, was it? I see now, Kanbei. So that's what you meant."

A keening whistle. Murashige looked up to find a black kite flying in circles above.

14

The war drums summoned an interim calling of the war council.

The sound of the drums percussed at the castle tower was repeated through the drums positioned in all the most fitting areas of Arioka Castle, relaying the will of the castle's lord out to every nook and cranny, including the outermost enclosure.

The townsfolk of Itami didn't know what the war drums meant. They just gave one another uneasy looks as the troops suddenly grew boisterous and noisy and the commanders rushed through town on horseback. They wondered whether the war was finally commencing in earnest.

The three forts constructed in Arioka Castle—Fort Kishino at the northern edge, Fort Hiyodorizuka on the southern edge, and Fort Jorozuka on the western edge—were also in attendance through their respective main commanders, whose horses galloped for the castle tower at the inner citadel. The commanders' faces were drawn tight. They were witness to Oda's forces encircling them closer and closer. Each one had taken what measures they could to make sure they could hold out even if they were away at the war council or there was a surprise attack.

On the first floor of the castle tower, Murashige was sitting cross-legged on his cushion. He wasn't wearing his helmet, but he was fully equipped with armor otherwise. His hands were on his knees, and his eyes were shut. He looked like he was meditating.

A short distance away from Murashige, six men were lined up in a row. They were the Five Spears of the Guard and the gunman, all of whom were on watch during the dawn of the day Jinen was killed. The Five Spears wore nervous expressions, while the one man who wasn't a member of Murashige's guard, Sagehari of Saika, had his back bent and something of an "I know everything" look on his face.

Murashige, who was still in his meditative pose, thought he now knew why Kuroda Kanbei had couched what he'd said as a riddle. Though the man's position was fairly humble, he was still a general on the Oda's side. If he unreservedly dispensed his knowledge for the purposes of removing a problem hampering Arioka Castle, it would be seen as a betrayal. On the other hand, he would resent being thought to be insufficiently intelligent, and much more importantly, if he held his tongue and Arioka fell, his own life would be in jeopardy. Murashige figured that because Kanbei was stuck between a rock and a hard place, he had no choice but to speak in veiled hints. And if that was true, then that fathomless abyss of a man was sweating in his own way.

The commanders gathered one after the other. They decided then and there where each should be seated in relation to one another based on their position as a retainer, their position in society, and their closeness to Murashige. Some of the commanders wore suits of armor, while others were wearing simple robes. Their roles and duties were varied, so not all of them were always in armor. When the commanders noticed the six men seated in front of Murashige, they were all nonplussed as to why.

Soon, all the commanders who needed to participate had assembled. "My liege," said Araki Kyuuzaemon, who was sitting in the front row. "We are all here."

Murashige opened his eyes. He glanced at the faces of the commanders in their rows and spoke.

"...Tidings have come that Takigawa Sakon, who attacked Ikuta and Suma, has pulled out. The Oda have set up camp, but they say the camp isn't sound—the fencing is short, and the ditches shallow. 'Tis a sign the war won't last long. They must be thinking of a way to take Arioka by brute force in a single assault."

The commanders were hanging on Murashige's every word. Not one let their hesitation show on their face, but Murashige understood that this was only because they were preoccupied with the enemy nearing their doorstep. Their apprehension was hidden in the shadow of their warrior valor. Their doubt in their general would blossom during a clutch situation that would make the difference between winning and losing.

"The Oda will attack as soon as possible. Today or tomorrow, I daresay. I'll have the extra provisions distributed today. Distribute the ammo, too. No doubt Oda agents are among us, so defend the gunpowder storehouse with particular prudence. Make sure you don't neglect any preparations, men."

The commanders replied in the affirmative and bowed their heads.

I knew it. Their hearts aren't fully in it. Their pluck—their readiness to look down their noses at the Oda—was slightly dampened. *Do it in time*, thought Murashige.

"Onto the next matter. 'Tis about Jinen's murder."

A low rumble of voices filled the castle-tower reception room.

"My liege, what is it?" asked Araki Kyuuzaemon.

There was a saying—*let sleeping dogs lie*. Kyuuzaemon likely wanted to say that if one didn't know something, it was probably better to stay quiet. But Murashige waved a hand to hush him.

"The investigation is over. The truth behind who killed Abe Jinen and how is now clear."

Nakanishi Shinpachirou's eyes were trained on Murashige. Even Shinpachirou, who admired and adored Murashige, was worried. Had his lord really uncovered the whole truth?

Murashige spoke dispassionately, as though it was some trivial affair.

"Why was Jinen's murder so mysterious to begin with? I'm sure you already know, but I'll get into it again."

He went over the points of contention. They could be encapsulated in two main points.

Number one: The corridor and the area outside it were under surveillance, so nobody could have approached the storeroom in which Jinen was confined.

Number two: Jinen died of an arrow wound, but there was no arrow to be found.

Due to those wrinkles in the case, many of the townsfolk and soldiers alike gossiped that the killing was either punishment from on high or by Murashige's hands. There were even those who suggested it was the work of the arcane inventions of the Christians.

The baffling nature of Jinen's death once again sank in among the commanders. Murashige paused. Then solemnly, he spoke again.

"The arrow did not vanish in a puff of smoke. Jinen's murder was affected using something like this."

At Murashige's signal, two men carried in some long objects. Not one of the commanders in the castle tower was unfamiliar with what they were.

"Are those not *sangen'yari*?" said one of them.

Sangen'yari were long spears used by foot soldiers. They were principally employed to form walls of spears meant to keep enemy warriors and horses at bay. In a clash, their length could help knock down the enemy from afar by lifting up the spear and then smacking them down; in that case, they were essentially used like long rods. A commonplace weapon, *sangen'yari* were found everywhere around the castle.

The spearhead of the long spear that was brought in had been removed, replaced by an arrow fastened to the tip. Still cross-legged, Murashige hoisted the weapon with relative ease.

"Stabbing with this will leave an arrow wound. Pulling the spear back will then take away the arrow. Once you figure it out, 'tis a simple trick."

The commanders murmured among themselves.

"He used something like *that*?" said one.

"I knew it all along," said another.

"My liege," said Kyuuzaemon. "Who does Your Lordship think made use of that?"

"Good question."

At this point, the commanders in attendance knew that the six sitting in front of Murashige were the ones who had stood watch over Jinen's storeroom. They all looked on with bated breath as Murashige lifted his hand and pointed at one of them.

"Itami Ichirouzaemon."

"...Yes, my lord."

Ichirouzaemon bowed his head. Though he was typically so calm and composed, his voice was wavering.

"Stand up."

Ichirouzaemon got to his feet.

"Now then—a nail was hammered ten paces behind you, so go find it. Everyone make way for him."

That was when they realized that Itami Ichirouzaemon hadn't been called Jinen's killer. Deep sighs were heard all around.

"My liege, I see the nail," said Ichirouzaemon, back to his calm self.

"Good. Now stand on top of it. You, fetch Ichirouzaemon a shield."

Following their orders, an attendant who had entered the room handed Ichirouzaemon a hand shield. Murashige gripped the long spear, gingerly got to his feet, and brandished it.

"Ichirouzaemon and I are now exactly five *ken* apart."

The spear was flexible, and the tied-arrow top was swaying.

"My liege," said Kyuuzaemon hesitantly, clearing his throat. "The spear does not reach him." It was only three *ken* long, nowhere close to reaching Ichirouzaemon.

"Indeed. And if it doesn't reach, you need to make it do so."

"Is Your Lordship saying the spear was thrown?"

"Don't be a fool. He'd have had to retrieve the spear, then. Just watch, Kyuuzaemon."

Murashige raised a hand, and another long spear was brought in. This one had also had its tip removed.

The soldier who had brought it left some straw rope behind, too, before leaving. Murashige relaxed his stance, put down the long spear he'd been holding, then tied the two long spears together using the rope. Since the two spears overlapped in the rope-bound middle, it wasn't quite three *ken* plus three *ken* in length, but it was still a frighteningly long spear measuring about five and a half *ken*. Murashige lifted it like a small stick.

"The spear of *itami*, huh?" he muttered, too quietly for any to hear.

Itami, not as in Ichirouzaemon or the land named Itami, but as in the homonym meaning "damage" or "injury." The riddle was referring to a spear that had been damaged by removing its point.

The spear was now long enough, but a spear that long couldn't stay rigid and straight. In its pliability, it drooped down, the arrow tied to its tip roaming unsteadily.

"With all due respect," said Kyuuzaemon, "if the spear bends that badly, I cannot see it being usable."

"I agree with you."

The combined spear still in his hands, Murashige looked at another member of his guard.

"Akioka Shirounosuke. Stand up."

"Yes, my liege."

He did so.

"Midway between me and Ichirouzaemon, another nail has been laid. Stand there and hold up the spear. You can stand to the side, but use both hands."

Again, he did so. The bend in the spear didn't go away, but the shaking of the tip was held in check.

"That morning, it was the stone lantern that did what you're doing now, Shirounosuke. The spear was fed through its firebox, which kept it straighter than otherwise and allowed the killer to take aim. Now, Ichirouzaemon, shield yourself. Hold your ground."

"Yes."

Itami Ichirouzaemon held up the hand shield, put one foot behind him, and lowered his waist. Murashige kept his left hand in place, thrusting the spear using his right hand only. The arrowhead pierced through with a *clang*. Murashige withdrew the spear and stabbed the shield again. The third strike knocked Itami Ichirouzaemon down, despite the fact that he'd braced himself for the blow. A shout rang out. Ichirouzaemon put aside the shield and prostrated himself, exclaiming while choked with emotion.

"As expected, Your Lordship's might is something to behold."

Murashige put down his combined spear.

"This is how Jinen was killed. As proof, a bloodstain remains on the lantern's firebox."

The arrowhead, which was drenched in Jinen's blood, left some of that blood on the firebox when the spear was pulled away.

"A long spear can easily be taken from the spear warehouse, as it isn't locked now that the Oda might close in at any moment. An arrow and rope are also easy to obtain within the castle what with battle so close at hand. Drawing a spear might get it stuck in the rampart, but passing it through the embrasure ought to suffice. It must have simply been discarded outside the castle. Jinen's killer is someone of immense strength who can handle a spear five and a half *ken* long. Moreover, the killer must have been outside, not in the corridor. The one who stabbed Jinen from across the snowy garden was you—"

Everyone's eyes landed on the accused.

"—wasn't it, Mori Kahei?"

Mori Kahei suddenly prostrated himself. He was drenched in sweat.

"Your Lordship is correct!" he shouted loudly, straining his trembling voice.

"But why?" Murashige asked. "For what reason did you kill the boy I wanted alive?"

Kahei lifted his head. "It was all for Your Lordship's sake!" he cried. "The child of a traitor is the enemy! The enemy of the Buddha and the enemy of my liege! And we must kill the enemy!"

His wailing filled the castle tower and spoke to the commanders. Murashige saw that more than a few were nodding.

"...And that's why you pulled a trick like this?"

"I killed Jinen, but so too did another!" he said, eyes aflame. "A dimwit like me hitting upon such a trick was truly the heavens guiding my hand. As such, Jinen's death must be divine punishment, as well as Amitabha protecting you."

Murashige had half a mind to say, "And that makes sense to you, does it?" but he swallowed those words.

The will of the divine was with those who always spoke of it. Even Kahei himself recognized he was a cretin, yet he had managed to pull off a trick that rocked all of Arioka. If he claimed that this idea came to him by the Buddha's grace, could Murashige really deny that?

For a short while, Mursashige wavered.

It would be quite simple to execute Kahei for the offense of disobeying his orders, but his commanders saw logic in what Kahei said. If

Murashige declared he would end Kahei's life then and there, someone would stand up for him, and that might spark enmity in his retainers. More importantly, many would not look kindly on the execution of an ally, no matter whether he defied Murashige's orders, when the crime was the killing of a boy they considered an enemy.

But a different line of thinking beat out those rationales in Murashige's heart as grounds for letting Kahei live.

Nobunaga would kill him.

So I will not.

Murashige had decided to do the opposite of what Nobunaga would do.

It was the reason he'd sent back the Oda overseers in the branch castles alive. Nobunaga wouldn't have hesitated to have them killed. It was the reason he'd spared Takayama Ukon's hostages, and why he'd meant for Abe Jinen to live, too. And it was why he hadn't executed Kuroda Kanbei.

In all likelihood, thought Murashige, *that man—that Kuroda Kanbei—sees through that policy of mine. He knows that I don't kill hostages because it is the opposite of what Nobunaga would do. He figured it out, and he laughed at me for it. He's laughing at me for doing nothing more than the reverse of monkey see, monkey do.*

And if that's the case—should I kill Kahei after all?

Murashige loosened his famed Gou Yoshihiro blade at his waist. Slaying the likes of Mori Kahei then and there would be no different from taking candy from a baby. Perhaps he ought to kill and inform Kanbei that he wasn't blindly doing the opposite of Oda. Besides, his own retainers so wished to see him slay *someone.*

Nay.

Nay. That would be asinine.

I will *do the opposite of whatever he does. And that's because if I was to walk Nobunaga's path, it would result in the downfall of the Araki clan. Kanbei can't have guessed that to be the reason.*

The sword clinked, fully sheathed.

"Kahei. You defied my orders. The punishment for that will not be light."

"Yes, my lord!"

"Be that as it may…" He subtly scanned the commanders' faces. "I'll listen to what you have to say. You will keep your life and make it up to me by performing great deeds."

Kahei's mouth was agape, tears leaking from his eyes. "I—I shall, my liege!"

Murashige noted the mood of relief and satisfaction in the air. He was fairly sure the clouds of suspicion that had hung over his commanders were gone now.

"Good. This council is adjourned and the investigation with it." Murashige tensed his abdomen to firm his voice. "Everyone, return to your posts and repel the Oda! Trust in the steadfastness of this castle. Arioka will never fall. Litter the winter fields with Oda corpses."

"Yes, sir!"

The sheer volume of their cries might have shaken the heavens as far as they were concerned.

15

The next day, the eighth day of the twelfth month, saw clear winter weather.

There was a palpable atmosphere of impending war, not least because of the troops who were mobilizing. If they succeeded in hiding the troops rising up, the battle would start with a surprise attack. Oda Nobunaga was going to launch an assault on Arioka, but it seemed he had no plans of hiding his intention to strike. Shields made of bundles of bamboo were lined up where the castle's gunfire couldn't reach. Murashige, of course, knew that Oda's brute-force assault would soon begin, and there wasn't a foot soldier or townsfolk who was unaware.

That evening, the bamboo shields surrounding Arioka started closing in. The scouts rushed to the castle tower.

"Attention! The generals of the attacking army are Hori Kyuutarou, Manmi Senchiyo, and Sugaya Kuemon!"

Murashige looked surprised. None of them were commanders of high rank or renown. Araki Kyuuzaemon was next to him, and Murashige gave him a faint smile.

"It looks like the Oda are underestimating Arioka Castle."

He called for a messenger.

"Tell my commanders not to be rash. They're to wait patiently for the moment they come within reach of the guns, and then let them rip. Tell them not to shoot standing, but rather on their knees. And have them keep troops in reserve so they can react to any enemy stratagem."

The Oda drew right before their eyes. Outwardly, Murashige seemed imperturbable, but on the inside, he was nervous. If there were betrayers in their midst, this was where they'd be. There was no chance that Oda's scheming hadn't sunk its claws into the castle. Would there be fires set from within the castle? Would the castle gates be thrown open by double agents? More than the enemy outside, Murashige feared the betrayers within.

It was the Oda that fired the first blow. For a period, they attacked the three forts, aiming for the seams in their defenses. They rushed in boldly and brazenly with their bamboo shielding and their sheer numbers. The cacophony of gunfire deafened the fighters like so much lightning pealing in the skies.

There were no betrayers. Murashige's men followed his orders and gave the defense of the castle their all.

The sun set, and down came the night. Every time the Oda foot soldiers pulled the trigger from behind their bamboo shields, Araki troops used the fire shooting out the muzzles to locate the enemy and bathed them with gunfire of their own. The Oda added archers to their offense, and they came to rain fire arrows on the keep. Murashige ordered the reserve troops to quench any fires, and there were no conflagrations.

A man dashed to Murashige. A warrior of large build, he had on old-style *do-maru* chest armor reminiscent of a samurai from the Muromachi period, and a small war flag at his back reading *Namu Amida Butsu*—"Hail Amitabha Buddha." It was Kahei; he fell to one knee and shouted in a thick, deep voice:

"My lord—I am most grateful for Your Lordship's compassion! I shall render unto my liege my final service and head to the Western Pure Land! I take my leave of you."

At that, Kahei flew out of the castle tower without waiting for Murashige to reply, disappearing into the night.

The next morning, the cadavers of Oda troops dotted the fields of Settsu, and there knelt Mori Kahei, lifeless and leaning forward. He was tightly embracing the decapitated and helmeted head of an enemy to his chest. They tried identifying the head, but even the Oda prisoners were befuddled.

"'Tis no face I know," said one. "He's a samurai, that much is sure. But he isn't a well-known one."

The battle was a crushing victory for the Araki. To top it off, one of the three enemy generals, Manmi Senchiyo Shigemoto, had been slain, which greatly boosted Arioka's morale. Cries of triumph echoed through the desolate fields of northern Settsu.

Nobody knew how Kahei had perished that day.

Chapter II

Great Feats Under the Petals

1

The time was spring. The colorful brushstrokes of flowers could be seen in the mountains of Minoh and Rokko visible in the distance. Plum trees were blooming in Arioka Castle, only for their blossoms to wither and fall. Araki Murashige, Lord of Settsu, was well-known as a master of the tea ceremony who had studied under the legendary Sen no Soeki—and of course, he dabbled in poetry as well. It wasn't that his heart was immune to the charms of the vernal flora, but seeing the fluttering Oda banners surrounding the castle a distance away had a way of dampening his enjoyment of said flowers, and he didn't compose any verse, either.

It was the start of the third month, replete with dazzling flowers in the springtime haze. A horseman wearing a protective mantle rode fast toward Fort Jorozuka in Arioka's west. Innumerable bows and guns were taking aim through the breaks in the wood fencing around the castle. One wondered whether the rider knew that as he remained composed, raising the longbow in his bow hand overhead and shouting at the top of his lungs:

"Attention, ye besieged! My name is Saji Shinsuke, retainer of Takigawa Sakonshougen! I bring word from my lord! May the Lord of Settsu pay it heed!"

He drew the bowstring. "Yah!" he cried, firing an arrow. His aim was true, and it soared over the gates of the fort. The rider must have felt gratified, for he smiled. Then he pulled the reins of his steed and left.

The foot soldiers crowded with curious eyes around the arrow now standing in the ground. The leader of the fort ran up to it.

"Out of the way! Move it!"

It was Nakanishi Shinpachirou. Due to his distinguished war service, he had been entrusted with Fort Jorozuka. The four foot-soldier commanders were now under him. A proud and imperious man, Shinpachiro could be quoted as saying that even if the other forts were to fall, Fort Jorozuka alone would hold out until the end as Arioka's shield.

Shinpachirou saw the writing tied to the center of the arrow's shaft. Even in the middle of war, it was commonplace for envoys to exchange correspondence; going out of his way to fire a letter tied to an arrow was somewhat pretentious. The look on Shinpachirou's face was less than pleased.

Takigawa Sakonshougen Kazumasu was a famed commander among the retainers of the Oda. His lineage was unknown, but he had been serving the Oda since Nobunaga was in Owari Province. Through his outstanding tactics, he had won Ise Province for the Oda.

It was truly questionable if this letter came from Takigawa, but in either case, words meant for the lord of the castle couldn't be ignored. Shinpachirou forcefully dislodged the arrow and ordered his nearby servant to fetch him a horse.

Viewed from above, Arioka Castle looked roughly like a moon with a distended center. The inner citadel was on the eastern edge, and it sported a castle tower enclosed by a moat. The samurai district surrounded it in a semicircular shape, and the samurai district was itself surrounded by wooden town houses. Outside that, to the north, west, and south, lay the three forts. Shinpachirou spurred his horse, riding from Fort Jorozuka through the town houses and the samurai district and over the moat, entering the inner citadel.

When Shinpachirou entered the inner citadel, Murashige was praying with clasped hands before a scroll of the deity Suwa Daimyojin in his residence.

A samurai's calling required them to constantly skirt death; there were none who didn't wish for divine protection. They prayed to the

Buddha or the gods they believed in to shield them from ill fortune in battle, to not be struck by stray arrows or bullets.

It was Murashige's policy not to be interrupted by trivial matters while he was worshipping, but matters of war were all of the essence. Upon receiving news that Shinpachirou had come to make a report, Murashige ordered for him to be let into his reception room right away.

Murashige met Shinpachirou in the otherwise empty reception hall. The Lord of Settsu received the arrow letter by way of an attendant; he unfurled it, giving it a once-over.

"The one who fired the arrow claimed to be a retainer under Takigawa, yes?"

"That is correct, my lord." Shinpachiro prostrated himself, his fists on the floor. "He claimed his name is Saji Shinsuke, and that he is a retainer of Takigawa Sakonshogen."

"Shinsuke, eh? I wonder if he's a relative of Kazumasu's. Hmm... Why the arrow letter, though?" he said with bitterness, then slipped into a morose silence.

Growing impatient, Shinpachirou at last asked, "My lord, what is it?"

Murashige suddenly folded the letter up. "Nobunaga's coming," he muttered, leaving it at that.

Shinpachirou exhaled, taken aback. Nobunaga had also come in the winter of the year prior. So what if he came again? Shinpachiro wasn't wrong to wonder why they'd sent such a tame letter through an arrow.

"Is that all, my liege?" he murmured.

Murashige looked Shinpachirou's way. Asking as to the contents of a letter addressed to one's lord was impertinent. A retainer making light of Murashige was not to be excused, for it snowballed into contempt, then into betrayal, thereby spelling the castle's demise.

Murashige saw anger in Shinpachirou's eyes. He could sense Shinpachirou's umbrage at Takigawa Sakon for sending such a trivial notice through an arrow. Murashige would forgive him for his speaking out of turn this once, as he knew he didn't mean anything by this rudeness.

"...There's more," said Murashige. "Sakon said that since Nobunaga will be doing some falconry, I should accompany him."

"What?!" Shinpachirou's face was growing redder and redder. "Such insolence!"

Falconry was conducted within one's territory. For Nobunaga to engage in a hawk hunt in Hokusetsu was akin to declaring to the world that Murashige had already lost. To be ordered to accompany Nobunaga was too blatant an act of provocation.

"Damn that Takigawa! That lineage-less lackey is getting carried away!"

"Cool your head. If you don't concern yourself with their petty tricks, then that's the end of it."

"But, Your Lordship, this insult is too great!"

"And I am telling you to pay it no heed. That a general as skilled as Sakonshougen needs to resort to a trick like this means that 'tis sunk in that they can't take Arioka by brute force, don't you agree? The feeling's exhilarating."

Shinpachirou was still scarlet in the face, but he bowed his head. "I did not think that far, my lord."

"No matter. You're dismissed. I'm sure Sakon knows I won't put myself out there because of a letter like this, but he may think it will agitate the rest of the castle. Be mindful as you continue to defend it."

Shinpachirou prostrated himself once again before leaving.

Murashige deliberately didn't swear Shinpachirou to secrecy, and by sundown, not one person in the castle was unaware that Nobunaga would be coming for a hawk hunt.

2

Once daily without fail, a war council was held at the keep towering over the inner citadel.

There was no way something new and discussion-worthy would pop up every day while the castle was under siege. It was a council in name only; in actuality, it was somewhere the commanders could eye one another to detect whiffs of betrayal. But at that day's session, things were uniquely more of a tangle.

"My lord. If Your Lordship lets that knave Nobunaga's arrogance go unpunished, our reputation in war shall suffer for it. By all means, we ought to take our spears to them! Let us repay Takigawa's letter with Takigawa's head!"

The man who voiced his belligerence so vociferously that he nearly teared up was Araki Kyuuzaemon. Many of the commanders seated there expressed their agreement.

"Forsooth."

"Right you are!"

A commander in a lower-ranked seat than Kyuuzaemon spoke. "Of course, Takigawa Sakon's insolence cannot be tolerated. Be that as it may, we cannot overextend without the assistance of the Mouri."

The man who made that remark was around Kyuuzaemon's age, but his face looked wise and discerning; he wore a stiff and solemn frown. His name was Ikeda Izumi. Due to his meticulous disposition in all things, he was tasked with patrolling the castle, as well as the distribution of arms, armor, and provisions within the castle.

Kyuuzaemon's face tinged red. "The assistance of the Mouri? Pray tell, when will they get here? Wait as we might, persist as we might, I daresay they shan't. We ought to repay this disgrace, unaided or no."

Levelheadedly, Izumi replied, "If the Ukita in Bizen are with the Mouri, then no obstacles stand in the way of the Mouri joining us. They may even come today or tomorrow. In fact, I suspect they are already as far as Harima. We must exercise caution, lest we act rashly."

Holing up in the castle was a strategy taken with a specific end point in mind. The idea was to buy time through the impregnability of the castle, waiting for reinforcements. Once the reinforcements arrived, they and the samurai in the castle could coordinate a pincer attack. So long as the reinforcements had yet to arrive, any battle was certain defeat, so they couldn't put up a true fight for the time being. Both Kyuuzaemon and Izumi knew that. Kyuuzaemon was simply signaling publicly that he wasn't tolerating Takigawa's affront, and Izumi was simply signaling publicly that they needed to bear it for now.

"My compatriots," said Nakanishi Shinpachirou, a lower-ranked seat on the council, who mustered a deep bass voice. "I bid you all to think of it thusly. A commander of Takigawa Sakon's caliber needing to resort to such petty trickery must mean that it has sunk into his heart but deep—he knows that Arioka Castle shall not fall by means of brute force. And that, if anything, is thrilling."

Shinpachirou set his eyes on Murashige, as though to say, "How do you like that?" Clearly, he wanted to impress on Murashige that by repeating what he'd said, he was being of use to him.

Murashige thought Shinpachirou's loyalty peculiar, somehow. Shinpachirou seemed to view Murashige as a god of war, and he revered the man to high heaven. Soberly, Murashige nodded, and a smile that was beneath Shinpachirou's years curled his lips.

Shinpachirou's remarks and Murashige's nod made an impression on the commanders.

Kyuuzaemon glared at Shinpachirou.

"Stand down, greenhorn," he said before adding, "Granted, that point of view, too, exists."

The more they murmured among themselves, the more the urge to go out and catch Takigawa off guard subsided. At the subsequent war council, when the mood in the air figured that was that, a voice spoke up from a lower-ranked seat than Shinpachirou.

"Lord of Settsu, may I be permitted to voice a different opinion?"

He was a small, thin man with a patchy beard and a harsh, unnerving light within his eyes. The other commanders made a small stir; no one had expected that man to say anything. Murashige raised an eyebrow, a little bemused.

"Magoroku? I'll allow it. Speak."

Suzuki Magoroku bowed his head deeply. He was the commander of the men from Saika who had entered Arioka Castle.

He was a younger brother of Magoichi, the man seen as the chief of Saika, but Murashige hadn't heard anything about him beyond that. Before the castle got besieged, all Magoroku had said when he joined Arioka Castle was "*I am here to assist on the orders of the head priest of Osaka.*" Murashige saw him as a man who thought only of battle and war. That wasn't becoming of a commander, as commanders had to think about how to operate their territories as well.

Murashige was borrowing the fighters from Saika, but he was the Lord of Settsu, while Magoroku was merely a fighter from Kii. The gap in rank between the two was yawning; under normal circumstances, it would be considered untoward for Magoroku to so much as meet Murashige. Magoroku had spoken at a war council for the first time; the commanders of the Araki were openly staring at him with curiosity and a modicum of reproach, but he didn't seem particularly riled up by this.

"Three years ago, we of Saika shot that cur Nobunaga with lead at the battle in Tenno-ji, but to our infinite chagrin, we failed to bring him down thanks to his divine protection. For three long years have we awaited our chance to fill Nobunaga with our bullets. What says Your Lordship? If you order us to go forth, we shall shorten his life without fail."

The war council suddenly went quiet. Everyone knew that men from Saika had managed to wound Nobunaga—and that was because Araki forces fought in that battle on Oda's side. Nobody had to tell the retainers of the Araki twice that many of the men from Saika were master-hands.

It would be rash to carelessly leave the castle, drawn out by the bait that was the arrow letter, but the fine folk from Saika might actually be able to shoot Nobunaga dead... And even if that fails, if the Saika men are the only ones who engage in that fight, we'd be grateful. That was what Murashige sensed was running through his retainers' heads.

"Wait, Suzuki."

A husky voice from a position nearer the higher-ranked seats. It was a gray-haired man wearing a superb suit of armor bound by black thread.

"If this is to be a battle, then we of Takatsuki should be assigned to the front lines. That would be in line with the way of war. We joined Arioka Castle in order to stand by our duty as warriors. The men of Saika are not the only ones who want Nobunaga's head."

This was Takayama, Lord of Hida. A devout and baptized Christian, he was an old and wizened warrior who went by Dariyo.

When Murashige turned on the Oda, Takayama Ukon of Takatsuki Castle temporarily sided with the Araki before changing sides to the Oda. Dariyo, Ukon's father, was already retired when it happened, and he'd been furious, calling his son's conduct cowardly and unbecoming of a samurai. Dariyo left Takatsuki Castle, commanding the officers and men who shared his sentiments, and so they'd joined Arioka Castle.

It was common practice for newcomers to be ordered to the front lines. However, if outsiders like the men from Saika and from Takatsuki were to exit the castle en masse and take the fight to them, then the forces of the Araki could hardly stick behind and watch. The whole affair would slide into an open field battle. Everyone waited with bated breath to see if that was where this was all going.

Murashige's boulder of a body didn't tremble or budge in the slightest as he observed Suzuki Magoroku and Takayama Dariyo.

After a short while, Murashige issued his orders in a heavy voice.

"Nay. Both groups are indispensable for our defense. We lack the manpower to be sending troops to die in vain. Do not exit the castle; keep defending it."

Neither Magoroku nor Dariyo looked particularly dissatisfied. They placed their fists on the wooden floor and prostrated themselves.

"Yes, Your Lordship," they said in unison.

The other commanders breathed sighs of relief.

The war council concluded, and Murashige, who remained in the castle tower, summoned Koori Juuemon. He arrived at once.

"Juuemon, you're released from your guarding duties. Probe into the Takatsuki and Saika groups."

"Yes, my lord. What should I investigate?"

"Their standing in this castle."

"Consider it done, my lord. Is there anything I must avoid?"

"Don't cause any quarreling."

"Yes, my lord."

He got to his feet and trotted out of the castle tower. In the springtime skies above, the sun was approaching its zenith.

3

Around when the sun was beginning to dip, Murashige was at the tower's top floor. Standing beside him was Araki Kyuuzaemon; there was no one else present.

"Is Your Lordship sure that is for the best?"

Murashige simply nodded.

It had been under Murashige's orders that at the war council, Kyuu-zaemon advocated for going to battle and Ikeda Izumi for refraining from doing so. The Mouri troops whom they'd been told would be sent over two months prior had yet to appear, and the samurai of Arioka Castle were more than a little irritated. It was quite possible that somebody would have rashly taken Takigawa's bait and advocated for going into battle. Of course, if that had come to pass and Murashige shot the idea down, he knew nobody would have disobeyed him, but that would have generated discontent in the hearts of the commanders, and Murashige couldn't have that. Murashige's plan had been to let that debate play out through his plants, Kyuuza-emon and Izumi, and by making it so that Kyuuzaemon withdrew his war advocacy of his own accord, Murashige aimed to bring down his commanders' ardor.

"When Hida—or rather, Dariyo—brought up the notion of joining the men from Saika into battle, I got chills," said Kyuuzaemon.

Murashige said nothing.

No matter what Takayama Dariyo or Suzuki Magoroku said, Murashige knew that it wouldn't gain acceptance in the war council. Though the two bore different social ranks, they were *both* outsiders. Moreover, they themselves must have known that their appeals wouldn't get anywhere. He thought there had to be a reason they'd bothered to speak despite being aware of that.

Kyuuzaemon heaved a sigh.

"Nevertheless, what I said at the council was not entirely an act. The Mouri truly are being too slow. In the unlikely event we were to fall, they would be next, and I cannot imagine the Ryokawa is unaware of that…"

The head of the Mouri clan, Uma-no-kami Terumoto, was still young. Two commanders, Kikkawa and Kobayakawa, propped up the head house, as they were both experienced, skillful in battle, and able to maneuver with the times. Since they both had the character for "river" in their names, they were collectively known as the Ryoukawa—the two rivers. And the belief that the Ryoukawas' competence would never permit them to forsake Arioka Castle was what kept the officers and men of Arioka going.

If the Mouri were coming by land, they'd come from the west. The Ukita clan of Bizen Okayama, a land located on that path, was allied with the Mouri, and the samurai of Harima largely yielded to the Mouri as well, so there was nothing obstructing their passage to Arioka Castle if they crossed the San'yodo. If instead they came by sea, they'd take boats through the Seto Inland Sea to Amagasaki and come from the south. When Kyuuzaemon served as a lookout atop the castle tower, he always gazed exclusively west and south.

Murashige looked in every direction. Amagasaki Castle to the south and Sanda Castle in the west were holding out well. In the north lay the ruins of Ikeda Castle, which Murashige had taken over in the past only to then abandon. Oda trips had set up camp in those ruins. Murashige shifted his gaze east.

"Hmm."

"...Does Your Lordship see something?"

Kyuuzaemon stood beside Murashige and strained his vision. To Arioka's east stretched a marsh, with Ibaraki Castle visible far in the distance. The castle, once entrusted to Nakagawa Sehyoue, had to be packed with Oda battle troops now. Kyuuzaemon flashed him a pained look, but it wasn't Ibaraki Castle that Murashige was staring at. His eyes were trained on the swamps. Kyuuzaemon followed Murashige's gaze.

"Ah!" Kyuuzaemon cried.

In the middle of the reedy wetland lay a battle formation enclosed by wood fencing.

"When did they reach a place like that?" he asked.

"They weren't there yesterday. It seems they built it in a day."

"...Those barefaced wretches!"

No fortress was built in the east of Arioka Castle; the inner citadel was totally exposed. One reason the east was so undefended was because Arioka Castle had been built to fend off its erstwhile threats to the west and south, Osaka Hongan-ji and the warriors of Harima. Another was that the Ina River, the marsh, and shore precipice provided natural defenses. It was thought that Arioka could not be attacked from the east.

To find an enemy battle formation amassed in the east felt to Murashige like he now had a sword at his throat. The sensation was not pleasant.

The wooden fencing surrounding the formation was square in shape, and its makeup looked fairly simple; it amounted to a handful of *jinmaku* encampment curtains. It lay around two *cho* away from the castle rampart, but while it was too far for arrows or bullets to reach, it was still relatively close.

"Whose encampment is that?" asked Murashige, appalled.

"...I cannot see their banners from here."

"Is this bait? If not...," he muttered nigh inaudibly.

"My lord. What did Your Lordship say?"

Murashige didn't answer. He shouted out for an attendant, who came up from downstairs.

"Call one of my guard. Koori..." Murashige remembered he'd ordered Juuemon to conduct another probe. "No, not Koori. Get me Itami Ichirouzaemon."

The attendant descended quietly, breaking into a run once he got to the base of the stairs. Murashige stared at Kyuuzaemon. "Leave."

Kyuuzaemon looked a little peeved, but he left the castle tower without a word.

When Itami Ichirouzaemon came up the castle tower, the skies in the west had begun to redden. Ichirouza had likely been standing guard, as he still had his armor on. Though he was merely a descendant of the Itami clan, he was definitely connected to it, very much up to date with his riveted helmet and smooth breastplate. Ichirouza's frame was slim, but when he was in full armor, he cut the imposing and stately figure of a true samurai. As was the way during war, he dipped his head without removing his helmet.

"You're here, Ichirouza. Look over there."

Ichirouza looked where Murashige pointed.

"'Tis bizarre to set up an encampment in the marshland. Do you think this means a battle?"

Ichirouza knew the topography of Itami like the back of his hand. He strained his eyes.

"The east of the castle may be badlands, but not unlike an island float-ing in the sea, there are spots of sandy soil that provide more purchase here and there. They should be able to build encampments on those spots, but only until rainfall. A shower will cause it to sink in short order. I do not believe those troops can stay for long."

"What if they set up solid ground using stakes?"

"If they can build it to that level, then it will last for some time."

"Hmm. It looks to me like that encampment is meant to lure us out. I want to know whose it is, and to what end they built it. Can you do that, Ichirouza?"

The man didn't take his eyes off the encampment. "Yes, my liege."

"Good. Anybody you'd like to take with you?"

"No, my lord."

"Anything you want?"

"I believe money would be helpful."

Murashige nodded, taking a small leather pouch out of the breast of his clothes and loosening its mouth. He retrieved several pieces of gold and placed them in Ichirouza's hands. Ichirouza held it reverently.

"Have I a daily limit?" he asked Murashige.

"The faster, the better, but do not rush so much that you fail. 'Tis of the essence that you uncover the truth."

"Yes, my lord."

"Are you ready and able?"

Ichirouza didn't reply immediately. He hung his head.

"Humbly, I would like to say one thing. I plan to pose as a camp laborer and infiltrate the encampment, but if my fortunes fail me and they see through my plot, they shall likely leave my lifeless body in the plains like some lowly churl, and I shan't have so much as my helmet on me. That this should be my legacy would be mortifying. If I do not return, I hope that Your Lordship deems Ichirouza of Itami as having died a splendid death on the battlefield, and that my child receives Your Lordship's patronage."

"Very well."

"I would be honored with that in writing."

"You shall have it."

Murashige called for someone to give him paper and a brush. He wrote, "Should Itami Ichirouzaemon's life take an inficete turn, his child shall receive patronage," and added his handwritten monogram, handing this to Ichirouza. *Inficete* meant "not fun or witty," and it was used here as a euphemism for death. Ichirouza read the contents of the letter carefully.

"I am most grateful, Your Lordship," he said, putting the document to his forehead.

"Good. Now go," ordered Murashige.

Ichirouza hung his head and drew back. Murashige was left alone in the castle tower, glaring at the unidentified encampment until the dark of the night swallowed it.

4

The next afternoon, Murashige ordered his personal guard to accompany him, and on horseback, he exited the inner citadel.

He brought his retinue out to patrol the castle area like this every once in a while. That day, he was accompanied by Akioka Shirounosuke and Inui Sukesaburou. Shirounosuke had two swords at his waist, while the giant Sukesaburou was carrying a lengthy spear on his shoulder.

Many castle lords thought it best to stay inside their residences to maintain their aura of majesty. They didn't show themselves before others lightly. Murashige didn't agree with that line of thought. He considered watching whom he should watch and listening to whom he should listen to with his own eyes and ears a good thing. Murashige only rebuked someone while patrolling like this once in a blue moon, but his retainers feared Murashige's eyes to an impressive degree.

The daytime samurai district was still and silent, devoid of even any shadows cast by things moving in the breeze. That was because everyone was concentrating on their allotted tasks. Arioka Castle had been completed less than two years ago, and the houses of the samurai district were all quite new. The texture and appearance of plain unlacquered woodwork were still there in the pillars and sliding doors. A baby was wailing in the distance, and it suddenly grew in intensity like a raging fire. One member of his retinue frowned in the voice's direction, but Murashige spurred his steed forward, his expression unchanged.

Between the samurai district and the town houses, a deep ditch called the Great Fosse had been dug. If the forts were breached and the town houses burned, this fosse was there as an additional defense so the fight could continue.

Nonsamurai common folk lived in the town houses. Artisans who were useful to the war effort—such as carpenters, woodworkers, and swordsmiths and other blacksmiths—lived there, as did paddy-field tillers, traders and shopkeepers, and low-ranking Shinto priests and Buddhist monks. That clanging must be someone pounding metal, while some peculiar chanting could be heard from a different quarter—a service observed by believers in Christianity that Murashige knew they called *missa*. There were Christians in the town of Itami as well, and here in Arioka Castle, where there were no padres to officiate, they put on these services through learning by imitation, as they desired a place to turn to. Takayama Dariyo was on friendly terms with padres, making him the Itami Christians' ray of hope.

Arioka Castle was extensively encircled by ditches and fencing. The vacant land, without rice fields and the homesteads, had been turned into fields and plots for cultivating whatever food they could generate to stretch the provisions. A number of people were working those fields with spades and hoes, and they didn't stop when Murashige passed by, though whether they realized he was their lord was unclear.

"That's the lord," whispered someone within earshot. The peasants and common folk were watching from within the doorways and behind the squalid cottages. The look on Murashige's face betrayed no recognition of this fact, but it was during times like these he was all eyes and ears.

Back when Murashige was a retainer of the Ikeda clan, whenever battle was fast approaching, he would always travel around eyeing the town. The people had become so accustomed to war that they'd go about their daily errands with utterly resigned expressions that screamed, "Who are the Ikeda clan fighting this time?" Even for them, however, there were times when a slight tension hung in the air.

Sometimes, he could read the mood in a way that earned him admiration as a vaunted general of the Ikeda. Other times, he couldn't. At the moment, Murashige was attempting to detect the mood among the populace while patrolling Arioka Castle, but that was no easy task. He was worried *something* was amiss, but he didn't know what it was. He couldn't even be sure anything actually was amiss.

Murashige and his retinue neared the monkey temple. During Arioka Castle's construction, a number of temples were moved to the inside of the castle, and this was one of them. In front of the gate, many commoners were gathered; was there a service in progress? Inui Sukesaburou seemed vaguely pleased.

"My lord," said Sukesaburou. "'Tis Lady O-Dashi."

Sukesaburou was looking at the women wearing veil kimonos. Even without seeing their faces, one could tell who they were through the quality of their garments. Sukesaburou had spotted Chiyoho.

Dashi was the name that Chiyoho bore before Murashige's faction moved to Arioka Castle, back when she was living in a fort projecting from the larger castle. Since only her husband, Murashige, could call her by her real name, others called her "Lady O-Dashi" or other respectful variations of that moniker.

"Look at that," replied Murashige. A faint smile curled his lips.

Chiyoho noticed his presence and nodded his way. Murashige didn't say anything; he just slowed his steed a little.

The group went past the temple. A man made a beeline for them. Akioka Shirounosuke stood ready, placing a hand on the hilt of one of his swords, but the man was a fellow member of Murashige's guard, Koori Juuemon.

"Juuemon," said Murashige. "What brings you here?"

Juuemon looked surprised. "I heard tell that Suzuki Magoroku would attend this service, so I accompanied him. I thought Your Lordship was coming here for that, too, so I came to present myself."

This was a temple for practitioners of True Pure Land Buddhism, which was why Chiyoho was visiting. Suzuki Magoroku was a zealous believer as well, so it was little wonder he would attend, too.

Murashige nodded. "How goes your mission?"

"I have attained a general grasp of the situation, my liege. I shall refrain from informing Your Lordship at this juncture."

"Then head for my residence."

With that, Murashige pulled the reins.

Murashige had a host of things to attend to. When the sun was beginning to tilt westward, he finally made the time to listen to Juuemon's tidings.

The coffered-ceiling reception room was aesthetically high-class, as it was intended for meeting other people as the Lord of Settsu. But now Murashige talked to any and all comers here. Juuemon sat cross-legged on the wooden floor, his fists on the ground and his head bowed.

"Speak," said Murashige.

"Yes, my lord," answered Juuemon, looking up. "First, I shall discuss the Takatsuki. There are none who bad-mouth them for discarding their own castle to join ours. Takayama Dariyo is praised for being the exemplar of a samurai. However, when they left their castle, they only took a few days' worth of provisions with them. As of now, they are using Arioka's provisions. Moreover, they did not achieve any military feats worth mentioning in the battle this winter."

The battle in question was defensive in nature. The men from Takatsuki could hardly be faulted for not racking up meritorious deeds in battle if Oda's troops never attacked the fencing they were guarding. Everybody knew that, yet it was in a samurai's nature to feel ashamed or inferior if he didn't achieve any boastworthy feats.

"The men from Takatsuki seem worried that they are useless eaters. No one in Arioka openly accuses them of such, but from what I hear, it cannot be said that whenever provisions are distributed to them, there is no air of disaffection there. Among the Takatsuki men themselves, there are signs of anxiety as to what Takayama Dariyo is thinking."

Murashige remained silent. After a slight pause, Juuemon continued:

"Next, I shall discuss the men from Saika. As they do not interact much with their Arioka allies, their reputation remains largely neutral, and they are not well understood. However, many Saika men are ardent True Pure Land believers who diligently visit temples. Therefore, I

searched for those with inside knowledge of monks and temple workers. From what I was told, there are grumblings among more than a
few Saika men that they did not come to strain their eyes atop
watchtowers."

The men from Saika had no reason to ally themselves with Murashige
to begin with, apart from the orders they'd been given by Osaka
Hongan-ji to go to Itami to fight against the Oda. When there was no
battle, there was no purpose for them to be in Arioka.

"Rumor has it that Suzuki Magoichi, who joined Amagasaki Castle,
has already returned to Kii. The Saika men at that castle have apparently said that if they have no business there, they wish to return as
well. Suzuki Magoroku is not a talkative man, and I hear that while he
has not voiced any discontent himself, he also has not reproached any
who do."

"I see."

"Shall I continue to investigate?"

"No, that'll be enough. You're dismissed."

"Yes, my liege."

And so Koori Juuemon took his leave. Murashige was left alone in
this room, lit by the westering sun, to meditate.

Koori Juuemon's report was brief and to the point, and Murashige
now knew the gist of why Suzuki Magoroku and Takayama Dariyo had
suggested going into battle at the war council. It was standard to hun-
ker down when besieged, but to not fire a single arrow when the enemy
was before one's eyes would inevitably cause morale to dip. The Takatsuki and the Saika had a reason for wanting to fight.

Murashige knew that not every concern was of equal weight. That
was the thinking of lesser men who looked outwardly prudent but, in
actuality, didn't know sense. That being said, Murashige had a hunch
that the Takatsuki and Saika groups' unrest might trigger turmoil. The
spark was yet small, but he couldn't ignore it. A castle with low morale
was like unto a dead branch—the most meager ember could set it ablaze.
Murashige was compelled to give the two groups their chance to earn
glory. However, he still couldn't afford to launch a frontal offensive on
the Oda, either...

So Murashige waited. As lord of the castle, he met with others, handed down orders, wrote letters, and prayed to the gods and the Buddha while he did so. While he had a feeling he couldn't afford to wait for more than two days, the tidings he'd been biding his time for arrived unexpectedly early—the next morning. An attendant came after he was done eating his morning meal.

"Itami Ichirouzaemon wishes for an audience with Your Lordship."

Murashige was wearing only his under-armor garments, but he figured he didn't have the time to dress himself fully, so he ordered Ichirouza be let into the reception room right away before grabbing the *tachi* long sword himself and getting to his feet.

Ichirouza was covered in dried mud; it was clinging to the locks of hair on the side of his head down to the hands he placed on the floor. He had also tracked mud onto the room's wood flooring.

"Raise your head."

Ichirouza sat up straight. His face was also filthy. He didn't seem to be ashamed of his appearance, but at the same time, he didn't treat his having rushed in while still dirty as a point of pride. Murashige approved of that frame of mind.

"That was quick, Ichirouza."

"My lord."

"I'll get right to it. How did your investigation go?"

He cast down his eyes and answered under his breath, "The one who set up camp in the east is Otsu Denjuuro of the Oda."

Murashige's eyes opened slightly wider.

"What? Otsu?"

"Yes, my liege."

Murashige stroked his chin. "Could it be Nagamasa?" he muttered. "Surely not."

Otsu Denjuuro Nagamasa was one of Oda Nobunaga's mounted guards. A mounted guard's number one duty was to defend their lord, but Otsu had Nobunaga's full confidence; he had been entrusted with the duty of an inspector patrolling the various commanders as well. More than a few of Nobunaga's attendant mounted guards had been promoted to commander, but Otsu was still young. That the man should be leading a party of soldiers and pitching camps struck Murashige as very surprising.

"During the first month of the year prior, when we were called to Azuchi Castle, one of the people entertaining us with food and drink was Nagamasa. Oddly, we missed meeting each other... To think our forces would clash here in Settsu," Murashige confided before waving a hand. "Continue."

"Yes. I heard that Otsu Denjuurou and other commanders were ordered to guard Takatsuki Castle, but since he was unable to clear away his chagrin over his comrade falling in the assault on the castle last winter, he has left Takatsuki to come here and fight to avenge him."

During that battle, another attendant of Nobunaga, Manmi Senchiyo, was slain. Murashige presumed that he was this comrade of Denjuurou's.

"In that case, does that mean his setting up camp to the castle's east is not under Nobunaga's orders?"

"Indeed, my lord, I believe it might be a solo raid. I was told that Denjuurou was talking big about how, just as Hashiba Chikuzen made his name by pulling an upset on Gifu Castle, so too shall he earn his glory through Arioka Castle."

"Hmm." Murashige glanced at Ichirouza. "Who did you hear this from?"

"I infiltrated the encampment disguised as a camp laborer. There was a familiar face among the laborers they rounded up from the surrounding countryside, and I heard all kinds of things from the fellow."

"Might that familiar face inform Otsu that you were there scouting?"

Ichirouza gave it a moment's thought. "He is not a loose-tongued man; he spoke to me because he owes me somewhat. I do not believe he would report anything to Otsu unless asked about it. Then again, he also likely would not risk his life by remaining silent if he was so questioned."

"I see. Do you know the enemy's numbers?"

"Under a hundred, I would wager."

If this was a solo raid, then that meant Otsu was commanding not the troops vested to him by Nobunaga but rather only the troops he could move by his own power. A hundred troops would actually be fairly many for that scenario. And there weren't so many as to be unmanageable, either.

"Can you guide me to Otsu's encampment?"

"Yes, my lord. I was born and raised in this land. I could lead the way even in the dead of night."

Murashige nodded and got to his feet. "Good. You did a fine job, Ichirouzaemon."

Ichirouza bowed his head silently. Murashige shouted for an attendant, who promptly opened the door. Murashige ordered him to bring his treasured Mino-forged sword. When the attendant returned, Murashige handed Ichirouza the sword himself.

"Your reward. Take it."

Ichirouza's face turned beet red. "This...this is the highest honor."

"I'll prepare you a room and a bath," said Murashige forcefully, "so do not leave the residence tonight."

Ichirouza seemed a little surprised, but he didn't ask why.

"Understood, my lord."

And with that, he prostrated himself.

5

That day, Murashige dispatched messengers to Suzuki Magoroku and Takayama Dariyo.

The messengers relayed orders from Murashige: The were to bring twenty elite soldiers at the twilight hour to be treated to food and drink. Suzuki Magoroku didn't look particularly reluctant; he simply picked his twenty men in silence, as if to say, "If you tell me to come, I have but to go."

Takayama Dariyo, however, proved not as simple. The Takatsuki group were outsiders, not part of Murashige's retainers, and they were unable to grasp the meaning of Murashige's feast. One of them even told Dariyo: "My master. Perhaps they trust us not and plot to attack us when our guards are down."

Yet while Dariyo didn't seem cleared of doubt himself judging by the look on his face, he shook his head all the same.

"If that was so," he said, "he would not have told me to bring troops. And at any rate, I cannot turn down an invitation from the Lord of Settsu."

Thus, come the evening hour, specially selected groups of Saika and Takatsuki men entered the inner citadel. Though they were summoned to a feast, this was still wartime, so they kept their armor and helmets on. They crossed the moat bridge and passed through the gates, where Koori Juuemon was there to greet them.

"Thank you all for your hard work. I shall guide you."

Those of high enough rank went up to the residence, while those who weren't of sufficient social standing were allowed through the garden. The most prominent men took seats alongside Murashige. The women-folk carried food and drink and served everyone equally.

The gates to the inner citadel were always closed after sundown. Some among the soldiers raised an eyebrow upon hearing the sound of the gates closing, but the majority just kept relishing their first high-grade sake in a while. Laughter could be heard over and over from the fete unfolding all around Murashige. When the food and booze ran out, Murashige had everyone gather in the garden.

"Tonight, we will conduct a night raid," he declared calmly. "Our target is the encampment set up to the east of this castle. The enemy commander is Otsu Denjuurou Nagamasa. The commanders for the night raid will be Takayama Dariyo and Suzuki Magoroku. I will also be there as the general, commanding my personal guard. If you lack the equipment, take what you need from the spear and gun storehouses. Any who feel too timid may stay here. We leave the castle when the moon reaches high in the sky. We're aiming to take Otsu's head. Give it your all out there."

The men were abuzz.

"For Your Lordship to go into battle would be dangerous," said Takayama Dariyo, red in the face. "Prithee refrain."

But Murashige looked unruffled. "Come now—I'm itching to put my skills to use."

At some point, Murashige's guard had gathered around the residence. They hadn't been informed of the night raid, either, but they were satisfied now that they knew this was why they had been summoned here that night.

The Saika and Takatsuki groups were ordered to make their preparations in the castle tower. There, the members of the guard conveyed to them the plans for the attack pattern, the passwords, and the arrangements for the war drums and trumpet shells. Those who weren't busy stuck grass in the gaps of their armor so that it didn't make noise. Many tried to sleep until the appointed time. The moon on the thirteenth night of the month was so bright that they didn't need torches or watch fires. Arioka Castle's inner citadel was heating up with the burgeoning zeal for battle.

The inner citadel had a path going down to the Ina River.

The path was thoroughly and scrupulously concealed so that it couldn't be seen from outside the castle. Needless to say, there were those among the men from Saika and Takatsuki who didn't know it existed, but so too were there those among Murashige's guard, whom he had trained from an early age, who were just as unaware. In times of peace, it was used to exchange people and cargo through the boats traveling the Ina River, but since the war began, the path was now obstructed by a gate.

The night-raid troops exited the inner citadel and crossed the Ina River using boats that had been secretly placed in the water as a makeshift bridge. If this bridge came undone, then their path back to the castle would be cut off, giving the troops no choice but to die in battle. Murashige called the name of the man who even among the guard excelled at swordsmanship, Akioka Shirounosuke.

"I'm giving you two men, so defend this bridge to the last."

"Yes, my lord," said Shirounosuke eagerly, "I shall defend this bridge even if it costs me my life."

The lord's guard formed the front, followed by the Takatsuki men and the Saika men. Murashige also wore armor and a helmet, but as he valued being light on his feet, he made attendants carry his equipment. It was a quiet spring night; only the babbling of the water could be heard. The enemy encampment couldn't be seen for the reeds. Itami Ichirouza took the lead, guiding the way.

Calm and quiet were the bywords for a night raid. Horses neighed too much to be of use. Since armor made noise when its parts scraped against one another, the thighs were instead protected by string-fastened tassets. Some carried guns, but since their fuses stood out, they carried them concealed. Troops who weren't used to this were often made to bite down on pieces of wood lest they start chatting or quipping, but since the soldiers in this night raid were all elites, that was unnecessary. In total, the men now trudging through the muddy marsh numbered no more than seventy, including Murashige's guard. It was a small force, yet the noise they made stepping through the mud, breathing, and brushing against the reeds was still enough to resound through the night. Beyond the reedbed lay a faint light; it seemed the enemy had lit a watch fire.

How much mud had they plodded through? Murashige looked behind him; Arioka Castle loomed vast in the moonlight. The watch fires burning like pinpoints of light made for a beautiful sight. Judging by the distance between them and the castle, Murashige realized the encampment wasn't far now. That moment, Ichirouza stopped in his tracks.

Murashige went up to him. "What is it?"

"The reeds are sparse from this point forward," he replied under his breath. "It may be best for me to scout the area first."

"I see. Stay here, Ichirouza." Murashige scanned the nearby troops, his eyes falling on Koori Juuemon. "Juuemon, you heard him, right? You go."

"Yes, my lord," replied Juuemon quietly. He took off his helmet and gave it to one of his comrades. This was so he could hear better.

Juuemon pushed his way through the reeds, and moments later, they couldn't see him anymore. The rest of the night raiders waited with bated breath, but they weren't made to wait to the point of irritation, for soon the reeds swayed once again—Juuemon had returned.

"Beyond this point, the reedbed does indeed break off, and the encampment lies just ahead. Two armored soldiers lie in front of the encampment, and they have not taken note of us."

"Very well."

Murashige summoned Suzuki Magoroku and Takayama Dariyo, who were both wearing tense, almost angry expressions; as one might expect, they had steeled themselves for the fight. Murashige spoke to them in a low whisper.

"We'll be shooting the samurai at the front of the encampment. If they get away, the enemy will catch on to the night raid and strengthen their defenses, so we must rush in before the encampment can prepare themselves. Just as we planned, the Takatsuki will take the right and the Saika the left. I shall issue commands as the rear guard. Go forth at the second beat of the drums. If you hear the trumpet shells blowing long, fall back. If the shell sounds before you cut our way in, it means the enemy managed to prepare, so retreat posthaste."

Magoroku and Dariyo voiced their consent.

"Good. Now go."

At Murashige's command, the two fell back. He then called Juuemon.

"Stand at the front. We're watching the enemy."

"Yes, my lord. This way," replied Juuemon, who now stood at the head of the party.

Murashige summoned two members of his guard who carried bows, as well as the drummer, the trumpeter, and an attendant who was carrying Murashige's bow. They pushed through the reeds and stepped through the mud, and before long, they found a clearing from which the enemy encampment's watch fire could be seen at a distance. Also visible in the moonlight were the two warriors hiding in the reeds a few dozen paces away from Murashige. Both of them were wearing armor, but the one on the right wasn't wearing a helmet. The one on the left must be relatively high-ranking, Murashige surmised. Perhaps the one on the right was serving under him. Perhaps he was a foot soldier serving as a sentry. They were talking between each other as they stared intensely at Arioka Castle; they hadn't noticed Murashige or the others with him. Murashige called for his attendant, handing him his helmet in exchange for the bow. A gun would have made too much noise, and Murashige took off his helmet because sometimes, when the bow was drawn, one of the helmet's side turnbacks could get in the way.

The two bowmen of Murashige's guard took their places beside him. "I'll shoot the one on the right. You shoot the one on the left." Murashige nocked his arrow.

In the clear moonlight, he could see the face of the man he was aiming at. His eyes were accustomed to the darkness. He could make out the face's features. He was young and handsome, but his expression was stern, and at the moment, he was saying something or other. The wind blew through the rustling reeds. Murashige pulled the bowstring.

"*Namu*," Murashige prayed. "May this arrow keep its mark."

Clouds drifted over the moon. The warriors turned their heads; who knew what went through their minds? The moment their eyes tried to make out Murashige, he fired the arrow.

The arrow pierced the warrior between the eyes. The man had definitely seen Murashige during his last moments; he'd opened his mouth before he crumpled to the ground.

The other two arrows followed suit, flying toward the one on the left. One arrow missed, but the other got him in the shoulder. For an instant, his eyes reeled wide, but the next instant, he was on his knees trying to help up his fallen comrade.

"They're here!"

They couldn't stop him from crying out, but his cries wouldn't last long. Murashige fired another arrow, which struck him in the back, while a third arrow fired by one of the other bowmen pierced his thigh. Their victim must have lost the energy to utter anything else, for he started running toward the encampment without another word. Murashige drew his third arrow, aiming at the man's back, but he didn't fire it, as the man melded back into the darkness. Whether the dead one had been a foot soldier or a servant of the other one, he was an underling either way, so to have taken him down while the samurai one managed to get away caused Murashige some consternation. For a short while, he hesitated, thinking their cover might be blown. It all hinged on how much time it would take the encampment to prepare for battle after the samurai who'd fled called out to them. Yet Murashige didn't waver for long.

"Beat the drum twice."

The drummer followed his orders at once. The sound of drums

reverberated through the reedbeds and broke the silence of the night. The reeds appeared to all sway at the same time—and that was because the Saika and Takatsuki groups were now dashing forward.

Murashige breathed in deep. "Unleash your war cries!"

Battle cries from all around. "Raaahhhhh!"

While Murashige's guard surrounded him to defend him, the soldiers grappled with the encampment's fencing. When the first gunshots punctuated the night, arrows rained down on the encampment, accompanied by a hail of bullets.

The troops' hatchets and wooden mallets managed to break holes into the fencing, and the forces poured into the encampment. In a night raid, every moment was precious—they could shoot at rank-and-file soldiers, but they didn't have the time to take their heads. Individuals showed their comrades the enemies they shot but abandoned the heads of the slain for the time being, instead going after the next enemy. A cacophony of gunfire, shouting, and anguished screams painted the night. Disconcerted, the enemy took to their heels. Murashige stood outside the encampment with his arms folded, eyeing the battle without a word.

The encampment's watch fire to their backs, a figure in silhouette tumbled out of the encampment. He was in a pitiful state, dressed in nothing but a loincloth and a helmet with his unsheathed sword carried over his shoulder. It seemed he was trying to flee, as he was running while looking the opposite direction; when he faced forward, he realized he was running right into the laps of Murashige and his group. Murashige's guard brandished their spears and aimed their arrows and guns. The man grimaced, but he must have realized this was the end for him, for he had an odd glint in his eyes. The man stretched his arms out and shouted:

"I am Otsu's retainer, Hori Yatarou. Despite my current appearance, I am a warrior. I presume ye are the general commanding this night raid. Take my head and remember me by it."

He stooped lower and started running right for Murashige. Guns and arrows fired; the wind blew the gunsmoke away, but strangely for the collection of master-hands that was the personal guard of the Araki, they missed their mark. "Oh," said Yatarou, who drew seven, six, five paces away from Murashige. A member of the guard threw his gun, drew his sword, and stood in between Yatarou and Murashige. It was Itami Ichirouza.

Murashige unfolded his arms and reached for the sword at his waist. He had left the blade he treasured, a Gou Yoshihiro katana, back at his residence. The sword he carried into this battle was a Nara sword, and Nara swords were infamous for being dull. Its sharpness was a far cry from a sword commissioned to a skilled smith, but these swords were cheap and therefore easy to buy in large numbers. Murashige had chosen it himself, figuring he could swing it to his heart's content on the battlefield without damaging anything of value. He unsheathed it, and the nameless blade glinted in the moonlight.

"Damned lout!" shouted Itami Ichirouza, who came at Yatarou with a thrust. The tip of his sword landed true, wounding Yatarou's right shoulder, but Yatarou shifted his sword to his left hand and thrust without hesitation. That thrust was unexpectedly sharp, and it was aimed at Ichirouza's throat; the tip didn't strike him quite at the throat, but it did gash him in the neck, causing blood to spray.

"Why, you!"

The rest of the guard grew incensed, swinging their swords and thrusting with spears, but Yatarou evaded these blows as well, impressively managing to make it before Murashige's eyes. He still wasn't within sword range, but Murashige brandished his dull blade and swung it down in silence. Flanked by blades on both sides, Yatarou didn't bother trying to dodge; he fended off Murashige's sword with his own. Sparks scattered in the moonlight.

"Hrnh!"

Murashige's physical might was beyond the ordinary. The sword fell out of Yatarou's hand. He held his wounded arm, only to be stuck by swords and spears in that moment.

"Kuhhh…"

Yatarou crumpled. His chin strap must not have been cinched, for his helmet came off and fell to the mud. One of the guard members wasted no time severing his head. Murashige glanced at Yatarou's mud-stained helmet, then at Ichirouza's fallen form.

Ichirouza was still breathing. His lips were pursed; his expression was an agonized one, as though he was fighting to endure the pain or, perhaps, to resist the shadow of death creeping over him.

"You served me well, Ichirouza."

Ichirouza nodded slightly, and his trembling, bloodstained hand went inside the breast of his clothes to grab the letter that Murashige had given him at the castle tower promising patronage to his progeny.

"Leave him to me," said Murashige.

Ichirouza's eyes smiled—and with that, he moved no more.

"Your Lordship, we have a signal."

It was Koori Juuemon who spoke. Murashige looked in the direction Juuemon pointed. Torches were tracing circles in the inner citadel looming in the moonlight. The soldiers in the watchtowers were informing him that the enemy were mobilizing to save Otsu's encampment.

"Sound the shells," Murashige ordered immediately.

The trumpeter put the conch shell to his lips and blew into it for a long, long spell. The din of battle didn't end abruptly, but the gunfire gradually grew more sporadic, the shouting less cacophonous. Shortly thereafter, Suzuki Magoroku and Takayama Dariyo returned. Magoroku was drenched in the blood of his victims up to the jaw, while an arrow was sticking out of the sleeve of Dariyo's armor.

"Oda reinforcements are coming," said Murashige. "Withdraw your men."

"Yes, sir."

The two commanders hung their heads and began aggregating their respective troops. Juuemon cut off a tuft of Itami Ichirouzaemon's hair as a memento. The night raiders arranged the rear guard as previously planned and put Otsu's corpse-strewn encampment behind them, heading back toward Arioka Castle in an orderly fashion. The moon was westering, but it was still too soon for the night to give way to the dawn.

6

Victory was theirs. Otsu's encampment had been in disarray, giving the Araki forces free reign to rack up glorious feats. The night raiders were bidden to gather in the garden; Murashige stood in the square corridor, spurring the men to unleash their victory cries.

"Ohhhh!" shouted the soldiers in triumph. "Ohhhh!" Their faces were all smeared, but their expressions were fired up by pure vigor. Yet this did not mark the end of that night's work.

Samurai's lives were about achieving meritorious deeds and converting them into land or renown. Following a battle's end, they needed to swiftly ascertain which individuals achieved which kills. In order to facilitate the severed-head identification process, the members of Murashige's guard who had stayed at the castle had set up *jinmaku* curtains under the inner citadel's peak-season cherry blossoms ahead of time.

No number of kills of rank-and-file foot soldiers would earn the slayer any glory. Meanwhile, killing a general or commander by way of bullets or arrows also tended not to yield any glory that could be easily claimed for oneself, as there was no way to tell whose projectiles were whose. One way to obtain glory was to rush at the head and score first blood. Another way that was undeniable was to take a head with a helmet that high-ranking samurai wore. That was the surest proof that one had slain an enemy whose name was widely known.

Each head was first handed to a woman of the castle, for funeral makeup needed to be applied to it. Though the head was the enemy's, it was considered tasteless and cruel to mistreat a samurai who had fallen on the battlefield. It was viewed as civilized to clean the head of its filth and make it look presentable. When the first rays of the dawn began to banish the night, the person in charge of the head informed the others that the preparations for the head-identification session were now complete.

Murashige took a seat using one of the camp stools that had been set up within the camp-enclosure curtains. At his flanks stood two members of his guard, one with a spear and another with a bow—just in case the heads' tenacity proved too great. The handler of the severed heads brought over the first head, which was that of an exceedingly handsome young warrior.

When the head identification was over, the skies in the east were beginning to grow light in earnest.

One of the two heads that the Saika men had taken was that of an old man, and the other was that of a young one. The same was true of the two heads that the Takatsuki men had taken. Murashige figured that of the under one hundred men whom Itami Ichirouzae reported to constitute Otsu's force, only around ten of them were samurai, or fifteen if he was extremely generous. In any case, they had four heads that had borne high-ranked helmets.

Under normal circumstances, the head-identification process required them to write down the names of the samurai they'd slain. Unfortunately, they didn't know whose heads these were. Otsu Denjuurou seldom entered the battlefield, and no one knew the names or faces of Otsu's retainers. Usually, when that was the case, the convention was to take prisoners, but this time around, the sole person they'd taken prisoner was nothing more than an encampment laborer who had been brought there from the surrounding countryside.

Each time he was asked whose head this one was, he could only reply, "Please forgive me; I know not."

They released him, noting the heads in the head register as "helmeted heads." An official notice was sent around the castle after daybreak asking whether anyone knew the heads' identities.

After the head identification, a register was created to record the dead and injured. Murashige's scribe was ordered to take the role of casualty surveyor, and he questioned the wounded, jotting down who had suffered injuries and how grievous they were. Just about all the injuries sustained during this battle were minor. The only one among their number who had died was Itami Ichirouzaemon. In addition, the group leader of the Saika men, Sagehari, had not returned.

While the register of injuries was being composed, Murashige drank in a room of his residence to calm his mind and body. The room contained nothing but a small dining table with legs. It depended on the watch fire shedding light through the shoji screen for illumination, and the sole snack was miso. Chiyoho was sitting next to him. She, too, had not rested that night.

"I am sorry to hear of Ichirouza's passing," said Chiyoho, her voice cool and composed.

"'Twas tragic," growled Murashige. "He died protecting me."

"I heard that the one who killed Ichirouza was a samurai bare of skin."

Bare of skin, as in he hadn't been wearing armor. Murashige nodded, and Chiyoho looked down at the floor.

"I am reminded of Nagashima," she said.

"...Nagashima, eh? You saw Nagashima?"

"Yes. I remember it vividly."

Murashige tilted his sake cup.

Five years prior, in Ise's Nagashima Castle near the Owari border, many people died during a siege. True Pure Land believers barricaded themselves inside and fought against the Oda for many long years, but in that year, the castle finally fell. A great number of believers attempted to flee Nagashima by boat, but Nobunaga suddenly fired a gun into the vessels, killing more than a few people. The revolters cried bitter tears over this sneak attack, and in their indignation, hundreds of men, bare of skin and braced for death, raided Nobunaga's own encampment. They killed one of Nobunaga's brothers, as well as a multitude more Oda kin. Oda forces couldn't stop soldiers who weren't even wearing armor.

Chiyoho's father served Osaka Hongan-ji. She'd accompanied him to Nagashima when he had business there, so she had been in that castle when it happened. She had seen the bare-skinned warriors battling with her own eyes.

"I became keenly aware of how terrifying struggles to the death are."

"You're too right. There's nothing more staggering than a suicide charge."

Murashige had deliberately chosen not to surround the Otsu encampment in all four directions precisely because he knew that. When left with an avenue of escape, the enemy troops would try to flee instead of becoming as fierce as cornered beasts. It was Ichirouza's misfortune that the one samurai who had stumbled into them had no choice but to attack in a suicide rush. Murashige didn't explain that whole sequence of events to Chiyoho. If he told her they had come to an agreement about Ichirouza's death, it would smack of making excuses.

"Ichirouza was a fine warrior," said Chiyoho.

"A fine warrior indeed," said Murashige.

The members of Murashige's guard often came to his residence to serve as sentries for him, so they and Chiyoho saw each other from time to time. It was only natural for people to die in war, but that did little to lessen the pain of separation and loss. Murashige celebrated his victory, yet at the same time, he understood Chiyoho's heartache.

Armor clanked outside the door.

"Your Lordship."

Koori Juuemon's voice.

"Speak," said Murashige.

"Sagehari of the Saika has returned. He says he has a matter he wishes to discuss with Your Lordship."

"Understood."

Murashige put down the sake cup and got to his feet. Chiyoho bowed her head and watched him leave.

Sagehari had cloth wrapped around his forehead and shoulder. Stained with blood, he was sprawled out on the sliding door placed on the garden ground for him. The men from Takatsuki and the lord's guard were surrounding him at a distance, observing him. When Murashige stepped into the corridor, Sagehari tried to withstand the pain and sit up.

"As you were," said Murashige.

And so Sagehari lay back down. "I have suffered an embarrassing defeat," he said unflinchingly. "Guns are not suited to a sword fight." Then he forced a grin.

Kneeling beside him was Suzuki Magoroku. As always, he looked like he was chewing on a bitter insect.

Magoroku glanced at Sagehari and said, "We have testimony from someone who saw that after Sagehari rushed into the encampment and fired at a helmeted soldier, an enemy swung at his forehead from the side. His practice of wearing face guards saved his life, but he was out of commission for a short while. Pray forgive him for his tardiness in returning."

Murashige nodded. "I understand. Sagehari, you did well."

At that, Sagehari shifted his expression. "I thank Your Lordship for gracing me with your words."

"I'm told you've something to tell me. I'll allow it. You may speak."

"I shall." He grimaced at the sting of his wounds, but he spoke louder all the same. "When I awoke, the enemy encampment was buzzing like a beehive. I hid in the reeds so as not to be seen, and while I was there, I overheard voices speaking about the general's death in battle."

"Oh-ho!" said some of the men gathered there as they murmured among themselves.

Murashige himself raised one of his bushy eyebrows and blurted out, "What?"

"I am sure of it," Sagehari continued. "They said the same thing two or three times. I also heard an elder warrior—a veteran of the enemy army, I assume—direct them to pull back camp and return to Takatsuki."

The aforementioned general was likely Otsu Denjuurou. If they had managed to kill Otsu, then the night raid was even more successful than they could have anticipated. And considering it wasn't Otsu issuing the order to retreat, that was more evidence Otsu was dead. Murashige called for Juuemon, who rushed over and knelt before his lord.

"Did you hear that?" said Murashige. "Go examine the encampment for me."

If Juuemon was fatigued from fighting all night, he didn't show it. His face was flushed with excitement, if nothing else.

"As Your Lordship wishes."

Then he started running.

Sagehari was taken to the castle tower to recuperate. The whispers among the remaining soldiers didn't fail to reach Murashige's ears:

"Is it true?"

"Did we slay their general?

"We do have four heads."

"But Otsu was young, and two of the heads are wrinkled."

"In that case…"

The same thoughts were playing out in Murashige's mind. One of the Saika men's two heads was that of a young samurai, and the same was true of the Takatsuki men's heads. If Otsu did die in the raid, then one of those heads had to be him.

But which one was it? Did the glory belong to the Saika contingent or to the Takatsuki contingent?

The heads had been left at the curtained-off *jinmaku* enclosure where the identification process took place. Murashige's eyes shifted to that enclosure, and the other men faced that direction as well. There it was, under the dawning sky, lit by the lunar afterglow.

7

The long night came to an end.

The gates of the inner citadel opened, and the night raiders headed back to their respective abodes, replaced by the servants who now returned to the inner citadel in order to set about their daily tasks, such as cleaning their lord's residence and tending to the horses.

Murashige was alone in the middle of the camp enclosure, opposite the severed heads. Rumor had it that severed heads occasionally sprang at onlookers to bite them, but Murashige didn't believe that to be possible.

It wasn't that he didn't believe the grudges of the dead could bring about misfortune in the world of the living. To him, it was wise to fear curses and divine retribution. Yet he'd been born into a world of constant battle, and war was all he'd ever known. He had clambered atop a mountain of heads, and not one of those thousands of heads had ever jumped at him. Why would he start believing one might jump at him now?

He didn't factor the wrinkled heads into his thinking. While those heads belonged to high-ranking samurai, too, neither was Otsu Denjuurou Nagamasa. Murashige stared at the two youthful heads. The young head that the Saika men had severed was gazing down at the ground, his face and eyebrows slender, his lips thin, and his nose prominent. The young head that the Takatsuki men had severed was gazing up at the sky, his cheeks plump and his lips thick, his eyebrows bushy and his nose big. He also had a bull neck. They appeared to be around the same age. Nobunaga had a habit of keeping pretty-faced young men at his side, and the Saika's slender-faced head was the more attractive of the two. On the other hand, Otsu Denjuurou had been a commander leading a company of soldiers. The bull neck of Takatsuki's head was more in line with what one might expect of the build of an accomplished warrior.

Both heads bore a peaceful expression; one gathered that they'd braced for death with bravery in their hearts. Both of them also sported faint facial hair, so there could be no doubt they were male. Now, which of these two heads was Otsu's? Murashige stared fixedly at them.

Koori Juuemon had yet to return. In time, Murashige retired to his residence and got some shut-eye.

Murashige dreamed a dream.

He was aboard a small boat alongside Chiyoho. Looking more closely, he realized that he was also there with Suzuki Magoroku, Takayama Dariyo, Koori Juuemon, and Itami Ichirouzaemon. The boat had just left the fortress of Nagashima in Ise. Nagashima Castle had negotiated a peace agreement with Oda, so Murashige and the others were escaping unscathed.

"It was a tough battle," the ferryman said amicably. "But that battle is over now."

The ferryman was Hori Yatarou.

Murashige didn't know where the boat was headed. He scanned the waters to find dozens, no, hundreds of other such small boats departing from the castle.

This won't work, thought Murashige. *There's no way Nobunaga will ever let the besieged go unmolested.* No matter if they'd sworn they gave in through reams of written vows and multiple deponents, he was confident Nobunaga would kill them.

Sure enough, that was what came to pass. Gunmen lined up on the water's edge opened fire in unison. The sun had set before they knew it, and the fires lighting the fuses flickered like lightning bugs. The officer overseeing the gunmen was Otsu Denjuurou. Murashige leaned out of the boat to see what Denjuurou's face looked like, but try as he might, he couldn't catch a glimpse. All he could tell for certain was that Otsu was grinning from ear to ear.

With the bullets in the air, the scene soon turned hellish, agonized cries and pandemonium ruling the water. A hole was blown into Juuemon's chest, and he collapsed. Blood gushed from Ichirouza's neck, and he collapsed. Hori Yatarou had swords and spears stuck all over his body, but he was still rowing with a smile on his face. Murashige turned his head to check on Chiyoho. She had the seat of honor aboard this boat.

Riddled with dozens of bullets, she smiled and told him, "I must say, I am reminded of Nagashima."

The castle was burning. But it wasn't Nagashima Castle.

That's Arioka!

The heads leaped out of the burning castle, laughing. Suzuki Magoroku brought out his rosary, and Takayama Dariyo his cross, and they were quarreling over who could lay claim to those kills. Meanwhile, the heads closed in on Murashige's throat.

"Your Lordship. Your Lordship!"

An attendant was calling from outside the room. Murashige's eyes opened.

"What is it?" he asked.

"Koori Juuemon has returned."

Murashige came back to his senses and forgot about the dream. He got up, opened the sliding door, and stepped outside. The sun was still in the east.

He met Juuemon in the reception room. Juuemon was as dirty as Itami Ichirouzaemon had been the day before. In Ichirouza's case, it made sense as he'd posed as an encampment laborer, but Juuemon didn't have that excuse. Murashige raised an eyebrow.

"Why so filthy?"

Juuemon prostrated himself. "My deepest apologies. I ran into armor scavengers and engaged them. I slew three of them, but they called for reinforcements, so I hid amid the reedbed for a short while."

"I see."

After a battle, deserter hunters crawled out of the woodwork to strip the armor off the dead and resell it. Yet if Otsu's encampment was going strong, then why would deserter hunters emerge? Murashige had a feeling he half followed Juuemon's statement. Juuemon had certainly been attacked.

"So what's the state of the encampment?"

"Just as Sagehari claimed, the enemy pulled out. They left behind a great deal of arms and provisions, so I believe they must have been in quite the hurry."

"What of Otsu?"

"I asked a laborer who was there to pilfer provisions. It seems Otsu's forces did speak among one another of Otsu's death in battle before retreating."

Murashige had entertained the notion, however unlikely, that Sagehari had made that up as cover for fleeing the battlefield, but Juuemon's testimony had banished that doubt. There was no denying it now—the night raiders had indeed slain Otsu Denjuurou.

"Good."

Murashige was about to dismiss him then and there when he thought to ask him what he thought about the heads instead.

"Juuemon, come with me."

He had an attendant fetch him sandals before dropping down to the garden. As they headed for the camp enclosure situated under the cherry blossoms, Murashige asked Juuemon a question.

"How does Otsu's head differ from others'?"

Understanding what his lord was driving at, Juuemon replied with prudence, "I know not... I hear that Otsu was a favored retainer of Oda's, but a head alone is not enough. That said, I know that the general of a company would wear a high-quality helmet."

"Hmm. The helmet, you say."

Murashige kicked himself; it hadn't dawned on him to try identifying Otsu through the quality of the helmet. It seemed fighting all night and attempting to identify the heads until daybreak had dulled his wits.

The helmets that each of the two heads had worn hadn't been carried with them to the head-identification area, so Murashige had yet to see them. The helmets had to have gone to the Saika and Takatsuki men as their spoils; Murashige could command they show them to him. He was about to order Juuemon to fetch him the helmets, but he thought twice. The man hadn't gotten any rest yet. He realized he ought to use someone else as the messenger instead.

When Murashige drew nearer to the camp enclosure, Juuemon opened it up. There were four heads on the head stand, all turned away from Murashige.

"Two of them are the heads of older samurai. Otsu's head must either be the one on the far left or the one on the far right. Look them over carefully, Juuemon."

"Yes, my lord."

They both rounded the head stand and stood in front of the four faces. That moment, Koori Juuemon shouted out, "Ah!"

Murashige was likewise wide-eyed. The last time he'd seen the heads of the younger warriors, their expressions had been normal. Yet now, one of them had one eye closed, while the open eye gazed to the left. The teeth bit through the lips, drawing blood. Even a warlord like Murashige shuddered, his hair standing on end. The head was now brimming with hatred.

In war, there were various portents both good and ill. One could divine the nature of one's fortunes through everything from the date, to their food, to the way one fell off their horse. The expression of a severed head was no exception. A head with its eyes shut peacefully was said to portend good fortune.

Juuemon stared fixedly at the aberrant head, his voice trembling. "Your Lordship, this head, it…it bodes calamity!"

To Murashige's eyes, the head seemed like it was *sneering*.

8

The rumors spread like wildfire. By the time the sun had reached its zenith, not one person among the rank-and-file soldiers and the common folk had not learned of the night raid that had taken place, and that it had been victorious. Given that they'd taken the head of another enemy commander, Manmi Senchiyo Shigemoto, during the winter battle, adding Otsu Denjuurou's head to the list ought to have lifted the soldiers' morale a great deal, yet a strange air hung over the castle; people were waiting to see with bated breath how things unfolded, wondering whether they were allowed to rejoice. That was because while the Takatsuki and Saika men should have been boasting of their glorious deed, they all wore grim expressions, and none of them spoke of what happened that night.

At a crossroads of the castle, bulletin boards were placed soliciting help from any who might know Otsu's retainers. A member of Murashige's guard suggested he display the heads there instead, but Murashige dismissed that idea. He had no desire to expose the heads of blameless samurai against whom he held no grudge.

Talk of the omen could be heard from behind.

"They say the head transformed!"

"They say Otsu's features contorted into something resentful…"

"No, no, that's not what I heard…"

The common soldiers and townsfolk murmured in hushed tones, never growing tired of talk of that shocking event.

The commanders, on the other hand, were naturally discussing the developments concerning the troops' exploits. The fact that Murashige hadn't used his retainers but rather only men from Takatsuki and Saika sparked surprise and discontent among the commanders, but upon further reflection, they nodded to one another that it stood to reason. As fellow samurai, they more than understood the two groups' pain at feeling like they didn't know what to do with themselves. After all, they realized, the Takatsuki men hadn't so much as crossed spears with the enemy during the winter battle, and the Saika men had been grumbling about their boredom serving as dolittle reinforcements. As such, the matter of which side got to lay claim to what feat was of significant importance.

"Which side slew Otsu?"

"Must be the Takatsuki side. Takayama's a true warrior."

"No, it must be the Saika side. They're elite soldiers."

There were those who viewed the Takatsuki cohort affectionately, since Takatsuki was not too far, and there were also those who felt compelled to give the Saika cohort their due respect for being so battle-hardened. Such arguments were unfolding in places all around the castle.

Murashige took a short nap. The moment he woke up, he started the investigation. His first order of business was to have his scribe note down in letter form his intention to give his patronage to Itami Ichirouza's orphaned son, thereby making the boy a samurai in status. In that time, the helmets of the heads were delivered to him from the Saika and Takatsuki contingents.

He examined the helmets in a room of his residence. The older warriors' helmets both had rather large turnbacks, and they were on the more old-fashioned side. As for the younger warriors' helmets, the one once worn by the slender-faced head taken by the Saika sported a crescent-moon crest and a peach-shaped helmet-crown. The one once worn by the bullnecked head taken by the Takatsuki sported a sun crest, and while it was of a different style, both helmets were in the styles of the day.

The Takatsuki man who had slain one of the older samurai was one Kunou Tosa-no-kami, and his Saika counterpart was named Oka Shiroutarou. The Takatsuki man who had slain one of the younger samurai was none other than Takayama Dariyo, while his counterpart was none other than Suzuki Magoroku. Putting Magoroku aside, it was difficult to believe that Dariyo had taken the young warrior's head in a direct sword clash; he'd likely done so with the help of one or more vassals of his. There was no custom dictating that a head must be taken in single combat. The feats of the vassal were said to be the feats of their master. However it had actually shaken out, it was Takayama Dariyo's name that was written in the register as the man who'd taken the helmeted head.

Murashige took the helmets of the younger warriors in his hands and examined them, scrutinizing every detail. Some samurai who accepted that they might get their heads taken if their luck in battle failed them perfumed their helmets by burning incense so as not to be untoward. Yet none of the helmets were redolent of such lingering aromas.

There was no way to tell for sure which of the two helmets was more suited for the general, Denjuurou Nagamasa. In Murashige's eyes, the helmet-crown looked shapelier at first glance, but the other one seemed quite dependable given its careful and elaborate construction.

A voice from outside called him. "Your Lordship."

"What?"

"Nakanishi Shinpachirou wishes for an audience. He said he brought someone who recognizes Otsu's retainers."

"Understood."

Murashige placed the helmets back on the floorboards and slowly got to his feet.

Shinpachirou was waiting for Murashige nearby in the garden, since the man Shinpachirou had brought with him was a foot soldier who was past middle age and it would be rude to go up to Murashige's residence with someone so low-ranked. Murashige brought two attendants with him, and when he stamped down to the veranda, Shinpachirou fell to his knees on the bare earth while the foot soldier prostrated himself.

"Is this the one who recognizes Otsu's retainers?" Murashige asked.

"Yes, my lord."

"Who is he?"

"He is a foot soldier posted to Fort Jorozuka. The man claims he was once a rear vassal of the Azai clan of Omi, where he served as messenger to the Otsu clan."

Murashige nodded. "Raise your head," he told the foot soldier. "I permit you to reply directly to me. If you served as a messenger, do you know Nagamasa's face as well?"

The foot soldier straightened up, his lips curling with frustration. "Unfortunately, I am only familiar with the faces of Otsu's retainers. I would not recognize Otsu's face."

Judging by his tone of voice, he was vexed that he was missing out on a host of rewards for not recognizing Otsu's own face.

"...Very well."

With that, Murashige put on the sandals placed atop the stone that held footwear.

The camp enclosure, which had been set up underneath a giant cherry blossom tree, had been left untouched following the head-identification session the night before. Though the flowers no longer reflected the bewitching allure of the moonlit night, the way they swayed in the gentle breeze was a vivid sight to behold. The attendants stepped out in front and raised the curtain.

There were three heads on the head stand; two of them were the two older warriors, and one of them was one of the two younger warriors. Since a general was not to gaze upon a head of ill omen, that head was in a bucket. The foot soldier strained his eyes.

"...The heads of the two older gentlemen look familiar to me. As for their names... Let me see..."

He struggled to remember, and then he listed the two's names.

Murashige asked him how he came across the older samurais' faces, and he inquired whether that was what they'd called themselves. To each question, the foot soldier replied haltingly. Shinpachirou went down on his knees, watching the questioning with bated breath; if the man he'd brought here was a liar, then he'd lose face.

Murashige asked one last question. "Tell me, what orders were you following when you went to Otsu as an envoy?"

The foot soldier made a face as though something had gotten lodged in his throat. "I..."

"What's the matter? Can't you answer?"

His hands and forehead met the ground.

"I beg of Your Lordship, have mercy! At present, I am merely an underling of scant importance, but back then, I was a samurai. My former lord ordered me never to divulge that information, so I cannot inform Your Lordship."

Shinpachirou looked furious. "The gall of this drudge! Your lord asked you a question! Answer him now!"

Murashige stayed him with a wave of his hand. "No, no, pay it no mind. I'll grant him his reward."

He shouted for an attendant, who brought the silver coin that had been readied in advance. The foot soldier received it before flopping back down to prostrate himself again.

"I am most grateful, my liege!"

"Those who achieve glorious feats may receive my patronage. Put in the effort."

"Yes, my liege, yes, of course!"

He was overcome with emotion.

"Do not return to the fort just yet. Wait for Shinpachirou," Murashige said, dismissing the man.

Now it was just the two of them in front of the heads.

"So, Shinpachirou…what business have you?"

Shinpachirou looked uneasy, but he bowed his head right away. "My liege."

It was a matter of course that the foot soldier who recognized the faces of Otsu's retainers should come to the inner citadel, but that didn't mean Shinpachirou, commander of Fort Jorozuka, was obligated to accompany him. Had the foot soldier been the one to show Shinpachirou to the inner citadel, that would have proved less conspicuous. Murashige had sensed from the beginning that Shinpachirou was here due to a separate matter.

"To tell the truth, my lord, there is a matter I wish to discuss."

"Speak."

"The troops talk among themselves that a head transformed. They say a head that had tranquil eyes during the identification session grew more and more upset, transforming into a frightful omen."

Murashige didn't reply. Shinpachirou must have thought it was out of scorn for his fear of this strange phenomenon, so he deepened the timbre of his voice.

"Of course, I know 'tis foolish drivel, but rumors are spreading among the soldiers who are partial to the Saika that this bodes ill."

"…It bodes ill?"

"Yes, my lord… They say that the reason the head taken by Takayama Dariyo so changed is because, according to them, a warrior slain by a Christian who disparages the path of the Lord Buddha cannot rest in peace. They claim this is punishment meted out by the Buddha, and a sign of his wrath…and the ones making such remarks are not few in number. The troops who side with the Takatsuki contingent are at a loss, and the Christians are all quite perturbed."

Murashige scowled. It was nothing out of the ordinary for people to read good or ill omens into things whenever something unforeseen occurred. Devout Buddhists often saw the rain as the Buddha's grace and the blowing of the winds as a sign of divine retribution. But it wouldn't do for those believers to turn their zeal against the Christians among them.

"'Tis but a triviality," Murashige declared. "What sort of rumors did you hear about the head?"

"My lord." Shinpachirou gulped. He hesitated before awkwardly replying, "If the head truly did change, then...how strange and mysterious."

"Strange and mysterious?"

"I have no intention of siding with the folk clamoring that it is the Buddha's punishment, but I cannot think of it as a trivial matter, either."

"Hmm."

Murashige stroked his chin. If even his commanders were taking the changing of the head seriously, he couldn't ignore this. His hand left his chin.

"Shinpachirou. How did the night raid's course of events unfold?"

"My lord," replied Shinpachirou swiftly. "I heard that the chosen elite of the Takatsuki and Saika groups were summoned for a banquet, that they exited the castle late at night alongside the lord's guard, that Your Lordship was there to issue commands, and that we attacked the encampment."

"And the battle itself?"

"The Takatsuki and Saika contingents attacked the encampment from both sides, while the lord's guard lay in wait in front. Also...I heard that Your Lordship drew your sword and, in the same stroke, slashed a samurai who stumbled through."

Murashige glanced at Shinpachirou as he spoke with passion, still on his knees.

"We did cross swords, but I wasn't the one who slew him," said Murashige. "If I'd had to, then my guard would lose face."

"My lord..."

Shinpachirou looked massively discontented by those words. He revered Araki Murashige as a brave man of Settsu whose glorious reputation preceded him. He would have loved to hear that Murashige himself cut the man down.

"What did you hear about the heads?"

Shinpachirou frowned quizzically. "I heard that the two groups both scored two helmeted heads, and that both groups' commanders distinguished themselves... If I may ask, why is Your Lordship asking such a question? The heads are right there," he said, eyeing the head stand underneath the cherry blossoms.

Murashige looked at them, too.

"Shinpachirou, if you're going to ask me that much, then know that you mustn't breathe a word about the head having changed on its own. It would agitate the troops."

Shinpachirou suddenly prostrated himself at this unanticipated rebuke.

"My lord, I have no excuse!" he shouted. Yet before long, he looked back up and added, "But, Your Lordship, did ye not say that the head did not change at all? I simply thought that the ill-omen head was stored in yonder bucket."

"The head you speak of is indeed in that bucket."

Shinpachirou shook his head, more lost than ever. "Earlier, that foot soldier did not look at the head in the bucket. However portentous that head may be, it could still be Otsu's... My lord, what are ye thinking? I do not understand in the least."

"You don't?" Murashige muttered. "Count the heads that were taken during the raid, one by one."

Bewildered, Shinpachirou did as he was told and counted them on his fingers.

"The young and old warriors' heads that the Takatsuki took. The young and old warriors' heads that the Saika took."

"...Keep going."

"Ah! I...I beg Your Lordship's pardon. There should be a fifth head as well. The head that Your Lo—that the lord's guard took."

"His name is Hori Yatarou. Though he had lost his presence of mind during the raid, his last moments were splendid. It seems that head was the one with that evil expression."

"If there are five heads, then this is no mystery. The head that Dariyo took did not transform... 'Twas simply switched out with this Hori man's head."

Murashige nodded. "I'm having my servants search for the head as we speak. They'll find it before long."

A head that was surmised to be a terrible portent was not shown to the general during the head-identification session. Instead, its evil was exorcised through a memorial service conducted afterward. No one had been posted to watch over the head in the meantime. The point of the heads was to be proof of the soldiers' deeds in battle; if a head didn't belong to anyone of notable rank, it wasn't treated as all that important.

Somebody had taken Hori's head and covertly switched it out for one of the heads the Takatsuki had taken. That was how it was made to seem as though the head had changed expressions. The fleeting moment that Murashige and Koori Juuemon saw that the auspicious head had "turned into" an unlucky one, it made their breaths catch, but looking at it calmly, there could be no doubt that it was in fact a different head altogether—that of Hori Yatarou. That was why Murashige ignored the head's supposed transformation, but even the cunning Murashige hadn't foreseen that this would be all it took to lead to talk of retribution from the Buddha and whatnot.

"Be that as it may...," murmured Shinpachirou. "Who would do such a thing? Switching out the heads?"

"That, I do not know." Murashige was a candid man. "There are many who envy others for their glory. In fact, no samurai knows not envy. This might just be the work of one who, against his better judgment, committed a wicked act out of jealousy of the distinguished deeds of others, having failed to achieve any feats himself during his one golden opportunity. It could be a Saika man, a Takatsuki man... It could even be a member of my guard."

Shinpachirou sank into silence. During battles where he himself had failed to perform any great deeds, even if he praised his comrades for their feats, some level of chagrin remained in the recesses of his heart. As he was a samurai himself, he knew that feeling all too well.

"When it comes to competitions of glory, some do aim to deceive. Of course, as this is an injustice, and we uncover the perpetrator, they must be executed, but do not think for a second that 'tis the Buddha's curse. If you understand that and agree, then tell the troops the same. Tell them the head did not change."

"Yes, my lord," Shinpachirou replied, his voice deep.

Just as Murashige had declared, the head was found not long after; it was discovered in a corner of the inner citadel—amid the vegetation near the castle tower, stored inside a head bucket. Upon inspection, it was indeed the head of the young samurai that Takayama Dariyo was credited with taking.

The foot soldier who was familiar with the faces of Otsu's retainers was summoned at once. He was asked whether he recognized this head.

"I do not," he said, to his infinite chagrin.

The sun was already high in the sky. Murashige was sure that no matter how long he waited, no one else would come forward claiming to know Otsu Denjuurou's face.

9

The daily war council didn't take place at a set time each day, as establishing an appointed hour where the commanders would leave their posts would give rise to an exploitable hole in their defenses. Sometimes, the drums signaled the convening of the council before the crack of dawn. Sometimes, they did so as the day was beginning to give way to night.

Murashige called Araki Kyuuzaemon to his residence and issued the following order:

"At today's council, act as my representative."

"I shall," Kyuuzaemon replied instantly.

When Murashige was busy, he often set up a representative for himself at the council, and that representative was usually Kyuuzaemon.

Kyuuzaemon wasn't taken aback, but he did ask, "What for, my lord?"

"I've business to attend to."

"The heads, I presume?"

"Indeed."

Of the five helmeted heads, three of them were known names, and none of those three were Otsu Denjuurou. That meant that Otsu was either the young head that Dariyo took or the one that Magoroku took. If the castle faction that favored the Takatsuki men and the faction that favored the Saika men only ever quarreled through their words, then that might even serve them well as an outlet through which to vent the day's frustrations away. However, if it meant the castle's Christians fell into ill repute and it thereby caused true discord, that was no laughing matter. Murashige had to clear up who took Otsu's head and earned the glory without a moment's delay.

"My lord," said Kyuuzaemon, "what do ye plan to do? I heard that the head identification is over and done with. We can hardly rehash it."

Murashige said nothing.

There wasn't much to be gleaned just by staring at the heads. In order to determine which of the two young warriors' heads was Otsu Denjuurou, he had to first question the takers of the heads. But as Kyuuzaemon had said, the head-identification session was over, and they hadn't known then that they'd killed Otsu, so the session hadn't been any more thorough than usual; all it had confirmed was who had taken the heads, who attacked first, and whether any assistance came during the fight. Despite that, the inspection was definitively finished. If he asked about things in minute detail, it would cast doubt on the accomplishments that had already been acknowledged, and that was likely to come across as an insult.

Samurai did not take insults lightly. They were quite wont to repay the insult with bloodshed. Whether that blood would spill from the perpetrator of the affront or from the belly of the disgraced committing seppuku, it would spill either way. Of course, both Takayama Dariyo and Suzuki Magoroku had to be well aware that the head-identification session wouldn't be enough to ascertain to whom the glory belonged. Nonetheless, if doubt was cast upon him, Takayama

Dariyo, the head of the Takatsuki contingent, would certainly draw his sword in response. And Suzuki Magoroku would not shut his eyes to it in front of his men. That was because if there was no retaliation against the affront, they would be branded as cowards and lose face, or even lose their positions as commanders.

But by the same token, thought Murashige, *if it is for the purpose of safeguarding their honor, I imagine both Dariyo and Magoroku shan't be too tight-lipped.*

"I need to meet them alone…," said Murashige, talking to himself.

Kyuuzaemon frowned. "I believe that might be difficult, my lord. If they were retainers under Your Lordship, ye could summon them under some sort of pretext, but Takayama and the others are not."

"I've thought up a way," muttered Murashige.

"My word!" Kyuuzaemon slapped his knee and laughed. "I expected no less of Your Lordship! What method did ye devise?"

Murashige didn't answer. He cast his eyes downward slightly, and for a moment, he seemed to forget Kyuuzaemon was even there.

Murashige wasn't one to speak of his own ideas or opinions very often to begin with. Whether it was when he attacked the Itami clan, when he chased out his former lord Ikeda Katsumasa, or when he turned against the Oda, Murashige basically never gave voice to his inner thoughts. Yet Murashige's equals and vassals always had to accept his decisions and say it was like him to be so clever. As such, Murashige growing silent wasn't terribly surprising to Kyuuzaemon. That being said, to Kyuuzaemon's eyes, Murashige's giant frame looked smaller, somehow.

"…Your Lordship."

Murashige lifted his gaze, taking note of Kyuuzaemon once more.

"Kyuuzaemon. Make sure the council never gets unruly and set not anything in stone… You're dismissed."

"Yes, my lord."

Kyuuzaemon prostrated himself, then got to his feet and exited the room. The sun was almost at its zenith in the sky.

Thickets and bamboo groves were deliberately left to grow within the perimeters of Arioka Castle. Both bamboo and wood were indispensable for the war effort, and being able to cut some down within the castle was a strength unique to the castle's outermost enclosure, which encompassed a wide swath of land. The small bamboo grove right next to the inner citadel, on the other hand, was off-limits.

There was a narrow path in that grove, a path that the wizened commander Takayama Dariyo was now treading. It led to a small hermitage, and a stone for placing one's shoes was laid out in front of the external corridor. The double shoji doors were slightly ajar, signaling that there were one or more people inside. Dariyo stopped in his tracks.

"Enter," called a voice from within.

It was Murashige's voice. Dariyo did as he was told and stepped up onto the outer corridor, opening the shoji wider.

The room was four and a half tatami mats in size. One of the walls was the double shoji doors Dariyo just opened, and the other three walls were covered with blank white wallpaper. A sunken hearth was in the floor. Water was already boiling in the cauldron hanging from the ceiling by a chain.

This was Murashige's tea-ceremony house. It was designed in the Jouou style, and while the castle's besiegement started before the structure was finished being built, it was still the tea-ceremony haven Murashige was most intimately acquainted with.

Dariyo placed his fists on the tatami. "Lord of Settsu, I am delighted to receive your invitation."

"I want you to feel at home. Let me make you some tea."

Dariyo subtly scanned his surroundings. There was no one here besides him and Murashige, and no sign anybody else would be showing up. Dariyo knew little about tea ceremonies, but he wondered: If there was no one else present, then who would be the one to actually perform the tea ceremony? Meanwhile, Murashige took the teacup and tea container in hand.

"Lord of Settsu," Dariyo said despite himself, "ye mustn't go to such lengths for me!"

Murashige fetched the rest for the teakettle's lid.

"Put yourself at ease. Just think of us as host and guest."

It would be one thing if Murashige were a commoner, but Dariyo was surprised by a host being of such high social standing. Murashige wasn't making a show of eccentricity, either—he was simply performing the ceremony in a serene manner. Seeing that Dariyo's confusion wasn't abating, Murashige smiled a little.

"Having someone here to perform the ceremony would be superfluous, don't you think?" he said. "Oh, I didn't come up with that. I'm quoting Sen no Soeki of Sakai."

The host making the tea himself and not employing a dedicated tea maker was a new method of performing the tea ceremony. And Takayama Dariyo was old enough now that he tended to reject anything new. But when his initial confusion passed, Dariyo found himself unexpectedly at ease.

Dariyo felt he owed Murashige a debt of gratitude. Back when Dariyo was a vassal of the Wada clan, which had been in decline due to losing its head in battle, they had viewed the high-status Takayama clan with suspicion, and he was looked at as an enemy. Not knowing when his lord might send an assassin after him, he thought that if he was going to die, he might as well muster his forces in his defense. The head of the Wada clan must have thought that Takayama had indeed turned traitor. In the resulting battle, Dariyo's son Ukon suffered a neck injury so severe that all thought his life was forfeit, only to survive, to everyone's surprise.

Everyone around Dariyo was an enemy. He asked for aid, and it was Murashige who took up his request and sent out reinforcements. Depending on who one asked, Dariyo cast aside the Wada clan, whose fortunes were declining, to switch over to a clan that was making waves, the Araki clan. Whatever the case, Murashige was a man to whom Dariyo felt greatly indebted.

On top of that debt of gratitude, there was also a gap in their standings. Dariyo called himself Lord of Hida, but this was not a title he gained through an appointment. It was just a tile he'd given himself. On the other hand, Murashige had been granted the title of Lord of Settsu, and he truly was what his title suggested. In many different ways, Dariyo never would have dreamed of having a pleasant conversation with Murashige, just the two of them.

By that moment in time, as he waited for Murashige's tea in that four-and-a-half-mat room, Dariyo was certainly enjoying himself. Gone were the days of his youth when all he could rely on was his spear.

Dariyo drank some of the tea.

"Most delicious," he commented. "I enjoyed myself."

Murashige nodded. "A thing of beauty, tea is. Only during the tea ceremony can we doff our helmets."

"Our helmets?"

"Indeed."

That was all Murashige said. While Dariyo didn't know much about tea, he had a feeling he understood what Murashige meant by that, for Dariyo, too, had worn a helmet for a long time—the metaphoric helmet known as head of the Takayama clan and lord of Takatsuki Castle. The helmet weighing down on Murashige, meanwhile, went by the title of head of the Araki clan, Lord and Governor of Settsu. How much did *his* helmet weigh?

"Tell me about Ukon," said Murashige. "Is he in good health? I heard his neck wound has healed a great deal."

"I thank Your Lordship for your solicitude. He is a dunce, albeit a lucky one... I swear, that fool causes me naught but embarrassment."

Dariyo bowed his head deeply.

"Your Lordship, I am utterly ashamed! I know not how to apologize for what Ukon has done. He, too, owes Your Lordship his life; he should have staked his life out of loyalty to you, and yet he threw open the gates without any resistance!"

Dariyo was referring to how Takayama Ukon had surrendered Takatsuki Castle and switched sides to the Oda.

"I hear the Oda made use of a Christian padre," said Murashige. "Something about Nobunaga stamping out the Christians if Ukon didn't surrender."

"Right you are. Nevertheless, no true warrior would choose his creed over his army."

Murashige's eyebrow twitched. "You're a Christian, too, yes? You must know where he was coming from."

"I do not," Dariyo replied promptly. "Samurai rely on divine powers for no other reason than to bring success to their army. We pray not only to Deus, but also to Hachiman the Great, Suwa Daimyojin, Marici, Bishamonten, and others, all in the name of war. Your Lordship must know that full well."

War and battle hinged on the vagaries of fortune. Fate so often shifted in ways one could not affect by their own might. At times, people died abruptly and unceremoniously. Other times, people survived despite the odds. And upon closer examination, one realized that performing glorious feats and falling into disgrace also hinged on luck. Amid the chaos of chance, who could go without praying to the powers that be? Murashige agreed with what Dariyo said. A samurai clasping his hands in prayer was, in all respects, to emerge victorious in battle.

"Of course, my baptism in the sixth year of the Eiroku era stemmed from how moved I was by the teachings of the god that the padre Vilela called Deus. My devotion to Deus is no lie. Yet if we do not win in battle, there is neither *inferno* nor *paraíso*—doesn't Your Lordship agree? Praying for bullets to miss oneself is how a samurai must be."

Marici was the Buddha of sunlight. Light could not be grabbed hold of by anyone, nor could it be harmed by any means. Samurai revered Marici so that they, too, might be like sunlight—invulnerable. It occurred to Murashige then that if guns didn't exist, Dariyo might not have ever converted to Christianity. To protect himself from guns, which hailed from the West, he sought the saving grace of the Westerners' god… That simplistic piety was something Murashige could relate to.

"Yet if our fortunes in war should take an unlucky turn, 'tis incumbent on a samurai's honor that he should become a helmeted head that inspires admiration of one's final moments. Surrendering the castle in order to protect Christians makes no sense!"

"I'm sure Ukon had his own thoughts on the matter," Murashige said quietly. "After all, it can advance the interests of one's army or clan to rebel or to supplant one's lord. Returning to the lord one rebelled against and surrendering the castle—'tis all to further his group's position."

"Lord of Settsu," said Dariyo, bowing his head with tears in his eyes. "Ye would defend my fool of a son? Ye have my gratitude. But for this fight between father and son, if the Hogen and Heiji eras have set an example, when Ukon draws near, I should like to take his head by my own hands."

"...Let me ask you a question." Murashige sighed before straightening his posture. "Dariyo. There is something that, rightly or wrongly, I'd like to ask you."

"If I may, Your Lordship—ye would like to inquire about the night raid and the head I took."

"So you gathered. I expected no less."

"'Tis all anyone is talking about in the castle. How could I fail to?" Dariyo similarly straightened his own posture. "I am greatly obliged by Your Lordship's consideration. In a place such as this, I, Dariyo, can speak without paying appearances or prestige any mind. Now, what should I tell Your Lordship?"

"Tell me about the lead-up to your taking the young one's head."

"Understood."

Dariyo bowed, then began saying his piece.

"Obeying Your Lordship's orders, the Takatsuki contingent I command went around to the right-hand side of the encampment. At the signal of the drums, they held fast to the encampment, cutting the ropes binding the fencing and breaking it with our mallets while the archers fired their arrows. The fencing must have been constructed in haste, for it collapsed in nary a moment, and we rushed in, each of us crying out the names of saints. The people of Otsu had been asleep, and they panicked. All they did was scream and clamor for their lord; it was hardly a battle at all. We slew a great many rank-and-file foot soldiers, but there was one praiseworthy warrior who hadn't the time to put on his armor, wearing only a helmet and leaving his skin bare, and wielding but a single hand spear. Kunou Tosa, a man of valor known even among us Takatsuki, took him on, and I went deep into the encampment in search of glory."

Dariyo looked younger and more full of life when talking about all things military. A refreshing wind blew through the rustic and quiet tea house.

"Long I have lived my life on the battlefield, but never have I witnessed such a successful night raid. With the exception of that samurai who was bare of skin, all of Otsu's men shrieked and turned tail the moment they saw our faces. Then I saw a warrior wearing contemporary armor and a helmet visible in the darkness. Two men wearing *jingasa* hats were guarding him—I know not whether they were foot soldiers or servants. Our eyes met, and he tried to about-face. I mocked him, saying, 'Don't ye want to take this wrinkled head of mine?' Then he drew his sword and came at me; perhaps he saw me as easy prey. When you wield a spear, then no matter how old you are, you shan't come close to losing when attacked by a sword-wielder. My forces took on the rank-and-file soldiers as their enemies, and just as I was brandishing my spear and standing in wait, a stray arrow flying from I know not where struck the enemy's helmet."

Dariyo must have been getting excited, for a smile curled his lips and his voice was growing louder.

"He cried out and flinched, and I thrust my spear. The young warrior was either imprudent or hadn't the time to suit up, for he wore no throat guard. The tip of my spear tore through his throat, and that was the end. During a night raid, one must abandon the heads one takes, so I was searching for the next adversary, but then I heard the trumpet-shell signal to pull out, and since I knew the battle was over, I picked up the head of the young samurai before returning."

Dariyo took a deep breath and closed out his account:

"To what can I attribute this outcome? I am nearly sixty years of age. That I can achieve such glory without sustaining any injuries is, I believe, due to the protection bestowed upon me by my lord God, Deus."

Seated inside his tea-ceremony house, Murashige watched Takayama Dariyo leave.

There was no one to come for the *atomi*, the viewing of the tea ceremony tools, nor a server for the *hango* postmeal ceremony. Murashige was accompanied only by the rustling of the bamboo grass in the wind as he added more charcoal to the fire. His guest had left satisfied, and when it came to the tea ceremony, there ought to be no greater outcome. Yet Murashige's expression was displeased. He continued adding charcoal, his face a raw window of emotion that he never showed his retainers.

Soon, he heard the distant drumbeat—the war council had commenced.

10

By the time Suzuki Magoroku visited the tea-ceremony house, the sun was already beginning to set. A candlestick holder was at the ready within the room in case it got too dark. Magoroku noticed it and thought that it probably would never be of use.

After the customary greetings were exchanged, Murashige set about making them some tea. Unlike Takayama Dariyo, Magoroku wasn't surprised that Murashige was making it himself. That wasn't because he knew about Sen no Soeki's new ideas. He was merely observing under the assumption this was what the tea ceremony must be at base. And he had no concept of being able to lower his guard at such a ceremony.

He hadn't forgotten for one second that Murashige, as the lord of the castle and ruler of Settsu, could cut down a mere Kii fighter such as Magoroku himself on a passing whim. For all Magoroku knew, Murashige's tea had poison in store for him, or an assassin could be lurking outside the shoji door. But Magoroku's face betrayed none of that, as he sat there upright.

Despite his suspicions, Magoroku found himself gazing intently at Murashige's every movement, each of which *seemed* casual and effortless but in reality was not. Murashige conducted himself in a way where it was clear he understood what was where, what he'd do next, and exactly how his body was moving. And incredibly, through it all, he showed no opening through which he could be readily slashed or stabbed at.

"Impeccable," he muttered.

Murashige stopped. "What is?"

Magoroku hadn't planned on talking, but he couldn't fail to reply to an inquiry from the castle's lord. He cursed his own carelessness.

"'Tis, well... How ought I put it into words?"

"You may speak your mind. I'll allow it."

"Yes... If Your Lordship permits it, then..."

Magoroku was not an eloquent or articulate man. It took him time to string sentences together.

"...In Saika, we have a saying about guns. When one loads the gun-powder and takes aim, even if those motions are quite simple individually, doing it in one fluid sweep and firing often leads to a break in form at some point. In fact, one's execution might go awry *because* of the saying."

Murashige thickened the tea as he listened to Magoroku.

"That being said—pray forgive me for praising my own older brother—Magoichi's skills are a cut above. Everything from his stance to his shooting form is in accordance with the sayings, and he carries it out without a moment's delay. I always find myself thinking such fluid motions be the definition of beauty... I say this because I have Your Lordship's permission: Your motions remind me a lot of my brother's... That is what I was thinking."

Murashige gave Magoroku the fully thickened tea. "I see."

Magoroku took the teacup. His eyes fell on the tea jar on the shelf, and he went silent for a spell.

"Something catch your eye?" said Murashige.

"Torasaru."

Murashige raised his eyebrows. "Oh-ho."

He possessed a great many treasures: the tea-ceremony pot entitled Kobatake, along with the Azuki chain that was suspending the pot and had been granted him by Sen no Soeki. Then there was the famed painting *Returning Sails off the Distant Shore* by Muqi, and the tea jar Torasaru. There were more than a few tea-ceremony and fine-arts appreciators who would pay an arm and a leg to be invited to this very room.

"I underestimated you," said Murashige. "You have an eye for such things."

"I have no such eye, Your Lordship," replied Magoroku, shaking his head. "I merely hear what folk say, nothing more. For someone like me who lives off war, rumors are part of how I put food in my mouth… So I know that this teacup is probably a treasure, too."

"That thing?" Murashige said amusedly. "That's just an ordinary tea-cup made in Bizen. But 'tis the best of the tools I own. It has a nice style to it."

Magoroku looked like he didn't know whether he was allowed to smile. At last, he put the tea to his lips. There could be no foul play here, considering they were surrounded by priceless, fragile treasures.

Besides, he thought, *if he wanted to kill me, there are plenty of easier ways to do it. This is probably not poisoned.*

He partook in the tea.

"You said rumors are part of how you earn a living," said Murashige. "Let me ask you a question. Have you heard the rumors about the Bud-dha's divine retribution?"

"…If Your Lordship speaks about the rumors concerning the heads, yes, I have."

"Have the rumors spread far and wide?"

"Yes, they have."

"I hear that all the Saika men holing up in Arioka Castle are True Pure Land devotees. Are they living in fear after hearing about the Bud-dha's supposed punishment?"

"I know not, Your Lordship."

"What about you, Magoroku?"

Murashige's eyes were fixed on Magoroku. Murashige had his suspi-cions regarding the origins of the rumors. The heads had been taken during the dawn's early light, and the rumors had reached all corners of the castle before noon. Gossip flew quickly, but it seemed a touch *too* quick to him. Perhaps the rumors were started by the Saika men out of envy for the Takatsuki men… Magoroku caught on to the lead-ing nature of Murashige's question, but he pretended not to.

"The very thought is absurd," he murmured. "The Buddha would never punish anyone."

Murashige said nothing. Magoroku looked down at the tatami.

"'Tis my understanding that Amitabha assists those who fervently and wholeheartedly ask for help. Why would the Buddha curse or punish anyone? Personally, I am not much for dragging the Buddha into such sordid affairs."

"Well, well," muttered Murashige. "'Tis not often one hears that. That's not what the bonzes say."

"I am not a bonze. I know not whether divine punishment exists or existed. A common soldier like me counts it a great success if he races across the countryside with gun and spear, leaving behind a helmeted head when he dies, and inspiring those who live to say, 'So this was Magoroku of Saika? He was a worthy opponent.' Nothing can beat the good fortune of being able to die knowing one's afterlife is secured upon beseeching Amitabha for salvation. As such, being induced to fight through the phrase *advance to reach heaven, retreat to know hell* does bother me. I..."

He hesitated a little, but in the end, he sighed and said it:

"I cannot say I like bringing the Buddha into war."

Murashige was no priest of the faith. He subscribed to the Zen sect and didn't know much about the True Pure Land sect, so he couldn't be sure how valid Magoroku's words were. However, he couldn't help but see an irony to it all, and his lips curled.

"Why the smile, Your Lordship?"

Murashige reverted his expression. "Ah, 'tis merely a tea ceremony thing."

Magoroku said nothing, so Murashige continued:

"Soeki of Sakai has a disciple named Soji. He is neither terribly straightforward nor frank by disposition, but I cannot measure up to his knowledge of the tea ceremony. He wrote the following tanka listing topics that oughtn't be broached in *renga* poetry, but he said it also applies to topics not to be broached in a tea ceremony: one's gods or tenets, the fortunes of others, family matters, battles and politics, and tittle-tattle."

Murashige eyed his treasures before averting his gaze.

"I saw the wisdom in what Soji said. All who call themselves samurai engage in battle—and everything from when one wakes and sleeps to the meals one eats, to the gods or Buddha one worships, to the wealth one possesses, to the family one interacts with *is* battle. As

such, I thought that tea and tea alone, I would never so weaponize...
and yet here we are. To wit, you must know why I invited you here."

Magoroku nodded slightly. "In the end, I can only assume this is
about the heads."

"'Tis so. I need to decide whether you or Takayama—whether the
Saika group or the Takatsuki group—can claim the glory for Otsu's
head. Yet as the general, I cannot be alone. I couldn't think of a way to
meet with you face-to-face except through using tea as a pretext...
which, of course, means I've gone and made tea a weapon of war. And
you said something similar. That was what I found amusing. I wasn't
smirking *at* you."

Magoroku fell silent once again. Yet there was no wrath or blood-
thirst in his demeanor. Before long, Magoroku placed his fists on the
tatami and bowed his head deeply.

"Your Lordship's thoughtfulness is wasted on a lowly man such as
myself. As my talents are meager, I am sure I am being impolite. I humbly ask Your Lordship's forgiveness."

"That is fine." Murashige paused to take a quick breath. "Suzuki
Magoroku, raise your head. I've a question for you. How did you take
that young samurai's head? Tell me from beginning to end."

Magoroku sat up.

"If Your Lordship asks, I shall answer."

With that, Magoroku launched into his account:

"The Saika contingent took the encampment's left flank and awaited
the time for battle. At the signal of the drums, we fired at the encampment, and men wielding hatchets hacked away at the fencing, but the
footing was muddy, so it took a surprising amount of time and effort.
Before long, we started hearing peculiar war cries—it was the Takatsuki contingent. We gnashed our teeth, for the Takatsuki men beat us
to the punch, but then I realized that this afforded us a fine opportunity, so I waited for the fencing to go down and then ordered them to
rush in silently. Otsu's bunch was so taken aback by the Takatsuki men's
war cries that it was like they forgot we were there shooting at them;
for the most part, they simply turned their backs to us. There were even

some who saw me and told me, "'Tis a night raid,' or asked me, 'Has our lord been found yet?' As we all slew the rank-and-file soldiers, one of them finally realized the threat we posed and shouted hoarsely that the enemy was behind them, too. Oka Shiroutarou shot him forthwith and ran up to finish the job."

There was no excitement in Magoroku's manner of speaking. He was simply recounting what had occurred.

"Thus, I let others handle rank-and-file soldiers and went deep into the encampment in search of a worthy adversary, only to find Otsu's folk had fallen into a panic, knowing not what to do. They knew not whether to advance or retreat; they appeared to be simply awaiting orders. I had to wonder whether there was any glory in slaying cowards like them. I pitied them, I did. Not to tell this to an enemy of his in your person, but the Oda we saw at Tenno-ji was truly formidable. We were all expecting a battle that fierce, but just when I was thinking what a letdown it felt like, a young samurai dashed before my eyes without saying a word."

Magoroku stopped talking and stared into space as he tried to recall the events of that night.

"...From the front part of the encampment," he continued, "they were running toward Arioka Castle. He had two or three soldiers accompanying him, and one of them noticed me there and cried, 'The enemy.' I shot the man down, and the small fries ran away frightened and amazed. The young samurai, however, wasn't so daunted. He shouted how dare I and came at me with a hand spear. He was brave, but regrettably, his youth came through in his inexperience in battle, for he rushed headlong without calling for allies. In addition to my gun, I was wearing a sword at my hip, but fighting a spear with a sword is something of a pain. I was thinking about pulling back, but the samurai's spear pierced through the camp enclosure, and its tip got caught in the curtain, and so I drew my sword and slew him, feeling sorry for his poor luck all the while. Since the trumpet-shell signal to retreat was sounded just then, I took the warrior's head with me."

His eyes looked distant.

"War is truly a dance with fortune. That warrior was far too inexperienced. As such, I do not think of the deed as all that glorious, but if Your Lordship is asking me whether he might have been Otsu Denjuurou, I do think 'tis possible."

By the time Suzuki Magoroku left, the sky's hue had gone from red to ultramarine. Murashige lit his candle and brewed himself some tea. He had committed every minute detail both Takayama Dariyo and Suzuki Magoroku had told him to memory. Alone in the candlelight, he drank his tea. Both the painting of the boats and Torasaru were drowned in darkness. The bamboo thicket obstructed the moonlight, and almost none of it could reach the tea-ceremony house.

11

When Murashige left the tea house, two warriors shook the bamboo grass as they appeared and fell to their knees. They were Akioka Shirou-nosuke and Inui Sukesaburou, two of Murashige's Five Spears. A guard room had been set up within the grove in such a way that it could not be seen by the guests, and they had waited there while Murashige and his guests drank the tea. Of course, in order to protect Murashige in case of an emergency, they'd been listening with rapt attention, sometimes putting their hands on the hilts of their swords as they waited. That level of precaution was a matter of course, but Murashige's heart frowned upon it; he had now learned that a tea ceremony, when surveilled by soldiers and when its topic of conversation was war, could be *this* dreadfully tiresome. Even the fact that Suzuki Magoroku had admired Murashige's performance aloud was somewhat regrettable, given the impure nature of the ceremony.

There was one thing that Murashige had gleaned through his two tea ceremonies. Neither Takayama Dariyo nor Suzuki Magoroku believed with pride that he was the one who killed Otsu. Of course, neither outright stated that, but someone who believed that he was the one who deserved credit for it wouldn't have been so detached or indifferent about it. If Murashige wasn't wrong, both of them thought that while it would be grand if the warrior he had defeated turned out to be Otsu, it wouldn't be strange if the other had slain Otsu instead... No samurai alive was selfless enough to not want credit. That was true of non-samurai as well. The reason neither Dariyo nor Magoroku made the case that they were the one who deserved the credit for the greatest glory was because neither of them had the confidence to say with certainty that the head they took was Otsu's.

Astride the horse led there by his horse tender, Murashige returned to the citadel. It was a night of the full moon, but the cloud cover was too thick, and the moonlight trickled hazily through the clouds. Upon passing through the dead-quiet samurai district and coming to the bridge over the fosse, he saw a torch swaying on the other side of the bridge. He arrived at the gate sectioning off the citadel. Those who guarded the gate were suspicious of the approaching mounted warrior; Akioka Shirounosuke called out to them:

"Our lord returns. Open the gates."

"Understood," replied the gatekeeper, but the gate didn't open until Murashige and the gatekeeper drew close enough to be able to make out each other's faces in the torchlight, after which the gate finally opened. The gate was hard and heavy, with iron rivets hammered into it, and as such, it took time to open and close. Without waiting for the gate to open completely, Murashige spurred his horse onward. When he dismounted his horse in front of his residence, it seemed that the advance notice had made it there, as the guard knelt down to welcome him.

"Attention, my lord. Araki Kyuuzaemon awaits."

"I see. Call him to my reception hall."

Murashige entrusted his horse to his horse tender.

It was already night. Murashige entered the reception hall alongside his sword bearer; the room was darker than it was outside. Lighting the candle, he couldn't even discern Kyuuzaemon's face from Murashige's place at the seat of honor. Kyuuzaemon was prostrating himself, but it seemed a shadow was hanging over his heart.

"Good work, my proxy," said Murashige.

"Thank you, my lord."

"Tell me, how did the council go?"

"Nothing of note occurred."

Kyuuzaemon spoke smoothly and without faltering. In fact, he spoke *too* smoothly. Murashige detected some kind of undertone to it.

"Tell me what happened."

"My lord, I..."

"'Tis all right. Give me the unvarnished truth."

Kyuuzaemon drew back his body within the darkness.

"'Tis a trivial matter, but I shall tell Your Lordship. Nothing much happened at the council, but the matter of the credit for Otsu's head did seem to garner the commanders' interest, and they asked me incessantly what Your Lordship said. Among them, that Nomura Tango said that there was no need to investigate to whom the credit should go, and that there was no way that luck would favor Christians who were led astray by barbarous foreign customs to turn their backs on the Buddha. The Christian commanders turned pale and retorted, 'Let's see which of us has divine protection,' going so far as to put their hands on the hilts of their swords. Ikeda Izumi stepped in to mediate, and the spat subsided, but..."

He then spoke more softly.

"...if it had not been Tango, I might have seriously considered there was double-dealing afoot."

"By that, you mean Oda's hand could be at work?"

"...Verily."

Vying for glory on their names was common among samurai clans. It wasn't rare for people to slander those with enemy heads in their hands as simply having picked up another's kill, nor was it rare for people to say it was a lie when hearing someone else served as rear guard. However, Nomura Tango, the one who picked that fight, hadn't even been involved in the night raid. It was beyond the pale for him to wade into a glory dispute he had nothing to do with and almost cause blood to be shed in so doing. As such, it was only natural that Kyuuzaemon should begin to suspect that Nomura Tango was in touch with Oda and actively planning to kick up discord in the ranks.

Nomura Tango's bravery was unmatched on the battlefield, but

Murashige didn't think he was clever enough to be brought over to Oda's side to perpetrate such schemes. Tango was entrusted with Fort Hiyodorizuka in the castle's south edge, and that was the fort that contained the Saika men.

"Is Tango backing the Saika by saying that?" muttered Murashige.

Tango was good at taking care of his subordinates, which was why his soldiers loved him, but that very quality led to rank favoritism. Murashige wouldn't put it past Tango to speak ill of the Takatsuki contingent to curry favor with the Saika contingent, with whom he worked on a daily basis.

"I thought that may be the case, too, my lord," said Kyuuzaemon. "But all the same, I do not believe it is right for a commander to rebuke another commander at a war council."

Murashige didn't reply.

He couldn't say that Nomura Tango's reckless remarks sprang only from playing favorites and no other reason. The commanders, the soldiers, and perhaps even Murashige himself were getting impatient waiting day after day after day for the Mouri to arrive. The fact that whether they won or lost—and whether they lived or died—depended entirely on the Mouri chafed against the samurai spirit, which prized individual self-sufficiency. That was what had them on edge. Their hearts were so shaken that a single letter from Takigawa Sakon could create a chink in their armor.

Murashige knew the best cure for such times was securing a victory. He'd ordered a night raid, and as expected, they'd won. Moreover, they'd scored a victory they hadn't even been hoping for, killing the enemy general. And now that great victory had morphed into discord within the castle. *They do say fortune and misfortune are ever intertwined, but...*

"The heavens..."

Murashige swallowed the rest of the sentence: *The heavens are not with us.* He couldn't tell a vassal such a thing.

In any case, it all came down to the heads. Murashige used the tea ceremony to glean how Magoroku and Dariyo took the heads they severed, but he still couldn't say for sure which one killed Otsu.

Everything about the raid that night seemed to have melted in the springtime haze.

If the war hadn't been the way it was, he probably could have sent a messenger to the enemy and ask their help in identifying the heads. After all, it dishonored not only the side of the taker of the head but also the side of the fallen samurai of high rank if the head was not treated properly. They would have had reason to reply which head was Otsu's.

But in this case, that was next to impossible. The Araki had betrayed the Oda and killed two of Nobunaga's favorite retainers. Nobunaga's resentment was undoubtedly profound, and any messenger sent to determine which was Otsu's head would assuredly not return alive.

The candle flame kept wavering. The silence spoke volumes of how fruitless his information gathering with Takayama and Suzuki proved.

"My lord," said Kyuuzaemon gloomily. "Pray listen, for I have an idea."

Murashige snapped back to the present moment. "Speak."

"Yes, my lord." The man's silhouette bowed, then straightened back up. "I believe the glory should be attributed to Suzuki Magoroku of the Saika."

"...State your case."

"I would ask Your Lordship to clear the room first."

Murashige waved his hand and dismissed the sword bearer. Kyuuzaemon waited for the shoji door to close before speaking.

"First and foremost, Takayama Dariyo may say he is on our side, but there are more than a few who begrudge him his son's betrayal, and not everyone would greet news of the glory belonging to him as something to celebrate. Suzuki Magoroku, on the other hand, is here on the orders of Osaka Hongan-ji. A credit to him is a credit to Hongan-ji."

If reinforcements distinguished themselves, it earned honor for the side that sent those soldiers, and making Hongan-ji look good was no loss to Arioka Castle. Murashige stroked his chin.

"Continue."

"Yes, my lord. Secondly, we must consider Nomura Tango's careless remarks. While I have no stake in it personally, 'tis true that one facet of the current glory dispute is the rivalry between the True Pure Land believers and the Christians. As such, I believe we ought to take into consideration which side has more people in this castle."

Naturally, there were more True Pure Land believers than Christians. Besides the Takatsuki contingent, the Christians numbered only a handful.

"...Is that all?"

"I have a third point as well, my lord."

Still draped in darkness, Kyuuzaemon lowered his voice yet another octave.

"There is no guarantee that the side to whom the highest glory is not attributed will not bear any ill will. Whose enmity must we fear more, that of the Takatsuki contingent or that of the Saika contingent? Prithee take that into account, my lord."

Though they were from a different land, the men from Saika had Hongan-ji's backing. The Takatsuki men, meanwhile, had no backing, as they had turned their backs on their lord, Takayama Ukon, to side with Arioka. If they became too troublesome, no one would complain if they were slain.

Araki Kyuuzaemon was originally one of the most prominent commanders in the Ikeda clan. His words were not to be taken lightly. If they knew not to whom the credit actually belonged, then they soon had to reckon with which side was more politically expedient. Murashige had to admit that Kyuuzaemon had a point.

Kyuuzaemon put his fists on the floor and prostrated himself.

"Of course, if there is a way to convince everyone that one of them took Otsu's head, I believe that would be best."

"...You speak the obvious."

"My lord?"

Murashige stifled a sigh. "Your advice is sound, but I cannot act on it. We can't win this war without both contingents."

The castle lacked enough soldiers to be able to discard that many troops. If obtaining Otsu's head meant that either of the two contingents would be leaving their side, the night-raid victory would be Pyrrhic.

Kyuuzaemon didn't belabor the point. "Pray forgive me my impertinent remarks. I thought it would do our clan good."

"That's fine. You're dismissed."

"Yes, my lord."

Kyuuzaemon exited the reception hall. For a short while, Murashige stayed there, motionless in the scant candlelight.

12

Bringing a light into his bedchamber, Murashige looked at the head register and the register of injuries.

Five heads were taken during the night raid, but the raiders slew more than five men. Both Takayama Dariyo and Suzuki Magoroku said that their troops killed scores of foot soldiers and ordinary rank and file. Perhaps Otsu Denjuurou had been among them.

However, the more he flipped through the pages, the more he realized that couldn't be it. A glorious deed was proof that one risked their life. Whenever they killed an enemy—any enemy—a warrior's heart skipped a beat: Had they just slain a famous one? And when the battle was over, a samurai proclaimed his feats for all to hear. Sometimes, the battle was too fast-paced, and there was no time whatsoever to take the head, and sometimes, they were forbidden from taking heads, but it wasn't so for that night raid. Besides, if circumstances prevented one from taking the head, they had the testimony of their peers to fall back on, but the register bore no such record.

The fact that four heads had been submitted for inspection meant that the number of samurai killed by the Takatsuki and Saika contingents was definitely four. Two of those four were clearly not Otsu Denjuurou. That left two heads as candidates, a bullnecked head and a slenderfaced one.

"Is Otsu the bullnecked one...or is he the slender-faced one...?"

Murashige closed his eyes and recalled the looks on the heads' faces. Both were young warriors. Otsu Denjuurou was young, but was he really *that* young? At the dawn of the first month, when Murashige wished Nobunaga a happy New Year at Azuchi Castle, Otsu Denjuurou

must have been somewhere there. An enormous castle, glittering cos-
tumes, a sumptuous array of delicacies so vast that one could tire of it
all, and his son's father-in-law, Akechi Mitsuhide... Murashige found
himself picturing it in his mind's eye. *Was that Koreto Hyuuga just now?*
He remembered all the trivial chatting and laughter he and the Hyuuga
lord exchanged. Hashiba Hideyoshi, Lord of Chikuzen was also there.
He'd usurped from Murashige the role of capturing Harima, but
strangely, Murashige found he harbored no resentment toward the
man. That New Year had been a good day, a good day indeed. But where
had Otsu been? He didn't remember seeing either the bullnecked or
the slender-faced man in Azuchi Castle on that day.

He wondered whether Otsu was there at that time five years prior,
when he went to Todai-ji as a messenger for a cutting of the famed aro-
matic agarwood log, the Ranjatai. It was said that the treasure was
enshrined in the temple's Shosoin repository, and that Ashikaga Yoshi-
masa was the last person to get a cutting. When Nobunaga was slated
to get a cutting, Murashige's group was entrusted with the task of protecting the Ranjatai from Shosoin to Tamonyama Castle, where Nobunaga was waiting. The Ranjatai was about six *shaku* long. Legions of
enemies didn't frighten Murashige, but the journey to deliver that sizable treasure terrified him to his core. He would never forget the excitement of being one of the few tasked with guarding a curious treasure
said to rank first among the sixty-one famed scented logs. It was a cool
day in the third month...right around this time of the year.

*Oh, the Ranjatai! What an honor it was! Even if my body rots away,
the sentence* Murashige Araki was among the magistrates who received
the Ranjatai at Todai-ji in the second year of the Tensho era *will persist
forevermore. But was Otsu Denjuurou there on that grand occasion? Did
I see anyone with that bull neck or that slender face?*

Murashige opened his eyes with a start. It appeared he'd dozed off.

While he was dreaming, the candle had gone out. Only its flame had
left this world. The bedchamber was in complete darkness... And yet
there was one small source of light, visible through the shoji screen.
Was it a watch fire?

No, thought Murashige, it couldn't be. Something about it seemed less controlled. Just when Murashige was about to summon someone, a silhouette knelt down on the other side of the door.

"My lord."

The strained voice belonged to a member of his guard, Akioka Shirounosuke.

"What's going on?" Murashige asked him.

"There's a fire."

Murashige slowly got to his feet.

"Where? Is it the enemy?"

"I know not, my lord. Koori Juuemon is heading to it to investigate."

His eyes had grown accustomed to the darkness, and he picked up his sword and opened the sliding door. The night sky was overcast, concealing the moon, but due south was a little bit brighter. An accidental fire was already grave, but even more alarming was arson at the hands of the enemy. If the fire made it to a gunpowder storehouse, the castle would fall in less than a month's time. Murashige had ordered his retainers to report news of any fire to him, no matter how small.

Murashige scowled up at the sky. "I'm going up the castle tower to survey things. Come with me."

"Yes, my lord."

When Murashige returned to his room, he put on his mail, a helmet, gauntlets, shin guards, and leather split-toe socks. In that time, his guard had prepared his sandals, and so Murashige descended from the open veranda into the garden. Murashige placed Shirounosuke in front of him, and together, they ascended the castle tower.

Amid the inky blackness of the night, he could see a small fire. Murashige knew all about the topography of Arioka Castle, but it was nonetheless difficult to measure the distance in the dark. Still, he knew it wasn't one of the forts, or the samurai district, that had caught fire.

Isn't that in the south of the town houses, by the vacant land with all those fields?

Murashige figured that whatever was burning, they didn't have a catastrophic fire on their hands. Scanning the perimeter, one saw no movement among the Oda forces encircling the castle. It didn't seem as though they meant to charge the castle in tandem with the fire.

And that means 'tis not grave enough to worry too much about...

So Murashige told himself, but he couldn't shake the unpleasant sense of foreboding he couldn't name. Fires were rare at Arioka Castle, which was blessed with water access. In spring, the firewood and the brushwood were too damp to reliably light a fire. And yet tonight, on the very day signs of discord throughout the castle started coming to the fore, a fire had flared up. Murashige couldn't think of it as anything but arson. Like his unmoving master, Shirounosuke held his breath. Only the whistling of the wind filled the castle tower.

They heard footsteps from below; someone was running up the stairs. Shirounosuke put his hand on the hilt of his sword, but it was Koori Juuemon who appeared.

"So this is where Your Lordship was," said Juuemon, panting.

"Is that you, Juuemon? What's going on?"

"'Tis arson, my lord."

Shirounosuke wasn't one to get perturbed, but that made him gasp with surprise. Juuemon knelt before Murashige, raising his breathless voice.

"Seven or eight commoners banded together and set fire to the Christian place of worship, chanting it was for the Buddha's sake. Christians gathered, and there was a scuffle between them and the arsonists when Nomura Tango of Fort Hiyodorizuka sent a large number of men to disperse the crowd."

"Did Tango capture the arsonists?"

"I know not. I ran over there only after the crowd broke up."

"I see." Murashige looked sharply at the fire and gritted his teeth. "Good work. You're both dismissed."

At the highest floor of the castle tower, Murashige remained silent as he watched the faraway flames grow weaker and weaker. His heart was aching from the remorse.

In Settsu as it was elsewhere, differences between sects didn't typically cause many conflicts. Back during the Tenbun era, a fierce battle broke out between sects in the capital, but that was already forty years past. And while Osaka Hongan-ji was a religious institution, Nobunaga was not crossing spears against them simply because he was not a True Pure Land believer.

To quote a didactic poem from the Zen monk Ikkyu, "Many paths lead from the foot of the mountain, but at the peak we all gaze at the same bright moon." There was a panoply of sects and denominations all over the world, but the goal was invariably the same. Though many were unaware of Ikkyu's words of guidance, few openly talked about the differences between their faiths during day-to-day life. Butting heads over such things was anything but commonplace, and one seldom ever heard people speak of who was a Shingon adherent, a Nichiren adherent, or a follower of Zen teachings. Any who would cast aspersions on another's faith simply because they did not revere the Buddha would themselves be seen as oddballs. But that was only during normal circumstances.

The castle's denizens spent unceasing days waiting for help with bated breath, and the anxiety that seeped into the hearts made them seek out enemies *within* the fold. They went looking for othering qualities: *They're not one of us. They're not from Settsu. They're a newcomer.* Murashige had seen many clans succumb to suspicion, where distrust turned to internal bloodshed and eventually to wholesale collapse. Wasn't that why the Ikeda and Itami clans fell to ruin? And now here at Arioka Castle, the Christians were being eyed with just such destructive suspicion.

"This is stupid. Sheer stupidity!" Murashige blurted out.

The Takatsuki and Saika groups were the ones whose glory was in question, but that didn't mean they were at each other's throats. Except for the incident where one of the heads "transformed" into a foreboding grimace, nothing had happened to indicate that the two contingents were on unfriendly terms. Despite that, somebody lost their presence of mind and took a dispute between parties unrelated to them into their own hands, spreading silly rumors, shouting abuse, and ultimately setting a fire within the castle.

Murashige was haunted by his own negligence—he hadn't noticed. When he'd gone on a patrol tour of the castle, he *had* been vaguely uneasy, but he'd failed to detect the truth behind it. He should have picked up on the suspicion of Christianity spreading among the people, and the diffidence of the Christians. Last winter, when Abe Jinen died so mysteriously, there were people who averred that it must be the work of some strange technique known only to Christians. Murashige was now faced with two choices: abandon the Christians and side with the many against the few, or defend the Christians and earn the distrust of the many. Yet no matter which path he trod, they both led to the fall of Arioka Castle.

"No. No, I still have time."

Even if the kindling that was the suspicion against the Christians was accumulating in great piles behind closed doors, the spark that ignited that firewood remained the intractable question—was the credit owed to the Takatsuki or the Saika? If Murashige managed to find the correct answer, he might just be able to keep Arioka Castle afloat. He might even be able to convert suspicion of Christianity into hostility toward the Oda. No, he was *sure* he could.

But there was precious little time left. The war council would be held at dawn, and there, he would have to convince everyone in attendance. By noon of that day, things would likely spiral out of control. But could he do it? Could he really solve such a thorny case he hadn't been able to after thinking so hard on it? And could he do it by the time the morning rolled in?

Murashige looked up at the thick, low-hanging cloud cover. He had been left with but one option.

13

A candlestick holder in hand, Murashige descended the stairs of the castle tower to the basement. He came alone, relying solely on the feeble flame flickering to light his path as he took each step.

The steps led to a small room that housed a well. In this room, a small man of about forty stayed all hours of the day and night—the jailer. Illuminated by the candle, the warden unhurriedly went down on his knees before Murashige, the keys at his waist jangling.

"My liege… What brings Your Lordship here during the wee hours?"
Murashige eyed the hinged door in a corner of the room.
"Unlock it," he ordered.
"Yes, my lord."
Slowly, the jailer got to his feet. Upon seeing how bloodshot the pair of eyes staring at Murashige in the candlelight was, Murashige knit his brow a tad. He softly placed the candlestick holder on the ground.
The lock clanked. The jailer pulled the door open, then turned his back on the rectangular portal into darkness and hung his head.
"'Tis open now, my liege."
"Go in front."
Confusion tinged the jailer's voice. "My lord…"
"What's the matter? Go in front."
"Yes, my lord. I shall."
Yet the jailer didn't budge.
Murashige feigned an expression of innocence. "By the way, has anything strange or suspicious happened?" he asked as he looked over his shoulder in the darkness.
That instant, the jailer drew his *wakizashi* short sword and shouted, "Prepare to die, traitor!"
The second the unsheathed blade glinted in the candlelight, the jailer found Murashige's own *wakizashi* slashed his torso. His shabby robe was sliced open, and blood and guts spilled out. The jailer breathed his last long breath before toppling and dying.
Wiping his blade on the jailer's clothes, Murashige looked down on the corpse. Murashige had noticed the undisguised bloodlust about the man's eyes, but he didn't know what sort of grudge the jailer may have had against him.
"But why?" Murashige murmured.
In reply, a voice could be heard from beyond the threshold. A laughing voice. At first, the laughter was subdued, but it soon turned loud and booming, echoing throughout the underground. Murashige sheathed his *wakizashi* and shouted angrily into the darkness.
"Silence! Silence, Kanbei!"
The laughter suddenly stopped.

Murashige picked the candlestick holder back up and held it aloft as he slowly descended the damp flight of stairs leading to the dungeon, where a man's silhouette did lurk. Murashige shivered slightly as he approached.

"Kanbei."

Murashige held the candle up. Kanbei's hair and beard were long and unkempt, his clothes blackened, his face filthy. What Murashige saw in that cage was akin to a lump of rags. Kanbei's eyes slowly opened and trained on Murashige; the whites of his eyes were yellowed, and the pupils clouded. His cheeks were gaunt, but he was grinning. Murashige had last seen him in the twelfth month of the year prior. In that time, his hair had of course grown, but the way he laughed was also different.

"Well met, Lord of Settsu. The gods save Your Lordship's life. How splendid," he said hoarsely.

Murashige's eyes opened slightly wider. "What do you know?"

"Whatever does Your Lordship mean?"

"That jailer was honest to a fault. He was not the type to try to slay his lord and master. Yet he blurted out that I'm a traitor."

"Pray do not tell me Your Lordship hasn't a clue?" Kanbei asked, puzzled.

That show of scorn and his earlier statement about his life combined in Murashige's mind.

"Kanbei, did *you* instigate that man?!" he asked, shouting despite himself.

Kanbei smiled contentedly. "I stand impressed by Your Lordship's powers of discernment."

"A mere prisoner like you, aiming for my head?"

Murashige placed a hand on the hilt of his sword, to which Kanbei waved his hand as though shooing a fly.

"I would not dream of it. I could never do anything so ghastly." Kanbei's tone was facetious, but it took an unexpected serious turn: "'Twas the jailer's head I was after."

Murashige was about to say "lies," but he swallowed the word. Just as Kanbei said, Murashige was still alive, and the jailer lay dead.

Murashige wanted to think that Kanbei had just made that up in the moment as a stopgap measure, but he couldn't honestly believe it.

"...What did he do to you?"

Kanbei looked down, saying nothing. The candle illuminated the top of his head. Even Murashige couldn't stifle the noise that welled up in his throat. Kanbei's head bore brutal scars that filled the warlord with horror. The wounds were festering, swollen and open. Moreover, it seemed that that flesh was preyed upon by insects.

Kanbei lifted his head, thereby concealing the scars in the darkness.

"As thanks for these blemishes, I engaged in a little chat with the man," he said softly. "Lord of Settsu, it turns out that killing from inside this cage is, contrary to expectations, not so difficult."

Murashige's hand remained on the hilt. "'Twas I who killed him. Are you saying you *used* me?"

Kanbei didn't answer.

For a short while, Murashige was of two minds. He was a mighty, muscular warrior, but he believed he had climbed his way to the Lord of Settsu title because his intuition was sharper than anybody else's. A samurai counted the bow and the horse among their physical tools, and intuition and luck among their immaterial tools. And his gut was telling him to kill Kanbei this very moment.

Murashige couldn't put the blame of the jailer's death on Kanbei. No matter what Kanbei had spouted off in this dark dungeon, the one who had drawn his sword on Murashige had been the jailer. And yet his gut was whispering for him to pay that no mind and to stick his sword through the bars into Kanbei. He couldn't afford to do that, however. If he slew Kanbei, his plan to restabilize his castle, which was getting torn apart between the men from Takatsuki and the men from Saika, would come to nothing.

Kanbei was curled up, no longer gazing Murashige's way. He looked as though he knew full well that Murashige would not kill him by any means. Murashige dismissed his intuition. He could kill Kanbei whenever he so pleased. It didn't have to be now. That was what Murashige told himself as he took his hand off the hilt.

"...Now, then," muttered Kanbei, "what business has Your Lordship with me? Though it was tit for tat, I acknowledge it was a crime to have killed an honorable servant of the Lord of Settsu. And as penance, I shall put my heart into listening to Your Lordship."

Kanbei had more or less surmised the reason Murashige had come to visit him. Part of him rued not killing him, yet he got into it anyway. "There are two heads we can't identify."

He told Kanbei about Takigawa Sakon's letter inviting him to Nobunaga's hawk hunt. He told him about the complication that arose at the war council wherein Takayama Dariyo and Suzuki Magoroku both advocated for battle, which ran counter to the backroom consensus Murashige had contrived beforehand. He mentioned how they spotted a thinly defended enemy encampment and his orders to scout it out, then the night raid and the four heads. He spoke of how they only discovered that they'd slain an enemy commander after the fact. He told Kanbei everything.

Kanbei closed his eyes. His body was still, as though he was dozing. He did slightly tilt his head to the side in puzzlement when he heard about the tea ceremony. While bugs crawled around at his feet and amid the burgeoning smell of blood, Murashige recounted the burning of the Christians' place of worship, and how he'd slain the jailer.

"As such, I must bring to light who killed Otsu Denjuurou once and for all. But I don't think even you can help me with—"

"Lord of Settsu, what on earth has ye so concerned?"

"...What was that?"

Kanbei opened his eyes and indiscreetly scanned Murashige's face. "I find the idea that a case this simple should elude the Lord of Settsu of all people—simply unthinkable. I take it Your Lordship has been distracted by a separate worry. Am I mistaken?"

Murashige unconsciously drew the candle away from him. His hand had acted on the spur of the moment to conceal his face from Kanbei's prying eyes. It was a subtle movement, but it was more than enough for Kanbei to catch on to Murashige's agitation.

"Those who would buy time invariably wax on and on. Kanbei, don't get carried away with your braggadocio."

"It is a given who took that head. What I do find somewhat vexing is, what is tormenting Your Lordship so? Was it Takayama, or was it Suzuki? Or going back further, was it that 'Nakanishi'...? Oh, no—it couldn't be..."

"Kanbei!" Murashige's roar shook the dungeon. "Earlier, you told me that killing you from your cage would be an easy task. Did you know that killing you from outside the cage is even easier?"

"...Ohhh. I say." His long-bearded face contorted with sarcasm, Kanbei bowed his head deeply. "Prithee forgive my rudeness. As of late, I have taken to valuing my life. I beg Your Lordship's mercy."

"Are you mocking me?"

Kanbei laughed low in his throat. "Mocking a castle lord from within a cage... The notion is quite a hoot, O honorable Lord of Settsu. Why does Your Lordship think that night raid turned out to be such a crushing success? If the Lord of Settsu is dim-witted and inept enough at war to not know the reason, then that makes all my suffering seem so very hollow."

Murashige reckoned that the night raid was successful due to Otsu letting his guard down. Murashige couldn't blame him, as he didn't know that Arioka Castle could deploy troops from its eastern edge, but Murashige chalked up their victory to the encampment not being prepared for such a sneak attack.

Kanbei didn't wait for Murashige to reply.

"Please allow me to belatedly congratulate Your Lordship for your victory. It must be by dint of the blessings of the great bodhisattva Hachiman, or the various *kami*, or Nikko Gongen, or Yuzen Daimyojin... Samurai are an iniquitous lot. I would like to pray for the repose of that jailer's soul."

Kanbei pressed his hands in prayer and closed his eyes. No matter what Murashige asked him, he remained that way, never opening his eyes.

14

At the crack of dawn, the large drum at the drum turret was sounded. It was the signal summoning the commanders for the war council.

Murashige heard the drumming from a room in his residence. Hang-ing in the alcove was a scroll with the characters reading *Hachiman Daibosatsu*, the great bodhisattva Hachiman. Murashige sat cross-legged facing it and closed his eyes. With each beat of the drum, more commanders entered the inner citadel. Normally, a war council didn't need every single commander to be in attendance, as removing them all from their posts at once would spell danger. However, the pattern of the drumbeats that morning was a summons for everyone to attend, barring an imminent attack by the enemy. Naturally, these orders came from Murashige.

Another beat of the drum. Takayama Dariyo and Suzuki Magoroku had to be at the castle tower by now, as did Araki Kyuuzaemon and Ikeda Izumi. Nomura Tango and Nakanishi Shinpachirou might already have entered, among others. Yet Murashige still had yet to con-firm who should be credited with Otsu's kill.

The sliding doors had been left open. Feeling the spring breeze on his skin, he opened his eyes. He glanced outside; the cherry blossom petals were scattering in the wind. One whole day had passed since their victory in battle, and Murashige was cornered.

Murashige didn't know whether paying Kanbei a visit had been the correct choice. Kuroda Kanbei was doubtless the cleverest man in Arioka Castle. He had a sharper mind than even Murashige. Yet there was too much he didn't know about him. Kanbei had no reason what-soever to aid Murashige and every reason to loathe him. As such, had the things he said in that cage been meaningless noise? He'd asked Murashige why the night raid was such a success, and after mulling it over all night, he understood the gist of what he meant. What Murashige didn't understand was how it tied into who killed Otsu Denjuuro.

"I've no choice, do I?" he murmured.

The war council's appointed time was fast approaching. If he couldn't get to the bottom of the case in time for the assembly, his only option would be to adopt Kyuuzaemon's proposal. He knew it would earn him the displeasure of the Takatsuki contingent, but he would credit the feat to Suzuki Magoroku. That decision could very well lead to him hav-ing to forsake every Christian in the castle, but there was no other way.

"*Namu…*," he prayed, closing his eyes once again. He dived deep into his mind, but his thoughts were rehashing the same points and running in circles until the designated time was at hand.

An attendant kneeling on the open veranda whispered to him: "The commanders have all assembled."

"…Understood."

Murashige opened his eyes, before which hung the *Hachiman Daibosatsu* scroll.

He kept repeating the prayer in his heart: *Namu Hachiman Daibosatsu.* Murashige sprang to his feet.

The commanders were prostrate, and Murashige moved toward the chief seat, sitting cross-legged on the cushion. Next to it was a sword bearer.

"The council is now in session," said Murashige.

At that, the commanders bowed their heads even lower, then sat up. Murashige nonchalantly scanned them and found Takayama Dariyo and Suzuki Magoroku. Takayama's seat at the council was always a relatively higher-ranked one, while Suzuki Magoroku was seated in a higher seat than normal. Next to him sat Nomura Tango, who must have taken Magoroku to that seat.

The commanders awaited Murashige's words with bated breath. Like usual during these councils, Murashige's eyes seemed somewhat sleepy, and he began speaking slowly and deliberately.

"…Last night, a fire broke out in a town house to the south. It was arson. Izumi, explain the circumstances."

"Yes, my lord."

Ikeda Izumi bowed. In addition to being in charge of weapons, armor, and provisions, he also bore the responsibility of managing the castle area. He didn't need to be ordered to investigate the fire, as that was part of his role.

"The arsonists burned the Christian place of worship. It was surrounded by vacant land, so the fire did not spread, abating on its own. However, I was told a believer entered the blaze to retrieve a 'cross' or what have you, then was scorched to death. It was five commoners who set the blaze; we have already captured three, while the remaining two are on the lam. We have witnesses who say they saw them leave the castle."

"Excellently done. Execute the ones you captured and expose their corpses as a warning. Also, I want a thorough manhunt to see if anyone might be hiding the other two."

"Yes, as Your Lordship commands."

Murashige gave Nomura Tango a glance. According to Koori Juuemon's information, Tango had let the arsonists go, but at the moment, Murashige didn't pick up anything out of the ordinary with Tango. If Tango had stood up for the criminals, then Murashige couldn't overlook it, no matter if he was his sister's husband. But he concluded that that fear was unsubstantiated, which put him slightly more at ease.

No one else voiced a different opinion or version of events. That settled the matter of the arson, but it did nothing to soften the mood among the commanders. Everyone there knew that the next item of discussion was what mattered.

"Now, then," said Murashige. "Two days ago, we conducted a night raid on an enemy encampment and slew their general, Otsu Denjuurou Nagamasa. I'll now declare to whom the credit belongs."

One could slice the tension with a knife. Every man there was staring directly at him, from those in armor to those in plain robes, from the high-ranked to the low.

"None among you took Otsu's head. Takayama Dariyo and Suzuki Magoroku both proved their brilliance in brave battles and took helmeted heads. As rewards, I'll grant them Bizen swords."

This set the commanders abuzz; they looked at one another. Kyuuzaemon was the first to reply.

"Pray wait, my lord. Is Your Lordship saying that Otsu is alive?"

"No. Sagehari of Saika told us otherwise, and my guard confirmed it. Otsu was indeed slain."

"...I fail to comprehend Your Lordship's reasoning."

"Then I'll explain."

Murashige surveyed the attendees. While some looked skeptical and some looked indignant, the majority mostly looked baffled.

"Why did our night raid go so swimmingly to begin with? Why was the battle so easy when the encampment we attacked was surrounded by fencing and they neglected not their watch fire? That's not to say the Takatsuki and the Saika didn't battle with aplomb. Our tactics were also sound, as we picked the right moment. Yet those aren't the only reasons we won."

His eyes fell on Dariyo and Magoroku.

"Takayama and Suzuki both recounted the same sequence of events for the night raid. That is to say, they corroborated that Otsu's troops were searching for their master—for Otsu. I hear that this never stopped being the case. It wasn't just the rank-and-file foot soldiers but also the armored samurai who were running around like headless hens. Most importantly, not one of us heard any enemy gongs or drums or trumpet shells. I know what kind of battle this was."

No one else uttered a peep.

"'Tis a battle without a commander. Bereft of anyone at the helm, no one can fight. That night, Otsu issued not a single order from the start of the battle to its end."

"My lord," said Kyuuzaemon. "Is Your Lordship saying that Otsu ran away? I heard that it was the first battle the man oversaw as commander. It would make sense if, panicked by the night raid, he was the first to flee."

"But that wouldn't be consistent with Sagehari's testimony. He overheard talk of their general's death in battle. He was there on the battlefield, and he did die there."

"But, my lord…the night raiders took five heads, and there were no others. What is Your Lordship saying became of Otsu's head?"

"Otsu was slain, yet his head was not taken."

Once again, the war council was abuzz.

"It cannot be!" whispered one.

"That's absurd!" muttered another.

Murashige shot them a sharp look, and the commotion died in an instant.

"My lord," said Kyuuzaemon. "No one who slew the enemy general would then elect not to take his head. He would do it even if it cost him his life. Even if, hypothetically, he got shot by a stray arrow or bullet, that would mean Nagamasa died amid his allies, and that would not make sense, since Otsu's forces were searching for him."

"That stands to reason. Yet on that night, there were two who took no heads, despite the glory they would have won us."

Birds began chirping outside.

"The first was Itami Ichirouzaemon. He was the first to strike an enemy samurai with a sword, but he sadly died in battle. He was not able to take that head. And then there was one other."

Murashige harked back to that point in time. He recalled the moment he set his sights on the warrior standing in that Itami reedbed, illuminated by the moon of the thirteenth day of the month.

Praise to the great bodhisattva Hachiman, the gods of my land, Nikko Gongen in Utsunomiya, Yuzen Daimyojin of Nasu. I beseech you, allow me to strike the center of that fan.

"Me."

"...What?!" Kyuuzaemon had no words.

The war council was astir.

Murashige was a general. Even if he took a head, he had no one to show it to for clout. As such, he didn't take any heads himself.

"Before the battle, I shot a samurai who had stood outside the encampment."

What had been running in Murashige's mind when he drew the bowstring and pointed the arrow at the warrior bathed in the moonlight? He couldn't remember. But there was a prayer everyone was familiar with, recited when they wished for their arrow to hit their target. It was from the chapter of the legendary archer Nasu no Yoichi in *The Tale of the Heike.*

By invoking the names of the gods and the Buddha, Kanbei must have been hinting that Murashige hit the bull's-eye. Murashige realized it when he faced the scroll reading _Hachiman Daibosatsu_.

"He hadn't been wearing a helmet, so I assumed he was a servant or foot soldier, but no. He was none other than Otsu Denjuurou Nagamasa. "

To samurai, helmets existed to prove to others that they were of warrior rank in death as well. That was why everyone wanted to take a helmeted head, and to _be_ a helmeted head if they did die in battle. That the company's general was at the battlefield but not wearing a helmet came as a shock to everyone.

That being said, there were times on the battlefield when one did take off his helmet. When Murashige pulled his bowstring, he'd had to remove his helmet first lest it get in the way. Koori Juuemon had to remove his when he was ordered to scout for noises.

As Murashige reflected on Otsu's misfortune, he continued:

"The man must have taken off his helmet in order to scout out this castle with his own eyes. If we had inspected the body, we likely would have grasped his rank through the quality of his armor. But every second is precious in a night raid, so we didn't have the time to do so. How unfortunate, both for us and for him."

Takayama Dariyo and Suzuki Magoroku were bestowed with quality swords forged in Bizen. The arsonists who set the Christian place of worship on fire were burned to death. People stopped openly disparaging Christians, though since the rumors of the Buddha's punishment were firmly rooted, the unkind remarks continued to be whispered in secret.

The death of Otsu Denjuurou Nagamasa was concealed, as no one knew whether to classify it as an honorable death in battle or a cretinous death precipitated by a careless blunder. Later on, an Oda retainer would write that he heard Otsu Denjuurou died of illness on the thirteenth day of the third month of the seventh year of the Tensho era.

After the war council, Murashige went to his residence and retrieved a letter from inside the breast of his clothing. It was the letter Takigawa

Sakonshougen sent. Everybody in the castle knew the contents of the letter, but no one had read it apart from Murashige. It read:

"The Ukita are our allies henceforth. Why not enjoy each other's company on a hawk hunt?"

Takigawa had come to tell them that the Ukita had allied with the Oda. Murashige figured it was a ploy. It had to be. After all, it was only because the Ukita, who had their stronghold in Bizen Okayama, were on the side of the Mouri that the Mouri could come to Arioka Castle by way of the San'yodo. If it was true that the Ukita had switched allegiances to Oda, then the Mouri would never arrive...

The real reason Murashige had gone with the night raid was to distract his men from the contents of the letter. Nobody noticed that the letter had sparked feelings of panic and impatience inside their lord. Nobody...except for Kuroda Kanbei.

Murashige inserted Takigawa's letter into the unseasonal brazier and burned it. Thus, it was not preserved for posterity.

Chapter III

Chants amid Distant Thunder

1

Summer. The season of death.

Waves of heat battered that which drew breath, nipping away the life from the old, the ill, and the very young. Rapidly the cadavers of the dead did rot, afflicted by the sultry air. The water turned stagnant, and the vegetation wilted. But the pall of deathly silence covering Arioka Castle was not solely attributable to the season.

With the exception of the raid on the castle that took place in winter, the Oda had yet to attack Arioka. They built forts and branch castles one after the other; none could enter Arioka, and many were forbidden to leave. At first, the officers and men of Arioka mocked Oda's perceived cowardice and took pride in their castle's steadfastness. Yet after half a year of confinement, everyone was beginning to suspect, albeit in the backs of their minds, that the reason the Oda weren't attacking wasn't because he couldn't win, but rather because he could win without needing to. And if and when the Oda won, they wondered, what would become of them?

In the summertime, the specter of death was strong.

One moonless night, in Murashige's residence, the lord of the castle met with Ikeda Izumi.

"You cut down an enemy or two, I hear," said Murashige. "Give me the details."

Izumi replied while still prostrate.

"Yes, my liege. While my troops were guarding the castle, they spotted two brigands near the samurai district's gunpowder storehouse. Upon being asked their identities, they fled immediately. The troops gave chase, and the brigands, seemingly unfamiliar with the castle, found their way blocked by the fosse. With nowhere to run, they drew their swords and engaged. The troops were greater in number, but the brigands were desperate, leaving me no choice but to take their lives," he said apologetically.

Murashige had ordered that brigands should be captured alive to the best of the soldiers' ability.

"I see," said Murashige. "Is the gunpowder storehouse untouched?"

"Oil was scattered. Had the watchmen come a moment later, the storehouse would be lost to us."

Murashige nodded. The incidence of Oda subordinates running around inside the castle had increased in recent weeks. Brigand sightings were being reported on a daily basis, and more than one or two bodies of castle folk struck down by unidentified assailants had been spotted as well.

While Arioka was a strong fortress, it also covered a wide area. The troops couldn't watch over everywhere and everything, no matter how expertly they were distributed. There was no telling how many of Oda's saboteurs lurked within the ramparts of Arioka. That had been a given since the beginning of this war, and as yet, they had averted major incidents by maintaining high alert. But now the enemy was romping about the castle more freely. It could be said that the troops were ceasing to pay careful enough attention.

"The gunpowder storehouses are all supposed to have sentries. What were they doing?"

"My liege." Izumi lightly wiped the sweat from his brow. "Two foot soldiers were on watch. A posse of strangers offered them drink, and so they left their posts. Both have been arrested."

"I see. Kill them."

"Yes, my liege. Shall we behead them?"

In so asking, Izumi was asking whether they could get it done without having to use more grisly methods like crucifixion or burning at the stake.

"Do so," said a languid Murashige. "And expose the heads."

"Yes, my liege."

"From now on, you are to bar any traffic crossing the Great Fosse after dark. Place sentries to guard it all through the night and don't let anyone through without my permission apart from our soldiers."

"As Your Lordship commands."

Somewhere out west, thunder crashed, its reverberation reaching Murashige's residence. It was said that years with a lot of lightning yielded abundant harvests. Arioka Castle encircled a large swath of land and was blessed with a great deal of water. There were fields of rice and other crops, and in autumn, the first rice crop of the year would ripen. But would the castle last until then?

Murashige concluded there was nothing to worry about. The castle would not fall for the time being. They had enough provisions and gunpowder; they could continue confining themselves to this land for months, even years. What they ought to think about—what they ought to worry about—was whether what lay beyond that period of seclusion was victory.

"The lightning...," muttered Izumi.

"What of it?" said Murashige.

"Nothing, my lord, pray forgive me my stray remark."

"Very well. You're dismissed."

"Yes, my liege."

Murashige was thereupon left alone in the reception hall. He had a feeling he knew what Izumi had wanted to say, for he, too, was likely thinking the same thing:

If only the lightning would strike Azuchi and kill Nobunaga...

Murashige smiled faintly. The fact that this thought surfaced in his mind meant there could be little doubt that this war was, in fact, effectively over.

The following day before noon, at the war council held at the castle tower, news of the gunpowder storehouse and the beheading of the foot

soldiers who shirked their guard duty was relayed to Murashige's commanders, who didn't raise a fuss over it. They all figured these things
happened. Even when Murashige ordered them to strengthen the surveillance, one could say they were letting it go in one ear and out
the other.

But Murashige said in a low voice, "Onto the next subject. I've something to tell you all."

And that made his commanders straighten up and take notice.

"The Ukita have taken Oda's side," he announced. "Bizen Mimasaka
is now Oda's to use."

As one might expect, no one said a peep. A heavy silence permeated
the tower.

Word of the Ukita's betrayal had already spread far and wide. There
were those who contended that they wouldn't put it past the Ukita,
given their propensity to obey at times and disobey at others, while
many others argued, red in the face and spit spraying, that the rumors
were utter bunk. They didn't want to believe it. If the Ukita switched
to the Oda, then Mouri troops would never be able to come running
to their aid overland.

"If so...," said Araki Kyuuzaemon feebly, "then what does Your Lordship plan to do?"

That was the problem. What ought Arioka to do now that the Ukita
had changed allegiances?

"I have reflected on the matter, but I'm sure you all have thoughts on
the castle's future. I'll hear any opinions you may have."

One who sat at a relatively high-ranking seat placed his fists on
the ground.

"If I may, Your Lordship."

He was a handsome young warrior by the name of Kitagawara Yosaku
Kanekatsu, and he was a relative of Murashige's previous wife. The
Kitagawara clan served the Itami clan, but Yosaku had been banished
by virtue of being a relative of Murashige's through marriage. The
Kitagawara clan turned weak after losing its clan head in battle, but
despite his youth, Yosaku was working assiduously as the man who carried the Kitagawara clan on his back.

Yosaku learned horsemanship under Araki Motokiyo, Lord of Shima, who was known not just among the Araki clan but the whole world as a first-rate horseman almost without peer. As Motokiyo was currently defending a different castle, Yosaku was the most excelled at the art of riding in Arioka. Recently, he'd leveraged his mastery by carrying out the important mission of breaking through Oda's siege and delivering a letter to Amagasaki Castle.

"The Mouri troops in Amagasaki Castle have already pulled out in the lead-up to the Ukita's betrayal," said Yosaku. "There are virtually no people left there, and the idea that reinforcements would arrive at the castle is scarcely conceivable. My liege, prithee assume that the Mouri will never come."

These words were spoken by a man who had seen Amagasaki Castle with his own two eyes. The other commanders seemed a tad overawed, but before long, someone laughed. That someone was a man in his fifties in the attire of a Buddhist priest.

"My liege, even if Amagasaki Castle is as empty as Yosaku avers, we mustn't jump to conclusions. Soldiers are like unto waves; they recede, and they come back. Osaka stands strong, and if Tanba keeps supporting us, then the tide of war shall not change. The Ukita may be blocking the San'yodo, but the Mouri have access by sea. I believe there is naught to fear."

The speaker's name was Kawarabayashi Noto. He was a monk and a relative of a high-ranking monk of the Araki clan, Kawarabayashi Echigo, who was presently ill. While Noto was the only one among the commanders in priestly attire, he very much had a taste for the art of the blade, and he cared nothing for Buddhist teachings, as he revered the god Futsunushi. He was an impious warrior who never heard of the Nichiren Buddhist chant or the Amitabha Buddha chant.

Kitagawara Yosaku's wife hailed from the Kawarabayashi clan, which made Yosaku and Noto relatives, and yet they were somewhat distant with each other. Noto looked down on Yosaku as a little brat of the diminished Kitagawara clan who played at a full-fledged warrior; Yosaku viewed Noto as an unenlightened brute who spouted flippant twaddle while resting on the laurels of the Kawarabayashi name.

"'Tis as Noto says!" came a loud voice from one of the lower-ranked seats. It was Nakanishi Shinpachirou, protector of Fort Jorozuka. "After all, we are effectively pinning tens of thousands of Oda's troops in place. Even if support from the Mouri comes a month or two late, that shall hardly affect us. My liege, we elite warriors of Fort Jorozuka wait many a weary day for the time we may do battle. When that happens, we shall build a mound for Your Lordship with the heads of Oda samurai."

"Oh-ho, well said, Shinpachirou!"

So remarked the protector of Fort Hiyodorizuka, Nomura Tango. His throaty voice echoed through the tower.

"My liege. Oda breaking through this castle by brute force could never, ever happen. I hear the Saika men at Amagasaki Castle withdrew to Kii, but the Saika men in Fort Hiyodorizuka are a dependable group. By the way, Izumi, how many arrows and bullets do we have stored?"

Ikeda Izumi looked perplexed to be called out so suddenly, but he replied all the same, "If we can go by the winter battle as an example, we can fight seven, maybe eight more times."

"That is reassuring to hear," said Tango. "Then we may battle on for another seven or eight years."

Tango then roared with laughter. One after another, other commanders shouted out their agreement. By contrast, Izumi's expression was glum. Though he had something to say, it was difficult to express an opinion that differed from Tango's, as Tango was esteemed by the vassals.

Murashige gave the commanders' faces a cursory scan before setting his eyes on Araki Kyuuzaemon.

"What say you, Kyuuzaemon?"

"My lord..."

Kyuuzaemon sat upright and spoke with equanimity.

"While there is logic to Yosaku's statement, this war is one we fight alongside the Mouri, Hongan-ji, and the warriors of Harima and Tanba. We have sent hostages to Hongan-ji. We cannot be the only ones who steer the fate of the war. Moreover, Ukita, Lord of Izumi, was renowned for being craven and strange. None can say his betrayal was sudden. Since the Mouri have their own considerations to make, I believe that the best policy now is to continue to defend this castle as we wait for the Mouri's arrival."

The room was filled with the commanders' commending suspirations.

"Always so wise, Kyuuzaemon."

"Ahhh, yes, that is best. That's what we ought to do."

"My lord, I believe what Kyuuzaemon said to be most reasonable."

Even the commanders who could not agree with Nomura Tango's words expressed agreement with Kyuuzaemon's opinion.

Murashige nodded languorously. "So be it. This council is adjourned."

2

When Murashige turned against the Oda, he prepared to a flawless extent. He employed foot soldiers, stocked up on guns, built several provisions warehouses, and carried in rice and salt. What Arioka Castle lacked, if anything, was people. In particular, there was a shortage of messengers.

When it came time to discuss matters with a faraway correspondent, it only made sense to exchange word via letters, but the usual way messengers conveyed the most essential information was verbally. Envoys were tasked with relaying what their lord had to say to the other party without error, then bringing back the other party's reply without error. For that reason, no dolts or men who knew not etiquette were entrusted with the role, no matter how fleet of foot they were. By the same token, even the brightest minds were useless as messengers if they lacked the knowledge and the means to traverse the hills and fields, or the power to protect themselves and the letter.

The ideal messenger was a man who was familiar with the lay of the land, accustomed to traveling, of robust health and with strong legs, boasted high intelligence, always courteous, and moreover, bore high enough social standing for the other party to place their trust in him. Yet a lord would rather use a figure of such remarkable character who exhibited all those traits as a commander. And indeed, Murashige used one of his commanders, Kitagawara Yosaku, as a messenger to Amagasaki Castle. But that stemmed from the fact that not only was Yosaku a proficient horseman, he was also born here in northern Settsu and understood the surrounding geography.

As such, Murashige used itinerant monks and traveling priests as his messengers.

After the war council, Murashige returned to his residence.

Koori Juuemon suddenly went up to him. "Muhen has returned."

"I see." Murashige didn't even look at Juuemon. "Proceed as usual."

"Yes, my lord."

Juuemon deliberately didn't bow his head and left Murashige's side. It all happened in a split second.

Muhen was a traveling priest who was around fifty years of age. He was known since before the war as a monk of saintly virtue who manifested miraculous works. Of course, since the Oda had Arioka encircled, not only merchants but also monks were forbidden from traveling to and fro. Yet Muhen showed up before the castle gates one day that spring, asking they be opened because he wished to hold a service for the dead. Since then, he'd paid the castle a visit a number of times.

Arioka was pelted with rain that day. Once the rain lifted, the summer sun, which was approaching its zenith, beat down on the earth mercilessly. Muhen walked through the shimmering hot air of the townscape of Itami alone. He wore a worn-out, filth-caked *kasaya* stole, and his conical hat stood out conspicuously. His wicker luggage seemed light—almost empty, in fact—and the khakkhara staff in his hand was also stained with mud.

All around Itami, the common folk were going about their daily errands. Though they'd grown weary of being holed up for so long, they told themselves they were rather lucky after hearing that those who'd fled to the mountains were all slaughtered. They had no choice but to continue living their everyday lives while pretending to forget the ever-present specter of death. There were, however, those who were cut off from their livelihoods. No longer did the craftsmen and artisans receive commissions, and amid the oppressive heat, everyone else had glazed-over looks in their eyes, too. When Muhen passed by, their faces lit up.

"Oh, 'tis the great Muhen!"

"Praise be to you!"

Some prayerfully put their hands together and chanted the *nenbutsu* to him, while others spoke the Nichiren chant. A woman whose hair and garments were covered in dust ran up to him and fell to her knees.

"Pardon me, sir!"

Muhen replied, his hat still pulled down over his eyes, "What is the matter?"

"'Tis my father. He passed away three days ago. Please, may I ask you to hold a service for him?"

"I see. I was called here by His Lordship, so I must be off, but when I return, I shall do so."

She teared up, overcome with emotion. Then she rubbed her hands together and assumed the praying posture, venerating Muhen. There was no wind, and not a sound could be heard apart from the pleasant clanking of the rings topping Muhen's staff and the murmured prayers of the townsfolk. Four foot soldiers were walking down the main avenue, and upon seeing the monk, they laughingly derided the "bald-headed beggar," but when someone said, "'Tis Muhen," they all sank into silence and likewise pressed their hands in prayer.

Muhen passed by the town houses and came to the bridge spanning the fosse, where sentries were posted. Normally, when those without armor or helmets sought passage, the sentries demanded a small sum in exchange, calling it the bridge toll, but when they noticed it was Muhen, their grins vanished, and they opened the way.

Past the bridge lay the samurai district. Muhen first came across the row houses of the foot soldiers. Owing to the sudden downpour earlier, the streets were muddy. The mud covered Muhen's durable sandals, and more earth clung to his staff each time it struck the ground. Eventually, he reached the area where more and more commanding officers' residences lined both sides of the street. Since everyone who lived in this district was tasked with defending the castle, there was no one about the streets here. Even so, the same three words followed him as he walked, perhaps chanted by the womenfolk and errand boys who'd stayed behind—*Namu Amida Butsu. Namu Amida Butsu. Namu Amida Butsu.* Hail Amitabha Buddha.

The samurai district was separated from the inner citadel by a bridged moat. The bridge was defended around the clock by Murashige's guard, who made sure no unfamiliar or unknown people ever crossed. Muhen strode across, the rings of his staff clinking all the while. The guard didn't even ask his identity, as Murashige had ordered them not to. The gates in the bridge's vicinity, too, did not bar Muhen's path. He went down the deserted soil, always watched by the brawny warriors of the lord's guard, and made his way to the innermost zone of Arioka Castle.

At last, Muhen stood before Murashige's residence. Koori Juuemon must have been spying from somewhere, for he approached Muhen from behind.

"I shall guide you," said Juuemon.

Muhen nodded, not doffing his hat.

Murashige and Muhen sat facing each other under the coffered ceiling of the reception hall. The postrain sun was blazing down, and so the room was stiflingly muggy. Perhaps due to the intense heat, the summer cicadas weren't even crying. The room was as silent as the grave.

Murashige and Muhen were alone. There were no sword bearers, no attendants. Typically, whenever Murashige met someone at his reception hall, a guard member was in the next room in case of an emergency, but that, too, was done away with for the sake of Muhen and only Muhen. Needless to say, Murashige had his sword at his left, and he was paying attention to Muhen's bearing and behavior.

That day only, several wooden boxes lay in a row behind Murashige, some large, some small, all tied crosswise with cord. Muhen glanced at the boxes but made no mention of them.

Muhen, who took off his hat, had a face tanned a tree-trunk brown. His features were soft and gentle, but they hinted at the strong core at the heart of the man. Murashige first met Muhen some years back, but he still didn't have much of a handle on him. Muhen's reputation painted him as a traveling monk of tremendous virtue. Murashige couldn't quite get a read on whether he had any worldly ambitions. Conversing with him revealed the rumors on the winds of this world did reach his ears, but he spoke of them as though they pertained only to some far-away territory. One got the sense that he was looking down on the doings of man from above, but one also got the sense he'd resigned himself to a life outside society because it was too exalted for the likes of him. He would do anything asked of him. One could press him to perform the last rites of someone on their deathbed, or recite sutras for the dead, or pay heed to rumors of a distant land, and he would never pull a face. Murashige didn't place any trust or belief in the man, but he didn't dislike talking to him, either.

"Muhen. Come closer."

Muhen used his fists to come relatively close to Murashige while remaining seated.

"You're doing good work," said Murashige.

"Good Lord of Settsu, you appear to have lost some weight," said Muhen upon seeing Murashige's massive frame up close.

Those were the only pleasantries between the two.

Over the past two years, Murashige had made use of Muhen as a messenger. It had started with entrusting Muhen with a letter addressed to a friend, since Muhen said he was headed to the capital. Back then, Murashige would never have dreamed that he'd be sending Muhen off with letters from Arioka Castle as it was besieged by Oda troops.

"Did you deliver the letter?" asked Murashige.

"About that, Your Lordship. Saito has entrusted me with a letter."

"'Saito,' eh? You must mean Kuranosuke Toshimitsu. Show it to me."

Muhen fished the letter from his breast pocket and proffered it. Murashige took it and waited for Muhen to distance himself before opening it. The sender was Saito Kuranosuke Toshimitsu, a samurai serving a general of the Oda forces formerly named Akechi Juubei Mitsuhide and now named Koreto Mitsuhide, Lord of Hyuuga.

The letter that Murashige entrusted to Muhen had been addressed to Mitsuhide. Since Mitsuhide was now at the front attacking Tanba, it must have been Tanba that Muhen had gone toward. It was doubtful that the reply letter would be in Toshimitsu's name. While Murashige read the letter, Muhen closed his eyes and didn't stir an iota, as if he was sitting in meditation.

Murashige finished reading the letter and refolded it, scowling as he put the letter in his pocket.

"That louse Kuranosuke said he wouldn't pass on my correspondence. I did think it was a possibility, but the letter also says the particulars were communicated to you. What did Kuranosuke say?"

"I shall convey his words," said Muhen sonorously and clearly. "According to Saito, the Lord of Hyuuga came to a branch castle he shall not name, and no audience with him will be possible because other people are strictly forbidden from entering or exiting while encamped at the front. Be that as it may, Saito relates that the Lord of Hyuuga is concerned about the future of the Araki clan and that as Shingorou is Your Lordship's son, he wishes not to see anything tragic or unsightly unfold."

"...I see."

Murashige's son Shingorou Muratsugu took Mitsuhide's daughter in marriage. When Murashige split from the Oda, Muratsugu divorced her and returned her to the Akechi clan. Murashige figured it was only natural for Mitsuhide to harbor a grudge, so Muhen's words struck Murashige by surprise.

"What else did he say?"

"He said this was not a consideration of the Lord of Hyuuga's. He also said he could not quite make sense of what he was told."

"Hmm. What couldn't he make sense of?"

"He failed to understand why the Lord of Settsu would speak of capitulating after starting this war. He claimed it seemed suspect."

For a little while, Murashige said nothing. He didn't sense a soul nearby, but he was straining his ears to hear if anyone was eavesdropping nonetheless. He didn't hear a sound. That day was bereft even of wind.

The messenger mission Muhen had been ordered to carry out entailed handing the letter to Mitsuhide and requesting that he get the Oda to allow them to surrender peaceably. Negotiations between members of the same clan were invariably conducted through a role called a go-between. But Murashige did not have a go-between for the Oda clan. Manmi Senchiyo had filled that role, but he'd made the ultimate sacrifice during the winter battle of the year prior.

The fact that Murashige was attempting to go ahead with peace negotiations was top secret. With the exception of his personal guard, the precious few he could put his trust in, none among his retainers were aware.

"So that's it." Murashige let out a small sigh. "So that's what Kuranosuke said, is it? I'm certain the Lord of Hyuuga wouldn't say the same thing."

"Saito was puzzled. He said that Arioka Castle is not likely to fall anytime soon, and that Amagasaki and Hanakuma shall not fall if Arioka doesn't. He kept repeating how bizarre he found it that a man such as the Lord of Settsu should propose he should be a go-between conveying a fitfully conceived surrender."

Saito Kuranosuke had asked Muhen that in order to sound out Muhen's and, by extension, Murashige's true intentions. Kuranosuke suspected that Murashige's letter was in fact some kind of ploy.

Mitsuhide not conveying letters because he was absent from the castle while he was attacking Tanba was nothing more than a convenient pretext. He had never heard of a vassal turning away letters meant for his lord just because that lord was away. The letter wasn't rejected wholesale, so it was safe to assume it did in fact make it into Mitsuhide's hands.

In other words, Kuranosuke had just bought Mitsuhide some time. But Murashige didn't think that Arioka Castle had any time left to play with.

"I'll write another letter. Tell Kuranosuke that we must surrender because we cannot win. And that the Lord of Hyuuga would agree that is so."

Muhen replied with a detached, aloof expression.

"As I am not a man of arms, I cannot for the life of me understand Your Lordship's command. The whole world talks of how Arioka Castle shall not fall."

Murashige did not like speaking of military strategy with others.

When such tactics were discussed openly, they lost their power. But Murashige reckoned this situation called for it.

"Arioka won't fall. Not for a number of years."

"......"

"A war is waged to be won. To me, victory in this war does not mean the castle holding up. It means the Mouri reinforcements arriving, and taking Nobunaga's head after a decisive battle against his troops."

"Good gracious… With all due respect, even I know Your Lordship has not won. However, neither has the Oda."

"Is that how you see it? Kuranosuke did, too."

And it was also doubtless how the commanders who advocated for continuing to hole up in the castle viewed it. To them, the battle wasn't over, and they had yet to *truly* cross spears with the enemy.

"You're wrong," said Murashige. "To the Oda, victory means this war never reaches a decisive battle. Take the Battle of Okehazama as an example. The smaller force does not always necessarily lose in a field battle, and the larger force does not always win. As such, I started this war by picking a time and a place where the Oda can't avoid a decisive battle."

By turning against Oda in Hokusetsu, it isolated Hashiba Hideyoshi, Lord of Chikuzen, in Harima. Oda's forces were forced to choose between abandoning Hideyoshi or attacking Arioka Castle. As abandoning Hideyoshi meant Oda's dreams of attacking the lands to the west would fall through, that meant Oda was forced to attack Arioka, whether or not he wanted to. Murashige's strategy had been to seize on that opportunity to challenge Oda.

The war proceeded as Murashige anticipated. Oda did in fact encircle Arioka Castle with a large army, and he even came in person. All that was left was the decisive battle.

But one thing had gone awry. The Mouri had never entered the stage Murashige constructed.

"The chance has already slipped away," Murashige went on. "Now that the Ukita have sided with the Oda, the Mouri will never come. Oda will accept if we surrender now."

That was when something occurred to him:

"Muhen. Did Kuranosuke say anything else?"

If he conveyed word of Arioka Castle's surrender, that would be counted as a glorious achievement of Mitsuhide's. While Saito Kuranosuke might be suspicious of Murashige's intentions, there was also no way he could be glad to pass up this chance to hand his lord such glory. And if that was the case, it was inconceivable that he would simply turn Muhen away at the door.

"I am loath to say this, Your Lordship," said Muhen.

It was as Murashige thought. There was something else.

"I mind not," he insisted. "Speak."

"If I must, then I shall. Saito said that he could not believe the Lord of Settsu would surrender so abruptly, and so he wishes for collateral as proof. However, as it would be most difficult to take hostages from Arioka Castle to Tanba, he said an object would do."

A reasonable request. Murashige nodded.

"What did he say he wants from me?"

Even the stoic Muhen hesitated to name it.

"Yes… He said he wants Torasaru."

Murashige's eyes opened a little wider.

Torasaru, "Tiger and Monkey." A tea jar that was the most famous among all the many treasures Murashige possessed, alongside Hyogo. The bottom portion of the jar was wide, and it got narrower as it went up, and the jar was yellowish in hue. It was given that name because it was discovered at Tenno-ji, which played host to a marketplace on each Day of the Monkey and each Day of the Tiger.

"Torasaru, he says?"

Muhen frowned. "I heard that if one were to put a price on such a treasure, it would surpass one or two thousand *kan*. For Saito to say he will only convey your letter if Your Lordship hands him Torasaru, his avarice must be considerable."

A single *kan* could easily purchase a person. It was no exaggeration to say Torasaru alone was worth as much as a castle.

Thunder crashed from afar. Wordlessly, Murashige slowly got to his feet and chose one of the wooden boxes behind him, never showing

Muhen his back in the process. He put that box in front of Muhen and sat cross-legged once again.

"'Tis Torasaru. Deliver it to Koreto's encampment for me."

Muhen looked speechless. He stared at the box for a moment, his eyes peeled.

"Is it in here?" he said finally. "'Tis truly in here?"

"Do you want to see for yourself?"

Muhen began to reach for it before coming to his senses and shaking his head no.

"I would never doubt Your Lordship's words. If ye say this is Torasaru, so it must be. However..." Muhen straightened his posture. "As a disciple of the Buddha, as I received a stipend from Your Lordship, I have not expressed a differing opinion up till now. But pray pay heed to this. Saito...no, the Lord of Hyuuga does not so much as dream that Your Lordship would actually send Torasaru. When Saito told me to hand over Torasaru, it was just a pretext to send me away."

"I figured as much."

"Ye did, Your Lordship? Well, if that's the case, then why is Your Lordship giving it to them? The Lord of Hyuuga will look down on Your Lordship as easy to deal with."

"He may very well look down on me." Ever so subtly, Murashige's lips curled. "However, if they tell me to hand over Torasaru fully expecting I never will and then it *does* come to them, then it will be Mitsuhide who's cornered. The whereabouts of a treasure of this magnitude cannot be concealed. If word gets out that they got a hold of Torasaru by force, it will be Mitsuhide who loses face. He shall be left with no choice but to do as I wish."

Muhen studied Murashige's general air.

"...I must wonder. Your Lordship says that Arioka Castle shall not fall for the time being, but ye seem in rather a rush."

It seemed Murashige's words came across as him trying to persuade himself.

"Nobunaga would never accept my surrender if it happens after Tanba falls."

Surrender was only accepted on equal terms if that would benefit the winning party in some way. If one couldn't make them think that by surrendering, you were saving them time, effort, and resources, they would either refuse to stay their hand at all or only accept the surrender by imposing harsh conditions.

If Arioka Castle were to surrender now, it would open up access from the capital to the west. Consequently, Murashige's surrender would be beneficial for Oda as well. However, if Tanba, which Mitsuhide was attacking, fell into Oda's hands, the road would still lead between Kyoto and the west, however roundabout the route ended up being. And if that happened, gone was any hope of a surrender on equal terms.

Once again, the faint rumble of the thunder reached their ears. Murashige turned his head to look at the shoji screen, but the summer sun was shining so brightly that he didn't think there would be another storm.

"Thunder in the distance," said Murashige.

"So it would seem."

"I hope it doesn't come here. I hope it strikes us not."

"Indeed, Your Lordship."

"...I am a general. It does not suffice to simply wish the lightning doesn't come to us." Murashige turned to face Muhen. "Muhen. Arioka's surrender shall not be like Nagashima or Kozuki. I will leave no stone unturned."

"......"

When Nagashima Castle in Ise surrendered, the boats were fired on by guns as they attempted to exit the area.

When Kozuki Castle in Harima surrendered, they strung up the women and children to posts by the borders of the land and brutally executed them.

Murashige understood that in these turbulent times, clean-sweep massacres were no rarity. And if Arioka Castle repeated the mistakes of Nagashima and Kozuki, it would make his dear concubine, Chiyoho, weep.

"Think of this messenger mission as being for that sake. And Torasaru as being for that sake as well. Now go—and be careful."

For a moment, Muhen's lips were pursed in a straight line. Then he put his hands to the ground and bowed deeply.

"I shall even if it costs me my life."

Entry in and out of Arioka was surveilled by the Oda. There was no way to exit the castle undetected except in the dead of night, so Muhen waited at the castle for nightfall.

Normally, when the monk was ordered to serve as a messenger, Muhen would wait for nightfall at Murashige's residence, but now there was one thing that obstructed that. The other day, after brigands tried to set fire to a gunpowder storehouse, the castle bridge became closed to traffic after sundown. Of course, since the castle gates lay at the outermost part of the castle, if Muhen remained in the citadel until night, he'd be unable to leave the castle. One could exit to the east of the castle by using the hidden path that they'd utilized when launching the night raid against Otsu Denjuurou's encampment, but he couldn't afford to tell even saintly Muhen about that path. No one outside the castle could be allowed to know.

If Murashige ordered that only Muhen be allowed to cross the bridge at night, the guards would obey, but it would give rise to rumors, and that, too, would work against him. Muhen was forced to wait for nightfall at a town house outside the inner citadel.

"Do you know where you can find shelter from the elements?" asked Murashige.

Muhen tilted his head in puzzlement and glanced at the wicker luggage now holding the tea jar.

"As I am a traveling monk, exposure to the weather does not distress me…but currently, I am a mite encumbered."

Murashige nodded.

"In the southern edge of the town houses, a wizened old monk built himself a hermitage, where he lives a quiet life of seclusion. He has no reason to turn away a traveling monk."

"If that is so, then there I shall go," Muhen said readily, clearly not fussed about it. He prostrated himself so that he may take his leave.

Murashige looked at Muhen's wicker luggage.

"A moment, Muhen."

The monk looked up. "What is it, Your Lordship?" he asked gently.

"Nothing…" Murashige forced his eyes half-closed. "'Tis nothing. You may go."

Muhen frowned quizzically, and his face stiffened with a start, but he said naught else before exiting.

The thunder was as yet distant.

3

Murashige ordered his scribe to write another letter addressed to Mitsuhide. The letter read that they would send what was asked for, so they wanted peace negotiations to be carried forward. The letter was capped with a note stating that the details would be conveyed verbally by the man delivering the letter. If one put everything into the body of a letter, then if the enemy stole the letter, they would become privy to all of it, and the letter would spell disaster down the line. Not putting the details in writing was just due caution.

The scribe followed his orders and went to the drawing room. Murashige didn't leave the reception hall until the letter was finished. When the scribe brought him the letter, Murashige inspected its contents.

"Call Juuemon," he commanded.

Koori Juuemon was the only one among Murashige's personal guard who knew Muhen was serving Murashige as a messenger monk.

Before long, Juuemon entered the reception hall.

"I come answering Your Lordship's summons."

Juuemon's voice was the same as always, but Murashige was suddenly seized by doubt. Juuemon was not one to be perturbed or shaken by goings-on. Even during the night raid, his spirits were raised, yet he didn't seem daunted or self-conscious in the least. But now there was a vague stiffness to his bearing and his expression.

"Did something happen?" Murashige asked him.

"My lord…"

"Worry not. Speak."

Juuemon resigned himself.

"Yes, my liege. Kitagawara's troops and Kawarabayashi Noto's troops faced off on the street, and 'twas a perilous situation."

"Did they cross swords?"

"No, my liege. Noto's troops were mocking Kitagawara's troops as cowards who speak only of surrender, and another clan's troops joined in, causing a commotion. Had Ikeda Izumi not led his soldiers and come running to mediate, blood might have been shed."

"...I see. Such things do happen. Juuemon, why did you hesitate to tell me?"

"With all due respect..." Juuemon faltered, but only for a second or so. "My lord. Most of the castle is of the same mind as Noto. More than a few are cursing Kitagawara's name as a coward who is dampening morale, and there are those who go so far as to call him disloyal."

"Disloyal, you say?" muttered Murashige.

He smiled a little. Murashige had banished his lord, Ikeda Katsumasa, and taken over Ikeda Castle. He'd abandoned Miyoshi, with whom he'd formed an alliance, when he joined the Oda, only to then abandon the Oda to join the Mouri. Murashige didn't think of his behavior as "disloyal" per se. He thought everyone had to do such things in order to survive. However, it amused him that there were people in this castle who used "loyalty" as a shield to hurl invective at others.

That being said, he could not afford to avert his eyes from the import behind what Juuemon told him.

"Juuemon," he said, his voice a tad low. "Do you plan to advise me against going ahead with the peace talks?"

Juuemon turned slightly red in the face.

"That is out of the question, my liege. I shall obey Your Lordship's orders."

Those words entered Murashige's ears, but what he heard was "While I shall obey, others won't understand." In Murashige's estimation, Juuemon was a samurai who would make for a good commander, as he possessed both military prowess and scrupulousness, while being moderate and reserved in the face of all things. For a man like him to say that out loud, he must have something weighing on his mind.

However, Murashige had no intention of reversing his decision. He handed Juuemon the letter.

"Muhen is currently staying at a thatched hut in the castle's south. Deliver this letter."

"...Yes, my liege. As Your Lordship commands."

Juuemon took his leave swiftly. In fact, he all but ran away.

Murashige was left alone in the reception hall. The reason the room was built so spacious was to prevent any eavesdropping. It was far too wide for just one person.

The many wooden boxes were still set in a row behind Murashige's sitting cushion. Naturally, the contents of the wooden box were all tea utensils. Predicting that Mitsuhide would seek collateral, Murashige had them lined up in advance.

"Hark."

The attendants who had withdrawn when Murashige had discussed matters with Muhen opened the door. "Here, my lord."

These attendants were not the ones who'd been ordered to take out the wooden boxes from the storehouse. If he had used the same people, one or more might be able to guess which wooden box was missing after Murashige was done meeting with Muhen. As a precaution, Murashige had made different attendants wait nearby.

"Move these boxes to the storehouse. Handle them carefully."

"Yes, my liege."

The attendants tried to carry the boxes. Murashige saw they were having trouble and amended his command.

"On second thought, do not carry them to the storehouse. Put them in the drawing room."

Murashige's words gave them no pause; they did as they were told and carried the tea utensils to the drawing room. Once all those treasures were transported, Murashige ordered that no one be allowed near them unless there was an emergency.

The drawing room was eight tatami mats in size. This was the room Murashige typically used to read texts, and it was close to the inner room his retainers were barred from entering. Though the summer day was almost interminably long, the sun had near totally set, and the room was dark. Alone and surrounded by a plethora of wooden boxes, Murashige undid the string tying the boxes and opened them.

There were his famed treasures: the grand tea jar Hyogo, the pot named Kobatake, the Azuki chain bestowed to him by Sen no Soeki, a poetry card of Fujiwara no Teika, and the painting named *Returning Sails off the Distant Shore* by Muqi. The Bizen ware *kensui* tea-ceremony waste-water bowl, the Ubaguchi kettle, and the Yoshino tea bowl weren't famous, but they were aesthetically shaped and the apples of Murashige's eye nonetheless.

The Ikeda clan, which Murashige once served under, was from northern Settsu, as was the Itami clan, which was the Ikedas' old enemy; Murashige's allies Kitagawara and Kawarabayashi, along with his betrayers Takayama Ukon and Nakagawa, hailed from northern Settsu as well. To clarify, the lands named Ikeda and Itami lay in northern Settsu, and the samurai who had based themselves in those lands called themselves Ikeda and Itami. However, there was no land called Araki in northern Settsu.

Murashige's kinsfolk were wanderers. As a retainer of the Ikeda clan, Murashige's father did carry weight, but not enough weight to have a house to himself. The Araki clan in its present form had essentially been built by Murashige in a single generation. Moreover, Murashige had collected all the treasures now stored here himself.

Murashige went about the work wordlessly. The sun sank past the horizon, and though the moon could be seen in the sky, it was merely a thin sliver. The tea utensils were illuminated instead by the starlight; some sparkled in the light, while others absorbed the light. Surrounded by several of the most beautiful pieces in all Japan, Murashige didn't move a muscle.

How much time had passed? Murashige could hear footsteps approaching the drawing room. They were not the footsteps of his attendants, and he could hear the rustling of clothes, albeit only faintly. Murashige reached for his sword but thought better of it. Before long, a subdued voice came from the other side of the sliding screen.

"My liege. Are ye there?"

It was Chiyoho's voice.

"Is there something you need?" Murashige asked.

"It may be impertinent of me, given I heard none were to approach while Your Lordship was in the drawing room, but I came to check on you."

"I see." It was then Murashige first realized night had fallen. "I'll allow it. Enter."

The door slid open, and candlelight shone inside. Illuminated by the flickering flame, the tea utensils took on a different sheen.

"Is Your Lordship here to polish them?" asked Chiyoho, convinced that was the case.

"No," Murashige murmured. "I'm not doing anything in particular. Just looking, that's all."

"Is that so?"

There was no suspicion, astonishment, or exasperation in her voice. She gently sat herself behind him and to the side.

"Would Your Lordship mind if I admire them alongside you?"

Murashige didn't say anything in reply.

A slight night breeze blew in through the open *katomado* bell-shaped window, and they could hear the chirping of insects. The summer humidity became a little easier to bear. Murashige stared at the tea-ceremony utensils, and Chiyoho remained silent. The candle's flame kept on wavering.

"I relinquished Torasaru," said Murashige.

"I was wondering why I had not seen it," said Chiyoho, a smile evident through her voice. "I liked that one."

"Someone said he wanted it. I gave it up for the war effort."

"I do know Your Lordship to be a generous man."

"Generous, eh?" Murashige smiled a little as he gazed upon Hyogo, the famed tea jar with sundry bumps dotting its surface. "Perhaps I did it because I wished to be praised thus."

Murashige recalled the expression Muhen wore when he left, the stiffness in the monk's face when Murashige had briefly stopped him from departing. At that time, Muhen must have sensed Murashige's intentions. What Murashige had wanted to say was: "Bring back Torasaru. And if that's not to be, at least give me one more look."

He knew that this lingering affection was absurd. And even more shamefully, Muhen had picked up on it.

It was certainly true that Torasaru was useful in battle. He did think that delivering Torasaru would force Mitsuhide to act. And yet...

"Perhaps I simply wished to hear myself praised by others as a man who wouldn't hesitate to give up a treasure on the level of Torasaru to a request. 'That's Araki for you. He's of a different caliber from Matsunaga.' Perhaps I did it because that's what I wanted people to say."

A year and a half prior, Matsunaga Hisahide turned against Nobunaga, relying on Uesugi to come out on top. Yet Uesugi never came, and soon, Hisahide turned desperate.

At that time, rumor had it that Nobunaga would pardon Hisahide if Hisahide handed over the teakettle named Hiragumo. Murashige didn't know whether those rumors had any truth to them. For all he knew, they could. However, in the end, Hisahide killed himself without handing over the kettle, and the famed Hiragumo disappeared in the conflagration, never to be seen again.

Some commended Hisahide for his samurai obstinacy, but Murashige found precious little to commend there. It wasn't just that losing Hiragumo was a tragedy. It was also because the fact that Hisahide had not handed over Hiragumo was thought of as stinginess, and that was untoward of a samurai. If he'd wanted to show the world he was a true warrior, he should have handed Hiragumo over to Oda so the victor could pass that treasure on to future generations, and only then should he commit seppuku.

Wasn't the real reason Murashige had relinquished Torasaru because he wanted to tell the world he wasn't some petty miser? Wasn't the real reason because he was putting on airs, telling the world that if it aided him in war, he would not hoard such treasures? And if so, didn't that mean that the reasons he gave up his Torasaru were *not* for the sake of the war, but for his own vainglory?

"I miss it," said Murashige at last. "I miss Torasaru. But I mustn't pine

for a single tea jar, for I am a man who has consigned countless soldiers to their deaths. Chiyoho, do you find me laughable?"

"I could never," she replied at once. "In this impure world, attach-
ment leads to suffering."

"Heh," said Murashige, a smile sneaking on his lips. "You sound like
some bonze. You can say 'all is void' as much as you like, but that won't
make the enemy troops leave."

"I am most gladdened that Your Lordship has shared his feelings with
me. Ye are a soul of few words, my liege."

"I see." Murashige looked out the window at the sliver of a moon.
"The sun has set. You're dismissed. I'll get some rest as well."

"Yes, my liege."

It happened the instant Chiyoho grabbed her candlestick holder. A
violent, rumbling *bang* ruptured the hush of the night.

There was no mistaking it. It was the sound of gunfire.

4

The unexpected gunshot was followed by the sound of voices from
within and without the residence. Murashige got to his feet, sword
in hand.

"What's the meaning of this?!" he roared, loud enough to rattle
Chiyoho nearby.

Dull but hurried footsteps. Someone beyond the sliding door
was running.

"Attention, my lord!"

It was the voice of an attendant stationed at the residence.

"Speak," said Murashige.

"It was a brigand. I am told that a watchtower foot soldier questioned
him, and he took aim and fired with his gun. The brigand is running
as I speak. Pray be careful!"

"Understood. Stay here and guard Chiyoho."

"Yes, my lord!"

Murashige locked eyes with her. "Worry not. I'll send someone over
right away."

He glanced at the treasures lined up on the floor, then left the draw-ing room without another word.

Upon stepping out into the residence's square corridor, he was greeted with the sight of torch-wielding soldiers running around shouting "Where?" and "Over here!"

Before long, a hulk of a warrior spotted Murashige and rushed over, kneeling on one knee in the garden. It was Inui Sukesaburou, one of Murashige's Five Spears.

"My lord!"

"I heard we've some brigands. How many of them?"

"Likely only one. I regret to say that we have lost sight of him."

"Come now, the bastard can't have left the citadel. He has pluck, I'll give him that. I'll don my armor. Come with me."

Murashige headed to the room where his armor was located, with his guard pacing in front. He ordered another member of his guard, whom he happened to encounter, to protect the drawing room, and a third member to secure the gates that led away from the inner citadel. In the room Murashige sought, an attendant was already preparing his armor. While it was a warrior's wisdom to don armor and a helmet whenever there was an emergency, if he suited up fully for a single brig-and, he wouldn't have enough time. He was only partially armored when he stepped out onto the veranda.

The troops were moving in a calmer fashion than before; someone had to be issuing orders. Murashige spotted Koori Juuemon among the soldiers and called out to him. Juuemon immediately rushed over and fell to his knees.

"We have tracked down the brigand. It appears he has hidden in some bushes near the castle tower, and while they say a cornered cat is a fierce one, we have him surrounded at a distance with bows and guns."

"Good. Tell them not to kill him until I arrive."

"Yes, my lord."

Murashige descended into the garden, following in Juuemon's wake as the man broke into a run. It was a nearly moonless night. A guard member who followed Murashige promptly procured him a torch from somewhere. The voices of the soldiers had gone from panicked questions about the location and number of enemies, to venomous abuse cursing the brigand.

A good many troops had gathered under the tower looming jet-black in the dark of the night. Numerous torches were held in the air, and the surroundings were bright enough to be as day. Soldiers aimed their spears, bows, and guns at the small bush, staring intently lest their rat slip away.

Murashige ordered the soldiers encircling the brigand to give way, and the circle opened for Murashige, who came to the front of the bush. He was defended by his guard. The bush rustled, and something glinted in the torchlight.

"Pray be on your guard," one samurai called to Murashige.

It was hawkeyed Akioka Shirounosuke. Murashige noticed the freshly made horizontal sword cut on his armor's corselet.

"A deft hand, the bastard has."

Shirounosuke could safely be called a master, but he was hardly a haughty man. When it came to appraising someone's sword skills, Shirounosuke never overstated or understated. Murashige nodded and stopped in his tracks. He took a deep breath, then shouted at the bush in a deep, rough voice.

"To have made it all the way to the inner citadel of Arioka Castle, you have my respect. Be a man and come on out."

Of course, Murashige didn't think the brigand would actually respond. He was, however, slightly intrigued by the brigand who'd snuck this far in.

"How absurd," replied the brigand, to Murashige's surprise. "Look at Yasuke of the Ikeda, running his mouth like some great general."

Yasuke was a former name of Murashige's. Speaking that name was to insult Murashige, who had clawed his way to the Lord of Settsu. As one might expect, Murashige's whole face flushed bright red. The bush rustled, and a small man with a drawn blade appeared.

"Here I am," said the man. "What will you do now?"

The soldiers around Murashige were more incensed than their leader, who raised his hand to stay them from stabbing the brigand with their spears. Murashige examined the man's face. Since he'd insulted

Murashige by calling him Yasuke, he couldn't be a soldier of Mino or Owari. Murashige reckoned he had to be from a neighboring village. Upon closer inspection, the torchlit face seemed familiar.

"I know you..."

Then it dawned on him.

"You're Zensuke of the Kuroda, aren't you?"

At the sound of his name, the man relaxed his arm. He sheathed his sword half-heartedly like this was a hassle to him, and he hung his head.

He was about thirty years of age, and his face exhibited a mix of both prudence and recklessness. A samurai who served the Kuroda clan in Harima, he must have been a personal attendant of Kuroda Kanbei, who was close to his age. Despite being small of stature, he was known all across the neighboring villages for his fierce fighting style. Ten years ago, during a bitter battle where the continued existence of the Kuroda clan hung in the balance, Zensuke had taken two enemy heads.

"Zensuke," said Murashige. "What made you sneak in? I heard nothing of the Kuroda joining our attackers' ranks."

"Ye ask why? Ye know the answer." Zensuke's lips curled sardonically. "I came here to ascertain whether my lord is still alive, and to rescue him if so... What other reason could there be?"

Murashige looked at the bevy of spears, bows, and guns pointed squarely at Zensuke. "Are you a lone agent?"

"Perhaps I am. Or perhaps not."

If he did have accomplices, he would have said he was alone in order to cover for them. Murashige inferred he was acting alone.

Zensuke possessed a foolhardy courage. Kuroda Kanbei was indeed imprisoned in this citadel, but to the outside world, word of that was nothing more than a rumor whose veracity was unclear. To go off such shaky rumors and sneak unaided into one of the most impregnable fortresses in the world was insanity. Zensuke couldn't even know where Kanbei was being held, and on the off chance he somehow made it to Kanbei's cage, he had absolutely no way of absconding with him. And yet Murashige couldn't sneer at Kuriyama Zensuke's show of valor as feral and brutish. He'd staked his life on this reckless gamble, and he'd managed to make it all the way to the inner citadel.

The soldiers, their passions tempered, lowered the points of their spears. Reverence and respect for men of valor and the art of war were ingrained in the heart of samurai. They, too, couldn't help but start to see Zensuke as admirable in his own right.

"I see. So you've come to rescue Kanbei, have you?" murmured Murashige.

At that, Zensuke fell to one knee, spent. His hemp clothing bore tears here and there, and blood was dripping from his loosely dangling hand.

"Lord of Settsu," said Zensuke, his breathing labored. "Is my lord alive?"

Murashige hesitated.

"...Yes."

"He is? My lord is alive? Kanbei is alive?"

Murashige nodded.

That very moment, Zensuke covered his face with his hands and wailed, weeping.

"Why?! Why have ye not put an end to his misery?!"

Zensuke's words struck Murashige like a flung stone.

"When my lord decided he must depart for Arioka Castle, he was smiling so sweetly. He expected he would not return alive, so he told me all the things I should do after he died. It is precedent to send a messenger who does not suit one's fancy back alive, and it is precedent to send back only his head. If our lord had been executed, we would have simply seen that as the wages of war. Tell me, Lord of Settsu, why do ye keep our lord alive and yet not return him?!"

Murashige had no words of reply. Zensuke must have known this was the end of the road for him.

"Our lord left for Arioka Castle, never to return. We heard the rumors that he remained alive. Lord of Settsu, did ye spare any thought to how those rumors would sound to Nobunaga? We retainers of the Kuroda clan spent every day waiting with bated breath, wondering if that would be the day our lord returned to us or, barring that, if his head would. If he died, it would be an honorable death spurred by loyalty and devotion. It would have been a lucky break for the Kuroda clan...and yet we received no word back..."

Zensuke looked up at the sky. The sliver of a moon cast scant light down on the scene.

"Nobunaga has taken our lord, and thereby the Kuroda clan, as siding with Arioka Castle against him. And who can blame him?! Who would believe that he has actually been taken prisoner?!"

The Kuroda clan could not survive after earning the enmity of the Oda. Their sole option for survival was to claim that while Kanbei alone had switched sides, the clan itself remained loyal to the Oda. And even if that claim was deemed true, the Oda would want a price to be paid.

Murashige had heard from Kanbei in the eleventh month of the year prior, back when the war had yet to begin, that he'd given his only son, Shojumaru, over to Oda as a hostage.

Unceasing tears streamed down Zensuke's face.

"Did ye know, Lord of Settsu? Nobunaga killed young lord Shojumaru. The Kuroda will be no more!"

Murashige was silent.

This war held the fate of the Araki clan, as well as the Mouri clan and Hongan-ji, in the balance. Murashige hadn't the time or energy to take other clans into consideration. Whether the Kuroda clan perished or persisted made no difference to him.

On the other hand, Murashige never thought that capturing Kanbei would lead to young Shojumaru's execution. As far as he recalled, the poor boy was a mere twelve years of age. If he'd known that killing Kanbei meant Shojumaru would be allowed to live, Murashige wondered what he would have ended up doing.

If Murashige thought about a matter from every angle before making a decision, he would accept any outcome, good or bad. If, however, he neglected to consider something in his deliberations, it would generate a small, minuscule kernel of regret.

Even so, as a general, there was only one thing he could say.

"Silence, cur. I care not!"

"Murashige!"

"Some common soldier deserves not death. Bind him and toss him someplace. If he gets to be a handful, you may slay him."

Murashige turned his back on Zensuke. The soldiers rushed him, and his furious cries filled the night.

Murashige returned to his residence and had an attendant help him take his armor off. Koori Juuemon came and informed Murashige that Kuriyama Zensuke was bound as ordered.

"Shall I withdraw the troops, my lord?" asked Juuemon.

The furor that Kuriyama Zensuke kicked up brought not just the soldiers who guarded the inner citadel, but also off-duty soldiers into the citadel. Murashige was about to order Juuemon to do so, but he hesitated for a moment. Juuemon frowned.

"What ought I to do, my lord?" he said.

"Hmm..."

While Zensuke was proficient in the martial arts, Murashige didn't believe he could be so skilled at stealth on top of that. Granted, Zensuke had been driven by one, all-consuming purpose, but he'd made it all the way to the inner citadel. Murashige grew uneasy about the castle's defenses.

"Have the guard defend the hermitage where Muhen is staying. Post a man north, east, south, and west of the hermitage and let no one else get near it. When the sun comes up, have them escort Muhen to the gates."

"As Your Lordship commands."

Juuemon didn't pry; he simply accepted his orders and withdrew. Murashige's armor now off him, he felt the weight on his shoulders lifted, and he had a momentary urge to call Juuemon back. The reason he hadn't posted guards to defend Muhen to begin with was because if he wasn't wise about how he apportioned soldiers, people would infer that this was an important mission. But now he'd changed his mind and deployed soldiers after all. Perhaps it had been shortsighted of him.

Murashige noticed the indecision in his own orders. He tensed his

stomach, telling himself that he was simply correcting an error, not reversing his decision. *Don't waver*, he thought. *Else death will come.*
The night wore on.

5

Murashige dreamed.

In his dream, he was young. He was not the Lord of Settsu, Araki Murashige. He was simply Araki Yasuke. He found his lord—Ikeda Katsumasa, the Lord of Chikugo—undependable, and while on the surface, he obeyed him, inwardly he was sharpening his fangs, intent on someday taking his place.

"You just might be the one who can pull it off, Yasuke."

His cousin, Nakagawa Sehyoue, was smiling beside him. Sehyoue was young as well, and he carried himself like he believed as long as he had strength in his arms and a sharp spear, there was nothing in this world he could not achieve.

"If and when you do, make me a samurai general," said Sehyoue.

"You're thinking small. I'll give you a castle."

"Oh-ho, a castle, eh? I like the sound of that."

"When we conquer Itami, I'll take Itami Castle and leave Ikeda Castle in your hands."

"Ha-ha-ha! In that case, we need to start surveying the castle interior now. What will you do once you take Itami, Yasuke?"

"Good question." Murashige gazed up at the azure skies. "I should go up to the capital. I want to see the tea utensils there. And I'll grab myself an official rank."

"What about Sakai? Don't you want it?"

So said Takayama Ukon, who appeared without Murashige noticing. He, too, was young. When it came to resourcefulness, he was no lesser than even Mouri Motonari, or at the very least, his sheer pluck would have one believe that.

"The padre will be pleased!"

Yasuke smiled wryly. "You're always so crazy about this Christianity business. Have you no *ambition*?"

Ukon facetiously made an exaggerated sign of the cross.

With Sehyoue and Ukon, Yasuke was even more of a force to be reckoned with. Taking Settsu would be child's play. After all, the current shogunate clan was undisciplined, to say nothing of Murashige's own lord, Ikeda. The Hosokawa and Rokkaku clans were naught to be afraid of.

Those lucky enough to be born to samurai ought to do something with their lives...

At the breaking of the dawn, it all came back to Murashige.

It was Oda who'd taken the capital, Oda who'd taken Sakai.

Nakagawa Sehyoue had switched to the Oda, and he was no longer by Murashige's side. The same was true of Takayama Ukon.

On the other side of the sliding door, somebody was kneeling.

Is that Sehyoue? Is he back? No...'tis an attendant. He has something to tell me.

"What is it?"

Stiffly, the attendant spoke:

"I have come to inform Your Lordship that Muhen has been slain."

6

Muhen had been stabbed to death in a room of the hermitage.

Murashige mounted his horse and dashed through Arioka at dawn. The lord's guard were unable to catch up to him on foot, so when Murashige crossed the Great Fosse and entered the town-house district, he was alone. Normally, Murashige would never be alone in public, partly for safety concerns, but also because it served as proof of his lofty status. He was fully aware that a man of commander caliber should never ride solo, but he was too impatient to hold off.

The hermitage stood alone on the southern edge of the town-house zone, on an untouched plot of land where the grass grew unimpeded. It was originally built by a priest of an old temple on the outskirts of the town of Ikeda so that he could spend his days immersed in prayerful chanting until he expired. Murashige and this monk were old acquaintances, and Murashige had lent him his power when building the hermitage. The monk—now the owner of the hermitage—was almost totally blind and deaf; he relied on a male temple worker to take care of him day and night, but he would gladly let itinerant monks and traveling priests stay the night.

When Murashige arrived, he saw countless commoners packed in front of the hermitage amid the uncut grasses. They must have heard the bad news somewhere. Every once in a while, an anguished scream rang out.

"Muhen!"

"Oh, my heart! Muhen!"

Their lamentations seeded the earth and shook the heavens, each plaintive cry inducing the next. Even Murashige hesitated to push his way in. When the throng noticed Murashige's presence, they stretched out their hands to him as if asking for salvation, every one wailing unintelligibly. Murashige's horse backed away in surprise.

The guard members who defended the hermitage took succor from Murashige's presence.

"Fall back! The Lord of Settsu is here! Go back now!" they shouted angrily, thrusting their spears skyward.

But those words went unheard. Commoners, who were not usually allowed to see Murashige's face, waved their hands at Murashige and drew closer, their faces wrinkled with grief.

Murashige looked at the people from his horse. With nary an exception, they all had sooty, sodden faces, frayed linen robes, and tears in their eyes. These were the people who, not knowing what the next day would bring during this time of besiegement, saw salvation in Muhen. And now Muhen was dead. Was it despair Murashige saw in the people's eyes? No, there was more than just despair.

There was also anger. Boiling, seething anger.

"Quiet!" Murashige barked. "There will be no forming bands!"

Murashige's voice was loud enough for his orders to break through the cacophony of the battlefield and carry to his troops' ears. Murashige had yelled so loudly that the folk who had drawn near fell on their backsides. Seizing on the chance provided by the people's dampened fervor, Murashige's guard swooped in to defend him from all directions.

"Go back!" Murashige ordered. "I'll kill any who don't!"

It was the command of the lord of the castle. Everyone understood it was no empty threat. As the commoners left in small groups and headed back into the town of Itami, they kept turning to look back at the hermitage.

When the vicinity quieted down, Murashige's guard all fell to their knees.

"My lord," said one of them, his head still bowed. "Our apologies!"

It was Inui Sukesaburou. His voice was quavering.

"We were guarding the hermitage, but we were helpless. As I am sure Your Lordship has heard, Muhen and Akioka Shirounosuke have been slain."

"Akioka, too?!"

"Yes, my lord. He was slashed in the thigh and stabbed in the throat."

Murashige gritted his teeth. Three of the Five Spears, the pride of the Araki clan, now lay dead. Murashige glared at the remaining people. It was then he realized that there stood among them a man who was not a member of his guard. He had a sword at his waist but no armor, and he was even wearing an *eboshi* hat. It was the outfit of a commanding officer.

"You over there! Raise your head."

The man did as he was told.

"Is that you, Yosaku?"

"Yes, my lord!"

Kitagawara Yosaku usually bore the mien of a brave young warrior, but on this morn, his face was white as a sheet.

What are you doing here?

Murashige swallowed those words. He didn't care what Yosaku was doing here at the moment. Time was of the essence. Murashige dismounted.

"We'll investigate. Sukesaburou, come with me. Everyone else, wait here."

By the time Murashige was about to enter the hermitage, the members of the guard who had been lagging behind caught up. He spotted Koori Juuemon among the breathless, panting soldiers.

"Juuemon, come with me," he ordered.

The hermitage was surrounded by brushwood fencing. The fencing was low, the brushwood barely maintained, but they served their purpose well as a borderline. When Murashige and the others stepped into the hermitage through the doorless gate, they encountered a ghostly figure standing in the darkness. He was skin and bones clad in priestly attire—it was the owner of the hermitage.

The man groaned, barely audible.

Murashige strained his ears until he could make out the man's words. He was saying, "Lord of Settsu…"

Upon witnessing the terrible decline of his old acquaintance, Murashige lost his voice for a moment. But now was not the time to rekindle a friendship.

"We're coming through, good sir," he said, leaving it at that. Then he turned to face Sukesaburou. "Lead the way."

The hermitage contained three rooms, one of which was a living room with a dirt floor and a sunken hearth. This was where the owner of the hermitage slept. Another was the Buddha statue room, which was cramped and smallish in size but otherwise well-made. The third was the guest room, and it was to this room that Sukesaburou guided Murashige.

To move from the living room to the guest room, one had to cross an outer passageway. Sukesaburou halted before a screen door riddled with tears, then knelt down.

"This way," he said, hanging his head.

Before he even opened the door, the room's heady odor hit Murashige's nostrils. It was the scent of incense…and two other smells quite familiar to samurai. The twin stenches of blood and a dead body.

"Open it."

"Yes, my lord."

Sukesaburou opened the door, and the moisture in the air surged their way.

In the center of the cramped room, a monk in priestly attire was lying facedown. A pool of blood had spread over the blackened wooden floor, and a swarm of flies was buzzing over him. Murashige was well aware that there was no hope that this could be anyone besides Muhen, but despite that fact...

"Turn him faceup," he ordered.

"Yes, my lord."

Without hesitation, Sukesaburou turned the cadaver on its back. The flies flew away and buzzed in circles within the room.

It was Muhen. His eyes were wide-open, his mouth agape, and his face a canvas of fear and shock. The monk's final moments had been far from peaceful.

"His wounds."

Sukesaburou obeyed his lord's brief command, searching for wounds on the body. His massive palms and thick fingers soon became covered in blood. Muhen's rigor-mortis fingers looked as though they were frozen in time while scratching the air. The blood on Sukesaburou's fingers didn't drip; it was almost completely dry.

The wound was plain to see. Sukesaburou wasn't even quite able to wipe the blood away.

"He has a stab wound in his chest," said Sukesaburou. "The weapon pierced through his *kasaya* and his back. I see no other wounds."

Murashige stroked his chin. Muhen was not a samurai, but he was a burly traveler who walked the hills and fields with ease on his own two feet. He must have known how to protect himself from brigands and their ilk. Moreover, it was no easy feat to pierce a chest plate in a single thrust.

Murashige once again surveyed the fly-infested room. The floor was wood and about four and half tatami mats in size. Blood was pooled, and there was also sprayed blood on the walls. In other words, this was the murder scene. The corpse was not moved after the murder.

The room was covered on three sides by walls, with the fourth side consisting of a shoji door leading into the passageway. There were no cabinets or closets he could see. And befitting the hut of a hermit, the room was quite sparse. There was only a futon and a censer. The censer was no glorious artifact but rather an unglazed earthenware vessel with little to no workmanship to speak of and the marks of burned incense still visible.

"'Tis not here," muttered Murashige.

"What isn't, my lord?"

Murashige didn't answer Sukesaburou's question.

Murashige noticed that the wicker luggage that Muhen had woven to store his travel tools and altar fittings was nowhere to be found.

The wicker luggage presumably still contained the famed tea jar Torasaru.

In all likelihood, Torasaru had been made off with, but it was still too early to jump to conclusions. Murashige stifled his nerves and asked Sukesaburou, "Where was Akioka Shirounosuke killed?"

Sukesaburou didn't even bother wiping the sweat dripping down his brow, and he seemed to be at a loss as to what to do with his blood-stained hands, but he straightened his posture before replying:

"Outside, my lord."

"Lead me there."

"Right away, my lord."

When Sukesaburou exited into the passageway, Murashige whispered in Koori Juuemon's ear, "Search for the secret letter. If you find it, take it. And check to see if there are traces someone read it."

The secret letter Juuemon delivered to Muhen, addressed to Koreto Mitsuhide, Lord of Hyuuga. The fewer the number of people who knew that peace talks were in the works, the better; it was a task he could entrust only to Juuemon.

"I shall make haste," said Juuemon.

"One more thing… I gave Muhen Torasaru."

The normally unflappable Juuemon opened his eyes wide.

"Your Lordship did? A treasure that great?"

"I did. But I don't see it anywhere. I'm sure the brigand stole it, but on the off chance Muhen hid it, try all possible means to find it. Check under the floor, above the ceiling—every nook and cranny. 'Tis thicker on the bottom, and yellowish in color."

"Yes, my lord. I understand."

With a stiff look on his face, Juuemon bowed his head.

Murashige knew that the likelihood Muhen had hidden Torasaru in this hermitage was, in fact, zero. His inability to let go of that vain hope and ordering Juuemon to do something so fruitless was sheer folly. But Murashige couldn't go on without telling himself that Torasaru would be found once more—that it had to be *somewhere*.

Nourished by the intense heat, the grasses had grown in abundance, as though they drained the life from those who had been baked under the blazing sun.

Akioka Shirounosuke lay dead in the summer grass. Although he was in full armor, his inner thigh, unprotected by any metal plating, bore a laceration, and his throat had been pierced. The damp soil absorbed the blood, leaving no pool of red, and the blood that stained the tassets and puttees was almost totally dry. Since Shirounosuke's armor sported a neck guard, his killer likely slashed him in the thigh and then stripped off the neck guard once his victim had fallen, stabbing him in the throat as the finishing blow. The murderer was clearly used to killing. Murashige, for one, would have gone about it the same way.

"For the sake of the investigation," said Sukesaburou, "I have turned him faceup, but he was originally facedown."

Shirounosuke's sword was still in its scabbard, totally sheathed.

"Did Shirounosuke have any other weapons on him?"

"No, my lord. He carried only his sword."

The blade master had no need for any other weapons. Shirounosuke had been killed without ever getting to draw a sword. It was an honor to die on the field of battle, but if one got killed without being able to protect a single monk, he would inevitably be disparaged as a blundering failure. Murashige did not, however, think that of Shirounosuke.

"That Shirounosuke was unable to draw his sword in time means the culprit must be quite formidable."

Sukesaburou lowered his voice mournfully as he gazed down at

Shirounosuke's pallid face. "Indeed, my lord. For a master on the level of Akioka to die this way… I cannot believe my eyes."

Murashige looked more closely at how Shirounosuke's *hakama* trousers were cut and the direction of the wound, which was thicker on the back of the thigh and tapered toward the front.

"Shirounosuke…," muttered Murashige. "He was slashed from behind."

Sukesaburou appeared unconvinced.

"Yes, my lord. And yet…in this patch of grass, he would have heard anyone approaching. How could anyone attack from behind without Akioka noticing?"

Sukesaburou's argument was sound; Murashige scanned their surroundings. This place was located behind the hermitage, which stood amid the grasses. The hermitage was surrounded by a brushwood fencing, with openings in the front entrance and the back. There was no wicket door or anything like it, which meant there was nothing to prevent trespassing. Shirounosuke lay about ten paces from the fencing.

"Sukesaburou. Tell me everything that happened between when you reached your posts guarding the hermitage last night and the discoveries of Muhen's and Shirounosuke's bodies."

"Yes, my lord. However, I believe it would be best if Kitagawara was with us."

Murashige didn't ask why.

"I see. In that case, let's leave this place."

They left the rear of the hermitage, walking around the fencing to the front. Standing there idly were the two guard members who had kept watch the previous night, the two who'd followed Murashige from the inner citadel, as well as Kitagawara Yosaku and the tender of his horse. Juuemon was still scouring the hermitage's guest room. The sun rose, enveloping them in the heat and the strong odor of grass.

"Last night, after the thieves who sneaked into the inner citadel were captured," said Sukesaburou, "guard leader Koori Juuemon ordered us four to guard the hermitage and protect Muhen, and so we rushed to this place. Akioka told me that if I held a torch, it would leave that hand unfree and that might spell our failure. Since there was the starlight to go by, we all did as Akioka demonstrated and forwent torches."

The guard members who defended the hermitage were Inui Sukesaburou, Akioka Shirounosuke, and two others. Each was stationed at one of the four sides of the hermitage, and collectively, they watched the grassy fields from four directions. Sukesaburou stood guard at the front, and Shirounosuke the back.

"That's all well and good. Continue."

"Naught happened until daybreak. At the coming of the dawn, Kitagawara arrived saying he wished to see Muhen."

Naturally, Kitagawara Yosaku approached from the front entrance of the hermitage, so Sukesaburou was the first to notice him.

"As I had been ordered to let no one approach, I could not let him pass, Kitagawara or no. He tried to pass anyway, and in the scuffle, the horse went berserk. While I and the horse's tender were quelling it, Kitagawara swiftly entered the hermitage."

"I shall describe what transpired next," said Yosaku. "I asked the owner of the hermitage to guide my way, but he did not appear to hear me. I was forced to be rude and enter unbidden, whereupon I searched for Muhen. I thought that it would not take long to find him in such a small building, but when I did find him, he was already in that state, slain."

Next spoke Sukesaburou.

"Kitagawara came back out and informed us Muhen had been killed. I stepped inside at once to find Muhen was indeed deceased. Alarmed, I called my fellow members of the guard, and though these two came right away, Akioka was nowhere to be seen. I searched for him and found him lying as Your Lordship saw."

Murashige glared at them. "Did it occur to none of you to occasionally call out to your fellows while you were guarding? Shirounosuke must have been slain sometime that night. If you had maintained contact with one another, you would have noticed far earlier that Shirounosuke had been murdered!"

Sukesaburou and the rest of the guard shuddered.

"Our apologies, my liege!"

It had been a show of negligence on their part, that much was certain. However, Murashige thought better than to excoriate them too heavily. The buck stopped with their commander, Murashige himself. He was also at fault for not giving more detailed orders when it came to watchman procedures. Besides, even if they had cottoned onto Shirounosuke's death earlier than they had through communicating, Muhen would have died regardless.

Juuemon exited the hermitage. Judging by the expression on his face, he had something to tell Murashige, so Murashige left the others. Juuemon half ran over to him and, with Murashige's permission, whispered into his lord's ear.

"I cannot find Torasaru anywhere."

"I see."

"The secret letter was sewn inside the collar of Muhen's hat. However, the threads of his collar were unraveled, and the seal on the letter is slightly off."

"So you're saying someone read it."

"Presumably, my lord."

"Tch!"

Murashige shifted his gaze toward the field of grass surrounding the hermitage, glaring as though the enemy might still be lurking there.

"He could be a henchman of Oda's. He approached from behind the hermitage, killed Shirounosuke, slipped through the gap in the fencing, stabbed Muhen…"

Murashige swallowed the words *then read the letter and stole Torasaru.*

If that was true, the enemy was a master-hand, in which case it would behoove Murashige to assume that Torasaru had already been whisked outside the castle. Murashige said nothing, and no one else did, either. Silent, too, were the insects and even the winds. There was only the blistering sunshine.

7

Muhen had simply shown up at the castle one day even when its occupants weren't allowed outside, preaching the way of the Lord Buddha. To everyone in Arioka, he was salvation in the flesh.

It was more than just the promise of life after death in paradise that provided solace. So, too, did the thought that Arioka was not an isolated island surrounded by the sea that was the Oda army, but instead connected to the outside world. Yet Muhen was now dead. Rumors abounded that Muhen's death was at the hands of an Oda subordinate who'd managed to breach the castle. Word spread in secret that the enemy killed Muhen in spite of all the guards Murashige posted to protect him. This told them that nothing lay beyond the Oda's reach and that there was nothing that the Araki could protect.

Murashige returned to his residence in the inner citadel, whose reception hall he sat in cross-legged. Koori Juuemon was prostrating himself before his lord.

"Juuemon. Tell me about what happened after you handed Muhen the letter."

"Yes, my lord."

Before Juuemon entered the hall, attendants had told him about Murashige's business with him. That was why he could speak without faltering.

"After Your Lordship entrusted the letter to me, it was in the early afternoon hours that I handed it to Muhen. I rode toward the hermitage and stated my purpose, but the hermitage owner's poor hearing hindered his grasp of my words. Shortly thereafter, Muhen arrived, so I communicated to him that I had a secret errand, and Muhen guided me to the guest room. However, I simply handed him the letter and did not converse with Muhen. I parted the hermitage with a good-bye to the hermitage owner, but he said nothing, as if he was sleeping."

"Was the wicker luggage in the guest room at that point in time?"

Juuemon didn't reply.

"What's the matter?"

"I apologize, my lord. I was so preoccupied with handing him the letter that I cannot remember." Juuemon's response was a touch frantic.

Murashige stroked his chin. "I don't blame you," he said. "Was there anyone besides the owner and Muhen when you visited the hermitage?"

"That, too, I know not."

"The owner is quite old and frail, as you saw. A temple worker from Ikeda is currently supposed to be looking after him at all times."

"Yes, I do know of that man," said Juuemon animatedly.

"Do you? Then tell me, was he there or not?"

"He was not, my lord."

Murashige raised an eyebrow. "Didn't you say you knew not whether there was anyone besides the owner and Muhen at the hermitage? How do you know the temple worker wasn't there?"

"I shall tell you why, my lord," Juuemon replied quickly. "When I returned from delivering the letter, it was already evening, and I saw that very man in the streets of Itami. I caught sight of him while he was buying greens."

Murashige nodded. "I see. I now know the particulars. Go find that man and bring him here."

The temple worker in question spent his life at a True Pure Land sect temple in Ikeda, and although no one, including himself, knew the year of his birth, he was believed to be over fifty. Hallmarks of his harsh life, his back was hunched, his head sported white hairs, and his face was deeply wrinkled. He was a good-natured man, and while he treated low-ranking monks and laymen alike politely, he didn't fawn on high-ranking priests or nobles, either. When Ikeda Castle was abandoned and the bonze built a hermitage in Arioka Castle, the temple worker moved in as well.

The temple worker was taken through the residence's garden, and he prostrated himself on the ground. Murashige walked along the external corridor and stopped in front of him.

"It's been quite some time."

As an old acquaintance of the hermitage owner, he'd also met this temple worker before. In his humility, the man said nothing in reply.

"You may respond. I'm going to ask you some questions. Answer carefully."

"Yes, my lord!"

"Koori Juuemon told me that last night, he saw you about town in Itami. Is that true?"

The man remained prostrate on the ground, not moving an inch.

"I did pass by a mounted retainer of Your Lordship's, but there are many samurai on horseback in Itami, and I cannot be sure the gentleman I saw was Koori."

The man's prudent answer made a favorable impression on Murashige.

"Very well. Now tell me in detail everything that happened afterward."

"Yes, my lord."

The man was silent for a while so that he could gather his thoughts. Little by little, he began to speak.

"Since I have business in town during the day, I come to the hermitage once in the morning and again in the evening. Yesterday, the owner had asked me to purchase vegetables to be pickled, but it took me a while to buy it all, and my evening rounds were delayed. By the time I got back, it was on the cusp of twilight. I greeted the hermitage owner, and he told me that Muhen would be staying with us for the night, and that Muhen had a guest. I was so awestruck."

Both Kitagawara Yosaku and Koori Juuemon said that they were unable to exchange words with the hermitage owner. Even Murashige himself could not understand what the hermit was ever saying. Murashige wondered whether he should be suspicious that this temple worker could hear what the man had to share.

Murashige thought not. After all, it stood to reason that only the temple worker could understand the owner, given that his vocation was to take care of the old man.

"Then what happened?"

"I hurried to welcome Muhen, and I asked whether I could be allowed to offer his guest some sake. Muhen rebuffed me sternly, saying he had no business with me and that the guest had already left. I recall he told me not to interfere for he needed to perform his chanting."

Who was this guest he spoke of?

Muhen had said that the guest had already left. If so, could it be referring to Koori Juuemon, the deliverer of the secret letter? When

Juuemon entered the hermitage, he greeted the owner, who offered a garbled response. Juuemon had also testified that he'd tried saying farewell upon leaving, but the owner seemed to be asleep. Murashige surmised that the owner knew Juuemon had come but never realized that Juuemon had left.

Yet if that was the case, Murashige didn't understand why Muhen would be so short with the temple worker. This was the same Muhen who was meek and mild with everyone, irrespective of age, gender, rank, or social standing. That being said, it was commonplace for one's manner of speaking to change when they were dealing with a steward. Murashige didn't much like the idea of this hidden side to Muhen.

"Then I drew water and did other chores until nightfall, at which time the scent of incense wafted from the guest room, and Muhen seemed to be chanting what I assume was the Shingon mantra. I did see him go to the lavatory, and he had quite a grim look on his face. I was deeply impressed that Muhen, the man so saintly that they call him a living Buddha, was this fervent about his sutra chanting."

"...Go on."

"By the time I received the owner's permission and left the hermitage, it was the dead of night. That is not at all uncommon, my liege. I have good night vision, and if I have the light of the stars, I can walk paths that I am familiar with without much trouble. When I exited the front door, a very large samurai was standing there. I called out to him, and he asked me who goes there. I replied that I am a temple worker, and he did not censure me. Following that, I returned to my humble abode and laid myself to sleep."

The temple worker's speech was fluid, and he never stammered or faltered. He possessed a good memory, and he was neither timid nor skittish. The man did not once look up; Murashige gazed at his bowed head and surmised that if this temple worker were twenty, no, fifteen years younger, Murashige could see himself employing the man as an odd-job runner for a retainer.

The man was given some money before he left. Murashige returned to the reception hall and ordered his attendants to summon Inui Sukesaburou.

Sukesaburou, a corpulent man, was particularly affected by the heat of summer. He prostrated himself in front of Murashige; it was hard to watch his sweat drip down onto the floor of the hall.

"Sukesaburou. I only have a handful of questions for you. Last night, did you see the temple worker after he started headed home from the hermitage?"

"My lord...!"

Sukesaburou, who had kept watch for any who might approach the hermitage from the dark of the night, had been stunned when someone called out to him from behind. Sukesaburou replied to Murashige, certain that there was no way he could be rebuked for that.

"Yes, I did see the man."

"You did. Now, answer carefully... At that time, was the man holding anything?"

That night, Sukesaburou conversed with the temple worker from up close. Sukesaburou knew that the man paid the hermitage visits regularly, and there was nothing about him that might arouse any suspicion. Nevertheless, Sukesaburou had been watching him carefully. In the aftermath of Abe Jinen's murder that winter, Murashige had admonished him that it was crucial for a samurai to take note of the items one carried.

"No, my lord, he had nothing on his person."

"By 'holding anything,' I don't mean just in his hands. Was he carrying anything on his back, for example?"

Sukesaburou had also seen the temple worker's back as the man went on his way home.

"No, my lord, he carried nothing on his back."

"...I see."

Last night, Sukesaburou was one of the four who had stayed up all night guarding the hermitage. The members of the guard were rugged and strong, but not even they could work without sleep.

"Understood. You're dismissed. I relieve all of you who stood guard last night from duty today. Go tell the others."

"Yes, my lord!"

Sukesaburou took his leave of the reception hall, wondering whether there was some way to wipe his sweat from the floor.

Kitagawara Yosaku was the last to be called into the hall. Unlike that morning, he was now wearing a full suit of armor. The forces of the Kitagawara clan, Yosaku included, were reserve troops, always at the ready to rush anywhere in the castle if an enemy attacked. Last year, he was dispatched among the reinforcements sent to the hard-pressed Fort Kishino during the winter battle, during which he distinguished himself with meritorious deeds.

Yosaku prostrated himself.

"Raise your head, Yosaku."

"Yes, my lord!"

The reply was forceful, but Yosaku's expression betrayed his dissatisfaction. Murashige didn't press him on that front.

"At daybreak, you paid Muhen a visit… What business brought you there?"

"Is that what this is about?" Yosaku seemed dispirited. "The reason is this, my lord: One of my retainers is afflicted by illness, and he has not long to live. In his delirious muttering, he said that he would like to die while listening to Muhen's invocations. Though he is a mere servant, this was his final wish, and I would have seen it granted. I left to fetch him, for I intended to bring Muhen to the house."

"You went quite early in the morning."

"It was for the sake of a dying man, my lord. Time was of the essence. I did wait until daybreak. For an end so pitiful as his, I would regret it if I could not grant my retainer's humble wish."

In the room next to the reception hall, the members of the guard were listening. By now, one of their number had to be running to the Kitagawara clan household to see if there was actually any such retainer.

Yosaku was frowning.

"My liege, may I ask a question?"

"…I'll allow it."

"Well…your Lordship has summoned Koori, Inui, and even the temple worker. What is this investigation about?"

Murashige didn't reply.

"An Oda agent killed Akioka, entered the hermitage, and killed Muhen," argued Yosaku. "What else is there to investigate? I cannot see the point of this."

Murashige could understand why Yosaku would think that, yet he had to investigate the circumstances surrounding Muhen's death at any cost.

No one person was supposed to know that Muhen was a secret messenger who'd received orders from Murashige and also that he'd given the monk the peerless tea jar Torasaru. Murashige hadn't even told his scribe or Juuemon about Torasaru, and in order to make it less obvious whether the number of tea utensils had increased or decreased, Murashige had ordered one set of attendants carry the tea utensils out of the storehouse, another set to take them to the drawing room, and another set to return them to the storehouse. He'd gone through such great pains to protect the secret mission. And yet Torasaru had been stolen despite that.

That left one possibility—there was a leak. For all Murashige knew, even news of the forthcoming peace talks, which were supposed to be conducted behind closed doors, had leaked.

Who was the mole? *That* was what Murashige was trying to figure out. But of course, that was not something that Yosaku could be privy to. Murashige couldn't tell anybody else in all the castle.

No. There is one person.

Murashige noticed Yosaku's inquisitive eyes.

"I can't say," Murashige told him.

8

Murashige secluded himself in the drawing room, facing opposite the scrap paper he was reusing.

One could tell the time by ascertaining the rough position of the sun in the sky and the level of darkness in the vicinity. Depending on the time of the year, the length of the roughly two-hour periods by which time was measured (called *koku*) changed. If one were to ask different people about something that occurred at a given point in time, one might answer that it occurred at the Hour of the Horse, while another might answer that it happened during the Hour of the Sheep. That did not, however, have any bearing on the order of events.

Murashige took up his brush and wrote the sequence of events from the day before to this morning. It was more or less as follows:

Before noon
The war council ended. Muhen entered Arioka Castle. There was a sudden downpour.

Noon
Spoke with Muhen at the citadel residence. Handed Torasaru to Muhen.
Muhen went to the hermitage.

Early afternoon
Koori Juuemon visited the hermitage bearing the letter. He gave it to Muhen. The wicker luggage's whereabouts are currently unknown.
On his way back, Juuemon bade farewell to the hermitage owner, who did not respond.

Evening
Juuemon spotted the temple worker in the streets of Itami.

Before twilight
The temple worker entered the hermitage. He heard from the hermitage owner that Muhen would stay the night, and that Muhen had a guest over.
The temple worker went to greet Muhen.

*   *   *

Early night hours

A. The temple worker carried out errands such as drawing water. He smelled incense and heard mantras. He also saw Muhen standing in the lavatory.

B. Kuriyama Zensuke sneaked into the inner citadel and was confronted. Murashige ordered the guard to stand watch over the hermitage.

Unclear which happened first, A or B.

Dead of night

Four guard members, including Akioka Shirounosuke and Inui Sukesaburou, arrived at the hermitage and stood guard.

The temple worker was stopped by Sukesaburou when the former was about to take his leave of the hermitage.

Daybreak

Kitagawara Yosaku visited the hermitage in order to grant a dying retainer his wish of hearing Muhen's prayers.

Inui Sukesaburou tried to prevent Yosaku from entering the hermitage.

Yosaku shook off Sukesaburou and entered the hermitage, where he found Muhen's corpse.

Afterward, Akioka Shirounosuke's corpse was also spotted.

Morning

Murashige received the news.

The wicker luggage could not be found in the guest room.

That was everything leading up to Torasaru's disappearance and the discovery of Muhen's and Akioka Shirounosuke's bodies. However, no matter how much Murashige glared at the scrap paper, it wouldn't tell him what he wanted to know—who leaked the secret mission, and even more importantly, where did Torasaru disappear to? It was utterly opaque to him.

The Samurai and the Prisoner

9

The soil of Settsu was drenched in water.

Murashige descended into the basement of Arioka's castle tower. The basement was always wet, as water was always steadily oozing from the soil crushed by the castle tower directly above. Though the ground was exposed to intense heat, the basement was cold.

It was midday, and Murashige was holding a candlestick, unaccompanied. The jailer heard his footsteps and came out to greet him.

"My liege."

His voice sounded hoarse. The jailer, a man by the name of Katou Matazaemon, was around fifty years of age. He served as the warden for a singular prisoner, and he was the replacement for the jailer who had died a death none could see coming some time prior.

"Is he alive?" asked Murashige.

"Yes, my lord. Your Lordship ordered me to keep him alive."

"Unlock the door."

Matazaemon obeyed, retrieving the key hanging at his waist and inserting it into the lock of the wooden door before turning it. It unlocked with a heavy *clank*.

"…I have unlocked it, my lord."

The door seemed slanted, as it opened on its own after Matazaemon turned the key. Murashige held out his candle, but the darkness swallowed the feeble light that it cast, failing to illuminate the space beyond. He walked through the door without a word. Past this threshold, there were more stairs to descend.

As he went down the stairs one step at a time, the insects, repelled by the flame, fled from Murashige. Before long, in the ring of light created by the candle, a thick wooden lattice came into view. The cage might as well have been the coagulation of the stubborn determination never to let a man escape.

Behind the bars lay a black lump of a man.

"Kanbei."

The lump stirred, then laughed.

"To what do I owe the pleasure, oh Lord of Settsu? By my rough esti-mation, Your Lordship has come to see me a tad early."

In the flickering light, Murashige could make out the husk of Kuroda Kanbei, the warrior so well-known in Banshu and praised as a man of courage and wisdom. The thrash wounds on his head were ugly, the scar tissue shrunken and taut; they were clearly visible even in the dark-ness. His eyes were sunken, his back was bent, and perhaps his legs had failed him as well, for he seemed unable to sit up straight. Kanbei had been thrown in prison under Murashige's orders, but when Murashige dwelled on what became of a man who spent seven months stuck in a cage too cramped for him to even stand or stretch his limbs, he was frankly impressed Kanbei remained alive and could move or talk at all. The emaciated, unsightly wretch's hoarse voice echoed mournfully—and yet it was also still endowed with the insidious ring of a man who was not to be underestimated. The scorn in Kanbei's words was thinly veiled, and Murashige didn't think for a second that his words were simply sour grapes or him putting on a brave front.

"Early? What are you talking about?"

"Well, I predicted that it would be ten days until my next audience with Your Magnificence."

"What makes you think I'd come to see a dirty prisoner like you?"

"An odd question, Your Lordship... Do ye not see it for yourself?"

He said nothing more after that. When he was silent, he was indis-tinguishable from a mere shadow.

To Murashige, Kanbei was, like this shadow, ungraspable. Once a vas-sal of the Kodera clan, Kodera Kanbei was nothing more than a samu-rai who was proud of his wit and known for his martial prowess. So what made him so hard to understand? In Murashige's eyes, Kanbei had seemed to be a handful at times but ultimately easy to manipulate as a man who was always so eager for any opportunity to show his inge-nuity to the world. But after all these months, Kanbei had become an enigma. He'd thought Kanbei was sharp, but not *this* sharp. He could tell Kanbei wanted something, although he'd had no inkling what that could be. However, Murashige now believed he knew what cards Kan-bei was holding in hand.

Kanbei must have been prepared to die when he visited Arioka. But when he found out that he was going to be imprisoned instead, he was extremely dismayed, crying out to be killed. Now it was clear why Kanbei had done so. Kuriyama Zensuke, who had sneaked into the inner citadel the night prior, was right. Kanbei had known that the hostage would be executed if he did not return, either alive or as a head.

Getting a hostage killed is a source of great shame for a samurai. I would rather die than suffer such shame... That was what must have run through Kanbei's head during that fateful day. In these internecine times, it was not uncommon for samurai to leave hostages to die without batting an eye, bragging that this was just another strategy. Kanbei's point of view, while not broadly shared, was not particularly difficult to understand, either. If anything, it was *too* like an honorable warrior—too respectable for this new era of ruthless chicanery. Murashige felt the urge to look Kanbei in the eyes and tell him he saw right through him.

No, wait, thought Murashige. *If Kanbei had chosen death for fear of being disgraced, does that mean I have a lead to the Kanbei who's been stewing in this cage?*

No. No, I don't. I'm missing something.

Murashige grew frustrated when he realized that Kanbei's heart, which he thought he'd been beginning to see into, was still as opaque as ever. However, Murashige soon realized that he had something he could hold over Kanbei's head, so he smirked and blurted it out.

"Kanbei. Kuriyama Zensuke came to rescue you."

"......"

"The louse made it all the way to the inner citadel. A master-hand, you'll agree."

Relying on the candlelight, Murashige strained his eyes to see what tells would appear on Kanbei's face and movements...but he saw nothing. Kanbei simply looked down a little and sat there as if he'd heard nothing of note. The scant light shed by the candle wasn't helping Murashige discern whether Kanbei was bottling his emotions or whether he truly thought nothing of it. This wiped the smirk from Murashige's face.

It was then Murashige realized that he'd been swept up in a passion he couldn't name, and that this temper was now abating. A man of ambition, he was never too shy to deceive or swindle, and not only for the sake of warfare. That being said, he was not mean for its own sake. Verbally making sport of a prisoner without so much as a dagger on him was unlike Murashige, who looked inward with astonishment, wondering what was wrong with him.

Murashige clammed up, and Kanbei started speaking as to lend the poor lord a helping hand.

"And what did Your Lordship do with him?"

"A single rank-and-file soldier like him? That was not a battle to be lost by letting him live, nor a battle to be won by killing him. I expelled him from the castle."

"Goodness me…" Once again, Kanbei's raspy voice sounded some-what amused. "Racking up the good deeds by releasing him from certain death, I see."

Murashige had half a mind to say, "The fool cried out 'Why didn't you kill Kanbei?'" but this time, he held his tongue. By irritating Murashige with his mockery and purposeful obscurity, Kanbei was aiming to get the Lord of Settsu to divulge what he ought to keep to himself. And Murashige was disgusted at himself for nearly falling for Kanbei's trap.

"Enough with the bravado," said Murashige, doing his best to keep an even tone.

Kanbei cast down his eyes. "I do not wish to hear pretexts," he mumbled. "That cannot be the matter that the Lord of Settsu came all the way down to this dungeon to tell me about."

"Always so impertinent. You think you have me figured out from inside this dungeon, don't you?"

Kanbei didn't reply.

Murashige had consulted with Kanbei twice before, once last winter and then again this spring. It was little wonder Kanbei would expect there'd be a third time. Murashige put down the candle and sat cross-legged on the damp ground.

"…Very well. I do have a matter to tell you of. A brigand of unprecedented prowess has stolen into the castle."

Kanbei raised his head a mite, but he didn't say anything. Murashige continued:

"Information no one was supposed to know has gotten out, my secret envoy was killed, and the letter's contents were read. So long as I know not where and how the information leaked, Arioka is in imminent danger. And I'm sure you understand that the day Arioka falls is the day you die."

Kanbei stirred slightly inside his cage. "In that case...I shall peel my ears."

"Good. Listen to this."

Murashige proceeded to talk about the case surrounding Muhen's and Akioka Shirounosuke's deaths. The only door leading to the dungeon was closed, so there was no concern that Katou Matazaemon, the warden who'd remained upstairs, was listening in.

Naturally, Murashige did not reveal everything to Kanbei. He didn't tell him that he'd made a secret missionary of Muhen to drive peace talks. Other than that, he did describe in detail what he saw and heard, including the fact that he relinquished the treasured Torasaru. Kanbei was silent as usual, though he did what could be considered a nod on occasion. Until now, that hadn't been the case.

Murashige also gave Kanbei a full account of the capture of Kuriyama Zensuke, as well as the story behind how he'd dispatched his guard to stand watch over the hut. He apprised him of the construction of the hermitage, the state of the brushwood fencing, and how Muhen and Shirounosuke died. He talked about the bridge that connected the town houses and the samurai district, and the bridge that connected the samurai district and the inner citadel. He filled him in on Kitagawara Yosaku's claim that he visited the hermitage before dawn, that Inui Sukesaburou saw the temple worker leave, and that he'd conducted as thorough an investigation as he could at his residence in the inner citadel.

"...And those are the facts. Torasaru has disappeared. As far as I can tell, Oda has a rogue of such skill that he's possessed by a *tengu*. By some method, he sniffed out the top secret information, made off with my treasure, and killed a formidable swordsman before he could even draw his blade."

"...Lord of Settsu," muttered Kanbei, "ye, too, must be thinking what I am thinking."

Murashige was silent.

He didn't believe that a single formidable Oda agent perpetrated everything. There was no doubt that a considerable number of the Oda's people had entered the castle, but no matter how skilled they were, they couldn't do the impossible.

He'd imparted the secret mission in the middle of a large hall. Not only that, but Murashige had also brought Muhen closer and spoken to him in a particularly quiet voice. Even if one or more Oda agents had been lurking above the ceiling or under the floorboards, there was no way they would have been able to hear anything. So how did Muhen's killer know that Muhen was a secret messenger, carrying a secret letter and a famed treasure?

"Given how sharp Your Lordship is...I am wondering whether ye might be suspecting one of your honorable retainers."

Indeed. If one of his retainers was feeding information to Oda, leaking secrets to enemy agents lurking within the castle, it all added up. Murashige didn't need to be told that by Kanbei; he'd thought that far himself. What he didn't understand was anything beyond that.

There was only one person in the castle who knew that Muhen was a secret messenger carrying the letter discussing peace talks. That man was Koori Juuemon, the head of Murashige's Five Spears. Murashige's scribe knew the contents of the letter, but not that it would be handed to Muhen. The Araki clan's guard was made up of a select group of samurai, but among them, only Juuemon was thought to have the potential to be a competent commander. Juuemon, for his part, lived up to Murashige's faith in him, serving him without a duplicitous bone in his body...or so it appeared on the surface.

Juuemon was the one who showed Muhen to Murashige's residence the day before, and the one who delivered the letter to that hut. Yet Juuemon shouldn't have been privy to the fact that Torasaru had been given to Muhen.

There was only one person who knew Torasaru had come into Muhen's possession, and that was Murashige's wife, Chiyoho. Losing a masterpiece of that magnitude felt like getting torn in half. That was why Murashige ended up telling her about it. He scoured his memory of what he'd let slip, racking his mind for anyone other than Chiyoho who might know that he had handed over Torasaru, but sure enough, he concluded he'd told no one else. However, Chiyoho could not have known that Muhen was carrying that secret letter.

Juuemon and Chiyoho. In this wolf-eat-wolf world, those two were among the few people inside or outside the clan whom Murashige trusted. One of them had gone behind Murashige's back and informed Oda agents that Muhen was entrusted with a peerless treasure... Just thinking about it made Murashige feel like he was chewing sand.

"On the other hand," said Kanbei with a smile, "'tis truly a wondrous enigma, this crime. Your Lordship may consider me a tad intrigued."

Murashige thought the events of that night were lamentable, not wondrous.

"What's so wondrous about it?"

Affectedly, Kanbei opened his eyes wide.

"Oh, dear me... If what Your Lordship said is true, then the Oda agent who sneaked into this here castle learned of the secret mission from someone in the castle they were already familiar with, after which they killed a guard to enter the hut, read the contents of the secret letter before returning it to the collar, and absconded with the tea jar... If so, then verily, it *is* wondrous, is it not?"

Now that Kanbei mentioned it, it struck Murashige.

"It *is* strange. Why wasn't the letter taken, too?"

A secret letter from an enemy general. Bringing it back would earn the agent who did so glory. And even if, for some reason, they couldn't bring it back with them, it should have been easy to burn it, rip it to pieces, or throw it away. Why did he search for the secret letter, find it in Muhen's collar, and then put it back there after reading it?

"The letter wasn't what they were after," said Murashige. "That's the only way it makes sense."

"Precisely. What say we think about it thusly? The only thing the brigand was trying to steal was Torasaru."

Murashige ruminated on it for a moment, then discarded the notion.

"Don't be absurd. If they were just some robber, then why would they unfasten the collar and search for the letter?"

"Why indeed?" came Kanbei's hoarse voice.

It was Koori Juuemon who told Murashige that the secret letter had been stolen. Murashige thought for a moment that Juuemon had given false witness. But since Juuemon did not know about Torasaru, the idea that he revealed the secret mission to an Oda agent, and then for that agent to attack Muhen in order to take Torasaru, didn't add up.

"What is going on…?" Murashige couldn't help from mumbling.

Kanbei snickered, his shadow on the mud wall swaying. "I wonder myself."

Going by his tone, he clearly knew. Murashige raised an eyebrow. Before he could say anything, Kanbei continued:

"I can always count on Your Lordship to throw some tasty food for thought my way. For a brief moment, my boredom left me. Now, if I may."

Suddenly, Kanbei curled up into the darkness. He stared at Murashige from behind his disheveled hair.

"Pretexts are pretexts and nothing more. I have had my fill. What the Lord of Settsu wished to discuss with me cannot have been *this*."

10

The smell of fire hung in the air, and the sounds of the flame burning and of unseen crawlers plied Murashige's ears.

For a short while, Murashige said nothing. He could not find any words to say. To Murashige, Kanbei's words had been *that* off the mark.

"You said that earlier, too," he offered at last. In both his eyes and his voice, there were exasperation and scorn. "I'll ask you again. Why do you think I've come here? What do you think I'm here to tell you?"

"It would seem Your Lordship is not yet conscious of it." Kanbei shifted his posture. "What else could it be? Your Lordship has graced me with his presence in order to talk about the tides of this war."

"Nonsense. Why should I have to talk about the war with *you*?"

"Obviously," said Kanbei, "because there's no one else Your Lordship *can* talk to about it."

A chill ran down Murashige's spine. Vivid memories of the war council the day before sprang to mind.

"I believe there is naught to fear."

"Then we may battle on for another seven or eight years."

"I believe that the best policy now is to continue to defend this castle as we wait for the Mouri's arrival."

"Ahhh, yes, that is best. That's what we ought to do."

Just when Murashige had reached the realization that the Mouri would never come, at the council attended by all the commanders who led his retainers, the majority of them pressed to continue the war effort. Murashige heard a crash of illusory thunder that couldn't be real within this abyss untouched by sunlight.

Murashige had told Muhen:

"I am a general. It does not suffice to simply wish the lightning doesn't come to us."

And of course, that was true.

I am the head of the Araki clan, the lord of Arioka Castle, and the Lord of Settsu, Araki Murashige. I am the one who decides all things, and my orders can crush countless men and spare countless more. Officers and commoners alike must bend to my commands. And yet...

"Among Your Lordship's retainers, I am sure that there are quite a few men of valor who gladly stake their lives to swing their spears in your name. And I am sure that there are those who, in their loyalty, do run themselves to the ground in order to see your will done. And yet with all due respect, from what I can see, the number of men you can talk to about the war without reservations is...well, zero."

Murashige had nothing to dispute this.

He'd taken over the Ikeda clan, destroyed the Wada clan, and wrested control over Hokusetsu from the Itami clan. And during all that time, there wasn't a single person with whom he could discuss serious matters. Yes, Araki Kyuuzaemon was calm, Nomura Tango brave, Ikeda Izumi loyal, and the other commanders far from dolts. However, with Hokusetsu as a foothold, Murashige had his eyes on the world, and it was certainly true that there was no one he could open up to about the future. If he absolutely had to name one person he thought could be a general on his level, he could *maybe* see a scrap of that general in Koori Juuemon, and Juuemon was a long way off from attaining that sort of greatness. Murashige might have been able to talk frankly about his ambitions with Takayama Ukon, but in the past, Ukon was nothing more than a *yoriki*, and now he was with the enemy.

Kanbei's remark was correct. Murashige was all alone.

"I surmise that after Your Lordship gave himself over to the Oda clan, it was an exhilarating time. Hashiba Chikuzen, Shibata Shuri, Korezumi Gorouza, Takigawa Sakon, Koreto Hyuuga—they were just *some* of the glittering stars in that constellation, and not a one your inferior. Be it at a war council or a tea ceremony, ye must have been able to have conversations with substance with them. That was the only time ye could talk to fellows on equal terms as a *person* and not a lord. Am I mistaken?"

When Murashige was under the Oda clan, the generals whom Kanbei mentioned were at once Murashige's peers and his rivals. They often jostled for glory, dragged one another down, and got on one another's nerves. But they were all *people*, not pawns. They grasped the talk that the vassals might look uncomprehending about, and sometimes, they blew Murashige away with their insights.

Kanbei's voice was gentle, as though to make a child understand.

"Since the flow of time is sluggish in this dungeon, I know not what month it is. But pray ask yourself, how many times, in these months, has Your Lordship found himself exclaiming 'you said it' or slapping your knee, impressed by someone else's insight? Has there been a single time ye found someone ye could *talk* to?"

"......"

"There is not one man in Arioka Castle who can truly understand or appreciate what Your Lordship says. Not one man besides myself, that is… And that is the *true* reason Your Lordship is here."

Kanbei's words corroded Murashige slowly, quietly.

"There is no one a general who decides all things himself *needs* to talk to," said Murashige. "So long as my retainers obey me, I want for nothing."

"Oh-ho, how right, how utterly true. But, Your Lordship, know ye why your brave and valorous retainers talk in circles about fighting the good fight despite the fact that victory clearly does not lie at the end of this war?"

Murashige looked livid. There was no way the prisoner locked in the dungeon could know about what had happened at the war council or the state of affairs with his retainers. *If he did find out somehow, perhaps Katou, the jailer, told him?*

Murashige looked behind him cautiously, to which Kanbei immediately said, "Katou didn't tell me a thing. The fact that it would all turn out this way was clearer to me than a pure lake's waters."

"Oh, was it now?"

Still seated cross-legged on the floor, Murashige drew the short sword at his waist. The sharp metallic noise of the blade sliding out of its sheath echoed across the dungeon. The tip of the sword, now pointed at Kanbei, reflected the candle's flame.

"Tell me what backs up all that big talk. If you don't, I'll kill you for the crime of defaming me. And if you bore me or waste my time, you're dead."

Kanbei stared at the sword, dazzled. "What?"

Still staring, he dared to smile.

"...Firstly," he began, "Your Lordship must know that this war has no future. Why has time simply passed fruitlessly, with neither victory nor defeat? For no other reason than that the Mouri come not. So we must ask ourselves, *why* won't the Mouri come? Could it be friction among the retainers...?"

From behind his unkempt mane, he stole a small glance at Murashige.

"Or else, could it be that Hashiba finally persuaded the Ukita? Let us assume that is the case. To the highest bidders the Ukita do turn, and no matter how much silver the Mouri mine in Iwami, they remain on the back foot against the Oda, who conquered the capital and Sakai."

Kanbei had been in this prison since the eleventh month of the last year. Aside from what Murashige had told him thus far, he shouldn't have been able to catch wind of a single new rumor. In other words,

Kanbei had predicted the Ukita's treachery since last year. Murashige, his eyes fixed on Kanbei, slowly lowered the tip of his short sword.

Kanbei bowed slightly and continued, "The Mouri shan't be coming. But the retainers will only ever say they can still win despite having come to that conclusion themselves. And there's a reason for that. There are those who fear being mocked as cowardly should they mention surrender as an option. And there are those who fear drastic change rocking the lives they've been living, even if it means the war ends. When times get dangerous, the folk who wax on about bravery and valor always multiply. Such is the way of the world... But 'tis all appearances. And the real reason, Lord of Settsu..."

Kanbei's dark eyes were staring at Murashige.

"...is that ye are an Araki."

Murashige exhaled and sheathed his *wakizashi* with a *click*. "...Very well. If there's anything you wish to say, say it."

Murashige cast his eyes down a little. Loath that Kanbei should read into that, he forcibly erased the emotions from his face.

"Now then, there are three ways one can become the lord of a land," Kanbei explained. "One, the land can be handed down from generation to generation. A lordship inherited. The Ikeda and Itami fall under that category."

He lifted one soil-crusted finger before lifting the second.

"Two, the land can be appointed to an underling, who thereby becomes a lord. The Imagawa of Suruga and the Takeda of Kai used to fall under this category."

The third finger.

"Three, there are cases, however few, where a man possesses the indescribable and mysterious power to attract enough tens of thousands to revere him as their lord. I believe that the Hongan-ji territory was that way initially."

He folded his fingers back down.

"A man who fits none of these criteria may take a land by force of arms, but even if his military might is great in the short term, his fate shall be a pitiable one. Examples include the Asahi Shogun—Kiso Yoshinaka—or for a closer example, Saito Dosan."

Saito Dosan captured Mino Province as a father-son team. Though the duo's tactics were beyond compare, their reputation did them no favors. They were abandoned by the samurai from that land, and in the end, their lives were forfeit.

"Don't be so conceited, Kanbei. You're overstepping your bounds."

That was what Murashige decided to believe. Yet there was no force behind his voice.

Of the three patterns Kanbei raised, Murashige didn't fit the first. The Araki clan had no connection to Settsu beforehand, and lands like Takatsuki and Itami were merely regions they'd captured recently. And Kanbei's third pattern, the mysterious power to attract people, wasn't something one could actively obtain.

That was why Murashige had desired the second pattern—to be assigned the governance of the land. He'd made Oda's acquaintance, was entrusted with the governance of Settsu under him, and adopted the title of Lord of Settsu. Now that he'd broken away from Oda, it was no longer clear why Murashige necessarily had to be the one to govern Arioka, and his place there was less assured.

In the past, Murashige went by the surname Ikeda, as granted to him by his lord at the time. The Ikeda clan was an illustrious family in Hokusetsu, so it was a convenient surname to bear when it came to governing Settsu Province. Yet now that he had split off from the defunct Ikeda clan, he'd had to revert to the Araki name.

Consequently, Murashige had reverted to an outsider in the land he ruled in name, too.

"However…," muttered Murashige, under his breath so Kanbei couldn't hear. "I cannot return to Ikeda after all this time. I've come too far."

"Lord of Settsu," said Kanbei, in a tone that could be called kind. "Upon coming under the fold of the Oda, you moved heaven and earth not only to bring Hokusetsu to heel, but also to attack Saika, Kozuki Castle, and Osaka. Your Lordship is a great general bursting with energy, and everything went as ye wanted—ye left your former land to get covered in blood and guts and vie for glory. Your retainers, however, were born in Settsu, as were their forefathers. The Kawarabayashi and Kitagawara, the Koori, the Itami and Ikeda—all these clans are from hereabouts. Ye can say 'tis to further secure the territory, but are your retainers fully convinced they need to be fighting in far-off Kii or Harima?"

Kanbei was right on the mark. Fighting bloody battles to protect the land that matched one's surname was what samurai longed for. Murashige knew that dissatisfaction was smoldering within the Araki clan's retainers as to why they had to leave their homes for far-flung domains and give their lives killing men they'd never had land or naval battles with.

Murashige wanted to fight. The arena hardly mattered. Just like Hashiba Chikuzen, who was born in Owari, ran around Echizen the year prior and Bizen this year, and just like Koreto Hyuuga, who was born in Mino, was invading deep into Tanba. Murashige himself wanted to fight in Kyushu and Mutsu Province if given the chance. For Murashige, Arioka Castle was nothing more than a castle, and Ikeda was nothing more than the land of the lord he'd banished. Just as Nobunaga had moved from Nagoya Castle to Kiyosu Castle to Gifu Castle to Azuchi Castle, Murashige wanted to attain glory and make his name known and feared in the farthest reaches by continuously switching to bigger, more important castles.

Murashige's wishes differed from those of the rest of his clan. He had averted his eyes from that point of friction, but the powder keg was beginning to blow.

Did Kanbei infer all that? From inside this cage?

"The fine fellows among your retainers shan't die for you, Lord of Settsu. While they don't like Oda since they don't want to be recruited for wars in distant places, when you're driven to a corner, ye alone will be made to slice your stomach, while your retainers will simply say they were following the orders of that outsider. As long as they've that escape route, they can shout from the rooftops that surrender is out of the question, that they'll fight to the last man, et cetera, et cetera... Tell me the thought has not crossed your mind, Your Lordship."

"...That's *if* we lose the war," said Murashige. "'Tis commonplace for the general to take the blame. The commanders, who bear no such burden, aren't wrong to be so gallant."

"I know that. However, Your Lordship..."

Kanbei smiled affably, and to Murashige, it was as though a dim light was now shining in the tenebrous dungeon.

"It appears Your Lordship agrees that I am the only one in Arioka with whom ye can speak about the future of the war. Truly, I am most delighted."

Murashige turned his face away. "...Don't get so smug, you damned bighead. You can rot in there for all I care."

"Goodness, smug? Me?" Kanbei muttered, reverting to a forlorn voice. "If I don't offer Your Lordship a present for coming all this way to visit me, it would tarnish my good name. I must also thank you for sparing Zensuke's life. Though this gift is far too modest, allow me to paint you a picture."

Kanbei cast his eyes down; his face hidden by his hair, he once again became naught but a dark silhouette.

"Your Lordship's assessment that the Oda agent stole into the castle and killed the traveling bonze before carrying off the priceless tea jar is upside down in every way. Reverse the inside and the outside, the cause and the effect, the concealed and the unconcealed, the before and the after, and the necessary and the unnecessary. What did vanish from that hut? I believe that will be your lead, your stepping stone."

There was a slight pause before Kanbei added:

"Prithee keep an eye on the temple worker. I am sure the truth will be revealed then."

Then Kanbei started quietly chanting a sutra. As a Zen practitioner, Murashige could tell it was a sutra of esteem within the Zen faith, the Verse of Homage to Buddha's Relics typically chanted after cremations. His chanting echoed through the empty dungeon, leaving Murashige with the impression multiple people were chanting the sutra at him.

11

The next day was a dark, gray one, the clouds hanging low in the sky.

Rumors flew every which way in Arioka Castle. Word had it that the temple worker who frequented the thatched hut was apprehended by

Murashige's guard, who hunted for him all around the town of Itami. When they found him, they hit him with poles and kicked him in the abdomen before tying him up with rope and carrying him off to who knew where.

There were some who said it didn't happen that way. According to them, while it was true that the samurai dragged the temple worker off someplace, the "beating him with poles and kicking him in the abdomen" part was an embellishment, and in reality, the temple worker accompanied the guard of his own free will. Either way, many witnesses saw the temple worker leave the town, only for a man's corpse to be transported out of the inner citadel not long afterward. The corpse, which was wearing the temple worker's tattered robe, had a laceration in its neck, and it was thrown outside the castle, whereupon dogs and birds crowded around it in an instant.

Nobody knew what crime the temple worker had committed, which was why each rumor begot the next:

"The lord must have pinned Muhen's murder on the temple worker."

"The temple worker was doing his chores for the hermitage and, in so doing, let Muhen die. That's what the lord punished him for."

A variety of rumors gained purchase among both the commoners and the samurai. They were all trying to find the logic in the temple worker's execution. But every theory ended up at the same place.

Namely, no one believed the temple worker could be responsible for Muhen's demise. The general consensus in the castle reproached their lord for the inhumanity of what he'd done. Muhen's death could only have been at the hands of an Oda agent, and it was Murashige himself who hadn't been able to prevent Oda agents from doing what they willed. It was mistaken at best to put the blame on the temple worker. That was what many thought, though they dared not speak it aloud.

At the same time, a different rumor was also spreading. Was Muhen's killer really an Oda agent? There was no doubt that spies under Oda's patronage were indeed in the castle, but why would they of all people kill Muhen, who was adored far and wide for his virtue? Those who didn't think the Oda had ordered Muhen to be killed speculated whom it could have been instead—and to a man, they whispered one name.

Several people were working on repairs for a defensive fence at Fort Koshino, located at Arioka Castle's north. They were retainers of the Kitagawara clan. And Kitagawara Yosaku was watching them work from close by.

Everyone in the castle knew that Yosaku had counseled surrender at the recent war council and that he had been immediately laughed off. Ever since then, the soldiers of the Kitagawara clan had been mocked and held in contempt as incorrigible cowards and forced to endure a wide array of snide remarks. If they were samurai, they could draw their swords and repay the indignity, but they were underlings, errand boys, and foot soldiers, so they could do naught but put up with it in silence.

Yosaku saw with his own eyes how few Mouri troops were at Amagasaki Castle and how many Oda troops surrounded Arioka Castle. No matter how much ridicule was thrown at him by colleagues who had yet to leave the castle's bounds since the war began, it did nothing to trouble his heart. What vexed him greatly was that ridicule reaching his soldiers. As such, Yosaku was, as much as he could be, present where his retainers were at work. Yosaku was a commander and a relative of Murashige's. Nobody would provoke Kitagawara soldiers in his presence.

That day, however, it was a different state of affairs from usual. Instead of disdaining Kitagawara soldiers, the rank-and-file soldiers stared daggers at Kitagawara Yosaku instead.

Yosaku knew of the rumors that were circulating. On the day Muhen died, Yosaku, seeking recitation of the *nenbutsu* invocation for a dying vassal, barged unaccompanied into the hut where Muhen was staying the night. He stepped inside without even asking for the permission of the hermitage's language-impaired owner, opened the sliding door leading into the guest room, and saw Muhen's corpse. As such, there were those who stated the following:

"It was Kitagawara Yosaku who killed Muhen."

"He saw that no one was there to witness him, and so he stabbed Muhen, then pretended to be the corpse's discoverer."

If anyone actually went up to him and asked him point-blank if he killed Muhen, Yosaku could defend himself, but no one did. So he simply kept watching over the fence repairs amid the suffocating silence. Inside the fort, everyone bore arms. The eerie sensation that unseen bows and guns were pointed his way had him sweating.

It was during just such a time that the drums signaled the war council. This pattern of beats meant that all should assemble at the inner citadel unless they were immobilized by illness or the enemy was before their eyes. At once, Yosaku called out to the group leader under him.

"'Tis the war council. I must be off."

The group leader replied respectfully, as though he'd heard nothing of the swirling rumors.

"Yes, my master. Leave the rest to me."

"Thank you for your hard work."

"Think nothing of it. Have no qualms, my master."

Yosaku mounted his steed and headed for the citadel alongside his horse tender.

Yosaku didn't think the war's future prospects would be called into question again. The mass meeting of the retainers had come to the consensus that they would wait and see how things went. Yosaku didn't think doing nothing proactive and merely waiting for the Mouri to come provide their aid was a winning policy, but he was young, and he knew he couldn't hit the older warriors with his differing opinion any more than he already had. Those who stuck out a little got laughed out; those who stuck out too much got killed. And given that, it wouldn't be odd for them to pin Muhen's murder on him on the basis of all those groundless rumors... When that thought ran through Yosaku's head, even the fleetness of his horse felt weighed down by the world.

He rode through the samurai district and neared the inner citadel; before the bridge spanning the fosse, there was a line of riders and horses. He saw the commanders who'd been summoned to the war council were being barred from passing, and he saw the lord's guard members who defended the bridge were questioning each of the commanders and allowing them through to the citadel one by one. Yosaku was about to ask the commander in front of him what had happened, but he caught himself. The man was in priestly attire. He was the first to gainsay him at the last war council, Kawarabayashi Noto.

Noto spoke reservedly, if anything, when Murashige was present—but afterward, when he and Yosaku met, he grimaced with a frown that screamed, "Yosaku the coward." Yosaku didn't bother talking to him, as he didn't expect a serious response. He dismounted, gave the reins to the horse tender, and got in line.

As he waited, Yosaku ruminated on many things. He thought about looking after his horse, he thought about the pain of his retainers enduring all that verbal abuse, he thought about the defense of Fort Kishino, and he thought about the rumors filling the castle. Yosaku, too, didn't buy Murashige's rationale. Did the lord of this land truly believe the temple worker stabbed Muhen to death? Is that why he executed the poor man?

That's ridiculous, thought Yosaku. Muhen may have been a monk, but he was also a burly man who traveled across various lands on his own two feet. The temple worker, on the other hand, was a feeble old man without so much as a sword to wield. Even if the temple worker somehow managed to kill Muhen, what of Akioka Shirounosuke? There were precious few within the castle who could best him in a swordfight. And even if the temple worker was a swordsman with masterful skill belying his appearance, killing Shirounosuke before he could even draw his sword was no ordinary feat.

What if he never actually *suspected the temple worker did it? That couldn't be. He, of all people, led astray by false rumors?* Yosaku told himself.

An angry outburst snapped him back to reality.

"What insolence!"

One of the commanders who was stopped at the bridge lashed out at the guard. It was Nakanishi Shinpachirou, whose hand was on the sword at his waist, threatening to unsheathe it any second.

As a rule, there was no assignment less desirable than sentry of a bridge or a checkpoint or the like. It did sometimes allow one to enjoy the side benefit of extorting entry tolls from commoners, but when it was a samurai who needed to pass, things became fraught. It was the way of the world that anyone who obstructed a samurai's path could be slain in the process, and that was even more pronounced with commander-level samurai, not all of who were amenable enough to let it go when they were told they could not pass. Shinpachirou was mollified by some means, as he at last took his hand off his sword, but he didn't bother veiling his chagrin.

The guard members defending the bridge had to be stopping the commanders on Murashige's orders, but from what Yosaku could see, more than a few didn't disguise the indignant looks on their faces, and Shinpachirou wasn't the sole commander with his hand on his scabbard. Despite that, the queue gradually progressed, until it was Yosaku's turn.

One of the men guarding the bridge was Inui Sukesaburou, who was wiping his sweat the whole time. When he saw Yosaku's face, he breathed a sigh of relief.

"Kitagawara!"

"I applaud your hard work," said Yosaku.

"I am unworthy of your kind words. Our lord has ordered us to create a register of names of those who shall attend the council, so I humbly bid you wait while I write your name."

"So that's what you've been doing. But couldn't ye simply see the faces of those who entered the tower from some vantage point?"

"Yes, I think so, too, but 'tis our lord's command…"

A member of the guard who was behind Sukesaburou—and who didn't seem particularly skilled at writing—clumsily jotted down the name *Kitagawara Yosaku Kanekatsu*.

"It is done. Please, by all means, you may proceed."

Yosaku couldn't say he understood what the point was, but he started down the bridge. Halfway down the bridge, Kawarabayashi Noto was waiting, standing in place. When he saw Yosaku's face, he grinned.

"Well, if it isn't Kitagawara. Our lord sure has peculiar ideas."

"I agree."

"What was that name register for? He can strike terror in the heart of a shirker who would fail to attend the council without resorting to such things."

"Verily, 'tis so."

"Then again, I can't say there's no one who *does* attend the council but exists there to dishearten and discourage."

"Is that right?"

"*Mettle, pluck, spirit.* A samurai's bywords. The battlefield is no place for the weak-kneed. Or am I wrong?"

"Ye speak the truth."

Yosaku gazed up at the sky. "Looks like rain," he muttered.

Noto snorted, and he began walking with long strides.

Usually, the commanders came for the war council inside the castle tower all but simultaneously. That day, however, since they'd been stopped at the bridge, the commanders were talking in groups of two or three. After Yosaku crossed the bridge and passed through the gates into the citadel, he found himself looking up at the castle tower. Lightning was flashing between the clouds, followed by the disquieting rumble of thunder.

The lightning's not that close by, Yosaku thought.

That very second—

"Now!"

"Right!"

There weren't many places to hide in the inner citadel, and yet scattered soldiers emerged from Yosaku knew not where. Before he realized it, he was surrounded by the points of hand spears. Yosaku unconsciously put a hand on his scabbard and loosened his sword. It was a motion he'd practiced since infancy, but inside, he was in pieces. *Does our lord really suspect me? Then there's no way I'll be heading back with my life.* Just when he screwed his resolve, he noticed that the warriors weren't looking at *him.*

Their eyes were all on the man beside Yosaku, Noto, who stood bolt upright from the shock. The one who stood directly in front of Noto was Koori Juuemon.

"Noto, this is by decree of our lord!" Juuemon declared solemnly.

Yosaku resheathed his sword and jumped out of the way. The ring of warriors that surrounded Noto closed in further. Noto must have come to his senses at that point, for he fired back, his face drained of color.

"Ye wastrels! What's the meaning of this?!"

It wasn't Juuemon who answered Noto's question. Murashige appeared unhurriedly from outside the ring. He had with him a man who appeared to be a common foot soldier—perhaps as a bodyguard. He was a small man wearing a *jingasa*, a common soldier's hat.

"You know full well what this is about," Murashige stated gravely and quietly.

"My lord! What on earth is this madness?"

The other commanders, seeing the commotion, gathered around at a distance.

It wasn't clear whether Murashige noticed that when he said, "Noto, you killed Muhen, just like you killed Akioka Shirounosuke. I will now ask you some questions, so behave yourself."

"Wh-what?!" Noto sounded dismayed, and the other commanders also made a stir. "We know Muhen was killed by an Oda agent. Why does Your Lordship suspect me?!"

"I don't think I have any obligation to tell you why. Feigning ignorance will not help you."

Noto scanned the sea of faces, and when he spotted Yosaku, relief colored his visage. He pointed a finger at Yosaku.

"Are you aware of the rumors surrounding that there Yosaku, my lord? They say *he's* the one who killed Muhen! Yosaku alone entered the hut, and Yosaku alone found Muhen's corpse. Before casting false aspersions against *me*, Your Lordship ought to question Yosaku!"

But Murashige paid Noto's objections no notice.

"Both I and the members of my guard have seen more than enough corpses in our lives. Did you think I wouldn't be able to tell whether a corpse was freshly dead? The blood was dry, and rigidity had set into the arms and fingers. Muhen had died long before Yosaku broke into the hermitage."

Yosaku sighed. His body had turned tense before he realized it, and as relief washed over him, his muscles relaxed. He wondered how he could prove his innocence if Murashige had accused *him* of killing Muhen, but he couldn't think of what he should do. Hearing Murashige's remarks, Yosaku knew he was no longer a suspect, and he had unconsciously bowed his head to Murashige.

Noto made no attempt to hide his rage.

"Even if it wasn't Yosaku, why does Your Lordship claim it was me who did it? Just because ye said it doesn't mean—"

"Enough, Noto!" shouted a furious Murashige. "You disgrace yourself!"

Murashige's booming, wrathful voice, which had both riled up his allies and intimidated his enemies in the field of battle many a time, now reverberated through the citadel. Yosaku saw Noto take a step back. But then someone he never expected spoke up.

"Pray wait, my lord! There is truth to what Noto is saying!"

It was Araki Kyuuzaemon, and he had a frantic look on his face. He waved his hand in front of the commanders and ran out in front of Murashige.

"Muhen's death is truly a shame, but, my lord, what reason do you have to say it was Noto's doing? Noto is not so low in standing that Your Lordship can decide his fate without so much as an explanation. The Kawarabayashi clan has been chief vassals for generations; they are not a clan that one may slight!"

Yosaku saw Murashige's eyes narrow. Did Kyuuzaemon understand how outrageously improper he was being? The Kawarabayashi clan, which once ruled their own castle, fell from that position and ended up under a different clan back when the head of the Ikeda clan was Katsumasa, Lord of Chikugo. Murashige had exiled Katsumasa and made the Araki clan prosperous in the space of a single generation. It had no predecessor.

Of course, Murashige had to have noticed Kyuuzaemon's error, but he didn't condemn him for his remarks. Instead, he replied so all the commanders could hear, his voice deep and full.

"In that case, hark. Noto killed Muhen because Akioka Shirounosuke was slain."

Kyuuzaemon frowned. "What makes Your Lordship say that...?"

"Shirounosuke was cut in the thigh from behind, and after he fell to the ground, his neck guard was stripped, and he was stabbed through the throat. Only a practiced hand could have accomplished that. And Shirounosuke was an outstanding swordmaster, at that. Even I might not have been a match for him without a sword. Granted, Shirounosuke was not the most skilled of fighters, but even so, to have slain him without him even being able to draw his sword in the slightest is unthinkable. Shirounosuke's killer used trickery to take him by surprise."

"Trickery?" repeated Kyuuzaemon.

Murashige nodded. "The orders I gave Shirounosuke's group were to protect the hut and to see that Muhen departed at the crack of dawn. The guard obeyed my command and let no one near the hermitage. Even if someone approached Shirounosuke as an ally, Shirounosuke would not have let his guard down. There was only one who could have gotten Shirounosuke to turn his back so that he could kill him without his ever drawing his sword."

Yosaku knew where Murashige was going with this. Who was the only person the man who'd been ordered to protect Muhen would let his guard down for?

"Muhen himself," said Murashige.

Lightning flashed in the distance, and claps of thunder reached the group from afar.

The commanders were hanging on Murashige's every word, and perhaps because Noto was searching for a reply, he opened his mouth to say something, only to then close his mouth. The guard's spears were still pointing at Noto without the slightest opening, and those spear tips showed no signs of lowering. The soldier standing beside Murashige wasn't wielding a spear and didn't have his hand on any sword. He was merely standing there.

Kyuuzaemon's voice came out shrill. "My—my lord, are ye saying Shirounosuke was slain by *Muhen*?!"

Murashige shook his head.

"Of course not. I'm saying Shirounosuke *thought* the man in front of him was Muhen. That's why he turned his back... There were things that vanished from the guest room where Muhen died."

"And those are?"

"The wicker luggage, the bamboo hat, and the khakkhara staff."

Yosaku saw a cynical smile form on Murashige's face.

"I had been under the mistaken impression that the brigand had designs on what was *inside* the luggage. But what was necessary and unnecessary was the reverse. He didn't want what was inside it. He wanted the luggage itself."

Yosaku didn't know that the luggage contained Torasaru.

"The culprit appeared before Shirounosuke wearing a bamboo hat, carrying wicker luggage on his back, and holding a khakkhara staff. Since Muhen always wore his hat over his eyes, few people knew his face, Shirounosuke included. Even if, hypothetically, he once saw Muhen's face from a distance, when he saw a figure with Muhen's belongings in the dim light of dawn, he was bound to mistake him for Muhen. The killer took advantage of that and tricked Shirounosuke into letting his guard down, then slew him."

"But, my lord, there is something I yet fail to grasp," Ikeda Izumi cut in.

Izumi was not the type to be so intrusive; he nervously stood in front of Murashige.

"With all due respect, I cannot understand what Your Lordship is saying. Noto is a samurai of virtue, and I cannot believe he would slay Akioka or Muhen or anyone else, but even putting that aside…the culprit slew Akioka *before* he slew Muhen. As such, it cannot be supposed that because the luggage was taken out of the guest room, he posed as Muhen."

Izumi's words gave Noto a second wind; the color came back to his face.

"Th-that's right! He speaks the truth!"

Far from shaken, Murashige simply nodded.

"Indeed, Izumi. The before and the after are actually the reverse."

"The before and the after… It couldn't be… That couldn't be, my lord…"

Izumi's mouth was agape; it seemed he'd been sharp enough to grasp the true sequence of events. Murashige nodded anew.

"Indeed. Since Akioka, who'd been guarding the hermitage, lay dead, and Muhen lay dead inside the hermitage, 'tis only natural we were all under the impression Akioka died first. But the opposite is true. Muhen was killed first, then the culprit disguised himself using Muhen's luggage and slew Akioka."

"But, my lord!" shouted Izumi. "If that is so, how did the culprit enter the hermitage? I heard that hermitage was defended all through the night by the guard."

"Which means there's no other way to think of it. He was already there."

"My liege, if the various whispers I heard are correct, the temple worker looked after the hermitage owner beforehand."

"Which means he was already there before even that."

"Before that..." Izumi shook his head vigorously. "My Lord, that would be absurd! If those are the grounds by which Your Lordship is implicating Noto, then I cannot agree with it. When the temple worker entered the hermitage, he greeted Muhen, and Muhen told him his guest had gone home. And that stands to reason, as I hear that guest was Kori Juuemon, who by then had already taken his leave."

When his name cropped up, Juuemon, who was still pointing one of the hand spears at Noto, budged a little. Yosaku spied his spear tip waver.

Izumi continued.

"Afterward, the temple worker told us he heard Muhen recite the Shingon mantra and smelled incense. Moreover, he also said he saw Muhen wash himself using the lavatory."

Muhen's death was a matter of great importance within the castle, and rumors regarding it flew wildly in all directions before anyone could ascertain their veracity. Yosaku couldn't conceal his surprise at the fact that despite the storm of rumors both true and false, Izumi had grasped the sequence of events to this extent, all while being entrusted with the responsibility of patrolling the castle. Murashige, too, opened his eyes slightly wider.

"Everything you heard is true," he said.

Izumi was confused. "If—if that's the case, then wouldn't that mean Muhen was the only one in the guest room? Is Your Lordship saying that Muhen invited the killer who would go on to take his life inside, but kept that a secret from the temple worker?"

"No, that's not what I'm saying. If he really did have a guest over, Muhen would have said so."

"I do not understand. I do not understand one whit, my liege. If we follow that train of thought, then by what means is Your Lordship saying Noto entered the hermitage?"

"Through the front door," Murashige said casually. "He asked to be led in."

"My Lord!"

Murashige glared, and the commanders, who had been watching nervously, glared as well. Crashes of thunder could be heard.

"Listen to me, Izumi, and all of you! Listen to me, and you will learn what happened at the hermitage on that day, and how Noto killed Muhen. Then you'll know that there's not a soul in Arioka, nay, in all of Hokusetsu who can escape my gaze! On that day, after Muhen withdrew to the hut, Juuemon visited the hermitage, just as Izumi said. After he did what he came to do and took his leave, Juuemon saw the temple worker in town. The temple worker bought some greens and came to the hermitage, then heard from the hermitage's owner that Muhen was to stay there, and that Muhen had a guest."

"My Lord," Kyuuzaemon interrupted, his eyes flared. "That hermitage owner may have been lucid when he was with the Ikeda, but nowadays, he can barely even tell people apart, and he has trouble with any manner of speech."

Murashige replied right away.

"Even the speech-impaired have functioning eyes and ears. It would be foolish to conclude that the man who ordered the temple worker to do his daily chores and who told him to go buy him vegetables to pickle wouldn't even know if the guest came or left. If you wish to know, I will be so kind as to inform you: In the time between when Juuemon took his leave and the temple man arrived, Noto visited that hut before dusk. I can't know what argument they had, but in a fit of madness, Noto killed Muhen! It was only afterward the temple worker arrived. It probably took a moment, if that—when the temple worker asked him about Muhen's guest and said he'd like to give him some sake, Noto decided to pose as Muhen, replying that the guest had gone home, and that he would be busy with his chanting so none ought approach him. He burned incense and recited the sutras so that the temple worker would not come to the guest room, pretending to be a very much alive Muhen. Thinking it over, the incense was also used to mask the smell of the blood. When the temple worker saw a man standing at the lavatory and never doubted it was Muhen, it was of course, because the man was in monk's attire."

Kyuuzaemon looked at Noto. Noto's heart wasn't truly in Buddhist teachings, and he had never once recited a single sutra, but his head of hair was shaven off and he was in priestly attire. Doubt colored Kyuuzaemon's eyes. For a moment, he wondered whether Noto truly might have impersonated Muhen.

It was Noto himself who spoke next.

"Even if the monk the temple worker saw wasn't Muhen, there are any number of men in priestly attire in this castle. Ye can't narrow it down to me!"

There were only two commanders in priestly robes, Noto and another named Kawarabayashi Echigo, who was currently in his sickbed. But if one looked past the commanders, there were a great many who kept their heads shaven. Yosaku didn't have the highest opinion of Noto, but he did think he had a point.

Kyuuzaemon pulled himself together and refused to back down.

"I cannot say I am convinced, either. I don't understand why you can assert so definitively that it wasn't Muhen who recited the sutras or burned the incense."

Murashige was unperturbed.

"I've never once heard of a monk conducting a service in a guest room. There was a Buddha altar in that hermitage. A proper monk would have recited the sutras in the room with the Buddha statue in it. Even more to the point, the temple worker said that what he'd heard coming from the guest room was the Shingon mantra. The concealed and the unconcealed were the reverse, I think you'll agree."

"I..."

Kyuuzaemon was at a loss for words, not comprehending what Murashige was getting at. But Yosaku understood. He'd gone to the hermitage in order to ask Muhen to recite the *nenbutsu* invocation, for that was the prayer that Muhen typically recited. That meant that Muhen's denomination was one of the exoteric Buddhist sects, such as the True Pure Land sect, or perhaps the Ji-shu or the Tendai sects. The Shingon mantra, however, was of the esoteric Shingon sect, with Mount Koya as its headquarters. The only ones among the traveling monks who chanted the Shingon mantra were Mount Koya missionaries.

Following Kyuuzaemon spoke Izumi.

"My Lord, we cannot comprehend the ways of a traveling monk. For all we know, Muhen might have chanted whatever was asked of him."

Murashige nodded. "Muhen was never the type to turn down any request. Perhaps what you're saying is true. But Muhen isn't the key. The temple worker is. That man lived his whole life in a True Pure Land temple. Let's say Muhen memorized sutras outside his sect, but why, then, did the temple worker say Muhen recited the Shingon mantra?"

"Well, I…"

Izumi shook his head feebly.

What was the reason that the man who had heard sutras recited all throughout his years said that what he heard coming from the guest room must have been the Shingon mantra. Yosaku had a feeling he understood why, and he found himself blurting it out.

"It wasn't a sutra…or rather, it was because it wouldn't sound like a sutra."

Murashige raised his eyebrows, not having expected Yosaku to interrupt, and he frowned at him. But Murashige's brow soon reverted to its usual position, and he nodded deeply.

"That must be the reason."

The temple worker assumed that because it was a monk of Muhen's caliber reciting them, they must be noble and exalted sutras—and yet to him, they didn't sound like sutras. As such, he assumed they were a recitation he'd never heard before—such as the esoteric Shingon mantra.

Murashige fixed his eyes on Noto.

"In other words, the culprit was in priestly attire, couldn't so much as mimic true sutra recitation, and is skilled enough to defeat Shirou-nosuke with a practiced hand, however much it was a surprise attack. Noto, do you still plan to play dumb?"

A flash of lightning, followed by the violent rumbling of the thunderclap.

With the spears pointed at him, Noto couldn't even move, and yet he cried bluntly all the same:

"Your Lordship...Your Lordship would arrest *me*, Kawarabayashi Noto, under such strained logic? There is no way ye could ever do such a thing!"

The blood rushed to Noto's face, turning it scarlet.

"I am a man of the highly esteemed Kawarabayashi clan, whose roots lie here in Settsu! You can throw a hundred pieces of circumstantial evidence at me, but I shall never accept that! If ye would execute me, then show us real evidence! Evidence that will convince beyond the shadow of a doubt every single one of the commanders here! All you've said thus far, Your Lordship, is naught but maybes and if so's!"

"With all due respect, my liege!" came a thick voice, which resounded across the citadel. It was the hawkish Nomura Tango, who always asserted the benefits of staying at war at each council. "Kindly hear Noto out! While what Your Lordship says may be reasonable, saying that they necessarily mean Noto was the one who killed Muhen and Shirounosuke is something I cannot agree with!"

Energized by the unexpected show of support, Noto let the spittle fly.

"Your Lordship! At this rate, no one will give the nod! If you insist I killed Muhen and Shirounosuke, then who bore witness to that? If I posed as Muhen, then tell us, who saw it happen?! There are none who saw, none who heard, no rumors that claimed as much; you absolutely cannot arrest me based on that, lord or no lord!"

Yosaku knew the tides were shifting. While what Murashige said made sense, no amount of logic would make up for the lack of a smoking gun. Murashige must have had the drums signal the commanders to convene at the war council in order to judge Noto in front of anyone who was anyone in the castle. But now, Murashige was cornered...

...or at least, one might have thought as much.

Murashige's eyes were slits. There was a sleepiness to his expression, and his tone was calm. "The witness, eh? You want to know the witness, do you?"

Noto's voice was choked, but he somehow managed to affect a smile. "The hermitage owner does not count! He can't speak; we can't know what he saw."

Murashige shook his head.

"It seems you've taken all the rumors to heart. I'm sure you feared one man: the one man who saw your face. I'm sure you were thinking of killing him too. You must have felt relieved when you heard he died. But there's no fooling the heavens."

He signaled something or other with a hand, and the soldier standing next to him grasped his headwear before untying the string and taking the hat off.

"Ah!" cried Yosaku.

Standing before them was the slightly hunchbacked temple worker, his hair speckled with gray and an uneasy look on his face.

Noto recoiled. "It cannot be! I *saw* his body tossed outside the castle! That corpse…"

"This castle has plenty of corpses to use," Murashige said nonchalantly. "If you want to know, I'll be magnanimous enough to tell you. That corpse was a foot soldier who shirked his duty guarding the gunpowder storehouse." He faced the temple worker. "Now answer carefully. On the day Muhen died, who was the man you saw?"

The temple worker was clearly unaccustomed to being in such a place. He was surrounded by high-ranking samurai he normally wouldn't even be allowed to look in the eyes, shivering as though the dozens of stern stares were giving him a bout of ague. Nonetheless, the temple worker extended a finger and pointed.

"It was that gentleman."

Naturally, he was pointing at Kawarabayashi Noto.

Another flash of lightning, and another crash of thunder. It was closer now.

"Now, then," said Murashige, "it seems I can finally ask you some questions. *Why did you kill Muhen?* is not among them. In this age of war, a samurai slaying a monk is nothing out of the ordinary. If you had simply said you killed Muhen because he was acting suspiciously, no one would have batted an eye. And yet you tried to hide it through trickery."

Yosaku could sense the commanders realizing for themselves how odd that was. However beloved Muhen was, resorting to trickery to hide his killing and going as far as killing an ally on top of that was not the behavior of a true samurai.

After pausing for effect, Murashige continued:

"Tell us, Noto. Why did you visit Muhen?"

A lump formed in Noto's throat.

"Why did you visit the hermitage wearing a *kasaya* to begin with? That *kasaya* is why all you had to do was pilfer the hat, the staff, and the luggage to pose as the traveling monk. What's more, you didn't even bring a horse or any attendants. My guard can attest that no horse was fastened outside the hermitage, and that there was no horse tender. For what purpose were you behaving so beneath your station?"

"......"

"You won't tell us? Then allow me." The glint in Murashige's eyes turned sharper. "There's only one reason a commander in a castle under siege would ever meet with someone from the outside in secret."

The commanders murmured among themselves. They all thought the same thing—there was indeed just one possible reason.

"Noto. You're communicating with the Oda."

Yosaku knew the truth behind Muhen.

Why did Muhen travel to Arioka Castle through a warzone? How would a mere traveling monk make it past Oda's forces many times over without getting halted or questioned?

Muhen could only have been a secret messenger for the Oda.

He had been ordered to pay Arioka Castle a visit and meet with the commander with whom Oda had contact. Muhen was the kind of monk who did whatever one asked of him. One could ask him to perform the last rites over the soon-to-die, or to recite sutras for the deceased, or to listen to rumors of a far-off land, and he would never pull a sour face.

Yosaku wasn't aware that Murashige had told Muhen to deliver a letter for him, or that Muhen accepted that request. He did know that Muhen must have been asked by the Oda to go talk to the lord of Arioka, and that he accepted *that* request.

"Why you!"

Noto drew his sword in the same breath. The guard members who surrounded Noto pointed the tips of their hand spears his way. Noto slashed at them sideways, and the guard stepped away, cowed by his fervor.

"Damn you, Murashige!" he howled. "How dare you dupe me! How dare you…how dare you *shame* me so, in front of everyone! Don't push your luck! Without the backing of us Settsu-born, you'd still be a stooge of the Ikeda! Yet here you are, dragging us into a losing war! As if there can be any doubt whether 'tis the Araki or the Oda that have a future!"

Noto scowled at his surroundings, his sword raised overhead. His eyes were not on the guard members encircling him, but on the commanders watching things unfold from outside that ring.

"Murashige! You're not going to call me a coward for communicating with Oda, I trust?! I know the truth! I read the secret letter! I know what ye told Muhen to do for you, and the truth will out! Everyone here, listen well!"

Noto lifted his sword high, high up to the heavens.

"Murashige, he—!"

Lightning. Thunder.

Yosaku didn't know what happened. For a while, he didn't even realize he'd fallen to the ground.

Yosaku got back up with difficulty; for a fleeting moment, he thought he was on the battlefield, for the thick stench of burning that he'd experienced in combat was hanging in the air. What was it that was burning? Vegetation? A home? A person…? As Yosaku's dazed eyes reverted to normal, the sight he was greeted with wasn't fire. It was the other commanders, also on the floor, and Murashige standing next to Kawarabayashi Noto.

"Noto, you bastard," Murashige said to no one in particular. "You went and died."

He looked up at the skies. Large drops started drizzling down, and then the rain turned torrential.

Another flash of lightning. Yosaku couldn't even keep his eyes open.

12

Before the end of that day, Kawarabayashi Noto's residence was burned to the ground.

Noto had been struck by a bolt of lightning. There were no other casualties or wounded. Noto's frantic suicide charge had caused the guard to move out of the way, making Noto to be the only one to die.

It was the head of the Kawarabayashi clan, Kawarabayashi Echigo, who burned Noto's residence. Despite his illness, he commanded his soldiers to chop off the heads of all Noto's vassals. Then he apologized to Murashige for the misconduct of a member of his clan. Before the building was set ablaze, guard members led by Kori Juuemon entered the residence and recovered Muhen's wicker luggage. The utterly priceless Torasaru was found, and the lid of the box had never even been opened.

"My Lord," said Juuemon when he returned Torasaru to Murashige. "I do not understand why Noto killed Muhen and Shirounosuke."

Murashige didn't reply.

Noto had been communicating with the Oda through Muhen as an intermediary. Noto must have spent every day extremely anxious, wondering if and when he would be found out. When Muhen was summoned by Murashige, Noto was likely unable to go on without learning what Muhen and Murashige discussed—and whether Noto himself had come up. Did Muhen answer Noto's questions?

Under normal circumstances, he almost certainly would have. However, he had, on that day, been entrusted with the safe transport of a peerless treasure. He would have been on tenterhooks, his behavior different from usual.

Noto and Muhen's back-and-forth was an exchange between a traitor and a secret messenger. One wrong word, and the secret messenger was as good as dead.

Murashige suspected that Noto pressed Muhen to divulge what was told to him in confidence, and when Muhen said he couldn't, things spiraled out of control and Noto killed Muhen, searching his body for proof that Noto himself was in league with Oda and thereby finding the secret letter sewn into his collar. The reason Noto didn't take the letter was because it didn't contain any proof that he was a mole. While he was examining Muhen's body, time passed, and the temple worker entered the hut, after which the guard stood watch over all four sides of the building.

Noto couldn't have known that the guard had been dispatched to protect Muhen. He must have wondered why they were there. Yet Shirounosuke had greeted Noto cordially:

"Muhen, are you departing now? Our lord has ordered us to escort you to the gates."

Then Shirounosuke turned his back to Noto. Noto must have thought that was his one chance.

Murashige didn't mention any of this.

He couldn't tell Juuemon to put himself in the shoes of a traitor.

A great many in Arioka were surprised and delighted to hear that Muhen's killer, one Kawarabayashi Noto, had been struck by lightning, and rumors permeated the castle:

"See? The Buddha protects Arioka Castle."

"Behold the grisly death of that infidel who laid a hand on Muhen!"

"The Buddha has meted out justice; 'tis truly divine retribution."

Occasionally, those who reveled in the Buddha's punishment peeked at the tower in the citadel—if Noto, who had slain Muhen, received the appropriate punishment, then how about the Lord of Settsu, who had failed to protect him?

That night, Murashige had Torasaru displayed in the drawing room. The winds had blown away the thunderclouds, and it was a cool night illuminated by the faint light of the moon. The treasure Murashige had thought was lost had returned to him. Murashige couldn't stop staring at its exquisite coloring.

Behind Murashige was Chiyoho.

"My liege. It ended up safe and sound, I see."

Murashige nodded slightly, his eyes still on Torasaru.

When Murashige had been about to have Noto arrested, Araki Kyuu-zaemon, Ikeda Izumi, and Nomura Tango had sprung to Noto's defense. But that just meant those three were the only ones who had stepped before Murashige, who understood that most of the commanders who had been staring from afar hadn't agreed with him.

Had the whole affair happened in the late autumn of the year prior, although the commanders may not have been able to swallow Murashige's logic back then, either, they would have thought Noto must have worked some kind of wicked act because Murashige was rebuking him. They wouldn't have doubted Murashige. But then winter and spring came and passed, with no sign of the Mouri ever actually arriving. It was clear as day that the war was not progressing as Murashige would have liked, and the commanders no longer assumed that whatever Murashige said must have had some truth to it.

It was as Kanbei had mentioned—not one person in Arioka Castle understood or appreciated the true meaning of Murashige's words. With the exception, that is, of Kanbei himself.

Murashige paid no mind to the drooling drivel of some prisoner. But even if Kanbei spoke the truth—even if Murashige was alone, at least Torasaru was back by his side. That alone had Murashige deeply satisfied.

Muhen may have died, but that didn't mean the negotiations with Koreto Mitsuhide, Lord of Hyuuga were necessarily hopeless. Murashige had but to appoint another person as messenger and send this treasure to Tanba. He needed the peace talks to progress before Tanba fell, and at all costs. And yet…

You would have me relinquish it again?

That was what Murashige kept asking himself in the moonlight.

Murashige continued staring at Torasaru. Having to let go of it once before had felt like ripping out a living tree.

On the eighth day of the sixth month, the Hatano brothers of Yakami Castle were executed via crucifixion at Azuchi.

Koreto Mitsuhide, Hyuuga-no-kami, captured most of Tanba. No historical text contains anything about Mitsuhide facilitating any peace talks for Arioka Castle.

Chapter IV

Alone Against the Setting Sun

1

When the night breeze started feeling a little cooler, the peoples who inhabited the lands breathed a sigh of relief:

The harvest season's still a ways off, so I can't let my guard down just yet, but I managed to survive another year by the skin of my teeth.

However, this year, the people confined inside Arioka Castle were an exception, and not in the good sense.

There were fields within the castle grounds, but the rice and greens harvested there were far from enough to feed the five thousand or so soldiers, let alone the rest of the populace. Since the beginning of the war, new fields had been opened up all over, but those places weren't particularly suited for agriculture, and they yielded a meager amount of vegetables. Inevitably, the amount of provisions brought into the castle before the war became linked to the number of days the people of the castle had left to live.

Every autumn, the villages reaped rice plants and turned them into edible rice, which was then sold for money. The samurai collected the money, used it for weapons, temple donations, or tea utensils, and bought rice. In villages, rice was converted into money, and samurai paid money to buy rice, so wholesale rice dealers could turn their trade even when profits were low. Recently, however, the all-important movement of money had grown stunted. The supply of the Chinese coins the people typically used had decreased, and only cracked or chipped coins were circulating.

That was true in Settsu, which was relatively close to the capital, which meant the shortage of coin was even worse in the Bando region and other parts besides, and some clans ended up collecting the land tax in rice form.

If the shortage of money doesn't abate, the Araki clan will eventually have no choice but to do likewise...

Murashige had often thought about such things since he founded the Araki family. But this year, those thoughts didn't even cross his mind. One of the duties of the samurai class was to examine the rice crop and make allowances for wind and water damage to determine the annual tribute owed them, but that was futile now. There was no traffic in or out of town, and all the villages of Hokusetsu were controlled by the Oda. This year, not a single cent would enter the Araki clan coffers.

On a sunny day late into the seventh month, Murashige was patrolling the castle grounds. Semiarmored and mounted atop a horse, he was accompanied by a horse tender and a spear bearer, as well as the guard members in front and behind. During such occasions, the swordmaster Akioka Shirounosuke and Itami Ichirouzaemon, who was familiar with the situation in Itami, often accompanied their lord, but they were no longer of this world. The people who accompanied Murashige on that day included Inui Sukesaburou, a man with the strength of ten men.

Now that the Bon festival and the service for suffering spirits were over, the temple district was deserted and silent save for the distant chanting of the *nenbutsu* invocation. When Murashige rode his horse to a corner with rows of shops, he and his party were the only ones outside in the sultry heat. The roads were blocked by the Oda, cutting off traffic, and all the merchants with any sense had left Itami a long time ago. The shops and merchants' homes that remained had nothing to buy or sell; the people there were simply eating every scrap of the rice that'd been saved up in order to survive. By this point, even small skirmishes had stopped cropping up in town, and as there was no need to repair armor or reforge swords, the pounding of blacksmiths' hammers could not be heard.

The silence was such that one might think ten thousand people had died out. All that was audible was the *clop, clop* of Murashige's horse, the clanging of the guard members' armor, and the cries of cicadas. The people of Itami didn't move an inch, and they remained silent, as though they were waiting for summer or for the war to end. No, not waiting— the people were in hiding. Spotting Murashige from afar, they were holding their breaths, not daring to come out, for they knew not what hardship would befall them if the lord caught sight of them. And Murashige knew that.

The group eventually passed through the town houses and headed to the south side of the castle, to Fort Hiyodorizuka. Amid the fields and wilderness, one could see the isolated thatched hut where Muhen had been murdered not long ago. Arioka Castle was vast, and only the inner citadel was protected by a moat and sturdy stone walls. The outer walls were fortified with nothing more than wood fencing and dry moats, with wooden planks for the most strategic points. Through the fencing, Murashige looked outside the castle. Amid the lush summer grass, there were still bamboo shields left behind by the attacking army. Bamboo shields were used by the attackers to block arrows. They were tools to aid rank-and-file soldiers in pushing through and approaching the castle.

Sukesaburou noticed that his lord had stopped his horse.

"My lord, what is it?"

"...Nothing. Let's move on."

Murashige's eyes fell back on the road ahead; he saw several foot soldiers dressed in rental armor walking in Murashige's direction, not having noticed Murashige yet. When Sukesaburou shouted and heralded his lord, the foot soldiers hastened to the side of the road and prostrated themselves hurriedly. Murashige was about to ride his horse past the prostrate foot soldiers, when he noticed that there was a man among them with a different mien. He was a seedy-looking man, dressed in shabby clothes and without even a dagger on his person. He was neither a samurai nor a foot soldier. The foot soldiers seem to be guarding the unarmed man.

"You there."

When Murashige called out to them, the foot soldiers bowed their heads even more deeply, as if they saw death flash before their eyes.

"Who is that man? I permit you to speak."

The foot soldiers exchanged glances. One of them replied, "He is a *geshinin*, my lord."

I knew it, thought Murashige.

The killing of someone in one's in-group was an unforgivable act, and that went for commoners as it did for samurai. If one person was killed, they had to be avenged by killing another, and if two people were killed, they had to kill two themselves. Those who did not demand blood in kind were mocked as cowards and viewed as weak, which would only invite more calamity. However, if the revenge continued indefinitely, it would be counterproductive, weakening the clans and villages they were meant to protect. An ancient method of justice first practiced in the Muromachi period recompensed the victim's side by having the killer's side offer up a person as a form of apology. That person was not the one who killed the victim, but rather a substitute or scapegoat, and that person was called a *geshinin*.

Murashige knew that if a man who didn't look like a noble was escorted by foot soldiers, he was almost certainly a *geshinin*, and where there was a *geshinin*, there was a conflict that'd led to a killing—yet Murashige had not heard tell of any such conflict recently.

"Who is sending whom this *geshinin*?"

"My lord," the foot soldier began respectfully. "He is sent by Nomura Tango to Ikeda Izumi."

"Tango and Izumi, you say? Give me the details."

The foot soldier put his forehead to the ground.

"Pray forgive me, my liege. I was simply ordered to escort him. I know naught else."

Murashige glared at the man's head from atop his steed before pulling the reins and returning whence he came. The members of the guard looked puzzled, but in their loyalty, they merely continued to defend Murashige's front and back without a word.

2

Two days passed. It was a rainy evening, and Koori Juuemon, the head of the lord's guard, requested an audience with Murashige, who entered the reception hall after letting Juuemon in and ordering everyone else to leave.

The pelting of the rain was quite loud. Juuemon was soaked, his shin guards and gauntlets still on. Water was dripping from him onto the wooden floor. Murashige had ordered Juuemon to find out the details that'd led to Nomura Tango's sending a *geshinin*. As always, Juuemon fulfilled his mission flawlessly, in rain as in sunshine.

"Raise your head and come closer."

Juuemon obeyed, using his fists to pull himself closer while remaining seated cross-legged on the floor.

"Now tell me."

"I have pinned down the story, my liege."

"Speak it."

"Yes, my lord. The incident happened four days ago, during the distribution of provisions. The group leader of Ikeda Izumi's retainers used the rank-and-file soldiers to carry the provisions to Fort Hiyodorizuka, and upon trying to distribute five *go* of rice to each man in accordance with military law, the foot soldiers of Nomura Tango aired their grievances, complaining that five *go* be not enough and demanding to be given more."

Five *go* of rice a day was close to the minimum amount given to foot soldiers, and it wasn't uncommon to give out double that amount while in battle. Murashige didn't think it odd that Ikeda Izumi, who was in charge of the weapons, armor, and provisions, would reduce the amount distributed during a siege, given the future was so uncertain. But Murashige also understood why the soldiers' dissatisfaction with five *go* would build over time.

"The quarrel became a full-on brawl. A young samurai among

Tango's retainers drew his sword and killed the group leader. Nomura Tango admitted the wrongdoing of his retainer and promptly sent a *geshinin*."

"And Izumi?"

"I hear he sent the *geshinin* back."

That was another aspect of the old *geshinin* practice. The *geshinin* was either killed or sent back alive without further incident.

"Yesterday, Nomura Tango and Ikeda Izumi sat opposite each other at the residence of Araki Kyuuzaemon. Kyuuzaemon served as the mediator, and both attended bearing no ill will."

Murashige looked sullen.

"Kyuuzaemon did?"

Araki Kyuuzaemon was Murashige's trusty chief vassal. They had met face-to-face and exchanged words that very day. And yet Kyuuzaemon had never told him that there had been a quarrel between Tango and Izumi.

The custom was for the lord of a domain to decide which side of an argument occurring within that domain was right or wrong. It was already established that if there was bloodshed and Murashige wasn't notified, both sides were subject to punishment. Of course, the idea that Murashige oversaw all things was just the public position. In actuality, it was often the case that the parties in question came to an agreement. Murashige couldn't claim that Tango and Izumi settling their discord by falling back on the *geshinin* solution constituted an injustice that violated the rules… But regardless, Murashige wouldn't overlook this.

"'Tis following a similar momentum," muttered Murashige, frowning.

"My lord. A similar momentum?"

Murashige nodded.

"Indeed… I speak of the momentum leading to our banishing the Lord of Chikugo, Katsumasa."

Juuemon turned stiff with a start. The rain kept pelting the ground noisily.

When Murashige's former master, Katsumasa, Lord of Chikugo, became the head of the Ikeda clan, a dispute arose. In order to become the head, he'd killed a key retainer who refused to accept him as his leader. The Miyoshi clan, the shogunate clan, and later the Oda clan were always reaching for Hokusetsu, and Katsumasa, who was in Hokusetsu, chose the Oda, surrendering to them and ably maintaining his clan. When Oda Nobunaga was betrayed by Azai Nagamasa, Lord of Bizen, casting him into a desperate predicament, Katsumasa was one of the generals who saved the entire Oda army from ruin, serving as a rear guard.

In time, however, the hearts of the Ikeda clan's commanders drifted away from Katsumasa. Eventually, he was banished by his own vassals—by Murashige and Kyuuzaemon, among others—and died in the grips of despondency.

"Loath as I am to gainsay Your Lordship," said Juuemon, dismay in his voice, "I do not believe that shall happen. While I agree that failing to report a casualty to Your Lordship is wrong, I suspect he was trying to save Your Lordship the trouble. Nomura Tango and Ikeda Izumi are retainers whose loyalty to you is second to none, and needless to say, that goes for Kyuuzaemon as well."

"Two days ago, I paid Fort Hiyodorizuka a visit," began Murashige, as though Juuemon hadn't said anything. "I looked outside the castle to find the summer grass overgrown and the Oda forces' bamboo shields undiscarded... Do you understand what I'm getting at, Juuemon?"

"My lord...I know not who is in charge of that fencing," Juuemon replied cautiously, "but I believe that to be rather lax on their part."

Needless to say, the foremost way to defend a castle was to prevent the attacking army from getting any closer. To do that, one had to detect the enemy quickly and rain arrows and bullets on them. It took longer to spot the enemy where the summer grass was tall and overgrown, and if the bamboo shields were ignored, the attacking army would simply use them again. The forces of the castle had to cut that grass and destroy the tools of their offensive. If they did it under the cover of the darkness of the morning and evening, it would not be terribly difficult. Murashige had repeatedly ordered his commanders to clear the view in preparation for battle.

"It is not the castle's defenses that are too lax. 'Tis their willingness to follow my order to protect it diligently."

Just like back then, thought Murashige. Before Katsumasa was banished, the repairs of the ramparts lagged, there wasn't enough rental armor to go around, the horses were skinny, and the summer grass was uncut and uncontrolled. Taken individually, they were too small to spell treachery. Taken together, that treachery was assured.

Katsumasa may not have been a general for the ages, but he was no fool, either. He ordered advance preparations be made when an inadequacy was spotted, but he didn't get into the weeds, leaving matters in the hands of his commanders. He admonished his commanders day in, day out to be ever diligent, but no one respected him enough to listen.

Here in Arioka, the fact that the summer grass had been allowed to grow tall and the fact that Kyuuzaemon hadn't reported to Murashige about the quarrel were indeed trifling matters, but it was also true that such trifling matters hadn't occurred until recently.

"In the past month, no, in the past month and a half, my commanders have grown careless and stopped reporting to me. Upon reflection, it started with that day."

The day Muhen and Akioka Shirounosuke were killed at the hut in the south of the castle. The day Kawarabayashi Noto, their killer, died due to an unforeseen twist of fate.

Murashige's physique and personality were both akin to an immovable boulder. He was a man of few words, and he rarely ever flew into a rage. In this age of all-engulfing war, he was an exceedingly easy general to serve. Nonetheless, in his hesitation, Juuemon swallowed what he was about to say. For someone who was a mere group leader to object to his general, he had to be prepared to die for it. Telling himself that he was the only one at the moment who could remonstrate his lord, he tensed his stomach and spoke his mind:

"With all due respect, my lord. Given the length of this war, a little laxness here and there is to be expected, and if Your Lordship commands it, all the officers and men shall obey with due diligence. We retainers of the Araki are resolved to support Your Lordship to the end. Pray do not doubt us."

Murashige didn't reply to Juuemon's brave back talk right away, and the sound of the rain alone filled the reception hall. Liquid dripped from Juuemon's chin. Juuemon didn't know whether it was rainwater or his own cold sweat.

Murashige exhaled. His expression wasn't one of wrath.

"Juuemon. Do you think I've succumbed to madness and groundless suspicion?"

"Of course not, my lord. I would never."

For a short while, Murashige stared down at Juuemon, who was prostrating himself, until he suddenly retrieved something from inside the breast of his clothes.

"I have my reasons for thinking something changed that day. Look at this."

In the palm of Murashige's hand lay a small bullet. Juuemon strained his eyes to spy it, though he was a bit far removed.

"A bullet from a gun...is it?"

"'Tis. Remember that day. The day Kawarabayashi Noto died."

Juuemon recalled that moment. He remembered the giant columns of dark clouds, the far-off thunder, the humidity.

On that day, Juuemon ordered the guard to surround Kawarabayashi Noto with hand spears pointed and, at Murashige's signal, either capture him or, failing that, kill him. Murashige's plan to divide the generals by the bridge to the inner citadel went as expected, and Noto was easily isolated from the commanders, who were made to walk to the citadel in small groups. In the face of Murashige's logic, Kyuuzaemon and Tango had been at a loss for words, and when the temple worker appeared, Noto's being in the wrong was obvious to everyone. Cornered, Noto had pulled out his sword and raised it skyward, shouting something or other...

Juuemon didn't remember anything after that. It was only later he learned that a lightning bolt had taken Kawabayashi Noto's life and had knocked back the members of the guard who had surrounded Noto.

A month and a half had passed since then, and the summer heat had abated, the raining turning much colder.

"You of the guard fell down, and I was the first one to approach Noto."

"Yes, my lord. I do think of it as a failure on our part."

"I'm not blaming you for that. You were simply close to the lightning, and I was farther away, that's all. I checked to see if Noto yet drew breath. It was then that I noticed this lead bullet."

He stared at the bullet before continuing:

"This bullet landed right next to Noto. It sank two *sun* into the ground, and when I dug it out, it was still hot."

"In that case…," said Juuemon, scarcely able to believe it, "Your Lordship is saying that before the lightning struck, someone shot at Noto."

"I know not if the gunshot came before or after the lightning strike," Murashige replied, gripping the bullet. "But yes, someone shot at Noto."

Juuemon grew animated despite himself. "But why?!"

By contrast, Murashige seemed listless.

"I know not. At a guess, 'tis the work of someone who found Noto being alive to be an inconvenience."

"Noto was in league with Oda. It follows that this was the work of someone else who is also in league with him."

"In all probability. But what we can be sure of is that someone sought to prevent me from executing Noto."

Juuemon finally realized what had Murashige so worried.

As a rule, within a samurai clan, the only one who could pass judgment and carry out a sentence on a samurai was the leader. Since Kawarabayashi Noto was acting suspiciously, only Murashige could bring his crimes to light and punish him accordingly, and that was the way it had to be. Shooting Noto from the sidelines while Murashige was questioning Noto about his crimes was infringing on Murashige's right as the head of the domain. That was treason.

The reception hall grew dimmer and dimmer. Perhaps due to how wet he was, Juuemon felt the shivers.

"There's a secret betrayer here in Arioka Castle. A fine fellow sharpening his blade in the shadows. This bullet is the one trace he so thoughtlessly left behind. Juuemon, I refuse to repeat Katsumasa's mistakes. I'm the only one who can defend this castle."

Murashige got to his feet. He then handed the bullet to Juuemon, who bowed his head yet deeper.

"I want you to find out who shot Noto on that day, who ordered it, and what their objective is. Investigate whatever you can."

Murashige lifted the bullet as though it were a piece of gold.

"Yes, my lord."

"Can you do it?"

"I can, my lord."

As always, Juuemon responded without hesitation or indecision.

Yet in his heart of hearts, Juuemon wasn't certain he actually could accomplish what he was ordered to. A month and a half had passed since Noto's death. There were probably a lot of things that had been forgotten or lost. Juuemon could only wonder why his lord had waited a month and a half before issuing him that order.

3

Several days passed. The changing of the phase of the moon signaled the arrival of the eighth month, which in the year 1579, or Tensho 7, corresponded to the ninth month of the Julian calendar used by the Christian missionaries. Summer was over.

In the eleventh month of the year prior, when the Araki clan decided to leave the Oda to join the Mouri, the daily review council was brimming with a peculiar nervous energy that could be likened to a cold fever. When the summoning drums were sounded, the commanders, some in plain clothes and some in armor, made every effort to outfit themselves, rushed to the castle tower, and leaned forward lest they miss a single word out of Murashige's mouth. It was like a new dawn; both young and old were so excited to take on the formidable Oda clan that it manifested as a redness in their faces. Ten months had passed, and too many things had changed since those days.

Nowadays, the commanders who assembled at the tower didn't care about how dirty their armor or how frayed their *jinbaori* surcoats were.

Their beards were long, and their faces were covered in dust. Most of
the commanders were hanging their heads, waiting for the end of the
council; some made no effort to hide their drowsiness. There were also
many commanders who weren't in attendance to begin with, as the
number who were unable to serve due to illness had increased. Since
Kitagawara Yosaku made the case for surrendering, he had not appeared
in public, probably because he came to feel his life was in danger. And
the statements exchanged during the council had not changed at all in
the past ten or so days.

"Their path overland may be blocked, but they still have the sea. If
they use Kobayakawa's or Murakami's navy, it wouldn't even take the
Mouri a day or two to come into Amagasaki as the rear guard. That
the Mouri haven't come means they had a change of heart. Actually,
no, they planned for us to be the shield diverting the spears of the Oda
from the very beginning. It was a mistake to place our trust in those
upstarts. We should forget about the Mouri, who will never come, and
show the Oda how gloriously we can fight. That will do us honor as
samurai!"

Speaking so passionately was Nomura Tango. Murashige's eyes
looked as sleepy as usual, but even so, he was giving Tango a once-over.

This long and grueling siege had done nothing to change Tango's
rigidity—his belief that if he but defended his allies and killed his enemies, everything in the world would go smoothly. Could Tango be aiming to overthrow Murashige? The social rank of Tango's clan was high,
and he had military power to boot, enough to supplant him. However,
Tango was the husband of Murashige's younger sister, which was almost
too close for him to be able to turn coat. Besides, Tango was not a man
with enough subtlety of acting or signaling to be outwardly obeying
Murashige but plotting against him behind closed doors. Or had he
been *pretending* to be that way all along?

Next to speak was Ikeda Izumi, who wore a pensive look.

"As Tango said, the Mouri are clearly no longer on our side. However, we do not have enough troops to wage battle by ourselves, and on
top of that, the Oda have already finished constructing branch castles.
If you ask me, taking on a castle containing many with only a small

number of troops honors not the warriors; it only reeks of desperation. What we need to do is work out a plan, and our first priority is to gain more allies."

Izumi hadn't performed any particularly glorious deeds since even before the siege, but he was good at working out ways to do things and was possessed of a strong sense of duty. As he was in charge of every-thing from weapons and provisions to bamboo and trees, there was not one commander in all the castle who had no interaction with Izumi. If Izumi said that their future was shaky with Murashige as their leader, many would agree. Could Izumi be eyeing Murashige's position? He didn't seem like the kind who'd take that gamble, but who could say for sure...?

Araki Kyuuzaemon looked stern and solemn.

"We said we sided with the Mouri, but that's not true. It was a mistake to count on clans that cook up so many schemes, such as the Mouri and the Ukita. The one we have sided with is Hongan-ji, subduers of the barbarians. Hongan-ji has been supporting us for nine years. We should just stand firm until the winds of the world shift direction. Takeda Shingen defeated Tokugawa, but then he fell ill... Even Nobu-naga is mortal, and his days are as numbered as anyone's."

As of late, Kyuuzaemon had counseled nothing but wait, wait, wait, which was more than fine by most of the commanders, given it meant they didn't have to do anything. Could *he* be aiming to turn against Murashige? While Kyuuzaemon was now using the Araki name, he was originally a member of the Ikeda clan. If Kyuuzaemon planned to chase out Murashige and restore the Ikeda clan to glory, more than a few would follow him. No one aroused Murashige's suspicions more than him. However, from what he could tell, Kyuuzaemon wasn't quite capa-ble enough as a commander to head a clan. Was it even possible for Kyuuzaemon to deceive Murashige and turn against him?

"What are you all saying?!" shouted Nakanishi Shinpachirou. "Work-ing together with the Mouri and destroying that cur Nobunaga here in Arioka Castle is a grand, far-reaching plan our lord crafted. Isn't it our duty to believe in that plan and strive to see it done? I believe in our lord. I believe in the Lord of Settsu. And because I believe in him,

I believe that the Mouri will come! For all we know, the Mouri could be arriving in great throngs tomorrow, so what in blazes are ye saying?!"

The council fell silent. No one reproached Shinpachirou, the newcomer, for his reckless remarks, nor did anyone agree with them. Going by the atmosphere, they were rather done with him. Murashige looked at Shinpachirou's face, which was flushed red; he didn't think the man had it in him to hatch a scheme to overthrow him. *Even if Shinpachirou has such ambitions, none would take his side...which doesn't then mean Shinpachirou has no sinister designs, of course.*

That day's deliberation was the same as the day before. The battle had reached a stalemate, and the commanders had nothing more to add. However, Murashige did notice that there were more and more blaming the Mouri for their perfidy.

It was Murashige who'd decided to leave the Oda and join the Mouri. Criticizing the Mouri for their unfaithfulness was akin to criticizing Murashige for a lapse in judgment. Were those commanders unaware of that? He had to wonder whether they *were* aware, and they were just telling off Murashige in a veiled manner.

Murashige honestly didn't know which it was.

Once the meeting was over, Murashige returned to his residence, escorted there by his guard.

Whenever Murashige appeared in front of his commanders, he wore his gauntlets and shin guards. As it wasn't a place where arrows or bullets could fly, wearing a helmet and body armor was a bit grandiose, but it was the samurai way to don a certain amount of armor just in case. In the past, he'd thought wearing gauntlets to a mere review council was on the theatrical side, but these days, Murashige started wearing chain mail under his clothes. His attendants seemed to think that this was to ward off a potential Oda assassin, but in fact, it was to ward off potential traitors within the castle.

Little wonder, then, how deep the sense of relief was when he could decompress at his residence. With the help of an attendant, Murashige removed his armor, cleansed himself using water carried there in a washbasin, and headed for the Buddha statue hall.

He crossed the square corridor and opened the sliding doors leading into the dimly lit wooden hall to find Chiyoho chanting the *nenbutsu* invocation there. Behind Chiyoho, a lady attendant was sitting on one knee, bowing her head as soon as she realized that it was Murashige who had opened the door. Chiyoho, meanwhile, didn't stop chanting. Murashige closed the door behind him and simply listened, not even sitting down first.

Murashige's silence must have made the lady attendant fretful.

"Lady O-Dashi…," she said softly to Chiyoho.

At that, Chiyoho stopped chanting abruptly. Her eyes still fixed on the statue, she asked, "What is it?"

"His Lordship…"

Chiyoho turned her head and looked over her shoulder. Despite the length of the siege, her face looked young, without any gauntness. Her eyes opened wide, and she moved out of the way so Murashige could sit before the statue.

"My lord. I do apologize."

"No need. 'Tis nothing." Murashige sat in front of Chiyoho instead of the statue. "You're praying so fervently. Are you making a wish or some such?"

Murashige was just making conversation; he wasn't expecting her to sink into silence. Finally, she spoke, her voice razor-thin:

"'Tis in memoriam," she said. "I'm praying for their happiness in the next life."

"Whose?"

"All those who perished in this war."

"Then you're praying for dozens—nay, hundreds."

"Yes."

Murashige looked at the statue. It was a seated figure of Shakyamuni Buddha, made by a Nara sculptor of Buddhist imagery.

The daughter of a Buddhist priest in Osaka Hongan-ji, Chiyoho herself was a zealous True Pure Land believer. Which was why Murashige thought it strange.

"I thought True Pure Land believers do not pray for the dead?" he said. Her sect didn't recognize the efficacy of prayer. According to its teachings, only Amitabha Tathagata could bring salvation to the dead, and no amount of prayer could help oneself or anyone else.

Chiyoho averted her gaze.

"Yes, I believe so... And yet while I hesitate to say this before Your Lordship..." She shrank a little. "I could not stand to sit around and do nothing while the castle suffers. If my father saw me, he would surely scold me."

Chiyoho, a follower of True Pure Land Buddhism, was praying for the dead in front of the statue of Shakyamuni Buddha, which flew in the face of the logic of her sect. Chiyoho seemed to be deeply ashamed of her behavior. However, when the faces of those who'd died over the course of the war sprang to Murashige's mind, he couldn't help but view Chiyoho's memorial service as noble.

There was Mori Kahei, who gave his life charging at Oda forces as his final gift to his lord. There was Itami Ichirouzaemon, who, while bloody and dying, requested patronage for his son. There was Akioka Shirounosuke, who was the best swordmaster in the castle but got slashed from behind before he could draw his sword. There was Abe Jinen, who kept crying that he wished to go to the Pure Land in the West. There was Otsu Denjuurou, whose face had been barely visible in the starlight. There was Hori Yatarou, who died while wearing little but a loincloth approaching Murashige. There was Muhen, who was beloved by all despite working with both sides of the war. There was Kawarabayashi Noto, who got struck by lightning upon drawing his sword and crying that this was the end of the line. There were the countless soldiers on both sides who perished in battle. And then there were all the citizens who fled to the mountains only to be cut down for it.

"With due respect to your father, I do not understand him. I'm happy you're praying for the people of my Arioka."

Chiyoho looked as though she'd been struck in the chest. She gently put her hands on the floor and hung her head.

"Your Lordship is too kind."

"Are you finished with your *nenbutsu*?"

"I do not have a set number of recitations to reach."

"I see. I'm not well versed with True Pure Land teachings."

She took her hands off the floor, raised her head, and smiled.

It was then something dawned on Murashige. There was something she had never asked him, despite having every opportunity to do so since coming into the fold, or at least since Murashige decided to break off from the Oda, or even since the beginning of the siege. And wasn't now a great opportunity as well? They were nine months into the siege, and the officers and men were getting utterly tired of this. Moreover, someone was now aiming to take Murashige's place.

Murashige looked at the statue.

"Chiyoho. You've never asked me to try reciting the *nenbutsu* myself."

"Indeed, my lord."

"Is there a reason for that?"

Chiyoho's eyes betrayed her confusion. She hardly ever spoke of her own opinions or ideas. When she was asked directly, she always seemed to wonder whether she should reply.

"Whatever it may be, it bothers me not," Murashige said to encourage her.

Chiyoho still seemed hesitant, but she spoke, albeit timidly.

"My father did, of course, instruct me to advise you to chant the *nenbutsu* whenever I had the chance. However, when I came to Ikeda, and when I moved to Itami, and I saw Your Lordship's duties, I figured that even if I were to implore you, that would just make ye think of it as a burden. As such, I never brought it up until now."

"A burden? What do you mean?"

"Well, if Your Lordship is asking…," she said, her voice clear. "Your Lordship is the leader of the Araki clan. The Buddha promises salvation for the powerless and protection of this life for the warrior clans of the horse and the bow. A general like Your Lordship looks to the Buddha for military tactics. I believe anything that would hinder your strategizing must be a nuisance to you."

Murashige felt like laughing. She had a point there. When the clan leader chose a sect, he could not afford to think solely of the ostensible benefits that, in so doing, he would gain in this life or the next.

Takayama Dariyo's former lord, Wada Koremasa, Lord of Iga, had
many followers of Christianity among his vassals, and he himself looked
favorably on that creed. However, he never abandoned his sect, Zen
Buddhism, until the very end. No one knew whether his fondness for
Christianity was genuine or merely a means of keeping his vassals
together. The only thing that could be said with certainty was that Koremasa could not decide whether to convert to Christianity or to remain
a Zen Buddhist without considering his position as head of the
Wada clan.

It was the same for Murashige. Even if, for argument's sake, Chiyoho
had strongly urged Murashige to switch to True Pure Land Buddhism,
he would have at least pretended to be receptive. But he didn't convert,
because if he did become a True Pure Land practitioner while here in
Hokusetsu, everyone would regard that as the Araki being at the beck
and call of Hongan-ji.

Murashige had never thought Chiyoho had surmised as much.

"You're not wrong," said Murashige. "Everything is tactics. *Zazen*
meditation is tactics. The Nichiren chant is tactics. Hongan-ji insisting
that going to battle will lead to a peaceful afterlife—*Advance to reach
heaven. Retreat to know hell*—that, too, is tactics. In this world at war,
there's nothing in all creation that's divorced from tactics."

Chiyoho knit her brow worriedly while still smiling, before bowing
her head. "My remarks were impertinent and uncalled for. I beg Your
Lordship's forgiveness."

"Don't be foolish." Murashige's lips curled up as well. "What's wrong
with a little impudence? What warrior would want to place an idiot by
his side?"

"I say…" Chiyoho smiled slightly, too. "I shall be wherever Your
Lordship likes."

Then they heard footsteps from outside the statue hall.

"Attention," came an attendant's voice.

"What is it?" asked Murashige.

"Koori Juuemon wishes for an audience with Your Lordship posthaste."

"I'll go now."

Murashige dismissed his attendant and got to his feet. The lady attendant was prostrating herself, and Murashige walked past her before turning around to face Chiyoho.

"Time for some more tactics, I suppose."

4

Wide, spacious rooms were ideal for confidential talks, since it was so difficult to eavesdrop. Once again, Murashige let Juuemon inside the reception hall. The appointed time was the same as days before, an hour not long before twilight.

Juuemon was in everyday clothing, a short, sleeveless *kataginu* jacket over his robe. Sitting on the wooden boards, he placed his fists on the floor and bowed his head deeply to salute his lord.

"Speak," said Murashige, sitting cross-legged on a cushion.

Juuemon didn't raise his head as he spoke, a tension in his voice.

"Yes, my lord. I shall report on what Your Lordship ordered me to do. I could find none who fired a shot in the citadel on that day."

"...None, you say?"

"None, my lord."

Murashige stroked his chin.

The soldiers of Arioka Castle could be divided into two broad categories: those who served Murashige himself, and those under the commanders who served Murashige. Naturally, Murashige led the most soldiers, but even then, that number didn't exceed half of the castle's total. And only Murashige's soldiers could defend the inner citadel, the sole exceptions being the small number of Saika men assigned to key strategic locations due to their unrivaled sharpshooting skills.

In addition, there were various standings among those who served Murashige directly, from Murashige's guard, the members of which were the closest to Murashige and who could be promoted to commanders, all the way down to the laborers used exclusively for transporting goods. It was the lord's guard and the foot soldiers who protected the citadel. The guard had their own weapons and armor, but the foot soldiers had dull swords at best, and so Murashige inevitably had to lend them spears, bows, armor, and guns, to be returned after the war was over. Only the guns, which were expensive and few in number, got passed around and reused.

Those among the foot soldiers guarding the citadel who were entrusted with guns first went to the gun storehouse in the citadel to borrow them. When their shift ended, they were to return the guns to the storehouse before leaving the citadel.

Meanwhile, some of the guard possessed their own guns, and the Saika men, who made a living on their gun skills, also came to the citadel bearing their personal firearms. Moreover, if some of the commanders and their security guards carried guns into a war council, they would not be reprimanded. However, Juuemon was telling him that on the day Kawarabayashi Noto died, no guns were brought to the citadel.

"I need not mention the foot soldiers," said Juuemon. "The guard members who stood watch over the bridge all said that none of the commanders or their attendants carried guns. They were aware of Your Lordship's intentions to execute Noto, and they were paying close attention to the commanders' weaponry, so I can say that with confidence. In addition, as we made the preparations to surround Noto with spears, the guard did not have any guns on them, either."

"What about the men from Saika?"

"I took the liberty of telling them on the day prior not to come to the citadel that day, as I thought they might get the wrong impression from the uproar surrounding the execution. They obeyed, and so there were no men from Saika on that day."

Juuemon paused for a short moment before continuing:

"As Your Lordship knows, the gun storehouse is locked and guarded. The sentries on the day were foot soldiers, but based on the testimony of several people, they didn't neglect their duties, and so it would be next to impossible for a gun to have been secreted out of the storehouse."

Sentries had always been guarding the gun storehouse, but ever since an Oda agent attempted to set fire to a gunpowder storehouse that summer, the security of both storehouses had been made more stringent. They had selected foot soldiers with particularly good work reputations and increased the number of sentries. Murashige couldn't object.

"That does sound impossible."

On that day, if not one gun was taken into the citadel and no guns were secretly taken out of the storehouse, then that left one possibility Murashige could think of for where the gun that shot Noto came from.

"If it wasn't taken out in secret, then it must have been taken there openly. Was it a foot soldier who did it?"

"My lord, the reasoning is sound. Under the orders of someone else, a foot soldier borrowed a gun from the storehouse and shot Noto... I thought so at first, too."

Murashige's eyebrow twitched. "At first?"

"Yes, my lord. I heard out the foot soldiers and checked to see if their testimony was trustworthy by comparing it to the testimony of others."

Passion tinged his voice—a rare sight from Juuemon.

"My lord, the gun-wielding foot soldiers who guarded the citadel that day didn't take their eyes off each other. In the citadel, those foot soldiers are assigned to watchtowers in pairs. One cannot leave the watchtower without being noticed by the other, let alone shoot Noto."

"......"

"One of the guard members is the storehouse administrator who lends out guns, and he never lends guns to suspicious people or to those whose role doesn't call for a gun. I have investigated who borrowed all the guns loaned from the gun storehouse that day, and where they were taken. The gun that fired at Noto was not one of the ones that was lent to a foot soldier."

Murashige had to suppress the urge to shout at him and ask if he examined things thoroughly enough. Juuemon was more than capable enough. If Juuemon was the one investigating, and Juuemon said the foot soldiers didn't shoot Noto, then they didn't shoot Noto.

Juuemon continued.

"The shooter firing from outside the citadel is also out of the question. Considering Your Lordship said the bullet was lodged in the ground, the shooter must have aimed for Noto from above, and there is no such place outside of the citadel where that is possible."

"I understand your point," said Murashige. "If you've nothing to add to that, I have two questions for you."

"Yes, my lord." Juuemon bowed his head. "By all means."

"Where did the shooter aim at Noto? Have you any idea?"

Juuemon sat up. "I do, my lord."

He spoke clearly and without any hesitation. Evidently, he'd given this careful consideration.

"Taking into account the place Noto fell, the gun's range, and the fact that it was fired from above, we can narrow down the place the shooter was lurking to three locations."

"Hrm, I see. And what are they?"

"Atop a pine tree, the second floor of the castle tower, and the roof of Your Lordship's residence."

Murashige assumed that the pine tree was the one planted near the bridge leading to the samurai district. It was true that the treetop was well-suited for sniping, but as there were no bushes or brushwood around the base, there was nowhere to hide once one descended the arbor.

As for the castle tower, it was where their war councils were held, and when Noto died, several commanders should have already been inside. If the shooter had fired from the second floor, there would have been no escape.

Lastly, there was Murashige's residence. While it had many blind spots, there was always a great number of people present both inside and out. It wasn't a place strangers could easily approach.

None of the three locations Juuemon mentioned were ideal. However, since Juuemon said that the hidden shooter could only have been in one of the three, that meant any other place would have been outright impossible. Murashige did have a follow-up question.

"Why only the second floor of the castle tower?"

"The first floor contained too many commanders and guard members in the way of the shot. The shot from the third floor, meanwhile, was too straight-down for it to make sense."

"Did you test it?"

"Yes, my lord, of course."

Murashige nodded. "Good. Now let me ask you the other question."

"Yes, my lord."

His wording and general tone turned slightly stronger.

"I ordered you to determine who shot Noto. I have taken note of how thorough your investigation is, and the time it takes to investigate even more closely. Be that as it may, you have yet to fulfill your orders. Juuemon, why did you request an audience before you completed the investigation?"

That instant, Juuemon prostrated himself.

"I beg Your Lordship's pardon."

"Did something happen?"

"My lord, I thought I should report back about Your Lordship's orders, and I ended up not reporting what I should have reported first. It is as Your Lordship has discerned—I came here because there is a pressing matter."

A man of Juuemon's caliber, making a blunder like that? Murashige figured that in reality, Juuemon must have hesitated to speak of it.

"Speak."

"Yes, my lord. I shall report what I heard while the rumor is circulating the castle."

The sky, some portion of which was visible through the transom, was blood red.

"The rumors about Nakanishi Shinpachirou."

5

At the review meeting the next day, the commanders merely kept harping on the Mouri, without any new ideas worth mentioning. From the first, the review meeting was a way for Murashige to keep tabs on his commanders, as well as a way for the commanders to keep tabs on one another; not a single thing was decided then and there. Murashige closed his eyes, tuning out the heated dissent for dissent's sake, and he ruminated about what Koori Juuemon had said the day before.

The commanders who were shouting at one another, flecks of spit flying, hushed down as though tiring of it. One could be forgiven for thinking Murashige planned the silence that fell upon them. He opened his eyes.

"Nakanishi Shinpachirou."

While Shinpachirou seemed taken aback, he replied right away, his voice throaty and deep.

"Yes, my lord!"

His face betrayed an unrest he couldn't suppress. Murashige looked at his expression and his full armor.

"I hear you received some sake from Takigawa Sakon."

"Oh, is that what this is about?" Shinpachirou slapped his thigh and laughed. "Yes, my lord, I certainly did. That Saji What's-His-Name, the retainer of Sakon, fired a letter arrow at some time or other. He brought the sake, calling it a comfort visit for the soldiers."

"I hear you had them deliver a gift in return, too."

"I did. I must say, Your Lordship, you're always so quick to hear these things," Shinpachirou said cheerfully, surveying the other commanders with pride. "I and the four commanders of Fort Jorozuka savored that sake, which was high-grade, as one might expect from an Oda general. But to my taste, I prefer sake made using the waters of Itami!"

Shinpachirou laughed boisterously, but that laughter melted like snow the second he noticed the look in Murashige's eyes.

The Lord of Settsu's glare was as icy as an autumn stream.

"And you thought that was just fine, did you?"

Murashige's tone of voice was also different from usual. Shinpachirou seemed totally lost.

"What is Your Lordship saying…?"

"Exchanging letters with another clan somewhere outside my supervision goes against military law, to say nothing of exchanging *gifts*."

Shinpachirou's eyes reeled wide, and his mouth was agape. "Oh—oh, no…" But then he flared up. "I don't know what I was expecting Your Lordship to say, but 'twasn't that. Your Lordship gave me Fort Jorozuka to watch over. I thought I was supposed to be in charge of everything. To think I would receive such a scolding over a cask of sake."

"Stand down!" Murashige roared. "Not even the general who governs the entire castle can exchange words with other clans without use of an intermediary. 'Tis an act of treason. Do not talk back to me! All you are is the overseer of a single fort!"

He thought he saw Shinpachirou retreat even as he remained seated, cowed by Murashige's fury.

Shinpachirou quickly prostrated himself. "My lord, I…I had no such intention…," he stammered, his dismay and panic coming to the fore. Murashige looked around at the faces of the other commanders.

That very instant, a chill ran down his spine, like someone had poured cold water on him.

All the commanders who attended the council looked confused and unconvinced—in fact, they looked positively dumbfounded. He was surrounded by expressions that told him they thought their typically taciturn general had suddenly flown into an irrational rant. Not one of them seemed to think Murashige had raised a valid point.

"But, my liege," said Shinpachirou, "'tis only courteous to repay a gift with a gift… 'Twould be terrible if the Araki come to be mocked as misers."

Ever since Shinpachirou was appointed as defender of Fort Jorozuka, he had brought together the quirky and idiosyncratic foot-soldier commanders there and successfully kept Oda forces from drawing near. Though one could chalk it up to the fact that the Oda had chosen to attack from afar and had not come rushing toward the fort, Shinpachirou's competence when it came to fortifying their defenses without committing gross mistakes was considerable. But his conscientiousness as a commander was utterly inadequate. Murashige was impelled by a farcical rage—*Kanbei would never give such a boneheaded reply.*

"You dunce! What did you send Takigawa?"

"My lord, I…I sent him a sea bass."

The *suzuki* sea bass was beautiful to behold. A summer fish, it was extolled as a high-quality ocean catch since times of old.

"What negligence! Shinpachirou, where did you get your hands on that sea bass?!"

Shinpachirou looked as though he didn't understand what he'd been asked.

"Arioka is encircled on all sides by the Oda! Where would anyone be able to get a sea bass?! Nowhere, apart from a black market!"

Wherever people crossed paths, money and goods changed hands. That much was natural, even for enemies who would take each other's lives the next day. At Osaka Hongan-ji, which was besieged even more heavily than Arioka Castle, there were endless rumors of rank-and-file Oda soldiers selling rice and miscellaneous goods on the sly for some coin. As such, it wouldn't be all too surprising if similar trade was taking place somewhere in Arioka Castle, but of course, such commerce was strictly prohibited.

Haltingly, Shinpachirou defended himself.

"While I'm sure that could be, 'twas the foot-soldier commanders who brought it, so I wouldn't know. My lord, I do not understand. I thought Your Lordship might *praise* me and say securing food by any means necessary is fine warcraft."

Murashige noticed some were nodding at what Shinpachirou said. On the battlefield, when soldiers ran out of provisions, they often boiled grass and licked rocks to temper their hunger. Murashige detected the commanders' confusion: *Obtaining a sea bass was resourceful. There's no reason to pick him apart...*

"I'm not condemning you for seeking food!" said Murashige. "What do you think Takigawa will make of the sea bass he was given in return? Takigawa Sakon is the Oda's most intelligent commander. He knows sea bass can't be caught aground. He'll think there's trade bringing things into Arioka. And once he learns that, he has free reign to set up a blockade or to hide an agent through that trade. You're essentially telling the Oda that Arioka Castle has a weak spot to exploit! 'Tis because such things can happen that correspondence with other clans is to be done through intermediaries. Shinpachirou, through your carelessness, you've committed a serious crime!"

Deathly silence permeated the hall. No one so much as coughed.

Murashige was getting flustered. While Shinpachirou himself was rightly crestfallen, there was no sign the other commanders understood what Shinpachirou had done wrong. Judging by the looks on their faces, they didn't know why he deserved such a dressing down. The only reason Murashige had rebuked Shinpachirou during the council was to make an example out of him, yet Murashige's words weren't getting through to the commanders, and the wrath he put on was falling on deaf ears.

This is just like the charge that was running through the Ikeda retainers right before they drove out Katsumasa, thought Murashige.

"My lord..."

The one who'd raised his voice so timidly was Araki Kyuuzaemon.

"I believe Your Lordship's anger is justified. However..."

Don't lie to me, thought Murashige. From Kyuuzaemon's expression, it was clear as day that he didn't think for a second that Murashige was anywhere near in the right. But Murashige chained his heart and gestured for Kyuuzaemon to continue.

Kyuuzaemon bowed slightly. "Shinpachirou's behavior was indeed careless, and according to martial law, he is not exempt from a grave punishment... However, he has served us well. It has not been long since he was appointed as a commander, and so such imprudence is understandable. I implore Your Lordship to forgive him this one indiscretion. Blindly charging allies with crimes while we are surrounded on all sides by the enemy cannot be called a winning strategy."

Once again, Murashige looked at the commanders seated in the keep. Gone was the air of opposition toward him, replaced by a silence whose significance was lost on Murashige. He almost thought that everything was now settled.

The commanders under the Araki clan were no fools. There was no way none of them understood how dangerous it was to show the Oda a chink in their armor, or how contrary to martial law Shinpachirou's behavior was. But at that day's council, the commanders averted their eyes from Murashige's logic and sympathized with Shinpachirou. As for why, Murashige was beginning to hit on the reason.

If Murashige wasn't wrong, they weren't actually pitying Shinpachirou. The true object of their commiseration was Kawarabayashi Noto. Yes, the man who had been in league with the Oda, the man who had killed the virtuous Muhen and thus pushed the populace into the pits of despair. Noto's death had mortified them. They still couldn't accept how Murashige had let a man who was a member of an illustrious clan in Hokusetsu die such a shameful death. Murashige was their head, but he was not a man of Settsu. And that was what spawned this pall of silence.

There was no helping it. Murashige pretended to meditate on things for a moment.

"Very well. In light of Kyuuzaemon's intervention and your work thus far, I'll forgive you this one time," he said. "Shinpachirou."

"Yes, my liege!"

"Be more discreet from now on. Strive yet harder and make it up to me through your feats on the battlefield."

"Yes, my lord, I shall!"

Shinpachirou's voice was trembling with emotion.

Following the council, Murashige went up to the top floor of the castle tower alongside Koori Juuemon and no one else. The winds and the color of the sky were suitably autumnal.

When Murashige obtained Ikeda Castle, after giving it some thought later, he destroyed it. The land where Ikeda Castle was located, which could be seen from the castle tower, was marked by fluttering flags, and it came to be called Old Ikeda. The Oda had built an encampment in Old Ikeda— No, they'd built an impressive fortress that was more castle than camp. Murashige no longer knew whether he would be able to defeat the Old Ikeda encampment even if the Mouri finally appeared en masse.

The war council that day was alarming and grievous.

Nakanishi Shinpachirou had exchanged gifts with another clan without the permission of his lord. It was extremely thoughtless behavior that could arouse enough suspicion to warrant execution. But Murashige was unable to censure him even for such a blatant transgression, and that was because the council would not agree with Shinpachirou's punishment.

Back when Murashige was under the Oda clan, for a time, Nobunaga thought of Murashige as the one and only master who governed Settsu, just like Nobunaga himself was. But that wasn't true, and Murashige was again reminded of this fact.

During the decline of the Ikeda clan, the samurai of Hokusetsu solved the crisis by installing Murashige as the new head. As Kuroda Kanbei once said, Murashige had next to no legitimacy to justify his rule over them, and without the support of the samurai of the land, the Araki clan would not see another sunrise. Murashige excelled at eyeing trends; he couldn't dismiss the attitudinal shift of the military council.

In the past, it wasn't like this. Once, the war council was a place where Murashige controlled the samurai, not a place where the samurai kept Murashige in check. The commanders once saw what Murashige had to say as important, and few ever gainsaid him. Even if Murashige had to deliver a hard pill to swallow, by working with key retainers such as Araki Kyuuzaemon or Ikeda Izumi behind closed doors, he'd generally been able to manage the assembly and have things swing his way.

But these days, even if Murashige listed Shinpachirou's faults, the commanders would not take his words to heart in the slightest. It was human nature—people always covered up what was on the inside. Even if someone was suspicious of Murashige's orders from the bottom of his heart, he would not openly display such feelings on the surface. That he could tell his commanders were apathetic at a glance despite that fact was frightening.

Murashige once again recalled the time when Katsumasa was expelled. By the time the war council had reached this level of momentum, the wheeling and dealing of the generals who wanted to chase Katsumasa out had already progressed a good 80 percent. Was that true today as well? Was someone 80 percent of the way toward driving Murashige out of Arioka Castle as they spoke?

He'd heard that after Katsumasa got banished from his castle, he fled to the capital before passing away at a later date. However, if Murashige was chased from Arioka Castle, which was surrounded by enemies, he would not be able to run to safety.

All that would await him was death.

6

Murashige looked up at the tower of Arioka Castle in the nighttime. The eighth month had just commenced, and the moon couldn't be seen.

The majestic castle tower was basking in the starlight alone. He headed to the dungeon, relying on the light of his portable candlestick holder. He had no soldiers to protect him, and if he were to be attacked by three or four assassins, even the mighty Lord of Settsu wouldn't stand a chance. Yet whenever Murashige went to the dungeon, he always went alone. When something happened to Arioka Castle, the only people who knew that Murashige descended into the dungeon were Murashige himself, the prison guard...and Kuroda Kanbei, the man imprisoned in the underground.

How many times had he stepped down these stairs? There were many dangers that could lead to the fall of the castle. Some of them were addressed by Murashige giving orders to his commanders, and some had been averted through Kanbei's words of wisdom. And it had all led up to the way this autumn was now unfolding.

The moment Katou Matazaemon, the jailer, caught sight of Murashige, he got to his feet, keys jangling. Murashige wondered when the man ever slept. He must sleep on the woven mat spread out in the corner of the room, but whenever Murashige visited, he was always awake. A samurai was never supposed to sleep too deeply, but was this warden also that disciplined?

"I appreciate your hard work," said Murashige.

"My lord... I shall open it," Katou replied laconically.

When the door leading to the basement was opened, a wave of cold air gently rose up. Lifting his candle aloft, Murashige descended. Something at his waist was making a tap, tap, tapping noise. It was a sake bottle.

A silhouette wriggled in the scant light. Kanbei was still alive in this hole in the ground, drawing breath within his wood cage. It came as no surprise to Murashige that Kanbei was awake. There was no way to distinguish between day and night here in the depths of the earth. Kanbei, who had been lying on his back, got up and tried to sit cross-legged, but after ten months of confinement, his legs were crooked and rigid, and his sitting posture was bizarrely slanted.

Murashige said nothing and placed the sake bottle in front of the cage. Kanbei's white eyes opened slightly, his face still black with grime.

Murashige took out two wooden sake cups from inside the breast of his clothing and poured the contents of the bottle into each.

Murashige remained silent as he held out a sake cup to Kanbei. Kanbei, too, said nothing, stretching out his withered branch of an arm to take the cup. The two generals brought the sake cups to their mouths and partook.

After drinking their cups dry, Murashige poured yet more sake. Their banquet for two continued for a while amid the darkness until at last Murashige spoke.

"What do you think of this sake?"

Kanbei gazed at the cup in his hands and muttered, "It hits the spot."

"What else?"

"Itami has good water."

"What else?"

Kanbei's eyes turned toward Murashige.

"...This sake is young. The castle's rice must have been turned into this sake recently. And turning rice into sake means fewer provisions to go around."

In the battlefield, rice was converted into sake fairly frequently. There were even soldiers who consumed all the rice that was apportioned to them in sake form, thereby dying of starvation. Consequently, a commander who knew the proper way to distribute rice to his soldiers did not distribute it all at once, but rather little by little.

"To brew sake despite that... So Your Lordship is a great general who would make use of rice that could go to the soldiers or common people for his own sake..." Kanbei drained his cup. "If not, then Arioka must have enough provisions to go around after all. 'Tis one or the other."

As long as the siege forced them to use the rice in the storehouses, Arioka Castle had no provisions to waste. However, the pressure wasn't so immense that a single bottle of sake could not be made. Murashige smiled sardonically for a moment before pouring cloudy sake into his and Kanbei's cups.

"Is that all?"

"Well..."

A note of mockery crept into Kanbei's tone.

"...I think the reason you're drinking with me..."

Kanbei partook a little at a time.

"...is because ye no longer have anyone else to drink with."

Murashige didn't confirm whether that was true.

"They say that a wise bird chooses a good tree in which to roost," he replied in a nice low voice. "You must have felt stifled under the Kodera clan."

Kanbei seemed unamused. He murmured even as his eyes lingered on the now-empty sake cup longingly.

"Does such a thing as feeling stifled bother ye so? Did the Lord of Settsu exile Katsumasa over that?"

Murashige stopped to reflect: Had he felt stifled under Ikeda Katsumasa, Lord of Chikugo? He couldn't say he *hadn't* felt stifled, serving under a lord whom one would be hard-pressed to call particularly wise or great, alongside colleagues one would be hard-pressed to call remarkable warriors. It was certainly true that Murashige had been itching to show the world his talents. But was that why he'd banished Katsumasa? When asked that question, he realized:

"No...that wasn't why."

Putting aside Katsumasa's caliber as a general, he hadn't been a bad lord.

"It was to survive. Everything has been to survive and to preserve my clan."

Samurai died with regularity. Of course, all men died. But for a samurai, death had to have a selling point. Samurai spent their days exposing themselves to the tips of enemy spears and the muzzles of enemy guns. It wasn't that they didn't mind dying, per se. Rather, they understood that while death would come eventually, they at least didn't want to die in vain. No—death's inevitability was the very *reason* they despised the idea they'd die in vain.

If a samurai was to die, his son would live on. If his son was to die, his family and clan would be left behind. They were told that their household existed only thanks to the brave and manly deaths of their forefathers, and it was that thought that allowed them to accept their deaths. If they followed a household on the wane and came down in the world, they would leave behind neither a family nor a reputation—and that was dying a dog's death. Murashige would die one day. As such, he had banished Katsumasa to secure himself a better death.

The booze had run out. Murashige tossed the sake cup into the darkness. The *thud* echoed hollowly.

"That said, the wheel of karma just keeps turning," said Murashige, power returning to his voice. "What goes around comes around. And as I chased out Katsumasa, now it appears there's someone trying to chase *me* out. Kanbei. I'm sure you already know, but anybody else would have killed you. And if I'm banished, it'll be off with your head if you're *lucky*. More likely, you'll be forgotten by everyone and starve to death here in this dungeon."

Kanbei tilted the sake cup to see if any more liquor was in it, but he gave up and put the cup down.

"That may well be true. I must say, such a thing would mildly inconvenience me."

"In that case, let me tell you a little anecdote."

Murashige began recounting what had happened when he tried to execute Kawarabayashi Noto.

Murashige told Kanbei about how Noto was in communication with the Oda and how he had Noto surrounded. He told him how, right as he was about to issue the orders to execute him, a bolt of lightning struck Noto. He mentioned the hot lead bullet found right next to Noto. He spoke of how Koori Juuemon's investigation found that not a single gun had been brought into the inner citadel from outside that day, and that all the guns lent out from the citadel's storehouse were accounted for. During Murashige's monologue, Kanbei had his eyes closed, and his body was shaking slightly, as if he was now inebriated after drinking for the first time in a long while.

"...As such," continued Murashige, "I need to find out who tried to shoot Noto. I need to uncover the traitor."

Kanbei stirred a bit. He stared up at Murashige from behind his unruly mane. Murashige didn't know if it was just his imagination, but to him, those eyes looked just like the eyes of a doctor taking the pulse of a dying patient.

"I wonder."

"What?"

"I wonder if uncovering this traitor…will be *enough*."

Kanbei had said that to no one but himself, but Murashige understood what he meant:

Would pinning down who shot at Kawarabayashi Noto be enough to win back the hearts of my commanders?

"It will," said Murashige. "It will be enough."

Kanbei just kept staring silently at him until, at last, he averted his gaze.

"In that case," he said, a vague note of resignation in his voice, "I have one thing to ask, if I may. I do believe around two months have passed since the sad affair with Noto. For what purpose did ye wait before ordering that Koori Juuemon person to investigate?"

Murashige was silent.

"No answer? That stands to reason… After all, 'tis obvious. Why don't I be the one to say it?" he added gloomily.

Murashige felt Kanbei did have an accurate read of things. There was only one reason Murashige didn't order Juuemon to investigate until a month and a half after Noto's death. It was because he'd suspected Juuemon might be the traitor behind the shooting.

Noto had been surrounded by Murashige's guard because he was to be executed, and the bullet hit the place Noto had been standing. Since it was difficult to hit a moving target, the shooter likely knew that Noto would be made to stand in place. Yet not many people had been privy to that knowledge.

When Murashige learned that Noto had been in league with the Oda, he ordered Juuemon to direct the guard in capturing him. Juuemon had finished making the necessary arrangements before night's end, and he'd told the Saika men guarding the inner citadel that he would not be able to be there the next day.

In other words, Juuemon knew more than anyone else in the castle except for Murashige himself that Noto would be held in place at the citadel. As such, Murashige suspected that Juuemon was in league with the shooter.

Murashige was examining Juuemon, checking to see if there was a commander with whom he seemed to have a close relationship or if he exhibited any suspicious behavior. He didn't come across any particularly close link between him and anyone else. It took Murashige over a month to conclude that even if he couldn't let his guard down entirely, it seemed safe to assume for the time being that Juuemon was innocent.

Murashige suspected the members of the guard sworn to protect him. He suspected even the one he had the most faith in, Juuemon. Murashige felt ashamed of Kanbei's having seen through him.

"Now then, who is plotting to take the position of Lord of Settsu...? I haven't the faintest clue. As a rule, plots are cooked up by people, and as I cannot read men's minds, I cannot help Your Lordship. However..."

Kanbei sneered a little.

"...I have resided in this dungeon since the day I paid this castle a visit. I know the names of the elders of the Araki clan and naught else. Divining their innermost thoughts is beyond me."

Kanbei caressed the sake cup in his hands, storing it in his bosom as though it was an unparalleled treasure.

"So you're saying you're of no use to me."

"As I lack the power of clairvoyance, I cannot say what I know not as though I know it."

This left Murashige dissatisfied to the utmost degree.

"If you're of no use to me...," he said, his voice taking on a slightly gloomy timbre, "then you would die now, Kanbei."

Kanbei stared at Murashige from behind his greasy forelocks. Murashige looked not at Kanbei's face, but at the candle's swaying flame.

"I see. As things stand for Your Lordship now, ye can kill me."

"Don't be foolish. You're at my mercy. I could kill you *any* time. I let you live because you were useful to me."

Kanbei shook his head. "No, that cannot be it."

"What?"

"Your Lordship may say that now, after all this time, but I cannot take you at your word. I understand full well the true reason the Lord of Settsu has kept me alive."

Last winter, when Murashige opted not to kill Abe Jinen as the hostage linked to Owada Castle, Kanbei saw into at least a portion of Murashige's mind.

Murashige didn't kill the people he was expected to kill, as if to tell the world he was different from Nobunaga. Murashige had sent the Oda castle overseers back alive, and he'd refrained from executing the hostage of Takayama Ukon after Takatsuki Castle surrendered. When Kanbei learned he wouldn't be executed, he screamed muffled pleas to be killed, only to be thrown into this dungeon. *Nobunaga kills, Murashige doesn't...* Their reputations now preceded them. It had all been just another tactic, meant to boost his reputation and prestige through rumors and net him allies.

But since then, everything had changed. Now it hardly mattered whom Murashige did or didn't kill. Not a single soul would switch to the Araki clan over such things anymore.

There was no longer any reason to keep Kanbei alive. It was true; as things stood, Murashige could, in fact, kill Kanbei.

Moreover, he couldn't bring himself to continue to torment Kuroda Kanbei, the renowned genius of Harima, in this dungeon. It was just then, when Murashige resolved himself to put Kanbei out of his misery, that Kanbei started talking:

"I do, however, wish to see the end result of this war. While I have no idea who the traitor Your Lordship speaks of might be, I do have an inkling as to Kawarabayashi Noto's shooter. So that ye may spare me my life, I shall give you a hint... Great Lord of Settsu. If that bolt of lightning had not struck, what do ye think would have become of the castle?"

What a strange question, Murashige thought. Wasn't it obvious? Even if there had been no lightning, Murashige would not have been able to execute Noto and maintain face. The only reason the gunshot missed was because the sudden lightning strike threw off the shooter's aim. Had there been no lightning, Noto would have died by the shooter's hands.

Kanbei rephrased the question. "If the shooter hadn't missed, what would have happened then?"

"Noto would have died all the same. Nothing changes."

"Indeed."

Murashige began to suspect that Kanbei was just throwing out some nonsense in order to stall and stay alive. If that was true, it was unsightly of him. But Kanbei had more to say:

"If the lightning had not struck, then Kawarabayashi Noto would have died by a bullet fired from who knows where. And how would the people of the castle view such a thing?"

Murashige had already thought about that. He grimaced a tad. "If a traitor got killed before a verdict was reached, they would have viewed it as bringing shame on my name. And given that, the lightning strike was a godsend for me."

"Pray tell me, what rumors spread through the castle after that?"

That took Murashige by surprise. "...What *rumors?*"

Following Kawarabayashi Noto's sudden death, Arioka Castle became a veritable whirlpool of gossip. While the way the idea was communicated varied, the general notion was that Noto's death was divine punishment from the Buddha.

And who could blame the people for thinking that? Muhen, the victim Noto murdered, was a traveling monk of tremendous virtue loved dearly by the masses. Muhen had been their link between Arioka and the outside world. He had been their salvation. His death plunged the people into the pit of sorrow and despair. If Noto's head had been laid at an Itami crossroads, the stones people threw at it would come down like so much rain.

For Muhen's murderer to have died by way of a bolt of lightning, it made sense for them to conclude it was the Buddha's retribution. But what if it hadn't been the lightning that did Noto in? What if the shooter had managed to kill him? What would the people have concluded then?

"I see...," Mutashige muttered. "Had the shooter succeeded, nothing would have changed. While a bullet is not as miraculous as a natural disaster...the rumors would still have called it divine retribution regardless."

"Verily, it is so, Your Lordship."

But the Buddha didn't use guns. It wasn't the Buddha who did it.

Murashige had a feeling he was catching a glimpse of a fragment of what he needed to know. But the rest of the iceberg was too hazy, too indistinct. *The Buddha doesn't use guns...* What did that signify? Did it mean anything at all, for that matter? As far as Murashige knew, it could all just be Kanbei's garrulity in action.

"I presume Your Lordship is already aware of the culprit behind the so-called divine retribution."

Kanbei was staring at Murashige from within his cage. His eyes, which had not seen the sun or moon in a long time and which were unaccustomed to even the meager illumination provided by the candle's feeble flame, brimmed with a strange, dark light. Murashige feared them—those eyes that seemed to be probing the recesses of his very soul.

What is he saying? Do I really know the culprit's identity already? And even if I do, would it help save me from whoever's plotting to betray me?

Murashige couldn't reply. Kanbei cast his eyes down, as though to wash his hands of Murashige.

"Has it not yet dawned on Your Lordship? Then pray forget old Kanbei's ramblings," he said, implying he'd only shared any of that to cling to life. He spoke no more, and he didn't even move an inch—he became nothing more than a shadow.

7

Murashige went back up the stairs, where he was greeted by the warden, Katou Matazaemon, and the light of a torch. A lukewarm night breeze was blowing in, tilting the flame of Murashige's candle. He didn't have to say a word; Matazaemon had already locked the wooden door leading to the dungeon, the clanking of iron breaking the silence of the late hours.

Murashige made to leave the underground. However, Matazaemon, who had never once spoken out of turn before now, addressed his lord in a hoarse voice:

"Going alone when the moon is so slight is dangerous, my liege. Prithee allow me to accompany Your Lordship."

Murashige glanced at Matazaemon, who was now on his knees. Surprisingly, the workmanship of the sword that Matazaemon wore was not bad.

"I'll allow it."

The whoosh of the winds was mixed with the chirping of the insects. Murashige ordered Matazaemon to walk in front of him. Needless to say, that was a precaution to prevent Matazaemon from being able to cut him down from behind. The two exited the dungeon; they were now directly under the castle tower.

The thread-thin sliver of a moon loomed amid the great tapestry of stars and celestial bodies. Relying on the moonlight and starlight, Murashige looked up at the castle tower. Gazing at the shadowed keep piercing the night sky, Murashige recalled the day Arioka Castle was completed. Back when they transformed Itami Castle into one of the stronger fortresses their world had ever known, whom exactly had he intended to fend off with this castle? Hongan-ji forces coming from the south? Harima samurai coming from the west? Or did he build such a magnificent castle with the intention of fending off the Oda, who would swoop in from the east? Murashige could no longer remember what he'd been thinking at the time.

The torch that Matazaemon bore illuminated the way. Murashige soon realized that they were approaching the very location where Kawarabayashi Noto was struck by lightning.

"Wait, Matazaemon."

Matazaemon stopped in his tracks unquestioningly. Murashige scanned their surroundings.

Murashige now saw how succinct and to the point Koori Juuemon's statement was that the shooter could only aim for Noto from one of three places. Murashige was standing right in the center of the triangle that connected the castle tower, the pine tree, and his residence. The castle tower was located at the northern end of the citadel, with ramparts and a water moat obstructing the way ahead. A lone, twisty-branched pine tree was standing in the thicket near the bridge that connected the citadel and the samurai district. Because a watch fire was kept burning all night at the residence, the area in its direction was dimly bright.

Murashige stayed there for a while, pondering. Matazaemon, too, remained silent, holding his torch aloft as he casually looked around.

"All right," said Murashige. "Go."

Matazaemon did as he was told and started walking toward the residence.

As he made Matazaemon walk in front, Murashige reflected on a variety of things. He thought about the council, the war, the Buddha, the Mouri, the Oda, the world, the shooter, the traitor, Kuroda Kanbei— and before he knew it, he found himself calling Matazaemon's name.

"Yes, my lord," replied Matazaemon, without turning, as looking at his lord's face from that close-up would be too presumptuous of him.

"What would you say is Kanbei's typical behavior?"

"My lord…" Matazaemon kept looking forward, walking at the same pace. "He eats and he sleeps."

"I see."

Murashige hadn't asked expecting a specific answer, and he didn't find Matazaemon's curt reply disappointing.

A few paces later, Matazaemon added, "He also flexes his voice."

"He flexes his voice, eh? I can see a man of Kanbei's caliber intoning poetry."

"Not exactly, my lord. It is more like singing, with a melody. When I stand guard, I sometimes hear him singing."

"…Singing, you say. Is it *sarugaku*?"

"Loath as I am to pass judgments, I do not believe so."

There was a noise. Matazaemon stopped walking. Nothing was moving save for the wind. Murashige looked behind him slightly, his head bowed.

"If it isn't *sarugaku*, then what does Kanbei sing?"

There were many different kinds of chanting, recitation, and song, from recounting of *The Tale of the Heike* to music, to *shomyo* Buddhist hymns, to more contemporary forms of expression. And yet…

"I know not what I would even call it. What Kanbei sings are silly little makeshift melodies."

Kanbei singing in his sunless cage. Songs heard from the prison below.

Matazaemon turned his back to Murashige and started walking once again.

"Kanbei's song—," said Matazaemon, his voice slightly drowned out by the sound of the flaming torch. "It must be a lullaby for soothing a crying child. I too am a father. It always sounds so terribly forlorn to me."

The gusts that blew through the night were chilly and desolate. The autumn winds were already upon them.

8

Murashige returned to his residence and entered the Buddha statue hall, dismissing the night guard attendant outside the room and sitting cross-legged in silence with his bracers and shin guards still on, alone with the one votive light.

The smallish statue in front of him was the Shakyamuni Buddha. While Murashige didn't take the teachings of the Buddha lightly, he only rarely revered Shakyamuni, the historical Buddha. This was because Gautama Siddhartha preached against killing, and was not one to confer divine protection on a warrior. There were gods of war to be worshiped, such as Suwa Daimyojin and the great bodhisattva Hachiman. And yet that night, Murashige was sitting opposite a statue of a figure who loathed war.

Divine punishment.

That was what Kanbei had told him to think about. Maybe it really was all about divine punishment.

In the end, what Murashige needed to know was who the traitor was. Investigating who shot Kawarabayashi Noto was nothing more than a snare to expose them. There were many things he didn't know about the shooting. Just like Kanbei said, part of the reason was because Murashige had waited so long before ordering the investigation. But

Kori Juuemon's search paid off regardless, making clear what remained unclear.

The first mystery was, of course, who ordered the shooter to fire at Noto. Then again, there was always the possibility that the shooter could have worked of their own accord, without being ordered by anyone.

The second mystery was the method by which the gun had been carried into the citadel. Juuemon's investigation had shown that on the day of that fateful crash of lightning, not a single gun had been taken into the citadel from outside it. Nor were there any guns unaccounted for. So where did the gun that shot at Noto come from?

The third mystery was where the gun was fired. According to Juuemon, it could only have been in one of three places—the second floor of the castle tower located at the citadel's northern edge, atop the pine tree near the bridge leading to the samurai district, and the roof of Murashige's residence. And Murashige agreed with that assessment. So which of the three was it?

Finding out what was unknown was invariably the first step toward settling any case. And the hint Kanbei gave him—the divine punishment rumors—was the one thread that tied that which remained hazy.

"The shooter..." Murashige began muttering to himself, the flame of the votive light wavering in the statue hall. "What did the shooter intend to do after firing at Noto?"

The shooter could not have predicted the lightning bolt. If the bullet had hit its target, Murashige and the members of his guard would have immediately determined where the gun had been fired, and if they found the shooter, they would have had him surrounded forthwith. They would have tried to capture him alive, and if he'd resisted arrest, they would have killed him then and there. That meant that the shooter did it under the assumption he would not escape from the scene alive...or so Murashige had thought. As a samurai, he was too used to the frame of mind that didn't balk at sacrificing one's own life if it meant certain death for the enemy.

Yet Murashige had thought wrong.

"If the shooter died in the process, no one would see it as divine retribution."

If the point of the shooting was to magnify belief in the Buddha's wrath, then the shooter could hardly afford to be slain directly afterward. If the shooter's identity came to light, the whole affair would be seen as a surprise sniping, not a miracle carried out by an invisible force. The shooter may not have minded dying on a personal level, but they couldn't risk being found on a pragmatic level.

That meant that the shooter must have had a place to escape to. A place they could hide. And that narrowed the possible location down to one.

That day, when the commanders answered the drum signal to convene for the war council, they crossed the bridge and traveled from the samurai district to the inner citadel. The pine tree near the bridge was the most conspicuous location of the three. A shooter firing from atop it would be detected in an instant.

Furthermore, the commanders who entered the citadel were on their way to the castle tower, inside which the war council was to be held. Firing at Noto from the castle tower's second floor wouldn't have worked, for the commanders would have been in the floor below. As samurai, the commanders would have started searching for an enemy the second they heard gunfire. The shooter couldn't have slipped into the crowd of commanders, either. The shooter wouldn't have had anywhere to flee.

Murashige's residence, meanwhile, lay some distance away from the paths trodden by the commanders who headed to the council and the soldiers who kept watch over them. If the shooter fired from the roof of that building, they could easily have at least escaped the eyes of the commanders, the guard, and Murashige himself.

"...Is that truly what happened?" Murashige mumbled to the statue. It simply kept smiling its maybe-smile in silence.

It was undoubtedly true that by shooting from that roof, the shooter could evade detection by the officers and men. But they could go undetected for only a brief span of time. Murashige's residence was not devoid of people. There were always the servants and attendants who carried out Murashige's day-to-day errands and chores, as well as the ladies in waiting who served under Chiyoho, and they worked day and night. Murashige's residence could be said to be the place containing the most pairs of eyes in all of Arioka. Once notice of a criminal in their midst got around, the shooter wouldn't have been able to safely descend from the roof. While the servants and the ladies in waiting didn't all know the arts of battle, they were acquainted with one another, so if the shooter tried to blend in among them, they would be discovered at once.

Considering that, didn't that make the roof of Murashige's residence even less of a possibility than the pine tree or the castle tower?

With the swaying of the votive light's flame, the look on the Buddha's face was in flux. There were supposed to be two attendants outside the door, but Murashige didn't even hear so much as anyone clearing their throat.

What if I suspected the folks stationed at my residence? How would that change the math?

Every one of them was born and raised in Hokusetsu, and all their identities had been confirmed. While they did give work to wanderers as well, those people couldn't make it to the residence, or at least, not at first. That being said, the hearts of men did change with time. Perhaps the traitor bought the loyalty of one of the residence workers and induced them to shoot Kawarabayashi Noto.

A ladder or some such would be necessary to get up and down the roof, but there would have been a way to procure it.

Two whole months have passed since Noto was shot at. Assuming a ladder was used, 'tis been either hidden or destroyed already. And a residence worker would be able to return inside the residence after shooting Noto and go through the motions searching for the culprit, pretending to be loyal to me. So is that what happened that day?

"That cannot be it." Murashige exhaled. "It wouldn't explain where the gun came from."

A residence worker wouldn't have much trouble getting on the roof or hiding, but they couldn't bring a gun in. Murashige supposed someone could have had a gun hidden in the residence for some time, but being in possession of such a fine weapon would have been a point of honor and glory. The idea that somebody would conceal their ownership of so valuable a status symbol wasn't terribly realistic.

Divine punishment.

Those words sprang back to mind. If there was anyone in Arioka Castle who deserved the Buddha's punishment, there was no better candidate for that honor than the man who killed Muhen. Murashige suddenly laughed.

No, no, it isn't Noto. The one who most deserves to be so punished is, of course, Araki Murashige, Lord of Settsu. Who but me threw the towns-folk and the soldiers alike into a pit of misery, dragging this war on day after wretched day pretending to wait for the Mouri, who were never to be counted on to begin with? But even if leaving the Oda meant smear-ing every single one of the people of Itami and Hokusetsu with mud and blood, I couldn't bear living under Nobunaga's thumb.

Still sitting cross-legged, Murashige stared at the statue and pressed his hands together.

And then he prayed.

Shakyamuni, Manjushri Bodhisattva, Akasagarbha Bodhisattva, I care not who. If the Buddha won't do it, then I'll even take an oni. Just give me the wisdom I need. Give me the wisdom to see the full scope of what happened in the castle I defend—the castle I built!

At that moment, Murashige almost forgot why he was this obsessed with Noto's death to begin with. It was all supposed to be to root out the traitor. But he had a feeling that the *true* reason that his hunger to learn the truth was so fierce that he'd just entreated the Buddha actu-ally lay elsewhere. Wasn't it because that one bullet had showed him a glimpse of something *bigger*—a conspiracy that totally enshrouded this castle?

What was it Kanbei had said again?

Oh, right. I remember:

"I presume Your Lordship is already aware of the culprit behind the so-called divine retribution."

He was absolutely correct.
Murashige did already know. And now he realized that.

This was far from the first time the term *divine punishment* was bandied about in Arioka.

It was only natural. Seeing the will of the gods in the falling of the rains and the blowing of the winds was all too human. Murashige was sure there were even those who stepped in horse manure and lamented it as a curse from on high. But there had been rumors that went beyond one of those everyday superstitions. Rumors that swept Arioka at a turning point that determined the castle's fate.

It had been during the spring of that year.

The Takatsuki contingent, led by Takayama Dariyo, and the Saika contingent, led by Suzuki Magoroku, hadn't yet had a chance to rack up glorious battlefield feats to their name. They'd been resigned to their lot of grumbling about the boredom of idling uselessly in the castle. Right then, Otsu Denjuurou, an Oda retainer, stood out from among the other Oda forces, perhaps in his own haste to achieve glory. Murashige capitalized on Otsu's strategic error and led the Takatsuki and Saika warriors in a night raid against Otsu's encampment; it was such a rousing success that they even managed to slay Otsu himself. The problem was that no one in the castle knew what Otsu looked like, making it unclear whether the Takatsuki or the Saika contingent had claim to the most glorious kill of them all. The castle's Christians sided with the Takatsuki warriors, while the True Pure Land believers sided with the Saika guns for hire. The successful night raid quickly turned into a Pyrrhic victory as the dispute over who would be credited with taking Otsu's head spiraled into a crisis that could have spelled the end of Arioka. It was then that something uncanny came to pass. The head that Takayama Dariyo himself took, the head that seemed perfectly normal during the head-identification session, had, at some point unbeknownst to them, seemingly changed into an alarming and grotesque rictus, biting its lips and with one eye closed.

Rumors swiftly spread through every corner of the castle: The head taken by Takayama Dariyo, an adherent of the creed of the foreign barbarians who slighted the old faith in the gods and the Buddha and who felt no shame burning temples and shrines, had shifted to a hideous expression presaging ill fortune to come. This could only be retribution from the heavens, they said. An omen. A curse. Proof that one could not take the wrath of the Buddha lightly. As a result of the furor, a hut where Christian masses were being held was set ablaze, leading to a commotion that costed numerous lives.

Murashige had brought the book down on the arsonists, but he hadn't followed up on the switching out of the severed head. Vying for glory was at once splendid and unsightly. After every battle, one encountered braggarts who talked up the beauty of their own achievements while casting mud on the achievements others boasted of. Murashige found the perfect excuse, chalking up the swapping of the head to a Saika supporter exploiting the custom of not showing the general a head with a sinister countenance.

It was normal and expected for warriors to compete among themselves for the greatest glories, but swapping out a head that had already been submitted to the identification session was out of the ordinary. One could even call it a wicked crime that held the general in contempt. Despite that, Murashige never launched an investigation into who had perpetrated it.

That was because he had been too afraid. Part of him knew all too well that if he got to the bottom of who switched out the head, he'd be faced with a truth he wouldn't want to look in the eyes.

When a warrior took a head, it was brought back to base, where makeup was applied to it before it could be presented for the identification session held by the general.

Who had been the one to apply that makeup? Or to put it differently, in whose reach did the head lie between when it was taken and when the general sat down for the identification session?

Thinking back, the rumors about the Buddha's wrath were circulating even before the glory dispute.
The rumors got their start on a winter day, didn't they?
During the twelfth month of last year, after Abe Niemon of Owada

Castle switched to the Oda, traffic between Hongan-ji and Arioka Castle became cut off. The surrender of Takayama Ukon's Takatsuki Castle and Nakagawa Sehyoue's Ibaraki Castle, which had to react to Oda troops at their doorstep, was probably unavoidable, but Owada Castle surrendering was beyond even Murashige's calculations. Murashige brushed aside his retainers' urgings to kill the Abe hostage and young Jinen's own pleas to be executed so that he may know bliss in the next life, throwing the boy into prison instead for the reasons that Kanbei inferred earlier.

Murashige could have tossed Jinen into the dungeon with Kanbei if he'd wanted to, but he'd had apprehensions regarding putting other people next to the man, so he decided to have another cage constructed for the boy and opted to have him confined in the storeroom of his residence until said cage was completed. The security guarding Jinen had been tight, and yet before the full day it would take to make the cage was over, he suffered a cruel and tragic death. It was murder.

It had been an enigma of a murder, too. Jinen had unquestionably died of an arrow wound, yet the arrow was nowhere to be found. The storeroom contained only Jinen, and the corridors connected to that closet had been watched over lest anyone entered. There was no other way to approach Jinen apart from through the garden, but there had been no footprints in the freshly fallen snow.

Once word of how Jinen died made the rounds, so too did the rumors—the one who paid the karmic price for Abe Niemon turning his back on the head priest of Osaka was his all-too-young son, and a miraculously invisible arrow struck the boy in the chest. While Murashige hadn't thought it made sense for the Buddha's wrath to manifest in the form of an arrow shot, the eerie circumstances of Jinen's death had unnerved even him.

In order to get to the bottom of Jinen's murder, Murashige paid a visit to Kanbei. He told the man in the dungeon about the details surrounding the mysterious case, after which Kanbei mocked him and let fly a satiric *tanka*. That poem was the clue Murashige needed, and the culprit and murder method were brought to light. The killer, Mori Kahei, was spared from execution, and shortly afterward, he died in battle.

That was not to say that every mystery had been unraveled. There were still aspects that eluded Murashige.

For Kahei to be able to kill Jinen, the boy had to stand in a specific spot, with the light he'd been holding as a guide for the spear. If Jinen had been the least bit off that spot, the strange death that could be reasonably mistaken for divine punishment wouldn't have transpired. Was it mere coincidence that Jinen happened to be in the right spot? Wasn't it more plausible that someone gave a willing, suicidal Jinen detailed instructions?

If so, who could have conferred with the imprisoned Jinen ahead of time? Who was the one who brought a source of heat into the storeroom? Or to put it differently, who was the one who had looked after the boy's needs?

There were three cases linked by the rumors of the Buddha's vengeance: the killing of the hostage that winter, the conflict caused by the enemy heads in the spring, and the shooting that summer.

What was the one thing that linked those three incidents?

The Shakyamuni Buddha statue was smiling. Its right hand was raised in the Abhayamudra gesture dispelling fear of the truth, and its left hand was held lower, the Varadamudra gesture representing how the Buddha heard out the desires of all humankind. Bonzes preached that the Buddha was a savior and that, as such, the Buddha never meted out punishments. Yet the people couldn't help but fear that one day, the Buddha's wrath might befall them. This world was the sinful cage before the Pure Land, and the people who lived during these internecine times were simply surviving amid a churning bloodbath. Someone had to be sinning somewhere, and if there was sin, there simply had to be punishment from on high. No matter how vociferously the monks spoke of the boundlessness of the Buddha's compassion, the people remained fearful of divine retribution. At present, the smiling, beatific statue of the man who disseminated the tenets of Buddhism in order to save the masses looked to Murashige as though it were sneering at him.

Regarding the crisis last winter, it had been a maidservant who had looked after Abe Jinen.

And during the spring crisis, a maidservant had applied the cosmetics to the heads.

And there was the summer crisis…

The sliding door opened with a faint rattle. Only one person ever opened the door knowing Murashige was in the statue hall without announcing themselves. He heard her graceful voice from behind.

"My lord. The hour is late. Would it not be wise to retire for the night?"

Murashige kept staring at the Buddha statue illuminated by the swaying flame.

"Chiyoho. You're the one behind the shooting, aren't you?"

9

Whoever tried to shoot Kawarabayashi Noto could only have done so while lying hidden on the residence's roof. However, even if the shooter had successfully shot Noto dead, they would have nowhere to run. Supposing they had been able to evade the eyes of Murashige or his guard, there was no way he could flee without catching the eye of the sundry attendants and lady servants stationed there. But there was another way to view it all. What if the people of the residence had been in cahoots with the shooter from the very beginning? What if they had sheltered the shooter?

Murashige's residence. The place where he laid his head down to rest, where he was given meals to eat, and where he could put on his raiments and armor. It could also be used as a meeting place. And the one in charge of all the residence's workers was Chiyoho and only Chiyoho. If the drudges of the residence conspired and hid the shooter, awaiting the chance to shoot Noto, then it was inconceivable that Chiyoho was unaware.

If the shooter had accomplices in the residence, it immediately cleared up the question of where the gun came from. Koori Juuemon's investigation confirmed that no guns had been brought into the inner citadel on the day Noto died, and that every gun in the storehouse was accounted for. That could only mean that the gun had been brought *before* that day.

The gun-wielding foot soldiers who served as security for the inner citadel received their weapons from the administrator at the warehouse, returning them there once their shifts were over. The whereabouts of the guns were always clear, and no guns were missing. This meant that even if such a foot soldier had the help of the residence workers, he couldn't have waited for Noto while carrying a gun. And that narrowed the suspects down to one possibility.

Murashige looked over his shoulder unhurriedly. Chiyoho was standing in the darkness like an immaculate snow-blanketed field.

"Was the shooter a Saika man?" asked Murashige.

"Yes."

Chiyoho gracefully approached him and sat down. Murashige was cross-legged, while Chiyoho had one knee raised. They sat opposite each other before the statue of Shakyamuni Buddha.

Murashige was beset by the urge to cut her down then and there, but it ebbed like the tides.

"You're not denying it."

Chiyoho replied, her voice limpid and clear, "Why would I ever lie to Your Lordship or answer you falsely? I did indeed have a Saika man fire at Kawarabayashi Noto."

It wasn't just the foot soldiers Murashige had directly under him who guarded the inner citadel. So, too, did men of the Saika contingent, and those men carried their own guns. The day that Noto died was the only day the Saika men were relieved of guard duty, but every day before that, they had brought their guns into the citadel. One of them must have pretended to leave the citadel once his shift was over, but he actually stayed, spending the night at the residence.

Murashige tried divining the meaning of the conclusion he'd finally managed to reach.

He had ordered Juuemon to investigate, paid Kanbei a visit in his dungeon, and even gone as far as entreat the Buddha to share his insight, all under the belief that finding the culprit behind Kawarabayashi Noto's shooting would root out the traitor who was trying to have Murashige banished from Arioka Castle. And now it was clear who had dispatched that shooter. But did that mean Chiyoho was the traitor?

Was *she* trying to oust Murashige, just as he himself had done to Ikeda Katsumasa?

Though his heart was rocked by bewilderment and suspicion, Murashige couldn't switch mental tacks that abruptly. Which was why he asked, "Did someone put you up to it? Did somebody incite you to shoot Noto?"

As he'd half expected her to, Chiyoho shook her head. "There is no such person. 'Twas all my idea."

"After the night raid this spring, a head that had already been through the identification session was switched out for a head with a contorted face. Was that your doing as well?"

"As ever, I stand in awe of Your Lordship's perception. Yes, I ordered a maid to switch it out with a discarded head."

"That incident fueled the fire of the True Pure Land believers in the castle. A Christian was burned to death, you know."

Gloom broke over Chiyoho's visage.

"It truly pains my heart. That poor soul perished believing he would pass on to the Christians' conception of heaven—'*paraíso*,' was it? Not a day goes by that I do not wish he hadn't died."

But feeling sorry for a single stranger's death during this era of constant war smacked of falsity. Then again, Murashige had survived thus far among samurai who couched their deceptions as stratagems, so he could hardly excoriate Chiyoho as duplicitous.

"What about the winter murder? On the morning Abe Jinen was stabbed to death, who was the one who told Jinen to stand there?"

Chiyoho answered with a smile. "'Twas me."

"Did Jinen know it would kill him?"

Chiyoho must not have seen that question coming, for her eyes opened slightly wider.

"But of course, my liege. 'Twas his dearly held wish to make up for his household's dishonor and to travel to the Western Pure Land. He meekly confided that he was positively grateful, and I was deeply moved by how gallant the son of a samurai could be."

Murashige couldn't be angry at her. Any wrath was superseded by how perplexed he was by her motives. He struggled to understand.

Last winter, spring, and summer, Arioka Castle was faced with crises that threatened to destroy it. Murashige used every trick he knew and defended the castle, sometimes through consultation, sometimes through the spear and gun. What on earth had Chiyoho been doing behind his back?

"Divine punishments…," he muttered.

It was as though he hadn't thought of it himself, but rather Kanbei had fed him the words from within his cage.

"Chiyoho. Did you try to deliver the Buddha's wrath yourself?"

"Oh my, Your Lordship, I would never." She was physically taken aback. "Why would I, as a foolish human being, presume to mete out punishments in the holy Buddha's place? All I wanted…"

Chiyoho put her hands together as though begging for permission. She cast her eyes down a tad.

"…All I wanted was to spread the *belief* that such retribution does occur."

"To whom?"

"Whom else?"

The votive light swayed. Chiyoho's countenance looked not unlike the bodhisattva of compassion, Kannon.

"To the people."

"The people, you say?"

Murashige was flabbergasted.

The people. The little folk who patiently endured the intense waves of heat and cold. The commoners who scrubbed the wells, built the houses, darned the textiles, and worked the hoes. Arioka Castle was surrounded by wood fencing, with Oda forces encircling it at a distance; without any means of fighting, the commoners simply existed in the middle of the besieged castle in their thousands.

"In order to show the people the Buddha's vengeance, you facilitated Jinen's death, swapped out the warriors' heads, and tried to have Kawarabayashi Noto shot."

"'Tis all as Your Lordship says," Chiyoho said, her hands still pressed together.

It was then Murashige remembered that Chiyoho was the daughter of a Hongan-ji priest. She was connected to the *Ikko-ikki* insurrectionists that ruled Kaga Province, subdued southern Settsu, and fought in sundry lands, including Ise, Mikawa, and Noto.

"So your plan was to show the people the Buddha does punish wrongdoers and, in so doing, stir up an insurrection here in Hokusetsu. Did you do all this on your father's orders?"

"My lord." Chiyoho unclasped her hands and spoke in a hushed tone. "I already answered that question. No one instigated me. 'Twas all my idea. I think riling *up* the people would be deplorable."

"I understand you not. I don't understand you, Chiyoho!"

Upon reflection, he realized this might well be the first time he ever raised his voice at his young concubine. Currently, Chiyoho was not his beautiful partner. She was some enigmatic entity.

"You would throw up a smoke screen against *me* with this sophistry? No one can have sincerely believed such trifling 'miracles' as Jinen's murder or the switching of the heads was the Buddha's retribution, no matter how uncanny they were made out to be. So what were you trying to accomplish?"

"My liege." Melancholy tinged Chiyoho's eyes. "I have answered all Your Lordship's questions, and not once have I uttered anything circuitous. If ye say ye understand not, that is because ye are a samurai—a strong and brave warrior."

"Do not twist my words, Chiyoho. I don't think that your behavior was harmless. You disturbed the peace of Arioka for no reason. As the general of this castle, I'm forced to cut you down."

"Please, my lord. When ye kill me, I implore you to make it painless and do it in one stroke. Death…death is inevitable, but I do fear and loathe pain."

Chiyoho straightened up a little.

"My liege. If ye would humor my foolish query, then prithee answer me this. What do the people fear most?"

"Death," Murashige replied immediately. "Man fears death more than anything."

"Does Your Lordship fear death more than anything, too?"

"I…"

Murashige's body shook a little, the platelets on his bracers clinking. They had fended off enemy blades on many an occasion, single-handedly changing the fate of a man who would otherwise have lost an arm and died.

"I am a samurai. I won't say I do not fear death, as samurai who don't fear death always die like dogs. But to fear death more than anything else would prevent a man from carrying on as a warrior."

"I truly believe so, too. Samurai have ways to resist death. They wield spears and guns, and they clad themselves in armor from head to toe. Commoners, meanwhile, do their best to fight off death through the thin armor and dull swords they scrape together. The commoners who cannot even afford that much simply die like so many worms."

The Shakyamuni Buddha kept watching the two, still seated opposite each other.

"…No," Chiyoho added. "While people might kill worms reflexively on sight, they do not go out of their way pushing through the bushes into the mountains to kill them. Yet if commoners' continued existence is inconvenient, they are rooted out of their hiding places and slaughtered. Thus, it can be said that the lives of human beings hold *less* weight than those of worms."

"Such is the world. Naught is colder than this life."

"Indeed, my lord, indeed."

The flame of the votive lights, feeble as the tip of one's little finger, was holding back the night threatening to engulf them from all sides.

"My lord, if I may. You said that what the people fear most is death. I do not agree. 'Tisn't death that they fear most. I have seen that with my own eyes."

"Where?"

"At Ise-Nagashima."

Her voice was sucked into the darkness of the statue hall.

Ise-Nagashima.

Though it was located within hailing distance of the Oda's homeland of Owari, the place had been swarming with the *Ikko-ikki* battle monks.

Fortifications were built on numerous sandbanks at the mouth of the Kiso River, a castle was built around them, and in the end, it resulted in the great fortress where believers barricaded themselves in multitudes. From the Oda's point of view, since they had already conquered Ise, it was as if enemy territory suddenly appeared in the depths of their domain.

The battle turned fierce. During his first bout, Nobunaga's younger brother Hikoshichirou Nobuoki was forced to take his own life, and Ujiie Bokuzen, who could be said to be the most distinguished combatant during the attack on Mino, died during the battle alongside chief retainer Hayashi Shinjirou. Nobunaga fought battle after battle like a raging Asura, and many of his vassals died in the process, but there was no battle in which generals died one after another quite like the attack on Nagashima. It was utter carnage.

"When my father betook himself to Nagashima on Hongan-ji business, I accompanied him due to unavoidable circumstances," said Chiyoho. "By then, the battle had become less intense. My father believed the rumors that while Oda never forgot about Nagashima, there would still be some time before the next brute-force attack. Nagashima's castle was built through unbelievable courage on the sandbar in the river. It looked like it was floating on the water. Any approaching boats were met with merciless volleys of arrows. The ramparts were high and the watchtowers numerous. Those unfamiliar with war tactics such as myself wondered how a castle like this could possibly ever fall.

"Even I know not how many people that castle harbored. Some said fifty thousand, some said a hundred thousand, others said just over ten thousand. The bonze warriors wielded weapons such as *naginata* and guns, and the believers used whatever tools they pleased, boasting that even the Demon King could not take down Nagashima Castle. *Advance to reach heaven, retreat to know hell,* they asserted, with a spirit strong enough to twain the heavens."

Chiyoho clasped her hands in prayer again.

"Then the Oda came. The Kiso River, which was thought to be a natural moat so impregnable that even demons couldn't get close, teemed with warships. The bonfires the Oda lit scorched the skies above, and their war cries echoed through the nights. The artillery cannons pierced through the wooden walls with ease, and all the tough talk dissipated like so much hot air. After that, all I heard people say was that if we died in battle, we would doubtless reach heaven."

For a fleeting moment, Chiyoho's voice quavered.

"...During the battle, I lost sight of my father, leaving me as nothing more than a hobbled weakling. Looking back, 'tis a wonder I wasn't killed, as I had no means of proving my identity. I lived alongside thousands of other abject weaklings in a hut with a rotten roof and walls in a corner of Nagashima Castle. The provisions were meager; in a day, we *might* receive a modicum of rice gruel. We could hear gunshots ring at all hours. In the hut stayed the emaciated, the ill, the maimed, the old, the very young, the deranged, and the feeble. The realm of hungry ghosts is likely very similar to such a place. And every one of us knew that death was near."

Murashige saw that Chiyoho's fingertips were trembling.

"That is the reason we chanted the *nenbutsu*. We clasped the stumps of skin and bones that were our hands and chanted through the day and the night for as long as our voices held out. We beseeched Amitabha to grant us salvation, to let us be reborn in heaven. My liege, do you know what we, who welcomed death, feared most?"

Murashige knew it wasn't death itself, but he couldn't think of what it could be.

Chiyoho's voice was beyond beautiful.

"We feared that not even death would rid us of such suffering."

"......"

"My lord. Though there are those who believe heaven is a land of plenty where they can indulge themselves in abundant luxuries, that is not what we were taught. We took heart when we heard that the Pure Land is a place with nothing in it. Just light, light, and more light... The infinite light emanating from the divine. We wanted to go to heaven as soon as we possibly could. I cannot express the distress our ravenous hunger gave us with words. Frenzied and bloodthirsty soldiers saw us as impeding the war effort; some killed us, others comported themselves abominably. Our anguish was hellish. We did not desire reincarnation, as life is hardship and pain, and we wanted to stop suffering. I find it difficult to believe that there is another faith as pure as what we exhibited in that decaying hut in Nagashima.

"...And yet we could not drive out from our hearts the anxiety of whether our prayers were truly reaching the Buddha. I'm sure Your Lordship understands, as you often speak the words that we heard day in, day out in Nagashima: _Advance to reach heaven, retreat to know hell_... The words that kept us tied down. Could we who lacked so much as a dagger with which to fight be said to be 'advancing' in any way? The priests, the laymen—they fought frantically, desperately, drenched in blood. Meanwhile, we were huddled in a corner of the castle, eking out a day-to-day existence. Could we be said to be participating in the fight to defend and maintain the Buddha's teachings? Is heaven open to those who _wanted_ to advance but couldn't? I cannot say that, even as we chanted the _nenbutsu_, we were untouched by the shadow of doubt. And then the end of the war was at hand."

Murashige knew of the fate of the Nagashima siege. He even saw it in his dreams.

"I am sure Your Lordship knows that the folk who swung around their naginata shouting at one another to die for the sake of the Buddha's teachings ended up wanting peace talks with the Oda. Boats were arranged, and we were to exit the castle. By that point in time, half of the people of the castle had died. Not by the sword, mind you. By starvation. The now-hobbling people of Nagashima Castle left the many scores of corpses behind them and exchanged glances while in their boats, for they could not believe the good fortune that had fallen into their laps. We wondered how our lives, which we were so sure were forfeit, had been saved. We had suffered so much for so long that we must have forgotten how to rejoice over anything. We suspected a dreadful trap was in store for us... An unspoken, vague anxiety spread within the boats crossing the great river. And then someone said it. They said that we were retreating."

The draft rocked the lamp light.

"Terror engulfed us like a wildfire."

Advance to reach heaven...

"If we retreated, would we not 'know hell'? Was it truly okay to *not* die? Wasn't it only right that we should die there, where so many had died while chanting the *nenbutsu* in unison, believing we were all in this together? Wasn't the only thing waiting for us if we survived...*hell*? That was when the guns of the Oda fired upon us."

Before Murashige knew it, Chiyoho's voice had gotten deeper, like it came from the bowels of the earth.

"The hell after the hungry-ghost realm is the Avici hell of unceasing suffering. Just when I thought death, which I once welcomed, had happily grown more distant, death swung back for us. We'd proven we didn't believe hard enough in rebirth in paradise, and right at the moment we had doubted we'd go to hell for it, I heard a shriek amid the gunfire: 'Blessed Amitabha, I have not retreated. I haven't retreated, so please, take me to paradise! *Please!*' Whether someone actually cried out to that effect, I honestly do not know. Perhaps that voice cried out inside my own soul. At any rate, I was surrounded by corpses wherever I did look."

"......"

"'Tis not as though I do not understand Your Lordship's fear of dying in vain. That, too, is what the warrior life drilled into you. And yet what I think...is that a death knowing there is even more suffering on the other side is the cruelest death of all."

After Oda forces shot at the boats leaving Nagashima Castle, they surrounded the remaining stronghold and set it on fire.

It is said that as many as twenty thousand died in the blaze.

"When I awoke, my boat was ashore, and there were neither Oda forces nor our forces. All I saw was a deserted fisherman's hut. My father tells me that I survived through the Buddha's grace. It was not something I could fathom. I fled into the mountains, and I saw Nagashima Castle survivors raid Oda's troop headquarters. I felt as though I was witness to man-eating rakshasa fiends here in the world of the living."

Chiyoho continued:

"I returned to Osaka, living my days as an empty shell. At Kadoma, a villa in Gantoku-ji in Kawachi, I met that chief priest of eminent virtue and requested his knowledge—did the people who retreated go to hell? Would *I* go to hell, too? The honorable priest had once been banished from Hongan-ji for committing a sin; others must have been listening in on what he said, considering it blasphemy. Yet he did impart his wisdom to me regardless. He said that the sect founder's teachings were not so. He explained that in this degenerate Age of the Final Dharma, a foolish commoner attempting to attain salvation through their own power is not in line with the teachings. Why would Amitabha ever claim that retreat led to hell? What a dim-witted *upaya*, he said. The idea made him indignant."

The *Ikko-ikki* always inculcated into its combatants that they were to lend their strength to the battles, for if they didn't, they would be expelled, which in turn would consign them to hell. To preach that this notion flew in the face of the sect's actual teachings was to expose himself to danger.

"When I heard that humankind and life would end while being led astray by such phrases that aren't even in the scriptures, the impermanence of all things sank deeply into my spirit, albeit all too late. I shall never forget that good man's lamentations. Since then, I have led a life I could have only dreamed of thanks to Your Lordship taking me in. When we were so unexpectedly besieged by Oda forces a second time, I vowed that as whether or not we emerge victorious is a matter of chance, in the unlikely event we did lose, I would not let the people of Itami die like those of Nagashima died. That is why the Buddha whisked me back here from the Avici hell that was Nagashima. And it is that belief that has been my salvation."

And then the siege commenced in earnest.

"I told those with whom I was able to speak that paradise also welcomes those who *cannot* advance, try as they might. Many heeded my words, and they lent me their aid. To those with whom I could not speak...I tried giving them a reason to believe that the Buddha stands beside them."

It was then that Murashige remembered how Chiyoho was adored not only by the lowly servants and maids of the residence, but also by the lion's share of the soldiers and townsfolk. When they caught sight of Chiyoho, they behaved themselves and bowed their heads. Part of the reason for that was her status as Murashige's concubine, but that wasn't the full picture. Those who listened to her teachings and took them to heart never balked at laboring for her sake.

That was why Chiyoho was able to orchestrate the Buddha's divine punishment.

"The unexplainable death of the hostage of Abe, betrayer of Osaka. The twisted countenance exhibited by the head taken by the barbarous Christian. The bullet that struck the heinous fiend who slew Muhen from out of nowhere. The people would naturally chalk them all up to divine retribution. In other words, they would come to understand that the Buddha truly is watching over them. That is the manner by which I tried to ease the suffering of the dying."

Murashige had never once entertained the possibility that those incidents were the result of divine retribution, but he acknowledged the existence of the rumors to that effect.

"Earlier, Your Lordship stated that there cannot have been any who believed my trickery to be divine punishment. That might be the case for mighty warriors who fight against death by outfitting themselves with armor. They may not have any use for tall tales of divine retribution. In fact, I would not be surprised if ye found such a thing laughable. Yet with all due respect, in this castle, and in this world, the weak who cannot fight outnumber the strong. And in this fleeting life where false phrases that aren't one of the sect's teachings can mislead man, then good omens, however fabricated, can *save* man—wouldn't Your Lordship agree?"

Murashige couldn't deny Chiyoho's assertions.

The townsfolk *had* been calm and peaceful as of late, the town houses wrapped in a hush that couldn't be explained solely by the notion they were letting the summer pass by with bated breath. It hadn't occurred to Murashige that this might be some sort of sign, but now he suddenly found it peculiar. Where had the sorrow, rage, and fervor induced by the news of Muhen's death disappeared to?

The answer was obvious. The people were mollified when word spread of the death of Muhen's killer, Noto, by lightning strike. In their eyes, the heavens had meted out a fitting punishment for a wicked murderer. Divine vengeance was slow but sure, and none could escape it. The Buddha was watching. So the people came to believe, deriving comfort and reassurance.

Even if what killed Noto had been a gunshot, that bullet might not have had as clear an effect as everything else up to that moment. It was true, however, that it probably did cast a ray of hope.

"All I was thinking about was helping the dying. If that ended up hindering Your Lordship's war tactics, then pray execute me. I...I would like to go to heaven, as I should have back in Nagashima."

Then Chiyoho closed her eyes and solemnly chanted the *nenbutsu*.

The Shakyamuni Buddha statue illuminated by the lamp light said nothing.

10

Murashige was in the dungeon.

He and Kuroda Kanbei were facing each other on either side of a wooden lattice cage hewed of thick pieces of chestnut lumber. Both were hunched over and staring down at the damp earth within the darkness. Kanbei had his injured left leg splayed out, while Murashige was sitting cross-legged. Murashige was wearing a *kataginu* over his robe as the Lord of Settsu, and his bracers and shin guards were still on. Kanbei was clad in the clothes he'd been thrown into prison in the eleventh month of the year prior, which were now filthy black rags. For a moment, Murashige couldn't tell which one of them was inside the cage and which was outside it.

The hour had reached the middle of the night...or so he believed. Murashige didn't know what time it was exactly. He wasn't even sure when Chiyoho had left the statue hall. Murashige had simply found himself back here in this abyssal dungeon.

Murashige told Kanbei what Chiyoho had told him. That wasn't his objective coming into the dungeon. He simply wanted to talk to someone, anyone. Kanbei said nothing, almost as though it was all going in one ear and out the other. When Murashige finished getting the man up to speed, Kanbei stared at him through clouded eyes and murmured:

"In such a short span...Your Lordship has grown awfully haggard."

Lacking water with which to see his reflection, Murashige didn't know how accurate that statement was. But now he thought that maybe something his body was supposed to be brimming with, some driving force no great general could go without, had fallen by the wayside.

"And who can blame Your Lordship? After all, to boil down Lady O-Dashi's intentions, there was no treachery to speak of."

Murashige jolted with surprise.

He had convinced himself that if he could trace the shooter who fired the gun at Kawarabayashi Noto, he could find the one who was trying to supplant him.

Yet he had been counting his chickens before they'd hatched, for while Chiyoho had acted inexcusably on multiple occasions and gone contrary to Murashige's desires, none of it was done out of a desire to oust Murashige and be in league with the Oda. Executing Chiyoho wouldn't restore any of what had been lost. Murashige wasn't so confused as to not understand that.

There is no betrayer...

Kanbei's words seeped into the bottom of Murashige's heart. If there was no traitor, then what could explain the negligence around the castle, or the unrest at the war council, or the commanders' cold stares? There *had* to be some kind of plot afoot. And if he could but find the mastermind behind it all, he could execute them, and everything would revert to normal.

But no such schemer exists!

And didn't that mean that the explanation for the laxity around the castle didn't hold up to scrutiny? There was no conspiracy for his position, no strategy to supplant him. That left no other way to see it—the hearts of his retainers had simply drifted away from him.

"No, there *is* a traitor," muttered Murashige. "All this means is that the gunshot isn't connected to the traitor. I haven't misjudged the situation. I'll have to take hostages for my commanders. Their wives and children will be brought to the inner citadel. Then if anyone tries to pull something, they won't be able to make their move very easily. What say you, Kanbei?"

"That may be, Your Lordship."

"My officers, they obey me. There are only two or three, no, five or six impudent ingrates. I am Murashige, Lord of Settsu. I am a general who has won battle after battle over all my years. Even if public sentiment veers away from me... No, something like that would never happen."

Kanbei nodded quite deeply and spoke, his voice hoarse. "That is all too true; the Lord of Settsu is a man of grandeur who obtained his loyal retainers through all his victories. And I'm sure that back *when* ye were earning all those victories, every single one of your retainers fought for you, come hell or high water."

"I haven't lost!"

Kanbei stared at Murashige.

He had not lost—but he wasn't winning, either. Nor was there any hope he might win. Murashige understood that better than anyone.

"Even if we are not winning, why does that mean I must lose my retainers? Nobunaga lost battles at Shiga and Kanegasaki, to name a few, and the chief retainer of the Oda left the clan. Hashiba Chikuzen disgraced himself gravely by leaving the army without notice or permission, and yet he was entrusted with the heavy responsibility of attacking China. Why should I lose them simply because I haven't won?"

Araki Kyuuzaemon, Ikeda Izumi, Nomura Tango, and many of Murashige's countless vassals had fought alongside him ever since he served the Lord of Chikugo, Ikeda Katsumasa. They had stuck together through thick and thin for over a decade since his first battle. And it wasn't as though Murashige had been a bad general to the younger ones like Kitagawara Yosaku or Nakanishi Shinpachirou. The loyalty and camaraderie he had forged over months and years of putting his life on the line, crumbling after less than a year? Murashige couldn't accept it.

Kanbei replied from within the shadow.

"That is because Your Lordship has only ever assembled retainers through your victories...but the hearts of men are not so easy to understand."

Murashige said nothing.

When neither of them was speaking, the underground prison was frighteningly silent. And what a cramped cage it was. Murashige, ruler of Hokusetsu, had lost Takatsuki, Ibaraki, and Ikeda, and now he felt like he'd been driven at last into the corner that was this dungeon.

"...If you would emerge victorious," said Kanbei, "then there is but one stratagem left to you."

Murashige couldn't believe his ears. Oda troops had kept Arioka encircled for nine months. If there was some way to win, they would have tried it a long time ago.

"Enough of your tomfoolery, Kanbei."

"Who would jest about matters of war?"

Kanbei straightened up within his cage. He couldn't sit cross-legged on account of his crooked legs, but his back and head were upright. He placed his hands on his thighs and bowed his head deeply. His clothes and his face were still covered in dirt, but Murashige once again saw the vigor of the old Kanbei return.

"The time is ripe. The reason I have endeavored not to die up until now was for this very day. Pray allow me to humbly propose a plan for the sake of the Lord of Settsu."

It was so unexpected that Murashige was left speechless.

"Have I Your Lordship's permission?"

"Speak," Murashige managed.

Kanbei sat up gingerly and threw out his chest. Just like Zifang and Kongming, the Chinese military strategists of old, Kanbei presented the stratagem to Murashige in a commanding and stately manner:

"Then I shall tell Your Lordship. Needless to say, the war will be decided entirely by how the Mouri shall move. However, now that the Ukita have switched to the Oda, even if you sent a letter without the Oda catching on, the Mouri would still not move."

Murashige nodded. Kanbei's manner of speech was silky smooth.

"However, if the Lord of Settsu was to leave for Aki in Mouri territory and engage in direct talks with clan leader Mouri Terumoto by way of the shogunate clan in Tomo, I do believe 'tis a different story. The Mouri have their own honor to uphold. If they do not return the favor of Your Lordship coming to them directly, it would be shame enough to rock their clan. They will send troops to Arioka without fail."

"What did you say?!"

Murashige had never heard of the leader himself standing in as a messenger for talks between clans. The tactic was so simple, yet it was so outlandish that it had never occurred to him. Getting the shogunate clan involved also made it quite plausible.

The act of requesting reinforcements from another clan didn't necessarily determine which clan ranked above the other. However, if the leader himself bent the knee and asked for help directly, the Araki clan would likely continue to stand in the Mouri clan's shadow in the future. That being said, Murashige had no intention of fussing over clan rankings. Not anymore. There was no reason why it couldn't be done.

"I believe you would be best served sending Kitagawara Yosaku first. I hear that he has served as a messenger for Amagasaki in the past. I'm sure that he didn't break through Oda encampments, but he knows paths that lead to Amagasaki while evading the Oda's notice."

"Oh-ho."

"After entry into Amagasaki, pray turn to Ura Hyoubunojou for help. He and I have battled against each other before, but he is an honorable warrior and pleasant company. While he shan't go as far as to speak to the head of the clan about it, he will assuredly pity that they cannot uphold their end of the bargain and provide assistance. If 'tis a request from the Lord of Settsu, he will prepare you a boat to Aki at any cost. I know not about overland routes, but the Ukita shan't lay a hand on you if you go by sea."

"I know Ura Hyoubunojou myself. All that very much stands to reason."

"After arriving in Aki, I believe Your Lordship should pay a visit to Ankoku-ji. The chief priest, Ekei, is trusted by the head of the Mouri clan, and he famously hates the Oda as well. He will assist Your Lordship and act as a go-between for you and the clan head."

Murashige nodded vigorously. Kanbei's remarks had a mounting intensity to them.

"The head of the Mouri, Uma-no-kami, is a narrow-minded man, but I believe that for that reason, a famed treasure shall work on him. I am sure ye of all people wouldn't be stingy, but do choose something quality as your gift. And by all means, pray do not forget a special allowance for Kobayakawa Saemonnosuke Takakage. Even if Uma-no-kami, as head of the Mouri, gives the nod, should Saemonnosuke say no, then things will not move forward. That is how the Mouri are."

"I see. I'll remember that. Kanbei, did you work out a plan like that within this cage?"

Kanbei bowed slightly, and his expression relaxed a tad.

"Everything up until now has been nothing more than preparation. Even if ye return with Mouri forces in tow, your chances of beating the Oda are fifty-fifty at best. I have nothing to say to the Lord of Settsu, whose skill in battle is oh so great. Fight to your heart's content."

"My word!"

Kanbei's plan was truly a gift from the heavens. Murashige found himself smiling. He could see it in his mind's eye.

Warships choking the Seto Inland Sea, carrying Mouri forces into Amagasaki Castle. The mouth of Muratsugu, Murashige's son and defender of Amagasaki Castle, agape with shock.

But the Oda's dismay will far outstrip Muratsugu's surprise. Nobunaga himself will probably enter the fray. While the man's battles exhibited a touch of the incredible and the fanatical, if an attack comes from Amagasaki, Oda would be trapped in a pincer between it and Arioka Castle. 'Twould make for a good fight. How long have I been scheming and strategizing all to see that day? I have the geographic advantage. At a guess, two or three enemy generals might respond to collusion beforehand. 'Tis a pity that Muhen died, but we can find another messenger monk suitable for our strategy. When it comes to messengers, I can always borrow a good one from the Mouri.

'Tis the eight month now, and the decisive battle will probably happen this winter. I'll rush across the desolate winter fields of Settsu, employing

every tactic in my book and engaging in a showdown with Nobunaga. I'll wear my Gou Yoshihiro sword at my waist, Iwai armor, and mount a strong Kiso steed. I'll wield the baton of command I've used all these years. What a joy that grand battle will be after this suffocating besiegement.

Murashige shuddered at the prospect of returning victorious to Arioka Castle and being greeted by his commanders. And even if he lost, there was no better end for a samurai than to die in grand fashion as a brave warrior who fought in a great battle whose tales would be passed down from generation to generation.

Murashige grew impatient; he wondered why he was spending any more time in this dungeon. He might have been about to get on his feet straightaway when he noticed a spider crawling on the back of his hand.

The spider was minuscule. It was colorless, perhaps because it lived in the dark, and it was treading Murashige's hand as though it owned it.

He was about to smack it dead, but his hand stopped; Chiyoho's words sprang back to mind. She'd said the life of a person was lighter than a worm. He was on the verge of recalling something else—what else had Chiyoho said? What had she said was the way of the world?

Good omens.

Good omens save souls. That was what Chiyoho had told him.

No, that wasn't what he was trying to remember. She'd said something before that, too. What was it?

Murashige had no idea why he was dwelling on this. He knew he should just crush the bug and leave this dark dungeon. He had to prepare for war. He had to make his arrangements quickly so that he could kill and kill some more.

That was when he remembered. Chiyoho's words came back to him: It was the way of the world that a *fabricated* good omen could save souls as well.

Why was this memory resurfacing? And why at a time when he'd received a stratagem from Kanbei—when everything might just come to a head? Were he a weaker man, he might have labored under the impression that such make-believe was true salvation and jumped at it, but the Lord of Settsu was different. *I'm different from them*, he told himself.

Am I actually *any different?*

Kanbei was looking at Murashige, eyes peeking from between his unkempt hair and beard. Murashige couldn't read those eyes. Kanbei was looking into the emptiness, as though he had totally forgotten about the plan he'd just related.

Murashige waved his hand and threw off the spider.

"I see," he said. "So this was your war, was it?"

A shadow crept over Kanbei's expression.

11

The Mouri would not come. He'd thought it through so many times. He *knew* the Mouri wouldn't come.

And yet somewhere in the recesses of Murashige's heart, part of him thought it was still a maybe. Humans clung to the meanest scrap of a good omen if it allowed them not to acknowledge their destruction, and that was what Kanbei took advantage of.

Come to think of it, when Kanbei cajoled that jailer into trying to kill me, didn't he say something to this effect?

"Lord of Settsu, it turns out that killing from inside this cage is, contrary to expectations, not so difficult."

"Kanbei…did you try to kill me from within your cage?"

Now that it dawned on him, it was all so clear.

No matter where, when, or who, those who flee never claim to be running for the hills. They always couch it in other terms. Of course, retreat was a valid strategy in war. In fact, if one side didn't know retreat was an option, it'd be less of a battle and more of a slaughter. But who on earth believed those who fled when they claimed they were running to "call for help"? Moreover, Murashige was a general. It wasn't unusual for all of a castle's retainers to evacuate during a losing battle, but he'd never heard of a general slipping away alone while the retainers held out, not even in fiction.

"If I carry out your plan, my good name would definitely be tarnished for ages to come. Was it not my head but my reputation you were after?"

Kanbei's expression was changing. His eyes glinted as though brushed with oil. Murashige had seen Kanbei's eyes turn that way before. It was when he spoke of the death of Abe Jinen the year prior.

Kanbei snickered.

"To think ye would stay. I must say I am a touch surprised."

"Kanbei!"

"My understanding was that Your Lordship would not hesitate to jump at the chance. What did I fail to notice, I wonder?"

Murashige thought it a gift from the heavens. If he hadn't heard Chiyoho talk about fictions woven to give people peace of mind, he wouldn't have been able to refrain from venturing forth. The dream Kanbei had fed him was too sweet.

Now Kanbei was rocking slightly, and even though Murashige saw through his ploy, he looked vaguely pleased. Murashige was relieved he'd averted the deadly trap, and he was dumbfounded by just how far-reaching Kanbei's plot was.

"Kanbei, were these ten months all for this?"

Kanbei simply chuckled to himself.

Whenever Arioka was in danger of falling, Murashige had descended to the dungeon and showered questions on Kanbei. And each time, Kanbei sounded Murashige out, probing into his psyche and prying information. Kanbei also made sure to always throw Murashige the lifeline he'd needed to overcome the castle's latest crisis. Kanbei had otherwise never had any real reason to answer Murashige's inquiries. Murashige had chalked it up to Kanbei's supposed need to flaunt his intellect. But he'd been wrong. It had all been for this moment. For the killing stroke that would bury Murashige's honor forevermore.

"Even if you drag my name through the mud, no one will recognize it as your own glorious deed. Why do you hate me so? I spared you your life."

Kanbei laughed loudly. "Your Lordship, you 'spared me my life' for your own convenience, and yet ye would be so patronizing about it? How utterly absurd. I'm sure Your Lordship hasn't forgotten that I *begged* you to kill me."

"So you begrudge me my sparing your life? Do you feel that much shame from getting thrown into this dungeon?"

"I care not about *shame!*" he spat, his cloudy eyes pointed at Murashige. "I can scarcely believe you'd ask at this late date why I hate you. That alone is reason enough."

Murashige could think of a whole host of grudges borne against him. He'd spent all his life engaging in war and intrigue. But one inkling in particular struck him.

"Don't tell me this is about Shojumaru."

No reply.

Which could only mean it *was* about Shojumaru.

Murashige winced, but he wasn't necessarily shocked. To act in a way that caused hostages to be killed cast shame upon one's clan, but it was also something that happened with regularity in this life. If one's child became a hostage, one could leave them to die in order to save one's own skin, and if one's parent became a hostage, they could save themselves by leaving *them* to die. That stubborn determination was another facet of the samurai, however despicable. Murashige couldn't believe Kanbei would hold a grudge over something like that.

"You're still stuck on that, Kanbei? I shan't say I don't understand the misery of losing your child, but such is the samurai life. And I find it very difficult to believe you didn't understand that."

"The samurai life?"

Kanbei grinned contemptuously.

"If Shojumaru had died on the battlefield, that would be an honorable warrior's death. If Shojumaru had been executed because I had turned my back on the Oda, that, too, would be an honorable death. If I had abandoned a weeping Shojumaru while being torn between the conflicting demands of my master's household and the Oda, I could at least tell myself that it couldn't be helped, as we are all warriors. But why did Shojumaru die?"

Then he flew into a rage.

"If I had been sent back from Arioka alive or as a head, either way, Shojumaru would be unharmed! Yet ye saw fit to do the unprecedented and imprisoned me here, twisting the ways of this world in so doing! I told you before—if ye bend the ways of the world, the wheel of cause and effect will turn, and turn it did, for now Shojumaru's life has been taken. Murashige, what killed my child was your vanity! Your desire to be seen as merciful!"

Kanbei raised his quivering hands from his emaciated frame, as if he was attempting to strangle Murashige right then and there.

"He was a bright one, my boy. Strong, too. He was the light of the Kuroda—*my* light. Murashige, I would kill you a hundred times, and it would never be enough. Ye called your vainglory 'tactics,' and my boy died for it! Ye took from him a chance to die a death befitting a warrior, and so I decided to take the same from you. May your name be tarnished forevermore!"

Struck by the sensation that the cage had disappeared and Kanbei was right before his eyes, Murashige lurched backward slightly. But of course, that was just a momentary illusion, and Kanbei was still in his cage, his hands far outside reach of Murashige.

"And that's your driving motive, is it?" said Murashige, masking his momentary fright. "Your plan's in pieces now. You've nothing left to try. Rot in that cage, and you'll join your boy soon enough."

"Know that ye are wrong. I said that the time is ripe. My plan has *already* come to fruition."

"What?"

Kanbei threw his arms open wide. "I could have made a simple suggestion at any time. Why does Your Lordship think I waited for ten months? For what purpose did I sit through your monologues and wag my silver tongue to solve your castle's crises? I did so because until today, I would hate it if the castle did fall. Does Your Lordship understand why that is?"

"To earn my trust, I'd imagine."

Kanbei laughed and slapped his knee. "Your *trust*! Ha-ha! Not so, Lord of Settsu, not so!"

Caressing his scarred head, he continued:

"Pray think of it this way: If Your Lordship had surrendered the castle too quickly, then just like Matsunaga Danjo before you, ye would have been allowed back into the Oda's service. You would have been a temporary traitor and nothing more, so you could have vindicated your honor based on your achievements. But that would be so banal. So I wedged myself into Your Lordship's problems to solve them, and it was precisely because you settled those problems that the war dragged on, wouldn't ye agree? Ten months have already passed. Nobunaga will never forgive you now."

Had it not been for Kanbei's help, Arioka Castle would have fallen long ago, or at least, there was a chance it would, thought Murashige. It was difficult to gauge Nobunaga's mood, but Murashige might have been allowed back in the fold even if he'd surrendered the castle as late as that spring. But in consulting with Kanbei, he'd solved the issues facing the castle one by one—to his own detriment. Now that the war had dragged on *this* long, he wouldn't be so pardoned.

The smile didn't disappear from Kanbei's face.

"There's another reason, a more *entertaining* one for me. I waited ten whole months for no other purpose than to see the day your honorable retainers would forsake their lord. I waited for the days of false rumors and baseless gossip, where everyone would start searching for betrayers and informers in their midst. So long as the Mouri never came, the Araki clan retainers would never last, and I could see that plainer than the noonday sun. At first, I was sure it would take less than half a year, but to my surprise, you held strong. I surmise that's thanks to the work of Lady O-Dashi."

Kanbei erased his expression and stared at Murashige. Kanbei's face was grimy, his eyes watery, and his voice was so gentle as to be called *kindly*.

"Lord of Settsu, what ever will ye do, now that you've no allies in your own castle?"

" . . . . . . "

"Does Your Lordship plan to continue the review meetings where nothing gets done until the very last grain of rice is consumed?"

" . . . . . . "

"'Tis true that my suggestion will end in failure nine times out of ten, resulting in disgrace upon your name. But there's no guarantee that it could *never* succeed, either. Is Your Lordship capable of forgetting your ambitions and twiddling your thumbs while awaiting death, even after catching wind of an all-or-nothing stratagem? Is it really in you to pretend you've forgotten your dreams of commanding large armies across the plains of Settsu? Nay, I say. Before long, Your Lordship shall be leaving this castle. I know that for a fact…and as such, I say to you that the time is ripe, and that my plan has already come to fruition."

Murashige didn't think that would come to pass. The dream that Kanbei spoke of was poison. And who would imbibe what they knew to be poison?

Yet Murashige's heart was already flying toward the battlefield.

"I now have no more reason to live. Do what ye will."

With that, Kanbei dropped his head. It was as though the strings that had been keeping him moving were gone now, and he was melting into the darkness of the prison where no sunlight would shine ere the fall of Arioka. There sat hunched the two warriors, facing each other.

Eventually, Murashige picked up his candlestick holder and languidly got to his feet. The man had no intention of killing Kanbei. Whether he lived or not was of no great import, and therefore, he didn't want to accumulate bad karma if he didn't have to. When Murashige mounted the first step, Kanbei spoke with the tone of someone asking after the weather.

"Lord of Settsu. No matter what fate may befall you, this is our last face-to-face as general and prisoner, so pray allow me to ask one question."

Murashige stopped in his tracks and looked behind him. The candlelight was too weak to illuminate Kanbei, so Murashige didn't know where in the sea of darkness he was.

"I'll allow it," replied Murashige.

"Then I ask Your Lordship this: What made you oppose the Oda?"

"Heh…" Murashige smiled despite himself—he hadn't expected that question after all this time. "You said it yourself, didn't you?"

"I did?"

"Very well. Hark," Murashige said into the darkness. "I have no justification for governing Settsu. 'Tis not the land of my forefathers, nor is it a land I'm ruling as my mission from the Oda any longer. And yet I also didn't find myself in that position due to any power of charisma to attract people, as you yourself stated. I won't say that there's no truth to that. Can you not see what reason I may have to go against the Oda?"

No reply.

"Has it never occurred to you that Nobunaga's the same?" Murashige continued. "He's from a deputy lordship's household in Owari, and a side lineage at that. Not exactly the lofty family status of one who would rule all the lands. So would he rule the lands as an assignment from higher up? No, that doesn't apply to him, either. The man made it all the way to Minister of the Right, only to resign from that post. Folk everywhere may acknowledge his might, but they don't understand why they ought to be governed by the Oda. A man who would win a land through strength alone will suffer a piteous end… I'm quoting you there, too."

Murashige recalled the day he visited Azuchi Castle. And what a majestic castle it was. But while the retainers of his clan and his fellows sang the praises of the giant fortress's imposing opulence, Murashige had one thought: *'Tis just like Epang Palace. Its opulence will do little to defend it.*

"What Nobunaga did have was the charisma. No one could take their eyes off the man. And I couldn't suppress the desire to risk it all in a bet against the Oda. Nonetheless…he lost that charisma. I've killed my share of people, but he killed far too many."

This was an age of civil war; it was kill or be killed. Yet even in a world where exterminations and scorchings were commonplace, Nobunaga killed dizzying numbers.

"That goes for Ise-Nagashima and for Echizen. Truly, the *Ikko-ikki* battle monks were a thorn in his side, but he killed *tens of thousands*, which is madness. Then there is Harima's Kozuki Castle two years ago…which you saw with your own two eyes."

Kozuki Castle, where Akamatsu Masanori had been holed up, fell at the hands of Murashige and Hashiba Hideyoshi. The Hashiba forces entered Kozuki Castle and massacred the last pockets of resistance among the Akamatsu. That was all par for the course, as Murashige was aware. It was afterward that the cruelty became extraordinary.

"The women and children were captured, lined up at the border, then skewered and crucified."

Two hundred people, two hundred corpses exposed for all to see.

"I've heard the rationale that it was all to intimidate the Ukita and the samurai of Harima, as they weren't sure to leave or to stay. However, that was hardly a respectable battle. Nor were the Ukita cowed, and Harima's samurai kept changing alignments anyway. The women and children died for nothing."

Murashige couldn't be sure Kanbei was even still there in the darkness; he heard not a peep from him.

"Everyone has seen how the Oda forces fight. While human beings are more than capable of tossing children into boiling oil if ordered to do so, there *are* limits. Both the common folk and the retainers of the Oda will abandon the Oda in the near future. Kanbei, one can avert punishment by a lord through an apology, and one can avert punishment by gods and the Buddha through prayer. But none can fight against punishment meted by the common man or retainers. That was what I feared. Everything I did, I did to preserve my clan. All I wanted was a means to survive as a warrior. And that meant not getting dragged into the ruin the Oda are soon to experience."

Perhaps I was a bit hasty, Murashige thought for the first time, with a slight bitterness in his soul.

"But I grew battle-drunk, and I forgot the purpose behind my turning against them. That was my foremost mistake... Farewell, Kanbei. I have horizons to conquer. As for Shojumaru, I do pity you. I'm sure you'll resent the words coming from my mouth, but this life is a sad one, and tragedies of all sorts take place in this world."

Murashige headed back to the surface, back into the carnage. All he left in his wake was pitch darkness.

On the second day of the ninth month of the year 1579, Araki Murashige slipped out of Arioka Castle.

The castle's fate was sealed.

Epilogue　　What Is Reaped

1

Blood splashed on the twilight-colored reedbed.

The enemy numbered six. Fighting alongside Araki Murashige, Lord of Settsu, were Koori Juuemon, Inui Sukesaburou, and Sagehari of Saika. However, Inui Sukesaburou had precious tea utensils in the wicker luggage at his back, and since he mustn't break them, he couldn't move freely. All six of their opponents wore *jingasa* headwear and *do-maru* chest armor, and judging by the long spears in their hands, they had to be patrolman foot soldiers. Viewing Murashige and his party as deserters, they very much looked down on them. One of their number recklessly stepped closer, and with a flash of Murashige's Nara-steel sword, the six became five.

"Bastard!"

The foot soldiers brandished their spears. Upon learning that they intended to avenge the man, Murashige grew relieved. If they had fled like rabbits and called for help, there was nothing more they could do.

"Don't let your guard down!" Murashige shouted in a deep, rough voice, his armor stained with the blood of the slain.

Koori Juuemon feinted with his short hand spear, then threw it at a foot soldier, who was too caught by surprise to try dodging. The tip of the spear hit his throat, and he breathed his last. Then Juuemon smoothly drew his sword.

Now that their numerical superiority was gone, fear ran across their faces. Seizing his opportunity, Murashige chose one of them and charged. Juuemon slashed at another. The remaining two foot soldiers flinched at their opponents' speed, but they, too, were soldiers in times of war, and they didn't panic indefinitely. One of them angled his *sangen'yari* for a stab at Murashige. Murashige saw it coming and evaded the attack; the spear instead landed a heavy blow against the shoulder of the soldier who had been assaulting Murashige with a blade. The man, in his agony, let his spear fall to the ground, and Murashige cut off his head.

"Don't use spears, use swords!" shouted the man who appeared to be the eldest of the three remaining soldiers.

A long spear could easily stop a brawny horseback warrior in his tracks, but they were difficult to wield to their fullest when there were multiple long spears near one another. The foot soldiers dropped their long spears and drew their swords, but Juuemon had been waiting for that moment. He pulled his hand spear back off his victim's corpse and continually thrust it once, twice, three times. His enemy couldn't handle it and immediately found himself pierced through the chest and covered in red.

Murashige was caught between the last two, who attacked from either side simultaneously. He fended off the blow from the right and, for the remaining strike, left it up to his faith in the protection granted him by Suwa Daimyojin. The sword missed his vitals, doing nothing more than damaging the sleeve of his armor. Murashige swung his sword down on the enemy to the right several times, and the enemy struck back by the skin of his teeth. The Nara steel chipped and bent right away, but in the end, Murashige's volley of rending thrusts pierced through the foot soldier's thin armor.

The last soldier threw away his sword and turned his back without a word.

We can't let him get away, thought Murashige.

That instant, Sagehari said, "I shall shoot him."

He'd readied his arquebus at some point, and he was taking aim at the fleeing soldier.

"Good. Fire."

No sooner than Murashige had said those words did the gunfire jet out. Sagehari's aim was true, for the bullet landed in the soldier's head.

The twilight deepened, and the skies were red as the flames of hell. Murashige tried sheathing his now-bent Nara-steel sword, tossing it aside when he saw it wasn't possible. Juuemon was gripping his left arm; had he sustained an injury? Sagehari was keeping a watchful eye on the reeds to see if there were any more enemies. He was holding the bamboo cartridge such that he could load more bullets at any moment. Inui Sukesaburou, who hadn't been able to join the fray, seemed somewhat chagrined by that fact.

"The sound of that gunfire might attract more enemies," said Murashige. "Come, let's go."

Juuemon knelt before him.

"My lord, this is the end for me."

"What?"

"I thought I should serve Your Lordship through my spear one last time. Now that I have done so, I can no longer accompany Your Lordship to Amagasaki."

While Juuemon had during the nine months of besiegement called tasks difficult, he had never said he could not do something. Murashige's eyes flared with anger.

"Are you quitting your post? Do you mean to abandon me?!"

Juuemon bowed his head deeply and tensed his stomach. "I would never abandon Your Lordship!" he shouted, his voice choked and anguished. "Though it is beyond my meager abilities, I am the leader of the guard. The guard follow my orders, and they have defended Your Lordship with all their might, sharing in both the hardships and sorrows that come with charging across the same battlefield. Why must I exit the castle and leave them behind?"

"I'm not abandoning Arioka Castle, Juuemon. I *will* come back. I'll come back with the Mouri in tow."

"I greatly look forward to that day. Yet I shall await it alongside not Your Lordship but the guard. My liege, I beg of you, prithee order me to lead the guard and take charge in your absence. I...I cannot abandon them!"

Juuemon was on the floor, and his arm was bleeding.

He had said all this knowing death might be his reward for doing so, and Murashige understood that. Murashige let his arms go slack.

"Very well," he muttered. "Return to Arioka Castle and support it until I return."

"Without fail, my liege."

"And in the unlikely event… No, in the near-impossible event that I never return, I want you to live, Juuemon. You have the talent to be a commander. It would be a shame to let you die under me right now. I want you…"

A note of self-derision crept into his voice.

"I want you to die a good death one day, under a good lord."

"My liege!"

"Go now. Obey your orders!"

"Yes!"

Juuemon looked at Inui Sukesaburou, whose eyes were tearing.

"Sukesaburou. I leave our lord in your hands."

"Please do, Juuemon. And pray give our brethren my regards."

Juuemon smiled faintly. "Message received. Farewell. Now, if you'll excuse me!"

He bowed his head deeply again, then clutched his hand spear before turning on his heels.

Carrying his arquebus on his back, Sagehari watched him go.

"I shall be off, too," said Sagehari.

"…Is that so?" replied Murashige.

Sagehari bowed his head lightly.

"I'm not a vassal of the Lord of Settsu. I'm a follower of Magoroku of the Suzuki. It was an honor and a privilege to accompany Your Lordship, but if I break from Magoroku, the villagers of Saika will criticize me behind my back."

Sagehari was speaking sense. Murashige nodded.

"I see. You did good work."

"An underling like me was not worthy to be in Your Lordship's august presence. I must express my delight at Your Lordship's kind words. Now…" Sagehari faltered a little; this wasn't the easiest thing for him to say. "Well, to be frank, I was the one who shot at Noto."

"...Is that right?"

Guns weren't the most accurate weapons. Murashige had figured that having been able to shoot Noto despite that inaccuracy meant it could only be of an elite sharpshooter even among the Saika gunslingers. And Sagehari boasted that level of skill.

Sagehari scratched his head.

"I could never refuse a request from Lady O-Dashi. I did think I could hit Noto, but that lightning bolt gave me quite a start... While I said this is the end—and it was no lie when I said that I would return to Magoroku—that is just an excuse. I am loath to say it before Your Lordship, but Lady O-Dashi is the one person who can make me think that the saying—*advance to reach heaven, retreat to know hell*—is a lie, because she taught me that a heaven exists right here. All my life, I've been told to fight, to press forward. For the first time, I got to *breathe*."

While Sagehari's manner of speaking was rather above his lowly station, it didn't displease Murashige. Seeing someone to whom Chiyoho had been such a shining star stoked a strange gratification in him.

"There's no knowing what might happen in an Arioka Castle without Your Lordship," Sagehari continued. "If I am to die anyway, I would like to die protecting Lady O-Dashi."

"Understood. Do as you please."

Sagehari bowed his head once more. "Farewell. I wish Your Lordship the best."

With that, he exited through the reeds.

The sun was beginning to set over the reedbed, where Murashige and Inui Sukesaburou stood alone. Sukesaburou was protecting the wicker luggage that Murashige entrusted to him as though it was as precious as his life. It contained the famed tea jar, Torasaru—the trump card with which they would beg the Mouri for help.

"Let's go, Sukesaburou."

"Yes, my liege!"

Lord and retainer left the corpses and pools of blood behind them, and together, they walked through the fields of northern Settsu as the day grew darker. Murashige looked to his rear. Arioka Castle was there, spanning the land of Hokusetsu like a pitch-black silhouette beneath a sky the color between scarlet and ultramarine.

2

The wheel of cause and effect turned and turned.

What became of Arioka Castle?

On the fifteenth day of the tenth month, Nakanishi Shinpachirou colluded with Takigawa Sakon and allowed Oda forces inside the castle. The forts defending the north, west, and south of Arioka fell, the town of Itami was taken by the Oda, and the samurai district was burned, leaving only the inner citadel as a holdout. The remaining vassals defended it for a little over a month, but in the end, the Mouri never came, and the castle fell altogether.

What of Nomura Tango?

When Fort Hiyodorizuka was attacked, he lost almost all his soldiers, including the men from Saika. He attempted to surrender, but it was not accepted, and he was summarily killed.

What of Araki Kyuuzaemon?

The commanders' wives and children were taken hostage, and Kyuuzaemon was given the role, along with another chief retainer, of persuading Murashige to give up Amagasaki Castle. Murashige refused, and Kyuuzaemon didn't return to Arioka Castle, instead escaping to Awaji Province.

What of Ikeda Izumi?

Izumi remained in Arioka Castle, serving as a caretaker, but when he learned that Araki Kyuuzaemon's flight sealed the fates of the women and children hostages, he put a gun to his head and pulled the trigger. He left behind the following death poem:

> *Though I shall vanish*
> *like a single drop of dew,*

my thoughts will linger
with the poor little children.
What on earth will be their end?

3

As for Nakanishi Shinpachirou, after he allowed in the Oda forces, he was installed as a retainer of Ikeda Shouzaburou Tsuneoki, who was given northern Settsu. History records no noteworthy exploits from him afterward.

Takayama Dariyo was spared following the fall of the Arioka Castle and placed under Shibata Shurinosuke Katsuie of northern Settsu. That was because his son Ukon, who had switched allegiances to Oda at an earlier date, was proving to be of great use to the Oda clan.

No one knows what became of Suzuki Magoroku. He may have been killed during the defense of Fort Hiyodorizuka, or he may have been tenacious enough to survive. His son would later serve the Tokugawa clan in Kii Province.

Kitagawara Yosaku avoided death and stayed in northern Settsu, living in an area named Onohara. It's said that he went on to take in and raise Murashige's orphaned grandchild.

There is no record of whether Sagehari survived or died, though history does state that nearly all the Saika men in Arioka Castle perished in battle.

In order to thrive off the saintly reputation of Muhen, who had disappeared without a trace in northern Settsu, a man appeared in Azuchi claiming to be him. He earned some fame, but his deceit was exposed not long after, and he was executed.

Inui Sukesaburou managed to defend Murashige and the treasured tea utensils all the way to Amagasaki Castle. Nothing is known of his subsequent fate. Perhaps he moved from one battlefield to the next alongside Murashige.

Koori Juuemon survived the battle in Arioka Castle, and he took part in the Siege of Osaka under Toyotomi Hideyori thirty-six years later. He was one of Hideyori's seven handpicked elite military leaders and given the title Master of the Stables. Juuemon was appointed a flag magistrate, and he fought all his life, ending it after more than seven decades of constant battle by committing seppuku.

4

Many, if not most, of the commanders' wives, children, and relatives were executed.

One hundred and twenty-two people were crucified near Amagasaki Castle.

Three hundred and eighty-eight women and one hundred and twenty-four men in Arioka Castle were pushed into their homes and burned to death.

At the capital, thirty-odd wives and children of high-ranking commanders were beheaded.

Chiyoho was sent to the capital. Wearing a white death kimono over her robe, she descended from the carriage that took her to the Rokujo-gawara execution ground, refastened her obi, tied her hair up, and pulled back the collar of her robe. She was not shaken in the slightest; her beheading was calm, peaceful. She left behind a number of death poems, one of which is the following tanka:

> *The moon in your heart*
> *that you saw fit to polish*
> *remains unclouded;*

now venture you with the light
toward the realm in the West.

"The realm in the West" refers to the paradise that is Amitabha's Pure Land. It is said that the majority of the women who were executed with Chiyoho were just as composed as her when they departed this life.

5

Araki Murashige survived.

After slipping away from Arioka Castle, he turned to Amagasaki and Hanakuma Castles, fighting on until the seventh month of the next year. He must have been waiting for the Mouri to arrive. When Hanakuma Castle fell, Murashige again survived, escaping to Mouri territory.

Afterward, he returned to Settsu as a master of the tea ceremony, living a full life and dying seven years following the fall of Arioka. He likely wrote a death poem or at least had dying words, but they are lost to time. Perhaps no one left his words behind.

6

Oda Nobunaga breathed his last at Honno-ji in Kyoto, three years after the fall of Arioka.

They say his body was never found.

7

What became of Kuroda Kanbei?

After Arioka Castle fell, Kanbei was rescued by his vassals, including one Kuriyama Zensuke. The jailer, Katou Matazaemon, provided them the needed guidance. Kanbei was emaciated, his cheeks hollow and his belly swollen like that of a *gaki* hungry ghost. His hands and feet looked like withered branches, the wounds on his head were pustulous, and his crooked legs did not heal for a long time. Hashiba

Hideyoshi, Lord of Chikugo, was extremely pleased that Kanbei had returned alive, and he suggested that Kanbei leave matters to him so that he may rest. Kanbei obeyed, facing his wounded body and mind head-on at the hot springs of Arima.

The more days passed, the more he became able to sit up and down on his own, as well as to eat rice instead of congee and to walk (albeit with the aid of a cane). His voice turned less hoarse, and his eyes adjusted to the light. It was now the twelfth month, and winter blanketed the land.

Kuriyama Zensuke and several others were at the lodging where Kanbei was convalescing, carrying out errands for him. Yet when Kanbei heard about Chiyoho's execution, he left with no companion save for his cane. The nights were long now, and the village of Arima, which was situated deep in the mountains, was covered with snow. When Kanbei was captured in Arioka Castle during the year prior, it had also been winter—a year had since passed. Strange, then, that to Kanbei, it felt like it had all transpired over the course of a single night.

Kanbei paced slowly, leaving prints of two feet and a cane in the snow.

His life in that dungeon seemed like a dream to him now. And what a horrifying dream it was. He had wielded his cunning to permanently tarnish a man's name, but what were the fruits of his travails? As the war dragged on, a great many soldiers and civilians died, and hundreds were crucified, burned, or decapitated.

The bamboo branches drooped, unable to bear the weight of the snow, which crashed down sonorously. Kanbei didn't even look in the direction of the noise.

While I was in that dungeon, I was possessed by an evil spirit... That was what Kanbei kept telling himself. Yet it was his own wisdom that refused to allow him that easy escape. *No, I was the one who sought to drag Murashige's name through the mud for bringing a dishonorable death upon my son—never once sparing a thought to what that might lead to.*

At the same time, Kanbei's intellect would not let him shoulder all the blame, either. He had reckoned Araki Kyuuzaemon and the other chief retainer might head to Amagasaki as messengers to ask Murashige to surrender, but even he could never have suspected that the chief retainers would make such a hasty escape after failing to persuade Murashige. According to what he learned via hearsay, Nobunaga expressed greater wrath at those chief retainers fleeing than when Murashige left Arioka Castle. While Chiyoho's days were at an end no matter what, if that unfortunate event hadn't come to pass, hundreds of others would not have been executed.

Thinking about it that way, it was quite possible to take a different view regarding the war persisting for so long. It was said that when Nobunaga learned of Murashige's mutiny, he dispatched soldiers to the mountains of northern Settsu and Harima to kill the commoners who fled. If Arioka had surrendered the castle while Nobunaga's fury had yet to dissipate, the people of Itami might have been massacred like at Ise-Nagashima. Could it not be said that his plan to prolong the war bought the time needed for Nobunaga's head to cool, thereby saving the lives of the masses?

"No..."

Kanbei shook his head.

Don't lie to yourself. In that dungeon, I was consumed by my wrath at Shojumaru's violent death and at Murashige for bending the ways of the world. I never thought that innocents would get wrapped up in the consequences of my revenge, and even if I had, and even if hundreds or thousands of people died, I would have chalked it up as just deserts for Murashige's crimes. Looking at it that way, all I can say is that I was possessed by an evil spirit of a sort. An evil spirit that still lurks within me.

The wind rustled the bamboo thicket.

Murashige's vanity killed Shojumaru, and Kanbei's resentment dwelled within him, spiraling around and around and getting the women and children of Arioka Castle crucified, beheaded, and set ablaze. However, Murashige had been trying to appeal to the people, whom he believed would never accept Nobunaga's ruthless method of waging war, by showing them he was different from him. If one pointed to Nobunaga's killing too many as the root of all this evil, one could just as easily counter that it was Nobunaga's thoroughness of killing that ensured there was little war within Oda territory for the

The Samurai and the Prisoner

time being. In these internecine times, the causes of these evils were intertwined, and those effects left no corner of this fleeting world of misery untouched. Could it be that in a world such as this, cherishing one's own child was itself an act that flew in the face of the ways of the world and consequently stood as another root of evil?

If that's so, then I am the one at fault.

In Kanbei's estimation, perhaps all samurai, all commoners, all monks, and all human beings were similarly weighed down by sin and trying to endure it through chanting the *nenbutsu*, making donations, converting to Christianity, or, as many samurai did, seeking to ease their hearts by oversimplifying things as all the fault of the weak.

And who can blame them? Isn't that inevitable?

Isn't it true that people have no way to resist the truth of this world— that evil causes produce evil effects, and evil effects produce evil causes? And if that is the case, will I continue as I have been doing, working out schemes and killing and killing and killing some more?

Before he knew it, Kanbei was going around the bamboo grove. Chilled to the bone, he dragged himself back toward the inn.

"Over there!" cried Zensuke, who came rushing over to him. "My lord, what are ye doing out in this freezing weather? I implore Your Lordship to take care of yourself!"

"Oh, this is nothing."

Irritated, Kanbei waved a hand dismissively, trying to shoo him away, but Zensuke didn't back down.

"Your Lordship has a guest."

Kanbei knit his brow. Hashiba Hideyoshi would have sent a messenger, not a guest. Kanbei didn't know who it could be.

The inn didn't have a room that was fancy enough for greeting a guest. Kanbei gave it some thought before issuing his orders.

"Lead the guest into the Buddha statue hall. I'll be there right away."

He let his vassals help him change into more presentable clothing. An anxious Zensuke had his lord warm up by drinking a decoction he'd prepared for him. Kanbei went to the statue hall, wondering who this guest could be and what business they were here for. The owner of the inn had been considerate enough to set up cushions and armrests on the wooden floor.

When the guest saw Kanbei enter, he bowed deeply; Kanbei didn't have to look at the sword at the man's waist to know he was a samurai, as his demeanor gave it away. The face that looked up at him seemed familiar, but the man was someone Kanbei ultimately didn't recognize.

"I'm afraid that, as my legs pain me, I must be so rude."

He sat on the cushion with his left leg outstretched.

"My apologies for coming uninvited while ye are resting," said the samurai, his voice clear.

Even as he was still trying to figure out who or what this man was, Kanbei gave his name.

"I am Kodera Kanbei."

As he still technically belonged to the Kodera clan, he had to announce himself as such. He didn't, however, think that would last for long, for inwardly he believed he'd be going by Kuroda again in the near future.

The guest nodded. "My name is Takenaka Gensuke. This is my first time meeting you, Kanbei."

Oh, so he's a Takenaka.

He bore a resemblance to Takenaka Hanbei Shigeharu, a retainer of Hashiba, Lord of Chikuzen, and a friend with whom Kanbei had often spoken of the future. Hanbei had departed this life in the summer of that year, while Kanbei was still imprisoned.

"Takenaka? So you're Hanbei's…"

"Hanbei was my cousin and my brother-in-law."

"Oh, is that so?" Kanbei cast his eyes down. "I am much indebted to your brother-in-law," he said humbly. "'Tis truly vexing that I was unable to see him one last time."

"I'm sure he is in the hereafter and is delighted to hear you say that after all the terrible hardship you faced."

Making the acquaintance of a former friend's relative soothed his heart, if only a little.

"Now, may I ask after your purpose?" said Kanbei.

"The truth is…" Gensuke sat up straight. "I do not think you're yet aware, Kanbei, that 'twas Hanbei who was ordered to execute Shojumaru."

"...What?" Kanbei muttered.

He was speechless. Nobunaga must have known that he and Hanbei were exceptionally close friends. Ordering Hanbei to kill his friend's son was far too cruel a command.

"He didn't concern himself about his status as a rear vassal, and he told our general that slaying Kuroda's hostage was folly. For that reason did he earn his disfavor. I believe making that remark only made things worse, as it caused our general to order *him* to kill Shojumaru."

"I see. So Hanbei tried to protect the boy, and that's how it happened. I know that Hanbei..."

He wrung out the words.

"...I know that he would not have caused my boy to suffer in his final moments."

Gensuke looked troubled.

"Is something the matter?" asked Kanbei.

"No... No, of course not."

"If I may, could I ask you to recount to me his final moments? Or did ye bring me a memento?"

Gensuke had his eyes lowered, and he spoke with a groaning tone. "Please forgive me this shame. As I am not a man of wisdom on par with my brother-in-law, I could not think of a better way to tell you, though I pondered it all this time. Therefore, I thought it necessary to come pay you a visit."

Kanbei looked puzzled.

"Come in!" said Gensuke.

Kanbei thought he heard a nice, crisp "Sir!"

The door was opened, and the chill of winter streamed into the statue hall.

Out in the external corridor, a young samurai was prostrating himself.

"My brother-in-law," Gensuke began, "told our general that if he were to kill Kuroda's hostage, 'twould be a mistake with regard to the administration of Chugoku, and also that it would draw the ire of the ever-watching sun in the skies, and that he would have no defense for his actions to give to you, Kanbei... He did everything in his power. And it took time to receive permission from Hashiba and our general. Please accept our humblest apologies for it being delayed until today."

The wee warrior raised his head.

"Shojumaru!" Kanbei cried.

Perhaps because he'd been made to wait in the cold hallway, Shojumaru's cheeks were bright red.

"Father!"

Kanbei's hands were shivering. His eyes were open wide, his lips trembling.

"Hanbei has done a good deed," he said. "Hanbei staked his life to sow a seed of good, did he? Are you telling me this is how one fights against this fleeting world, Hanbei?"

Gensuke just sat there, bewildered. Shojumaru wore a radiant smile.

"It has been too long, Father! I understand not a word you're saying!"

Kuroda Kanbei would go on to leave behind the following nuggets of wisdom:

Fear the punishment by your lord more than by your god, and fear the punishment by the retainers and by the people more than by your lord.

If you are shunned by the retainers and the people, you will invariably lose the country, and no amount of prayer or apologies will stave off your chastisement.

As such, you must fear punishment by the retainers and the people more than by your lord or your god.

Shojumaru grew up to be Kuroda Nagamasa, Lord of Chikuzen. He ruled over Hakata, changing its name to Fukuoka, the name that place retains to this day.

Kanbei's teachings were passed down through the generations, becoming the cornerstone of times of peace and bringing great prosperity to Fukuoka.

References

Amano, Tadauyuki. *Araki Murashige*. Ebisu Kosho Publishing, 2017.

Andou, Wataru. *Sengoku-ki Shuukyou Seiryoku Shiron* [Treatise on the influence of religion in the Warring States period]. Hozokan, 2019.

Hatakeyama, Kouichi. *Iwasa Matabei to Araki Ichizoku* [Iwasa Matabei and the Araki clan]. Tohoku University Graduate School Faculty of Arts and Letters Art History Course 30th Edition, 2009.

Hiraoka, Satoshi. *Joudo Shisou Nyuumon: Kodai Indo Kara Gendai Nihon Made* [A primer on True Pure Land Buddhist thought: From ancient India to modern Japan]. Kadokawa Sensho, 2018.

Kanda, Chisato. *Nobunaga to Ishiyama-Gassen: Chuusei no Shinkou to Ikki* [Nobunaga and the Ishiyama War: Faith and uprisings in the middle ages]. Yoshikawa Koubunkan, 2008.

Kuroda, Motoki. *Hyakusei Kara Mita Sengoku Daimyou* [Daimyo of the Warring States period through the eyes of the people]. Chikumashobo, 2006.

Marushima, Kazuhiro. *Sengoku Daimyou no Gaikou* [Diplomacy between Warring States era lords]. Kodansha Sensho Metier, 2013.

Mitsunari, Junji. *Honnouji Zenya: Saikoku wo Meguru Koubou* [The eve of Honno-ji: Jockeying for west Japan]. Kadokawa Sensho, 2020.

Nakanishi, Yuuki. *Sengoku Settsu no Gekokujou: Takayama Ukon to Nak-agawa Kiyohide* [Takayama Ukon and Nakagawa Kiyohide: Superiors overthrown in Warring States period Settsu]. Ebisu Koushou, 2019.

Nishimata, Fusao. *Shirotori no Gunjigaku* [The study of taking castles]. Kad-okawa Sophia Bunko, 2018.

Okuwa, Hitoshi. *Sengoku-ki Shuukyou Shisoushi to Rennyo* [Rennyo and the history of religious thought in the Warring States period]. Hozokan, 2006.

Ozawa, Tomio. *Buke Kakun Shuusei* [Collection of samurai family precepts and teachings]. Perikansha, 1998.

Satou, Hiruo. *Amaterasu no Henbou: Chuusei Shinbutsu Koushou-shi no Shiza* [Amaterasu's transformation: A vantage point on the history of relations between Shinto and Buddhism in the middle ages]. Hozokan Bunko, 2020.

Shimizu, Katsuyuki. *Kenkaryouseibai no Tanjou* [The birth of the both-parties-at-fault system]. Kodansha Sensho Metier, 2006.

Suwa, Masanori. *Kuroda Kanbei: Tenka wo Neratta Gunshi no Jitsuzou* [Kuroda Kanbei: The true picture of the "tactician with his eyes on the world"]. Chuko Shinsho, 2013.

Takagi, Hisashi. *Erizeni to Bita-ichimon no Sengoku-shi* [A history of the Warring States period through the prism of coin discrimination and tiny sums]. Heibonsha, 2018.

Takeuchi, Jun'ichi. *Yamanoue Souji-ki* [Chronicle of Yamanoue Souji].
Tankosha, 2018.

Takeuchi, Yoshinobu. *Saika Ikkouikki to Kii Shinshuu* [The Ikkou-Ikki Uprising in Saika and Shin Buddhism in Kii]. Hozokan, 2018.

Tougou, Ryuu. *Rekishi Zukai: Sengoku-gassen Manyuaru* [Diagrams decoding history: A manual on battles in the Warring States period].
Kodansha, 2001.

Yabe, Yoshiaki. *Episoodo de Tsuzuru: Sengoku Bushou Chanoyu Monogatari* [An illuminating episode: The tale of the tea ceremony and Warring States period commanders]. Miyaobi Publishing, 2014.

Yamada, Kuniaki. *Sengoku no Komyunikeeshon: Jouhou to Tsuushin* [Communication in the Warring States period: Information and the correspondence thereof]. Yoshikawa Koubunkan, 2011.

All background research was reviewed by Mr. Shin Mori, to whom I offer my deepest gratitude.